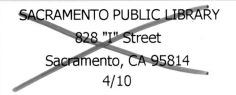

The

SIX-LITER
CLUB

The SIX-LITER CLUB

A NOVEL

HARRY KRAUS, MD

HOWARD BOOKS
A DIVISION OF SIMON & SCHUSTER, INC.
NEW YORK NASHVILLE LONDON TORONTO SYDNEY

Published by Howard Books, a division of Simon & Schuster, Inc.
1230 Avenue of the Americas, New York, NY 10020
www.howardpublishing.com

The Six-Liter Club © 2010 Harry Kraus

Library of Congress Control Number: 2009039531

ISBN 978-1-4165-7797-3
ISBN 978-1-4165-9262-4 (ebook)

10 9 8 7 6 5 4 3 2 1

HOWARD and colophon are registered trademarks of Simon & Schuster, Inc.

Manufactured in the United States of America.

For information regarding special discounts for bulk purchases, please contact Simon & Schuster Special Sales at 1-866-506-1949 or business@simonandschuster.com.

The Simon & Schuster Speakers Bureau can bring authors to your live event. For more information or to book an event, contact the Simon & Schuster Speakers Bureau at 1-866-248-3049 or visit our website at www.simonspeakers.com.

Edited by David Lambert and Lissa Halls Johnson

Interior design by Davina Mock-Maniscalco

For Evan.
With love, Dad

ACKNOWLEDGMENTS

THANKS TO MY fellow surgeons, the elite ones in an elusive club we call The Six Liter Club. It is my current hope that I never join you.

Thanks to Steve McMillan for sharing personal insights into the Simba Rebellion in Congo. Steve's father was murdered by the Simbas and yet Steve returned as a missionary to the very country that robbed him of his father. He has my friendship and respect. I wrote this story during a time when we both served together in East Africa.

Thanks to my literary agent, Natasha Kern, for loving this story, believing in me, and working hard to find the right home for this novel.

Thanks to the whole Howard team, especially David Lambert and Lissa Halls Johnson, who pushed hard to give the manuscript the polish it needed.

Thanks to my wife, Kris, for her love and patience and for her eyes in the proofing process.

And, of course, thanks to God. Creative. Full of grace. He enables imperfect fingers to do this stuff.

1

MEDICAL COLLEGE OF VIRGINIA, 1984

M Y HEART BEAT with the exhilaration of knowing I hid in enemy territory—a woman in a men's bathroom. Moments before, I had blown in to make a poignant statement about this sexist university, but right now, I felt a bit short-winded, like I needed to recover an ounce of the passion that had fueled my daily survival in this hospital for the greater part of the past decade.

There were trite metaphors to describe what I had just done. Threw down the gauntlet. Drew a line in the sand. Aunt Jeanine would have called it career suicide, but I never did give much for her opinion of my actions.

Thirty seconds before, I had thought my statement was precisely what this stodgy establishment needed. But at this moment, on the day I had become the first woman surgeon to join the prestigious Six-Liter Club, I cowered in a stall of the men's bathroom, desperate to find the fire that had emboldened me to barge into this inner sanctum of testosterone. I peered through a crack looking into the doctors' locker room, appreciating only a small vertical slice of the room at a time. It was much like the nurses', except larger, and it smelled a bit like my sweat socks after a run in the Virginia heat. I leaned forward until my forehead touched the cool surface of the metal door, tuning my ear to the voice of Dr. Bransford, my mentor and the chief of general surgery.

I closed my eyes and began to gloat in near euphoria. The Six-Liter Club! It wasn't exactly where I had expected to be on this first day as a surgery attending, but a coveted milestone nonetheless. I knew graying surgeons who, respected and dignified as they were, would never know the thrill of successfully pulling a patient back from so far over the precipice during his plunge into the next world. Oh, they'd often snatched patients back from the edge, made some "good saves," but rarely from six liters of blood loss—a hemorrhage of more than the circulating blood volume of medicine's prototypical normal human. "Normal" in the medical literature meant male, probably white, seventy kilograms, three-fourths fluid, five liters blood, one brain, one heart, and two testicles.

But today I cared little about the prejudiced medical literature. I'd fought for the arrival at this pinnacle every day for the past decade, slogging through four years of medical school and six more grueling years of surgery residency. Every day I had strived to be seen for something other than my physical equipment in a surgery world dominated by men who thought a woman's role should be assisting them toward greatness. But now, in 1984, I'd done what no other woman had ever done. I was the first female in the department to join the club on the first day as an attending. If I played according to the rules, the crack in the door would widen. If I failed, I'd confirm their suspicions, and the door would shut again for another decade of bigotry. Women were celebrated in other areas of medicine. Pediatrics. Obstetrics. But surgery remained the last holdout for the boys. I was determined to show them that a woman could be a cutter, too. I could play their game. Today I'd proved it.

Did I sense destiny, that I was the point of a spear thrust into the heart of a crusty, male-dominated field? Yes.

Was I up to the task? Today, I'd convinced myself that I was.

I listened to the chatter from the boys as they entered the locker room from the hallway and the operating rooms beyond. They talked about the Richmond Braves, a pitcher who was sent back from Atlanta to see if he could find his game again. I loved baseball, but today I was listening only for the approval of my hero. Certainly Derrick would tell him of my coolness under pressure, the swiftness with which I'd gained the upper hand against the hemorrhage. The Six-Liter Club was a definitive step toward gaining the respect of the guys.

Derrick was a brother, the best scrub tech I'd worked with, able to keep up with the quickest surgeons, handing them what they needed often before they uttered their request. He'd slipped into the banter of the hood, a relaxed style punctuated with his own laughter. I listened for my name as I inspected my nails. They were kept short, but manicured. Not polished. That's a no-no around here, another concession I'd made to enter this boys' club of surgery.

There was blood under my right index fingernail. It didn't surprise me after the bloodbath in room five. I knew the patient only as John Doe, the assigned name for anyone who came in the ER without an established identity. I'd taken time only for the essentials before rushing him to the OR. He didn't have the chance to give me his name before his blood pressure became a real problem. We focused our attention on the critical business of saving his life rather than the fluffy extras like name, age, and whether he liked basketball or soccer.

When I asked who shot him, he looked around with wide eyes as if he expected his assailant to jump from behind the curtain. The look of sheer terror faded from his face only as he slipped into unconsciousness. His mumbled reply was, "Some dude." It was a statement I'd heard hundreds of times in the last five years of surgery training in downtown Richmond, Virginia. Everyone assaulted was always minding their own business when some dude shot them. Or else they knew him and were afraid to say. The way this John Doe looked when I asked the question, I'd say it was the latter. Something had made my patient very afraid. And he came within a breath of seeing the other side as a result.

If my patient's fears were justified, and we found out there was a credible threat on his life, we'd admit him under an assumed name for his protection. It was all part of a day's work on the trauma service at the Medical College of Virginia.

I paused, thinking about the look of terror on my patient's face. I'd seen fear in the eyes of patients who were about to die before, but there was something different in the eyes of my newest John Doe. And something told me that I hadn't seen the end of his terror.

This John Doe appeared to be a young teenager. A thin African American with a pitiful growth of tangled chin hairs signifying a teen who wouldn't shave. He'd come in with three entrance and two exit wounds, a belly swollen like one of those obnoxious ticks I found on Max, my boyfriend's German shepherd. John Doe lived because the residents put in four big IV lines so we could squeeze blood in as fast as it flowed out of the injury to his vena cava, the mother of all veins. He lived because he was young and his heart could still compensate for the stress. He lived because I had the best anesthesiologist the U had available. He lived because an OR was open the very moment he had arrived, and because I was nimble at isolating and repairing his injuries. So no, I didn't fool myself by thinking I deserved all the credit, but attending surgeons were known to be forgetful of the little people around them. I was determined not to be one of them.

The locker room door snapped open with a thud and the sheer tenor voice of Ellis Hamilton overtook the baseball chatter. Ellis was a geeky white boy who served as the fourth-year resident on my service. He was book smart, author of over twenty papers in the surgical literature, and the nephew of one of the biggest names in academic surgery.

I wouldn't let him operate on my dog.

I heard hand slaps and peered through the crack next to the stall door. Ellis clasped his hand around Derrick's, his fingers curled around Derrick's thumb as if he were his homey. This didn't compute for me. Derrick hated arrogant white doctors. He tolerated them because it was his job. He even led the ones who fumbled in the OR without their attendings, helping them through their surgical cases. Once outside, he returned to his downtown hood, and they drove the opposite way to the west end or a stately home in the fan on Monument Avenue.

Derrick grinned at the resident. "You're one bad dude, Doc. What color are your drawers?"

Ellis wore a tentative smile and looked down.

Seth Patterson, another tech, rolled his scrub top into a ball and swished the laundry hamper. "He don't get it."

Ellis's face reddened. "My drawers?"

Seth chuckled and said something too low for me to hear from my hideout. Derrick roared.

Ellis didn't give up. "What?" He slumped onto the bench beside Dr. Bransford, his only advocate.

Bransford patted the young surgeon on the thigh. "Your shorts, Ellis. No resident ever scrubs on his first six-liter case and comes out with white underwear."

"My wife always complains about the blood on my clothes."

Derrick shook his head. "We ain' talkin' 'bout blood."

I sighed, tiring of this drivel. My thoughts drifted to Ellis's wife. God only knew what she saw in him.

Seth's next remark brought me right back.

"I'll bet Camille's are dry."

Derrick snickered. "You are dreamin' now, bro. You wish you could check that lady's black lacy bikini—"

My mind whirled. Black lacy underwear? How would they know? My thoughts stopped short as I clutched the neck of my male-cut scrub top. In my haste to rescue John Doe, I'd forgotten to pin the neckline! For years I'd worn men's large scrub tops that would fit comfortably over my ample chest, but I always pinned the neckline to avoid . . . Ugh! They must have certainly gotten an eyeful today.

My eyes fell to the drawstring holding up my pants. Blood-stains. Nothing new for a trauma surgeon, but I hated it that I'd thrown away three pairs of panties in the last month. I loosened the string and peered in before shaking my head in disgust. Make that four. I dropped my scrubs and slipped off the stained pair, rolling the black lace into a ball to drop into the trash can—if I ever summoned the courage to leave.

I pulled my scrubs back up and listened again as Dr. Brans-ford finally stroked my fragile ego. "She is cool under fire."

Seth grunted his agreement, but was stopped short by a back-hand slap to the chest by Derrick. "That girl is outta your league."

Ellis jumped in. "Way, way out of your league!"

Dr. Bransford sighed heavily.

Derrick slapped his back. "Out of your league, too, ol' man."

I took a deep breath, trying to digest the exchange I'd just witnessed. Here, in this locker room, all normal vestiges of status evaporated in maleness. Derrick was talking trash and slapping the chief of general surgery—a man old enough to be his father—someone he would always honor with the title "doctor" in every other social arena. But here their common male bond dominated, swelling like a tidal wave to dwarf the ripples of social status. I didn't understand. Outside, Derrick and Seth always called me Dr. Weller. Here, I was Camille, or "that girl," and Dr. Bransford was "ol' man." The weasel resident was praised for his role in *my* save. He was "one bad dude." They should have been praising *me*, not fantasizing over my lacy undergarments! I found myself want-ing to shout, What about me? Aren't I a bad dude?

Fortunately I composed myself and took another breath. A deep, cleansing breath. I wanted to make a statement about the stupid sign on the door outside, not eavesdrop on adolescent BS.

I was a doctor, a surgeon, to be exact. I had two X chromosomes, not one like all the other surgeons here. It seemed that somewhere in our evolutionary past, the Y must have taken a dive into the shallow end of the gene pool. I nodded my head in a confidence I didn't feel. *Here goes nothing.*

I opened the door and casually sauntered past the overflowing trash can, where I shoved my panties below the first layer of paper towels. No use showing everyone how right Derrick was about my taste in underwear. I tipped my head forward toward the male quartet, now all standing with slackened jaws. "Afternoon, boys."

"Cami—uh—Dr. Weller!" Derrick pulled on a T-shirt emblazoned with an emblem of the Richmond Braves.

Ellis was wild-eyed, backing quietly toward the door. It was as if I'd somehow contaminated their turf. Now he was in full retreat, a cat running from a mouse in a dog costume.

After a moment, Dr. Bransford found his voice. "Dr. Weller, would you mind explaining what you're doing here?"

"You hired me, sir. I'm working here as a part of the attending surgical staff."

Derrick and Seth retreated one step behind the senior surgeon. Both were trying not to smile.

"Camille," he began again, this time in the fatherly voice I adore. "This is the men's changing area. You know what I'm ask—"

"This is the *doctors'* locker room," I interrupted. "Do you want me to change in the nurses' locker room down the hall?"

Dr. Bransford gave me a stern look. "Don't do this."

"This?"

"Come in and start making waves your first week."

"What, I should wait a year before I change in the doctors' area? Then everyone would wonder why it's OK now, but not last week or last month." I kept my chin high and solid. "I decided I'd better start right from the beginning."

"Camille—"

"The door has a sign on it." I pointed to the one Ellis was touching. "It says 'Doctors.' Well, that's me." I fixed my gaze on Seth and Derrick for emphasis. "So why are you two in here?"

Derrick was poking Seth's ribs with his elbow, and deep dimples were forming at the corners of his mouth. "What're you doing?" he mocked.

"I'm going to get changed. It's been a long enough day."

Dr. Bransford sighed. "Camille, you can't just come in here and—"

"Then change the sexist sign on the door. If you mean *men*, say men. If you mean *doctor*, say doctor."

My mentor shook his head slowly. I knew I was skating on thin ice. I'd been changing in the nurses' locker room ever since I arrived at the Medical College of Virginia as a student. The sign had always bugged me, but it wasn't a med student's or a resident's place to make waves. I had planned on bringing it up at a department meeting, but I'd surfed the high from joining the Six-Liter Club right down the OR hallway and into the doctors' locker room. It was just one of those split-second, on-your-feet decisions that surgeons were supposed to be able to make to succeed in a life-or-death career. One second I was in the hall looking at that goofy sign. The next, I was marching into the nurses' lounge to get my clothes. And two minutes later, I had invaded Testosterone Central and was seeking refuge in a bathroom stall.

I shrugged with casual nonchalance. I turned and looked at the locker I'd chosen. It was time. Game on, as they say. If I walked out now, I'd be just another poser. I touched the drawstring of my scrubs. I waited a few seconds, trying to find real courage behind my bravado. I closed my eyes.

I couldn't do it. I couldn't bring myself to drop my scrubs in front of a bunch of leering vultures—especially with the black lace tucked inside the trash can. But how could I save face? I cleared my throat, searching for an answer.

"Dr. Weller!"

I spun around to face the chairman of the department of surgery, James P. Gilles. He didn't smile on a normal day. I'd personally seen him fire two residents, one just for being late to a morbidity and mortality conference. My eyes met his for a second, and in that moment I felt the weight of my fate.

For five years, I'd lived for the sparkle in this man's eyes as we stood facing each other across an open body. Gilles could fry you, scare you, or send a resident's heart soaring with confidence . . . with just one look. We'd all grown to know the eyes of the chairman. Above his mask, his eyes told the story of fulfillment or the demise of your dreams. He had the kind of eyes that seemed to look right through your clothes. Not lustful, but searching, able to detect a faltering constitution. I always felt bare beneath his gaze, yet at the same time, warmed by his approval.

But not today. His eyes were dead. I shivered and looked away. "Yes, sir." Calling him "sir" was survival instinct. We were formal in surgery. All of our attendings were "doctor" or "sir." We never bantered around with first names the way they did over in family medicine. Family doctors could afford to be casual. They probably had a case of sniffles to diagnose. Surgeons dealt with life and death, and we trained like soldiers.

"What are you doing?"

I cleared my throat again and looked at the blank faces of the boys. "The sign on the door says 'Doctors,' sir." I winced. I was saying "sir" too much. Made me look rookie. *Like the rookie I am.* "I was just planning to change—"

"I'm not referring to right now. I'm referring to the bloodbath in room six. Your patient received twenty-three units of blood."

I managed a small smile. "Yes, sir. A save, sir."

"Why didn't you call for help?"

The question caught me off guard. In retrospect, I should have seen it coming, but I was still blind, surfing the wave of exhilaration. I started to answer, but my brain couldn't catch up to my mouth. Instead, I stood there, jaw unhinged, searching for a response.

"Arrogance leads to patient disasters, Camille. You may have stroked your ego, but at what expense? This is your first day," he said, swinging his arms in emphasis. "You lost that much blood and you didn't call for help!"

"He's alive, sir."

"Barely. And now he'll fight a battle to overcome the profound effects of shock." He shook his head. "This isn't a game. A boy's life is at stake and you've already turned him into some trophy."

I tried to speak. I wanted to tell him it wasn't a game to me, that the patient wasn't a trophy, that I was a surgeon, but also a woman and capable of deep feeling, but his words had hit a sensitive mark on my soul. "I wasn't—"

He raised his voice and cut me off. "For God's sake, Camille, call for help!"

I nodded, suddenly numb and barely comprehending what had just happened. I'd taken my first lashing from the boss. My first day as a trauma attending, and already, I was cut down in front of a crowd. I turned and gathered my things. I needed to change, but I needed to retreat to the nurses' locker room—and fast—before I started to cry.

I clutched a small handbag with such vigor that I whitened my mulatto knuckles. Heading for the door without uttering another word, I knew I was toast. Six-Liter Club on my first day or not, no one misbehaved in front of Dr. Gilles. I bit my lip in disbelief. I'd gone from Everest-high to Death Valley–low faster than anyone in MCV history.

The nurses' locker room was empty, as was usual in the middle of a shift. I changed and scurried out at a surgeon's pace. I hit the stairwell at a near-run just as the tears started to well over my mascara. Cursed X chromosomes! Surgeons don't cry!

I descended to street level and headed toward the Broad Street exit. My last thought before facing downtown Richmond was, Maybe Derrick will tell Dr. Gilles I'm a bad dude and everything will be OK.

The languid air brought me back to my senses.

No one crosses the boss of the boys' club and survives.

2

THE SIMBA REBELLION, THE CONGO, 1964

I'VE NEVER SEEN a dead body walk before. Tomorrow is supposed to be the day. From my hiding place in the loquat tree on the edge of the banana grove I'd guess the bad Simba men haven't seen it happen either. A body has been lying in the street for two days and more and more of the soldiers come by to see. Yesterday one of them wanted to take the body's hat, 'cause it's a special one with leopard fur, but another soldier with a big gun said he couldn't. The dead man will come back alive by tomorrow and will need his hat. They said the witchdoctor cast a spell so the bullets will turn to water and anyone who dies will come back to life in three days.

My daddy says only Jesus or Lazarus came back after three days, and the Simbas will have to face the facts. I'm not sure where the facts to face are, but I know that soon the Simba men won't want to face this body at all 'cause it's getting stinkier in the heat. At least it rained this morning and washed some of the blood into the dusty road.

Before it rained it looked like nearly all that man's blood was on the road. Daddy says a body only has five liters of blood. It's all God gave you and without it, you can't live. I'm small and Daddy says I have about a gallon of blood myself. He only told me that 'cause I was bugging him to know. I'd spilled a whole gallon of cherry Kool-Aid on the kitchen floor, and I remember that it seemed like a lot, especially if it were blood. I cried that day 'cause Kool-Aid is very precious and we only get it when special white missionaries from Daddy's home come to visit.

He says that back in his home there are stores with more Kool-Aid than a kid could ever dream of. I wish he'd take me there. Some of our friends left for safety a few months ago, and some of them the bad Simba men carted off to Stanleyville.

I like it here mostly, but when it rains, it gets real muddy and my mom won't let me play outside. I've seen mud so thick you could practically lose your car. Mr. McMillan got his motor-cycle stuck in the mud once. They call motorcycles *piki-pikis* here 'cause of the sound they make when they drive by. Mr. McMillan got red in the face trying to push his *piki* out of the mud. Then he just walked off and left it there, standing straight up in the mud without the kickstand or anything. I think Mom thinks that would happen to me. I'd wade in and get stuck and I'd have to stay there, planted in the thick Congo mud like a baobab tree forever.

Gunshots alert me. I strain through the branches to see where the fighting is, and if the soldiers are bringing more wounded people for my daddy to see.

"Camille!"

It's my mom. I want to stay here a little longer to watch the dead body. "Coming!"

I'll come back tomorrow if I can sneak out of the house. I want to see if the witchdoctor is right.

I'm not sure what to believe, the men who call themselves lions, or my daddy. I guess I'll believe my daddy 'cause he's been right about most stuff so far, plus the fact that the bullets that hit the dead Simba didn't turn into water, so I'm not sure I can believe the rest. Just the same, I'm going to come down here early tomorrow and watch from behind this tree to see for myself.

RICHMOND, VIRGINIA, 1984

I SPENT AN HOUR walking the streets of downtown Richmond
before ending up at a park bench in front of the governor's
mansion where I shooed the pigeons away and sat in a defeated
slump. I'd traversed the minefield known as surgery residency in
Virginia long enough to know two things: You don't cross the
chairman and . . . well, that's about it. As long as the chairman
liked you, you were going to make it. I'd also learned that the best
way to diffuse a potential bomb was to fall on it early, take your
due, and say it was your fault. They crucified you if you lied or
covered a mistake. If you said, "I did it," the worst they could do
was get mad or fire you, but at least you got to live. The department of surgery had been good-ol'-boy Southern until Dr. Gilles
was brought in from Ann Arbor and he made history by hiring
the first female of color. Now I wondered whether I'd make history again with the shortest academic career on record.

Gilles had been so upset about my independence that he'd
completely overlooked my locker room antics. But as soon as the
grapevine had a chance to spill the story, I was sure he'd rethink
things, and I'd have two strikes against my record instead of one.

I enumerated my options. Pretend it didn't happen. Go to Dr.
Gilles and promise never to make waves again. Defend my actions
and force the sexist institution to change, and promise to call for
help, even when I thought I didn't need it. Or, I could hide from
Dr. Gilles for the next three months, the approximate time for
him to forget my antics. My modus operandi had always been the
second choice. If I had problems, I'd just work hard and ignore
them. But this wasn't going to go away. I'd offended the big boss
on the first day, and it was going to be hard to sleep tonight if I
didn't claim temporary insanity and promise to do better.

I spent another hour on the bench rehashing the options in
order, reverse order, and finally, in random order, musing until I
was either going to nudge myself over the precipice of sanity or

do something to correct my problem. Being a surgeon, I selected the latter. When given a choice between contemplation and action, the surgeon's choice was a given. I would go to Dr. Gilles, apologize, and pray that I could keep my job a little longer.

I walked back to the hospital, stopped in the misnamed nurses' lounge to freshen my makeup, and padded on little cat's feet down the corridor leading to Dr. Gilles's spacious office. His secretary had left for the day, and his door stood slightly ajar. I raised my hand to knock, but halted when I heard voices inside.

The voice of my chairman, Dr. Gilles, was unmistakable. "My wife didn't want me to hire her. She's so—" He paused. "Damned pretty." I heard the scratch of an old lighter. Gilles must be lighting a cigar. "Gladys doesn't trust pretty women."

I listened to a chuckle I recognized as coming from Dr. William Bransford. I could smell the aroma of a Nicaraguan cigar, something I'd shared many times with Dr. Gilles on late nights. Sharing cigars with the boss was another bit of the boys' club behavior I'd adopted to survive.

Gilles spoke again. "I'm starting to regret this decision already."

Bransford cleared his throat. "It's a challenge to be respected when you stay on as an attending in the same institution where you trained."

"It's more than that, Bill." Gilles kept his voice low. As he continued, I leaned against the door to hear, then startled as the door edged open. I froze, suddenly afraid of stumbling into the chairman's office. Thankfully, the door didn't fly open; I didn't tumble headfirst into the room. I held my breath, slowly exhaling when I heard Dr. Gilles continue.

"Blaine Stevens's son from Ann Arbor wanted this job. I doubt his father is very happy with me."

I knew Blaine Stevens. Everyone in academic surgery knew his reputation. He walked on water and everyone expected his son would follow in his shadow.

I heard tapping—fingers on a desk. Bransford spoke. "Why didn't you tell the committee?"

"The dean's office made it clear. Diversification is the order of the day." Gilles sighed and I heard his chair squeak followed by a thud. I imagined the chairman leaning back in his mahogany chair and plopping his feet on the desk. "Did you know that surgery is the last department to hire a black?"

His words hit me like a train from nowhere. *Black? What's that got to do with anything?* I shook my head. I hadn't thought much about it. My aunt had raised me white. I rapidly pushed the thoughts aside. I didn't have time to process this. I needed to know if I still had a job.

"She's qualified, Jim. So she's struggled with arrogance. What surgeon hasn't? And if she wasn't confident, we'd have other problems."

"What are the odds she'll make it a year?" He sighed. "How long did Peterson last?"

"Four months."

"And Garrett?"

"Six."

The chairman growled, "My bet? Camille makes it two months." He paused. "She joined the Six-Liter Club and didn't call for help."

"She saved the patient."

"Ellis told me he was afraid."

"Ellis is a wimp."

"It takes a *good* surgeon to pull someone back from losing six liters of blood, but a *careless* surgeon to lose six liters in the first place." I heard a thump. Gilles must have dropped his feet to the floor. "Not knowing everything isn't a crime. It's a crime not to know your limits, when to ask for help."

I consciously unclenched my jaw. *That's ridiculous! I didn't cause the injuries that led to the blood loss!*

Bransford came to my defense. "The patient lived, Jim."

"So far. But he's a long way from making it. If he doesn't survive, I'm going to make her answer for why she didn't call for backup on such a huge case." I could hear him exhale and imagined him blowing smoke to the ceiling. "It was her first day, for God's sake."

"She's making a colorful start, that's for sure."

"Two months. That's all the grace I'm going to give. If it's not working out, I'm going to cut my losses early on this one."

"You're going to let Gladys win?"

"It's not just about that. I don't like anyone, the dean or Gladys, pressuring me to make decisions. Let's just say I'm going to be keeping my finger on the pulse of Camille's work. In the meantime, I want you to find out if Blaine Stevens the Second is happy in his new position working in the shadow of his father."

"He stayed on in Ann Arbor?"

"Yes. But sometimes the father-son thing messes up a young man's desire to be something on his own." The chair squeaked again. "Look at the time. I told my wife I'd be home early."

I stepped out of my shoes, gathered them in my hand, and ran. Ran without looking back.

The glorious feeling of destiny I'd savored in the men's locker room had been replaced by a sickening dread in the pit of my gut.

And for the second time on my first day, I fled the hospital with my heart in my throat.

3

〰〰〰〰

T HE DARKNESS HELD private terrors, dreams that held back their meaning but left me in the grip of breathlessness. As long as I could remember, the blackness of night carried a vague discomfort, something I couldn't name and mostly ignored. I had used it to my advantage, avoiding the night scene in college, and, preferring the light of my studies, I excelled, entering medical school and surgical residency. Studying was my escape and my security. Being the best left little time for anxieties that lay beyond my consciousness.

Maybe, just maybe, that's one of the reasons surgery was such a good fit for me. Because darkness delivered her scheduled horrors to the surgeon. With clockwork regularity, the sun fled, and with it the urban man's sensibilities. Mugs of golden ale, or unseen bottles wrapped in brown paper bags, were lifted in celebration or escape. Those with ill intent crept from underpasses to commit the butchery that fed the trauma surgeon her daily bread. Automobiles sped along, driven by inebriated Indy wannabes, and life became death. Silence replaced breath. So for me, the trauma surgeon, night was my busiest time. And that meant less time to be distracted by my personal nighttime demons.

But tonight, I ventured out. Partly because I needed to unload my miserable day on Mark Lawson, and partly because he complained of my neglect. This wasn't my fault. Not entirely. His schedule as a pediatric oncology fellow competed with mine as a surgery attending, creating frequent clashes of our calendars. And partly, although I wouldn't admit it to Mark, I wanted to drive my new Honda Prelude—which I'd proudly made a down payment on using my first attending paycheck. Since buying it, I'd refused to go anywhere in Mark's 1978 Datsun.

Tonight we ate Nepali food, hot enough to satisfy my passion for spice. As darkness descended on Richmond, I busied myself with conversation, expounding my turmoil over my impulsive behavior and the conversation I'd overheard in the chairman's office.

Mark was typical male. And so atypical male. Perhaps that's why I found myself hoping he might be the one. He's motherly and compassionate with the kids he encourages through the chemical tortures of chemotherapy. He listens. Really listens. And so I regurgitated the whole ugly story of the stand I'd made in the men's locker room, and the tongue-lashing I'd taken from the chairman.

Mark didn't seem sympathetic. I doubted if he'd ever feared for his job. In fact, he seemed more upset about my little statement over the stupid sign than the rebuke I'd suffered from the boss. "I know you, Camille," he said. "You'd have never dropped your scrubs in front of the guys."

"How do you know?"

"You've never undressed in front of me."

After I had laid bare all my raw experience before him, his only thought was the thrill of seeing me undress. He was jealous and it wasn't pretty. One mention, or one glance, of a shapely backside, and a man's frontal lobes went on vacation. I knew this for a personal fact.

My response to Mark was curt. "Sulking doesn't look good on you." I paused. "I haven't finished the story."

He busied himself with a rice dish while I recited the conversation between Bransford and Gilles. I couldn't hold back my anger. I kept my voice low, but inside I was seething. "He basically said that he hired me because I'm black!"

"He wouldn't have hired you if you weren't qualified—independent of skin color."

"He said Blaine Stevens's boy applied for my job."

The name meant nothing to Mark.

"Blaine Stevens is one of the world's best-known vascular surgeons."

"So? Gilles hired you instead. You know your credentials. You know he wouldn't have hired you if you didn't stack up in other areas."

"That doesn't matter. The fact is, I got the job because of my skin color."

"Ridiculous. If you couldn't cut it, he wouldn't let you into the club. He trained you, Camille, he knows what you can do." He pushed aside a red pepper, dissecting it from his next bite. "You know you weren't hired for your skin color."

I slumped in my chair. "You know what's weird? For years I didn't think of myself as black."

I watched as Mark's eyebrows lifted. "You're serious."

"My father was white. My aunt Jeanine is white. She raised me white." I shrugged. "You're white. Why should it matter?"

"Doesn't matter. When people look at you, they see black."

"That's just not fair. I'm as white as I am black." I sat up straight. "How do you see me?"

He avoided the issue. "You're beautiful."

"White or black?"

He shrugged. "It doesn't matter."

"It matters to me."

He shook his head. "You don't seem to know who you are."

I thought about what he said. Perhaps he'd tossed it off the cuff, but I took it to heart and couldn't respond. Maybe my aunt Jeanine had protected me from thinking of myself that way.

Maybe that robbed me of identity. When I did respond, I quickly
wanted the words back. "I'm a surgeon."

"That's what you do." He set down his fork and touched
my hand. "You're a woman, Camille. An African American. You
should celebrate that."

Sure, I knew I was a woman, but in my chosen field, I'd spent
most of my adult life proving that being a woman didn't matter. That having two X chromosomes wasn't a handicap. I stayed
quiet. Maybe Mark couldn't get this. He was a pediatrician. He'd
joined a field where a motherly touch was celebrated as an asset,
not a disadvantage.

Mark probed again. "Why do you care so much about Gilles?"

I glanced at him. He was staring out the window. He should
know the answer to his question.

He continued, "We don't deify our chairmen the way surgeons do."

"Be fair, Mark. He's not God."

"Exactly my point." He looked back at me. "Maybe you can't
see it because you're too close. But look at your department from
the outside and you might see the worship they offer up to him."

I held back my reaction. I wanted to argue, but I knew he
wouldn't say it unless it merited some thought. In truth, dating a
pediatrician brought fresh perspective to my surgical focus. I took
a deep breath. "I love the man, I guess."

Mark nodded.

"And I fear him."

"I know." He shook his head. "A style of leadership that is OK
for military conquest, but inappropriate for a hospital. We don't
put up with that in pediatrics."

I knew he was right. "Surgery will be the last to change. Kinder
and gentler is for our medicine colleagues."

Mark slipped into silence. I paid the bill, we walked to the
car and drove into the moist night. As we approached the Nickel

Bridge toll, I shoved my purse in his lap. "I need some change."

He grunted and began a hopeless search for the needed coins.

"Check inside the front flap on my wallet."

He rummaged happily, a blind boy without a cane, a man helplessly looking for spaghetti noodles on the pasta aisle at Safeway. Finding anything must be an X-linked trait, and the poor man only had one X chromosome. I stuck my hand in and extracted exact change in less than fifteen seconds.

Mark sighed. A moment later, however, something else had his attention. He held up a priceless treasure. He flipped on the dome light and stared at a yellowing photograph I kept in the cellophane picture section. It's a favorite activity of adolescent-minded men: Check the wallet for pictures of the competition. He wouldn't find any in there. I only kept one picture in my wallet. And I had for twenty years. His voice almost squeaked with excitement. "Who's this?"

I let him stew. "My mother."

I listened for the predictable gasp. He didn't disappoint me. "But sh-she's topless."

"She's not topless, Mark. Topless is an American concept. I told you my mother was African."

"But I thought, African, well, you know, uh, sort of like you, African roots or something."

"She was native Congolese. For the women of her tribe, the breast was for mothering, nurturing, not like here."

After a few more moments, I had to close the wallet for him. I was afraid he'd start slobbering or something. Here he was, one of the most educated men I knew, and let him see a breast outside of a clinical setting and his brain was held hostage.

"Tell me about your mother."

I didn't know what to say. I was orphaned at age ten, raised by my white aunt Jeanine, who resented the intrusion of her brother's daughter on her social scene in the upper crust of Montgomery, Alabama. She sent me north to a prep school in Boston and refused to let me speak of the Congo. That was past. My father lacked common civility, she'd said. I'd been scarred enough by the loss of my parents, as primitive as they were, she'd said. My focus was to be forward, not backward. Education would be my salvation. The answer for the hell I'd been through in the Congo was an awkward silence. What did I know about my mother? Very little. I had islands of memory within a sea of deep blue nothingness. Aunt Jeanine's attempts to erase the past had worked well, mostly. She'd have choked on her Southern sweet tea if she'd even known I'd managed to keep this particular picture of my mom.

"Camille?"

I realized I'd been in the ozone. "I don't know. I don't remember much."

"How old were you when—"

"Ten."

"You must have some memories."

I shrugged. Rehearsing the stories with those you love preserved memories worth keeping. Without the rehearsals, I'd retained precious little. Besides, I didn't want to talk about my parents. Maybe it was a hang-up I'd inherited from my aunt, but I had the gut-level feeling that there were whispers from my African childhood that were too horrible to speak of. I didn't understand it; the subject always made me uncomfortable. Like a child staring at the stairwell leading to a dark, little-used basement, I wanted the door to stay closed. I kept quiet and hoped Mark would take the hint.

Night fell with full force, and with it, a summer thunderstorm began to threaten, bringing first drops, then sheets of rain. I slowed to a crawl on Chamberlain Avenue on my way to my northside apartment. My mind turned from Mark to my career. How could I have been so stupid as to—

A dark object darted into my path from between parked cars. My reactions were swift, but not swift enough to prevent the sickening crunch that followed.

Mark gasped and whirled to look behind as we skidded to a stop. A pickup truck behind me swerved, narrowly missing my side mirror. Horns blared. Something or someone was lying in the road behind my new Honda Prelude.

"Oh God," I whispered. "Oh God, oh God, oh God."

Mark jumped out. I followed. In a moment, we were kneeling over a large yellow dog. A sticky, gasping tumble of fur.

"Can you do anything?" Mark honored me with the question, yielding to my forte in trauma.

I lifted the dog's head. It bobbed loosely on its body as if the only thing keeping it attached were yellow fur. The dog gasped and blood fountained from its mouth, spraying across the gray pants of my suit. "Tumi," I whispered.

"What?" Mark touched my arm. "Camille?"

I'd not spoken that name for twenty years, yet here with a dying dog in my hands, the name of my childhood pet dropped from my lips. I let the animal slip from my hands. Repulsed, I stood and backed away. "Its neck is broken. There's nothing—" My voice halted, betraying me.

Mark surveyed the apartment houses lining the streets, then felt in the dog's fur around his neck. "There's no tag." He grabbed the dog by the thorax, his hands buried in the thick fur. He pulled the dog to the side of the road between two cars, hesitated, then hoisted the lifeless mound of bloody, wet mange onto the sidewalk. Our eyes met. I was stunned. I'd never killed anything. Mark didn't seem to know what to say. He shrugged. "His owner will find him. There's nothing else to do."

I checked the front of my car, tolerant of the rain. Seeing nothing but a patch of yellow fur hanging on the bumper—cringing, I flicked it off—I returned to the car and we drove home in silence.

Something about the image of the dog coughing blood affected me in a way I couldn't describe. It was déjà vu, a miserable dyspepsia that told me this had happened before. Or I'd seen this before. I sensed something lurking just beyond my retrieval. My pulse quickened and panic blew a cool wind across my neck. I braced myself against this thought. I was a scientist, a rational being. I couldn't be given over to such psycho-bull. Of course I felt bad. I'd just killed someone's dog, a family pet perhaps. It was no deeper than that.

But I couldn't make the image go away. Blood. Sticky and warm. A gasping dog hungry for air.

Fortunately, Mark knew when to draw me out and when to stay silent. His quiet presence was welcome.

Ten minutes later, I stood at my kitchen sink staring at myself in a rain-streaked window. Mark embraced me from behind, watching our reflection as he began to nibble on my earlobe. His strong arms were around me, caressing me gently. He knew my mind was in turmoil, both from my day, and now from the night. He was amorous, but I was cold to the idea and wanted to hide somewhere. For about twenty years.

He must have sensed my tension. He whispered in my ear, "Come on, baby. Everything's gonna be all right."

I shivered, but not from Mark's warm lips on my neck. Something freaky was happening to me. For the second time in a few minutes panic tightened my chest. I closed my eyes and my breathing quickened. Something, somewhere felt very wrong. This was alien to me. I was not prone to such emotional extremes.

I neared the edge of a cliff. Closer. My mind raced. What is wrong with me? I feared loss of control. Surgeons didn't do this.

Mark acted oblivious, taking clues only from my actions, not my mind. I closed my eyes. My breathing quickened. He thought I was responding to his caress, but as my chest tightened, I ran through a mental differential diagnosis: acute myocardial infarction, stroke, pulmonary embolus, viral pleuritis. I fought the thought that I was dying. Mark's tender words echoed in my mind as if bouncing off expansive canyon walls. *Everything's gonna be all right.* The whisper held a dread for me. He'd spoken so gently, but my mind had reacted with abject fear. His kisses became longer, searching. He turned me toward him and I kept my eyes closed, afraid he'd see my terror.

In a moment, I pushed him away, gasping for breath.

"What's wrong?"

I shook my head. "I don't know. I just feel . . ." I hesitated. "I just feel weird." I knew I was on the edge. A child staring down the stairs into the scary basement. I didn't know why or what, only that there was something down there. Very dark and very evil.

"Slow your breathing down. You'll hyperventilate."

I knew what he was saying. The doctor in me knew. And the doctor in me was embarrassed. I was fully aware of how stupid this seemed and how little I could do about the feeling.

"Sit down." He motioned to an easy chair in the den, his face twisted with questions and concern. "Camille?"

I forced myself to slow my breathing. Take a breath. Slowly breathe out, mentally counting one, two, three, four, five . . . After a minute or two I felt better, but a bit flushed and a lot foolish. I thought of Sally Pickford, who used to hyperventilate on the prep school playground during recess. I couldn't be like her. She was prissy and afraid of everything—even going to the bathroom at school.

I waved Mark away. "I'm OK." I shuddered and attempted to reassure myself. "Really." I offered a weak smile. I was a horrible liar.

He handed me a glass of white wine. It was overfull. I didn't complain. My day had been entirely too weird to protest.

I studied Mark. He sat across from me drinking nothing, wearing a doctor face of concern. I felt bad. My reaction had ruined the tender moment.

After ten minutes, my glass was empty. I stood and picked up my purse from the kitchen counter. The wine and the intensity of the emotions had prompted me forward, to dare a second look into the basement, something I'd been avoiding for a long time. I retrieved the picture of my mother and laid it on the coffee table in front of Mark.

"I remember a few things, phrases of a language I no longer understand. I think she sang to me."

Mark spoke softly, "She was beautiful."

Just like a male. All he knew of her was what he had seen from a faded little photograph. Mark is a breast man, I thought. He's already infatuated with my mother. Luckily for me, I'd taken after my African mama in that way. But equipment of that caliber wasn't always an advantage. I'd worked harder in medicine to be noticed by my work instead of my breasts. I sighed. *At least I'm not blond.*

"What happened to her?"

"My parents were killed by the Simbas."

"Simbas?" Mark's ignorance of reality outside his small United States life was woefully common among Americans. But, truth be known, I only knew of the Simbas because I'd researched them in college on my own, not because my professors thought they were important.

"There was a rebellion to overthrow the young Congolese government shortly after Belgium granted the Congo independence. Those in the rebel party were fierce fighters, often proceeding into battle in opiate-induced frenzies, advancing after witchdoctors cast a spell convincing them that the enemy's bullets would be as harmless to them as drops of water."

Mark nodded, urging me forward. This was his gift to me. He loved to explore, to find what I was about. If he was right, and I didn't really know myself, maybe we'd discover it together. The thought made me feel warm. Maybe I could find the strength to take a step down the stairs of my past.

"*Simba* means lion. They wanted a name that would carry fear into the heart of their enemies."

"Your parents supported the government?"

"My parents were caught in the cross fire. The government

had called upon the West for help, so any white man was assumed to be a part of the established power. My mother was killed because she was my father's wife."

"Your father was a doctor?"

I knew I'd told this to Mark before, but he was drawing me out, looking for more. This was one reason I was falling in love. "A surgeon. A missionary who came and stayed."

Mark grunted. "From the looks of your mother, I think I'd have stayed."

I punched him in the arm, and he whined. After a few moments, we fell into a comfortable silence. I was tired of talking, and Mark must have been fantasizing about my mother. Or me. Hopefully me. He fidgeted, most likely wanting to—but not daring to—try anything romantic.

He seemed restless. "Are you sure you're all right?" He checked his watch.

I read him like a book. His body language said, This is going nowhere tonight, so I'm outta here. Typical male.

I nodded and shooed him out the front door, kissing his cheek, and telling him while reassuring myself, "I've just had a bad day. New job. Domineering boss. Hitting that poor dog . . ." I shuddered in spite of myself. "It's the stress. I'll be fine."

After he left I poured another glass of wine. I felt like cussing myself for reacting the way I had. I'd known that eventually, if Mark and I continued down this road, he'd want to stay over, and just when he was feeling the time was right, I'd freaked. It's not that I hadn't thought about it. But my feelings were a maelstrom of conflicting emotions. I'd dreamed of it, run from it, debated it, and agonized over it.

I'd spent the better part of my reproductive years chasing a career in surgery and pushing love to the back burner. Although I wouldn't admit it publicly, I'd started to wonder if I could lay down my perfectionism and trust a man with everything. I looked in the mirror. I still looked young for thirty. I was sure my biological clock had a few hours left. I puckered toward my reflection. There was no reason to rush love just because I'd finally finished my residency.

As I touched my kinky hair, the accusation that Mark had thrown out over dinner resurfaced. *I don't know who I am.*

I rehearsed my answer, whispering to myself, "I'm a surgeon."

I pressed my lips together. No. There was another part of me—a huge part of me—that I'd been shoving aside.

I'm a woman. I sat straighter. *A black woman.*

I plodded to the phone and dialed my best friend. Kara Schuller was the only person in the world who would understand the mess of a day I'd had.

Her answering machine picked up. I didn't feel like pouring my heart out to a tape recorder. "Kara, it's me." I paused, wondering how much to say. "We need to talk. It's getting late. I'm going to bed. I'll call you tomorrow." I set the receiver in its cradle and fought back a tear. Kara and I had been a team since my prep school days in Boston. When I'd come to MCV for medical school, she came along for nursing. Later, when I stayed for surgery residency, she'd landed a nursing job in the pediatric intensive care unit. Her love of Red Sox baseball and her ability to make me laugh at myself had been my sanity through surgery residency hell.

Now, just when I thought my arrival as a staff attending would bring the satisfaction and acceptance I sought, I found myself on a very short leash held by a chairman convinced I would fail. A chairman who'd admitted he kept me on the leash because of my skin color.

I knew how to react to that. I'd work harder than the white men who wanted to keep me out of the club. I'd prove to myself and the world that I was better than they were at their own game.

I undressed and crawled into bed. Staring at the ceiling, unable to sleep, I cataloged my anxieties. *Will I ever find true love? Can I overcome my boss's prejudice and keep my job?* I shivered at the next thought: *What evil lurks in the basement of my past?*

I played a mental game, willing every part of my body to relax in search of sleep. Hands, fingers, shoulders, neck, focusing on each to distract my mind from worries.

I yawned. My only relief was that my horrible day had come to an end.

When I closed my eyes it wasn't the image of a dying dog that robbed me of sleep. No, it was the eyes of my six-liter boy, wide with naked fear.

I'd pulled him back from the precipice of death. Now, for his sake and my own, I needed to pull him further from the edge.

4

I WAIT TO RESUME my hiding place in the loquat tree until my mother goes over to cook stew for Mr. Mutambo. I want to watch and see if the dead man is going to walk. Since Mr. Mutambo's wife died, my mother helps him out. He does pretty good on his own, considering he only has one hand, but my mother thinks a good Christian should help out the neighbors. Mr. Mutambo has done odd jobs around the hospital for as long as I can remember. He used to work in the rubber factory. He said the managers were cruel and cut off his hand when he didn't meet quota. I used to think quota was the name for the boss 'cause everyone wanted to meet him, but my daddy says meeting quota just means you got your work done.

Lots of guys in this country only have one hand, 'cause a lot of them didn't have a chance to meet quota.

My daddy says that the Congo is the wealthiest place on earth. There is gold here. Diamonds. Rubber. Lots of great fruit like mangos, pineapples, and sweet loquats like the ones I suck now that I picked from this tree. But these people just fight, fight, fight and can't seem to come to a place where they work together and use the good part of this land in a way that will keep the women singing and the men meeting quota.

By near night, the dead man hasn't walked, and I watch as a soldier steals his nice leopard hat. The dead man didn't have shoes or I'm sure he'd have taken them, too.

I'm not sure the witchdoctor is wrong about the dead rising, but I think the only way this guy could have walked is if he'd have kept his blood.

Mother and Daddy have been whispering about going away. I think Daddy wants Mommy to go away to keep her safe, but she's afraid to go alone and Daddy won't let me go with her.

Daddy has been scaring me lately. I never saw him cry until yesterday. The Simbas had brought a little boy soldier in. He bled all over the ground outside the operating theatre and Daddy didn't have a chance to save him. Daddy rubbed the tip of his rubber boots in the dirt beside the little soldier's body. My daddy wears rubber boots in the theatre. Daddy shook his head and mumbled about the red dirt. "Sweat, tears, and blood," he said. "It's what makes this dirt African."

RICHMOND, 1984

THE CHARDONNAY QUIETED, but did not annihilate, familiar demons that haunted my night. I awoke only once, at 3:00 a.m., my bladder screaming and with only blurred images of a gasping dog, blood, and being caressed in a dark place. After emptying my bladder, I laid awake until four, wondering how long I'd have until Dr. Gilles summoned me into his lair to tell me to find work elsewhere. Would I last two months? Would he give them to me? I reviewed what I knew of the bleak local job market. Surgical groups in Richmond were not closed to women, but gender seemed a handicap. The boys were suspicious of new partners who might become impregnated and want time off. And no group in Richmond had ever hired a female African-American surgeon. Dr. Bransford said nice things like "Their loss, our gain," but now I knew better.

It was in the darkness when I was alone that I fought back the tide of doubts that assails any trend-breaker. Gilles had hired me as a token female. *And* as a token person of color. I was riding the coattails of a system that granted reverse discrimination as a privilege to those it had considered second-class a generation ago.

Those were the lies I told myself at three in the morning when I'd just offended the chairman. But I knew the truth. I was the best resident to finish the program in years. And I'd had to be twice as good as some of the men just to stay in. Surgeons in the South seemed to have forgotten the Civil War and the ERA.

I awoke with a headache, probably from the alcohol, but I ran through a list of other causes for morning headache. Brain tumors cause morning headache, because nighttime brain swelling is worse when the patient is supine. Cursed medical education. It's bad enough to suffer from one's overindulgences. It's worse when you have to worry about obscure pathologies that haunt you every time you have a physical symptom.

The memory of the sheer terror I'd felt yesterday evening was still fresh. Almost palpable. I'd never experienced that kind of panic before. That worried me, making me anxious it might happen again. That's what I hated about worry. Pretty soon, you worry about worrying. You feel panicked about the possibility of panicking. I excused the episodes to the pressure I was under at work, and the horror of hitting someone's pet. I certainly hadn't been unstable for the past six years of surgery training. Of course, when you are in training, the buck stops on someone else's desk. Now, it stopped on mine. Nothing was different now, I told myself. I was still in control.

Four Advil, two Tylenol, and two cups of strong black coffee later, I drove to work and walked straight to my clinic, avoiding the hospital hallways that would be juiced with the news of my face-off with the boys. My new MO was to fly under the radar. Out of sight, out of mind.

Post-op patients filled my clinic, mostly motor vehicle accident survivors or penetrating-abdominal-wound patients who were in various stages of healing from their assaults. I paused at the reception desk before heading to the exam rooms, studying what was to be served up today. There were a few general surgery referrals for hernias and gallbladders, and even one patient that a GI guy had sent me for a colon cancer. That was cool with me. I enjoy an elective, low-tension case now and then.

Vanessa, a clinic nurse, saw me first and gave me a high five. That was bad. The news must be out.

I slumped in a chair and avoided her eyes. "Where are my boys?" That's what I always called the residents on my team.

Vanessa pointed a bright red fingernail toward the first door. "Ellis is in room one working up a potential gallbladder. Alton is in room two with the medical students, teaching them everything he knows about inguinal hernias."

I sighed. "That should take about three minutes." Alton Young wasn't the sharpest knife in the cutlery set, but he was too honest for a career in law. Besides, he worked hard, and in the end, I believed, would make a good surgeon. "Who's in room three?"

Vanessa smiled. "Private patient. A woman. She says she isn't here to see a resident or a student doctor. She wants to see the woman surgeon."

I nodded. It's not uncommon for someone to select her surgeon based on something other than skill. Gender is a favorite criteria.

"You OK?" she asked.

I was not confessing to anything. "Sure, why not?"

She lowered her voice, but could not conceal her delight. "Did you really barge into the doctors' locker room in front of Dr. Gilles to change?"

The MCV rumor mill had pushed my actions up a notch. If I didn't stop it, by evening, I could be a mythical hero. Or unemployed. Or both. "No."

Vanessa tapped her red nails on the counter. She grinned, revealing a small gap between her front teeth. "The residents think you've got the biggest cojones in the department."

"Wonderful." Unfortunately, their opinion didn't help. My fate rested with the chairman. "Please do what you can to squelch the stories."

"I knew you'd bring some spice to this dull department." She leaned in and spoke with a giggle. "Maybe I'll ask Dr. Gilles his side of the story during the reception tonight."

I slapped my forehead. "The reception! I'd hoped to stay out of sight of the chairman for a while."

"You can't exactly miss your own welcome reception, can you?"

I grumbled under my breath, "I'd rather go to bed early."

Vanessa pointed a red nail in my direction. "I'll see you at the country club. I wouldn't miss it."

I shook my head and picked up the chart in the rack. One thought made me smile. Certainly Gilles wouldn't fire me on the same day the department was shelling out big bucks for my welcome reception.

Then I frowned. This was a university surgery department. Anything could happen.

THAT AFTERNOON, I conducted teaching rounds on the trauma service. It was like leading a small mob. I had a chief resident, a senior resident, a senior assistant resident, two interns, a fourth-year med student doing an acting internship, and two third-year students. From the looks I got from the men on the team, they knew all about yesterday. I'd be on a pedestal for a week or two only because most of them secretly hated serving under Dr. Gilles. Anyone who dared stand up to him or the policies around his OR was either brain-dead or an idol. Or both.

Teaching rounds were my favorite activity outside the OR.

We traipsed from room to room checking vital signs, urine out-puts, and examining surgical wounds. I asked questions starting with the medical students and moving up the ladder.

In the ICU, our team moved en masse around my patient who'd put me in the Six-Liter Club. John Doe had a name now. Kendrick Solomon. He was still on the ventilator and showing early signs that he might be going into adult respiratory distress syndrome, a complication with a flip-of-the-coin chance of sur-vival. I went over every piece of data one by one, every lab result, and the hourly ins and outs. I couldn't let this one get away. I knew my pride was wrapped up in the case, but I justified my feelings. I'd put more than blood into this dude to lose him now.

My senior resident, Mike Dearborn, slapped a chest X-ray on a view box on the wall outside the patient's cubicle. I sighed. It didn't look good. There were fluffy infiltrates throughout both lung fields. "He's in trouble," Mike mumbled.

We discussed the titration of his oxygen and optimizing car-diac output. Here, I was home. This stuff made sense, pure sci-ence at work. Here, you dialed up fluids and watched the cardiac output respond in kind. I was tempted to hide out here for the rest of the day. Here, Dr. Gilles wasn't likely to find me. And if I surrounded myself with pathology that I understood, maybe I wouldn't have time for ghostly images of gasping dogs or fears beyond conscious retrieval.

Unfortunately, I couldn't stay. My residents and students all had lives outside of medicine. Not that I had anything to do with that. If I had my way, they'd show the same sick dedication to surgery that I did. To deny I had a life outside surgery was the only acceptable way a woman like me could rise to the top.

I forced myself to focus upon Kendrick Solomon, giving care-ful instructions on optimizing his numbers.

Mike obediently copied them onto his scut list. I had no doubt that he'd immediately turn around after rounds and hand the duties to an intern or resident below him. That's the way the system worked in surgery training. You implicitly obey the person on the rung above you. And the smelly stuff doesn't roll uphill. The problem at the top of the ladder is the responsibility. The problem at the bottom is the smell.

A large woman in a flowered dress and a purple hat waited just outside the patient cubicle. As I turned to leave, she touched the arm of Ellis Hamilton. "That's my boy, Doc. How's he doing?"

It was only mildly irritating that I was closer, and yet Kendrick's mother had asked a man. Ellis looked at me and deferred. Smart boy. He knew his place in this crowd.

I extended my hand. "I'm Dr. Weller, the trauma surgeon who operated on your son."

The woman's hand was plump and soft. Her eyes were wide. "I'm Nadine Solomon."

"Your son is very sick. His injuries were serious, but not immediately fatal." I hesitated. "He lost a lot of blood, more than almost anyone I've ever seen."

Her hand went to cover her generous lips. "He's going to make it."

"His lungs are starting to fail. It could go either way."

She pressed her lips together before she spoke. "I wasn't askin' a question. I was tellin' you the truth. I believe the Lord's gonna spare my boy."

Great. This woman wasn't going to listen to reason. I smiled, sweet and plastic. "I sure hope you're right. We're going to do everything we can."

"I've called on the elders," she said. "They're going to bring in the anointing oil."

I imagined half of her church showing up for the ceremony. I nodded as I felt a tap on my arm. I turned to see the unit's head nurse, Tracy King.

"I've already explained our visitor's policy to Mrs. Solomon."

I studied Tracy for a moment. This was a test. She wanted to see if I was going to bend the rules she so adored.

I took Mrs. Solomon's hand. "As long as the other patients' care is not interrupted, I'm sure it will be fine."

"You want me to arrange the elders to visit them, too?"

"No," Tracy interjected, smoothing the front of her white coat. "Dr. Weller means that no more than two people can visit at a time so as not to interfere with the care of other sick patients."

Nadine frowned. "We have five elders. I called them all."

"Perhaps they can come in two at a time," I offered.

She shook her head. "We have a healing team. They all come and pray together. The Bible says, 'Where two or more are gathered in my name, there I am in their midst.'"

Tracy stood firm, arms braced across her chest. "Maybe we could consult one of our chaplains. They can offer a prayer for your son."

The purple-dress lady frowned. "I trus' my elders."

Tracy smiled with plastic concern. "Two visitors at a time," she said. "I'm afraid you'll have to abide by our policy."

I traded glances with Tracy. The look told me not to cross her. I knew her modus operandi. In the past five years she had taken great pleasure to make sure I followed all of her ICU policies. Now, as the interim staff director, I finally outranked her, and she'd bared her fangs like a threatened animal. I suspected any deviation of the rules that I allowed would find its way to my superiors. I offered Tracy a smile, then paused for a minute to give her a chance to walk away. Fortunately, she took it.

When Head Nurse Godzilla was out of earshot, I turned to Mrs. Solomon.

She lowered her voice and leaned forward. "Make an exception for a sister."

Now she was playing the race card. I didn't like it. I wasn't really sure I felt like her "sister." I was ready to make concessions for her request, but not because she was African American. I handed her a business card. "Call me at my office, Mrs. Solomon. I'm sure I can arrange a time for the visitors to pray." I lowered my voice. "It will have to be after day-shift hours," I said, looking conspicuously toward the head nurse. "The nighttime staff will be OK with it."

She smiled and gripped my arm.

My team started to step away as I had a flash memory of the look of terror on my patient's face after I had asked who had shot him. "Mrs. Solomon, do you have any idea who was responsible for your son's injury? Who shot him?"

Her face tightened. "I . . . I wasn't there. I don't know what happened. You know Richmond," she added. "There are some gangs around."

"Was your son in a gang?"

A look of fear crossed her face, prompting me to explain. "I only want to make sure your son is safe. If you think there's a chance someone still wants him dead, we'll need to have him protected."

"Oh no," she said. "The boys tol' me it was an accident. Kendrick was on the wrong side of a door when a gun was fired from the inside."

I studied her for a moment, pondering the information. One moment, she seemed to be blaming it on a gang, the next, she was saying it was an accident. Whatever had happened, she wasn't exactly forthcoming with the information. I couldn't quite shake the feeling that she was hiding something or covering for someone. "OK," I said. "If you are satisfied . . ." I let my sentence trail off.

My entourage moved on. Mrs. Solomon stepped into her son's cubicle. I heard her as I entered the next cubicle. She talked to her son, and something in her voice made me shiver. "Everything's gonna be all right, baby. Everything's gonna be all right."

I tried to pay attention as my intern presented the progress on the next patient, but a worm of dread gnawed at my gut. My chest tightened. I felt my cheeks flush, and I wanted to be anywhere but here. A minute before, I'd wanted to hide in here for the rest of the day. Now, I thought—no, I knew—I had to get out of here before I lost it in front of the same residents who thought I was a bad dude for invading the men's locker room.

What was happening to me?

I listened as my intern droned on.

"His chest tube output has been two hundred ccs in the past eight hours. His urine . . ."

I could conquer this emotionalism. I tried to slow my breathing and ignore the pounding in my chest. Panic was not part of the trauma surgeon's personal repertoire. We may carry emotional bags packed with arrogance, pride, and insensitivity, but we do not panic.

"His cardiac index is two point four, his wedge is twelve, his . . ."

I felt as if I were in a race, with the devil on my heels. My heart galloped, and I felt sweat on my forehead.

I endured the data presentation as the cubicle squeezed tighter around me. By the end, it seemed it had shrunk by half, and I was suddenly too close to everyone. "OK," I mumbled. "I'll round with the team after cases tomorrow." I looked at Ellis. "I'm the attending backing you up tonight. I'm on my beeper." With that, I turned tail and walked away.

In the women's room down the hall, I washed my face and then sat in a stall, hiding in private, where I monitored my pulse. Perhaps it was something I ate. I reviewed lunch. I'd had a cheeseburger at the Skull and Bones—the medical campus bar and grill. It couldn't be that. I'd eaten a million greasy burgers at the Skull. Other than an extra five pounds on my hips I didn't think I was any worse for the wear. Of course, no one could see the effect on my coronaries, but I loved the burgers and I lived in denial, so I put that fleeting thought out of my mind.

Maybe it was just a vagal reflex, the hyper-response that makes speakers faint in front of large groups. No, if it was that, my heart rate would have been slow, not fast, and I loved speaking in front of groups. Maybe I had a pheochromocytoma, one of those rare tumors you heard about in medical school, and then never saw. Pheos secreted adrenaline that could make you feel the way I did.

I closed my eyes and counted. By the time I reached one hundred, my pulse had slowed and the feeling passed. I exited my hiding place and walked to my office to work on a slide presentation I would be giving the med students the following week.

I was looking over a paper on ICU outcome predictors in patients with ARDS when I heard a soft knock on my partially closed door. I looked up to see Dr. William Bransford. "Hey."

"Got a minute?"

"No, but I'll talk to you anyway."

He stepped in and closed the door, a definite "uh-oh" for me. He let a smile escape and raised his bushy white eyebrows at me. "Have you been by the OR?"

I shook my head. "Not today."

"Score: Weller, one; Gilles, zero."

"What are you talking about?"

"Maintenance repainted the doors on the OR changing rooms."

I smiled. "You're kidding, right?"

"Nope." He held up his hands and pulled them apart as he said, "Men," and repeated the motion, saying, "Women."

"So did you come in to congratulate me?"

His face sobered. "Not exactly. You may have gotten what you wanted, but you need to play this game correctly if you want to stay around. Gilles doesn't look kindly to people bucking the status quo he's established."

"I hate that term." I twisted my mouth. " 'Status quo.' It's so, well, stodgy, full of inertia."

"No one will ever accuse you of following it."

"I know." I paused. "So why did you come by? If you're not going to congratulate me, stop wasting my time." I waved my hand playfully to shoo him away.

"I want you to toe the line, Camille. Don't make so many waves. The boss will not be happy." He leaned forward, standing over my desk. "Gilles isn't going to give you a long time to settle in. If you want to keep this job you've landed, start coloring inside the lines."

"Maybe it's not my style."

"Make it your style." He sighed. "Just start playing by the rules."

I pouted. I've got great pouty lips, another thing I inherited from my Congolese mother. Other women line up for collagen injections to get the look I was showing Dr. Bransford. "I hate rules."

"Don't blow this opportunity. If you lose an academic spot this early, especially in the institution where you trained, you will not find it easy to obtain another."

"So I'll work in town."

"Maybe on your own. But try that for six months without cross-coverage from the groups that didn't think this town was ready for an African-American woman surgeon, and you'll be looking back fondly at residency training."

"That's just it. I don't want to be known as an African-American woman surgeon. I'm a surgeon. Period." I dotted the end of my sentence with my finger in the air. "It shouldn't matter that I'm a woman. Or black."

He shook his head. Dr. Bransford was a good man. He'd taken me under his wing as a medical student and encouraged me. He was a mentor, yes, but also a little bit like the father I never had. When I was having a bad time, I'd retreat to his office for another Bransford-signature go-get-'em-Tiger talk.

"Life is what it is, Camille. You aren't going to change Richmond in one year."

"Or one decade."

He ran his hand through the side of his closely cropped white hair. "So start toeing the line. You're a good surgeon, Camille.

Gilles and I both know that. But remember, a good surgeon knows her limits, inside the OR *and out!*"

He stood for a moment, as if letting the words hang would give them more gravity. He paused before lowering his voice to add a warning: "It's no secret that I've been on your side during your residency. But there is only so much I can do if you insist on pushing the edge of a very slow-moving establishment. Push the chairman's buttons and you'll be on your own." Then he nodded and let himself out.

For an instant, I wanted to call after him, to confess to him the turmoil I'd been experiencing, to tell him that my own panic, not Dr. Gilles, was what I feared would keep me from success in this game. I longed for him to tell me that every new surgeon experienced such terrors and that I oughtn't worry.

I suppressed the urge to run down the hall after him. Weakness was not something I'd easily admit. Now that I was on staff, I had to be careful how much I let my guard down in front of those who might need to go to bat for me if the umpire threatened to take me out of the game.

I sat at my desk and worked for another hour until the downtown traffic thinned, and then headed toward my northside apartment.

My new Prelude soothed my soul. I loved the way it smelled. I drove along happily until I approached the place of my accident the night before. I slowed and scanned the sidewalk for a large, dead dog. The place was barren. Maybe all the neighborhood kids were inside mourning the loss of their favorite pet. Some poor kid was going to need therapy someday because of what I'd done.

The thought swung round and slapped me in the face. *Perhaps I'm the one who needs therapy.* No. Not me. I reminded myself of my solid constitution, of my ability to make it on my own. I was an orphan. I had learned early to be strong.

"Therapy" was for women who retreat into soap operas to find a happy life.

I had a happy life. I was a surgeon. Others wanted to be me.

I pulled into the parking lot in front of my apartment and thought about the reception at the Pinewood Country Club. An evening of glitz, schmooze, and pompous posturing. Suddenly, I wasn't so hungry.

I can toe the line at work. I'm the first woman trauma surgeon at MCV. So why am I so afraid?

I was about to reach for the door handle when a sharp rap on the window shocked me from my introspection.

And I thought my day had been bad enough.

Aunt Jeanine!

5

Y OU DIDN'T THINK I'd miss a reception in your honor, did
you?" Aunt Jeanine said.

"Well, I—" I followed her up the stairs to my apartment. "I
hadn't heard back and—"

Aunt Jeanine waved a diamond-studded hand in the air. "Fid-
dlesticks! I'm sure I replied to your invitation."

I took a deep breath. I'd invited her only because I was sure
she'd never show up. If any decision I'd made in my life was destined to separate me from my aunt, it was my proclamation that I
was going to follow in my father's footsteps. A reception to honor
my initiation into my father's occupation was as likely to attract
my aunt Jeanine as water would a rabid dog.

Aunt Jeanine pushed through the door and inspected my
little apartment.

"I've been planning to get a bigger place," I said, following
her into my kitchen. "I'm going to have a Realtor show me what's
on the market."

"It's quaint."

I knew she meant small.

"Do you want to freshen up?"

"Heavens, no, Camille. I've registered at the Jefferson downtown. I just stopped by to get directions to the country club."

I looked at her short red dress and prayed she'd change into something age appropriate. "You could have called."

"I wanted to surprise you."

I smiled, hiding my turmoil. "Of course." I'd survived in my conservative surgical residency by wearing navy blue and gray. Not that anyone would have guessed I had conservative leanings after the colorful stamp I'd left on the department my first two days on the job. Aunt Jeanine dressed bold and talked bolder. I was already trying to figure out how to keep her away from Dr. Gilles.

I found a notepad and a twenty-five-cent Bic pen. Aunt Jeanine frowned and handed me a silver ballpoint. I sketched a map, thinking twice about sending her toward Petersburg instead of the club.

"I want to meet Mark," she said, tucking my map inside her handbag.

"OK," I nodded, "but I'm going to show up fashionably late."

"But it's your party."

That's why I wanted to be late. I didn't explain. I'm a complicated woman. I loved to be better than any man at what I do, but I didn't crave being the center of attention. I tolerated it when being the best thrust it upon me.

Fortunately, Aunt Jeanine didn't wait for my answer. She waved her hand again and said, "I'll see you there."

I sat on the couch contemplating the hurricane that had just blown through. I hadn't seen my only living relative in months and she was in and out in under five minutes. No investigation into my life. Not even a cup of coffee or a shared memory of her brother—my father.

Of course, I knew better than that. Aunt Jeanine never talked to me of my father. She was pushing seventy years old and I never remembered her mentioning his name.

I DROVE THOUGH sparse evening traffic on Interstate 64 West, heading for Pinewood Country Club. My aunt Jeanine's arrival had me in a slight tailspin, but I'd recover as long as she changed out of the red dress. It seemed every time she showed up, I ended up doing a little soul searching. Maybe it was because I couldn't believe someone like me was actually related to someone like her. Or maybe it was because my mind was always directed toward our one blood link: my father.

For as long as I could remember, I'd wanted to be a surgeon. In the beginning, perhaps it was because my aunt Jeanine hated the idea, so I said it all the more: "I'm going to be like my father."

This stubbornness carried well into high school, as I built an image of my father around dim memories and my own fantasies. Orphans do that, I suppose. We don't have fathers, so the ones we invent are better than any of our friends'. My father was a cutter, someone who healed people by the touch of his hand, the careful dissection of a blade.

He became my idol, the man of my dreams, the father who loved me, praised me, comforted me. When Aunt Jeanine treated me with chilled indifference, I retreated to my fallback position, rolling statements around me like Linus's security blanket: My father wouldn't treat me like that. My father would let me stay out late. My father would let me have a friend over for dinner or a sleepover.

As I grew older and endured medical school and residency training, I understood at an unspoken level that no man could ever be as good as the father I'd created, but by then I was addicted to the game. "What would my father do?" became my mantra when looking at a difficult new patient problem. He was not only the perfect father, but the perfect surgeon. And I would be just like him.

When I didn't feel acceptable to my aunt, I brushed her off. After all, what did it matter what she thought? Certainly my own father thought differently.

I sighed and checked my lipstick in the rearview mirror. Perhaps I should thank Aunt Jeanine for my success. I'd always thought it was her indifference to my performance that drove me to do my best. I brought home the top grades to her casual approval, but learned quickly that everyone else praised me for what Aunt Jeanine cared little about. Since she hated my father, and therefore hated me, I would become just like him. It would be the perfect revenge.

For me, becoming a surgeon was far from being only a way to spite a loveless aunt. Riling Aunt Jeanine was only a side benefit. Medicine to me was the best of professions, and surgery was its pinnacle. Touching someone with healing in his time of greatest pain became addictive, the drug that crowded out my own hurts. In surgery I found instant gratification, a mechanical solution that could be manifested in a few hours, a vast contrast to the weeks and months my medicine colleagues waited to see the effect of pills and prescriptions. From the moments of my first exposure in the mission theater where my father operated, I knew surgery was a special gift to be shared by a select few. And more than anything else, I wanted to be chosen to wield a scalpel to heal.

I was glad my aunt was showing interest, but I was suspicious of her motives. I supposed she just wanted to see if she was right after all. She'd warned me not to come South to train. Stay in Boston. *The South has too much inertia for a woman. Stay where women are respected as equals.*

I'd learned to read between the lines when I listened to Aunt Jeanine. I think she just didn't want me that much closer to her comfortable white life in Montgomery. She wouldn't voice the message I heard: *The South is no place for a half-breed.*

I arrived only twenty minutes late and saw that Aunt Jeanine's Mercedes was already in the lot. I took a deep breath and entered the ballroom, where the party was just picking up.

I surveyed the room. It looked like the department had spared no expense. A string quartet played in the corner. Tables of hors d'oeuvres and a chocolate fondue fountain were surrounded by guests who lifted champagne glasses from trays carried by black boys in white coats. I spotted Dr. Gilles and Dr. Bransford in the far corner. Thankfully Aunt Jeanine had been cornered by Kara, who was holding two glasses of champagne. She lifted one in my direction.

"Congratulations, Dr. Weller," she said, handing me a glass. She lifted her own to her lips. "To you."

I took a sip and traded looks with my best friend. She'd fought a demon, alcohol, for a decade.

She knew what I was thinking. In front of my aunt, I had to ignore the drinks. "I see you and Aunt Jeanine are becoming reacquainted."

Kara smiled. "It's been a lot of years. She's been telling me stories about your childhood I've never heard before."

"All lies."

My aunt, now tastefully attired in an emerald green dress, smiled. "Where's this fellow I've been hearing about?"

Kara leaned over and whispered, "Things must be serious if you're telling Aunt Jeanine."

"She asked me who I was dating, that's all." In truth, I wished things were more serious than they were. Mark was smart, intellectual, and best of all, seemed to adore me—except when I rooted for the BoSox.

I strained to see around the room. So far, no Mark. Typical. He would be very fashionably late. Maybe he had a sick kid in the ICU.

Dr. Gilles appeared at my shoulder. "Camille," he said.

"Hello, Dr. Gilles," I said, extending my hand. "You know Kara Schuller, I'm sure. And this is my aunt Jeanine."

Dr. Gilles took my aunt's hand. I watched for a reaction. If he was surprised, he didn't show it. I'm used to seeing the look of question when people learn that I've got white blood. I can thank my Congolese mother for that. Congolese genes seemed to have trumped my father's white ones.

Gilles stared at my aunt. "We feel quite fortunate to have kept a surgeon like your niece."

"So nice to finally meet you," she gushed. "Camille can't seem to stop talking about you." Jeanine gestured wildly. "Dr. Gilles this, Dr. Gilles that."

Enough already. I looked at Kara, who was enjoying the exchange, pleading with my eyes: *Help me, girl.*

I gently took my aunt's elbow. "Let's check out the buffet."

Dr. Gilles was interrupted by Dr. Daniels, one of his buddies, and MCV's best plastic surgeon. I was rescued for now. I needed to get Aunt Jeanine away or she'd start asking the plastic surgeon about getting her eyelids lifted.

For the next three hours I steered Aunt Jeanine through the minefield while watching the time and glancing at the entranceway, waiting for Mark Lawson to make his appearance. We'd been discreet around MCV, but I was hoping tonight could be our first real public appearance within the university community. It's not like I hadn't given him enough forewarning about the date. He probably had a cancer kid going south in the ICU and couldn't leave. Relationships in medicine demanded flexibility.

The fact that it bothered me that he was so late was revealing to me in another way. I really did care about him. He'd been so good about taking things at my pace, supporting my new position as a surgery staff member, and, well, he was so easy on the eyes. In the last few weeks I'd found myself cautiously dreaming of a future with Mark. Tonight, I'd wanted to make a public statement: *This one is taken.*

I looked around the room and lifted a curtain to peer out the window toward the entrance. A valet delivered a BMW convertible to one of the heart surgeons. No Mark. I let the curtain fall and turned back to face my public.

At the end of the evening, I stood on a veranda bordered by tall white columns. I smoked a Nicaraguan cigar with Gilles,

Bransford, and Ellis Hamilton. We talked shop and drank amber ale from tall mugs.

My eye was drawn to Kara, who was holding yet another glass of white wine. I walked to her at the edge of the portico and leaned against a white column. I pointed toward the glass in her hand. "How are you doing?"

She looked away. "OK."

"Kara, I—"

"Don't even start. You're worse than my mother."

"Excuse me?"

"I know what you're going to say." She glared at me. "So don't start."

"I just—"

"I said don't." She looked at me with disgust. "Don't talk to me about compromise."

"I suppose you think I have a problem with this?" I responded, holding up my beer.

"You don't even see it," she said with a hushed tone. She looked away again. A large magnolia tree reached toward us with waxy leaves. "Your problem is you don't even like beer."

I looked at the mug in my hand.

"And you hate cigars."

I pulled the stogie from my lips.

"Why can't you be who you want to be, Camille? Instead of what Gilles expects of his boys?" When she spoke the last two words, they escaped in a sneer, dripping with contempt.

I wanted to write off her accusations, telling myself that Kara was being defensive because she knew I was judging her for drinking alcohol. Attacking me was natural. That way, she wouldn't have to give credence to my judgment. But her words had struck their target. Maybe my arrival in the boys' club was time for me to make an assessment of some of my concessions. Hey, I told myself, having a cigar and beer with the guys isn't such a crime, is it? I paused. But if it isn't me, why do it?

Why am I so desperate to be accepted?

Kara walked away, leaving me to rejoin the boys. I looked around as I approached them and sighed. It was official. My best boyfriend prospect in years had missed the party celebrating my new position.

I pushed aside the next thought: Will I ever find love?

I shook my head. He just has a sick child to look after.

It was time to check on my aunt. I didn't trust her being alone with my coworkers for too long. As far as I knew, she hadn't embarrassed me. Yet.

I dragged on the cigar, letting the sour smoke burn the back of my throat and resisted the urge to spit. Kara was right. I didn't really like cigars.

Dr. Gilles met me head-on at the edge of the veranda. I looked at him, searching his face. After all of the polite comments from everyone tonight, I had hoped Dr. Gilles had forgotten my locker room antics. I looked at the cigar in my hand.

He lifted his to his mouth and pulled hard before blowing smoke toward the glass doors leading to the ballroom.

The unspoken message was clear. Toe the line. Be a man.

I should be good at that. At least I had been for six years.

There was just one little problem. And the fact that I was ready to admit it struck me as a subtle change in me, a change I thought I would like.

I'm a woman.

6

I N THE PARKING lot in front of Pinewood Country Club, Aunt
Jeanine kissed my cheek perfunctorily. "I'm leaving early for
Martha's Vineyard."

"I'd like to show you around the hospital."

"I've seen enough."

Typical for Hurricane Jeanine.

"Dr. Gilles is a charming man."

"He's a good surgeon."

"Charming men can be dangerous, Camille."

"He has a worldwide reputation."

"You adore him."

I thought for a moment before answering. "Yes." I couldn't
have stayed under that pressure if I hadn't.

"His eyes . . ." Her voice trailed off.

I understood. They were his most striking feature. Eyes alight
with menace and delight. The searching eyes that residents knew.
And feared.

Aunt Jeanine looked away. "Be careful, Camille."

"You're being spooky. Stop it."

"I've seen eyes like that before, but not for a long time."

I grew impatient with her little game. "They would be hard
to forget."

She looked back and cleared her throat as if some lost memory had choked her with emotion. "Congratulations on your new job, Camille." She paused. "This is what Jack should have done. Johns Hopkins wanted him to stay on." She shook her head. "But his head was full of dreams."

Jack. My father. "You never told me that before." I paused. "And you told Kara stories from my childhood? You haven't shared much with me."

She spoke with a condescending tone. "I'm sure you remember the important things, Camille."

I shook my head. Perhaps the parking lot wasn't the ideal place, but Aunt Jeanine was getting away so I pressed on. "I don't remember him. My father."

My aunt gripped her car keys. "Some things are best left alone."

"I want to remember him."

"Listen to me, Camille. Your amnesia is a gift. When I took you in from the Congo, I thought you'd never sleep a night through without those terrors." She touched my arm. "Leave Africa behind you."

I started to protest, but she warned me with a look and by raising her voice. "No. There are stones better left unturned."

"What about Alabama? Was there pain there for me, too?"

She looked at me as if I spoke a foreign language. "You don't remember?"

I started to say no, but she waved her hand in my face and continued. "Alabama was no place for a black child in the sixties."

She gave me a polite hug, the kind you reserve for a fragile old relative.

It seemed she wanted to say more, but instead turned to open the door to her Mercedes.

"Who were you talking about, Aunt Jeanine?"

"Who?"

"The eyes. You said you'd seen Dr. Gilles's eyes before."

"Of course." She halted and took a deep breath. She reached

for my hand and gave it a good-bye squeeze. "Your father," she said, "had eyes just like that."

SOMETHING ABOUT BEING dissed by Mark Lawson and the hectic antics of my first days as an attending told me sleep would be elusive. So instead of heading home, I decided to visit my Six-Liter boy one more time before trying to face a night of staring at the ceiling of my apartment. I parked on the street to avoid the longer walk from the parking deck. It was after midnight and space was open in front of Sanger Hall, the medical school's teaching complex.

The lonely wail of an ambulance siren dissected the moist Richmond night as I entered the emergency room to see if I'd have any new players on the trauma service in the morning. The scene was all too typical—a madhouse of activity with crying children, sleeping drunks, and a crowd of brothers standing at the foot of a stretcher holding a white-haired matriarch struggling to get her breath. The sweet-sour smell of bloody vomit and clinical antiseptic mingled as a familiar odor and prompted me to quicken my pace.

On the last stretcher a high school boy in a football uniform sat with his foot propped on a stool as an intern applied an Ace wrap to his swollen ankle. The patient looked as exhausted and haggard as the intern. It wasn't uncommon to have to wait six hours to be seen, and from the look on his face, he was more than a little upset. He'd probably been sitting in the waiting room since his afternoon practice, a summer insanity inspired by competitive Virginia coaches. My eyes met his long enough for his expression to change, and in a moment I was aware of how unusual I must look in my black cocktail party dress. The corner of his mouth turned into a half-snarl and I felt his gaze until I pushed through the doors exiting into the lobby by the elevators.

I shivered and pressed the elevator button and tried to think ahead to the checklist I'd follow on my ICU patient.

"Dr. Weller. Dr. Weller."

I looked over to see Rick Arensen, a surgery resident, vaguely aware that he had been calling my name. I studied his face without speaking, still lost in a cloud from my past.

"Dr. Weller?" His eyes took the scenic route over my curves. "I—well—nice dress, Dr. Weller."

I nodded emptily. "I was at the welcome reception."

He cleared his throat. "It's late. You're not on call."

The dedication I modeled was meant to inspire. Rick's tone of voice indicated he questioned my sanity. "I wanted to check on Kendrick."

He looked away. "I need to get to the ER. Call me if you want me to do something different in the ICU."

The elevator doors opened, ending our conversation. Rick didn't know it, but I was glad for the interruption of my darkening thoughts.

Inside, a child in a patient gown stood holding an IV pole. I looked at the panel of the floor buttons. All eighteen floors were lit up. Evidently the little patient was playing a game to pass the night, having escaped from pediatrics. I knelt down and tousled his cropped Afro. "Where do you belong, sport?" His eyes were alight with mischief.

The doors opened on the next floor to reveal a peds intern standing with her hands on her hips. "There you are, you little stink!"

The patient retreated behind me.

The intern, a young female, frowned and stuck her hand against the closing door. "Time for your blood test, Tommy." Evidently her demanding time schedule had pushed away any shred of compassion for her young patients.

Something in me wanted to protect this little brother, and I narrowly dodged a motherly impulse to gather him into my arms and flee from the intern-monster. Instead, I touched his shoulder, and stared into his dark eyes. "It's OK, Tommy. We all just want you to get better." I stood and looked at the intern and spoke in a quiet voice. "I'm Dr. Weller, department of surgery. I hope I won't need to speak to your attending about your . . ." I paused. "Tact." I offered a smile.

The intern shook her head quietly. Softer, she called, "Come on, Tommy. I'll be sure and find a Popsicle for you." The boy stepped out from behind me and joined the intern. As the doors closed, he looked back and caught my eye for a last time.

In three minutes I was standing at the foot of Kendrick Solomon's ICU bed and silently running his board—the clipboard of information about vital signs and input and output data. Every few seconds, his ventilator sounded a high-pressure alarm. His oxygen saturations appeared to be headed south. I paged Arensen. In a moment, the phone rang. I picked up to give him my orders. "Dr. Weller."

"Dr. Weller. It's Rick."

"I want you to paralyze our boy. His oxygenation is crappy. He's fighting the ventilator. He's not going to last long like this."

"OK."

"Do it now."

A sigh from my resident. "Sure."

I hung up the phone and thought about what Gilles had said: *If he doesn't survive, I'm going to make her answer for why she didn't call for backup on such a huge case.*

I resolved again to fight for Kendrick's life. And not only to avoid the chief's wrath. I needed it to be more. I needed to believe I cared for my patient and not just my reputation.

I sighed. *Who am I fooling? I divorced my emotions a long time ago.*

I padded on heavy feet to the automatic doors of the ICU. There I was met by Nadine Solomon wearing the same flowery dress as I'd seen earlier in the day.

"How's my boy?"

I needed to hang black crepe. I needed her to be realistic. But it wasn't time for confusing details. I settled for intentionally vague. "He's very, very sick."

Her hand trembled as she held it to her lower lip. She squeezed her fingers into a tight fist. She seemed to want to be strong in front of me. Her eyes met mine. "I'm glad you're takin' care of my boy."

The tenacity of her spirit amazed me. Her son was clearly dying. She had to know that. But from the blanket of darkness, she'd teased up a positive thread. It was a single strand, and she gripped it with a knuckle-blanching persistence. She'd found the essence of something that keeps people plodding forward: hope. And at that moment, right or wrong, I realized that who I was seemed important to the people of downtown Richmond. They wanted to see a brother or sister of color on their side.

She enveloped me with her soft arms and a thought embraced with the same force: she was comforting me. I knew it must be her way, giving in the midst of pain, to ease the rawness of her own experience.

We released each other as I felt a rush of emotions. I was in a fight just like Kendrick. Not for my life, but for finding my way. I felt like a little girl in the arms of her momma, scared and confused. I turned away from Nadine, not wanting to dissolve in front of her. I held my breath for a moment to swallow and collect my voice.

"I'll see you tomorrow," I said.

I was met at the elevator by a breathless Tom Ashby, a surgery intern on call for the trauma service for the night. "Dr. Weller, I'm glad I caught you. Dr. Larimore got wind you were around and wondered if you might be able to lend him a hand."

"What's up?" I asked as we stepped onto the elevator together.

"Twenty-two-year-old guy with a gunshot wound to his left groin. He's headed to the OR now. The guy's lost a ton of blood."

Dave Larimore had been a trauma attending for five years. Hiring me meant that finally the staff would have someone less experienced than he was to criticize. He'd taken his share of grief from the old guard, and if I understood things correctly, he had come to MCV from a high-powered intellectual program but lacked operative experience. That he'd obtained at the hands of the poor in downtown Richmond. Among the residents, he was tolerated because he always let them do everything. I'd never been sure if that was because he was unsure of himself or because he realized the residents needed experience. I trailed the intern to the OR and changed. Two minutes later, I entered room three, where the patient was being transferred to the operating table.

Dave was thirty-five, tall, and Hitler-approved blond. He looked at me through gold wire-rimmed glasses. He was a sixties holdout, played Beatles music during every case I'd scrubbed with him as a resident. In fact, I'd always thought he looked a bit like John Lennon. "I need you to put on a pair of sterile gloves and hold pressure over his femoral vessels. He must have a major arterial injury. I need you to control the wound while I open the belly to control the vessels above the inguinal ligament."

"Sure." I slid up next to an ER nurse who had been holding pressure on a gauze packing over the patient's left upper thigh. "Here," I said, slipping my hand over hers. "I've got it."

The patient was put to sleep and the wound prepped. Dr. Larimore opened the abdomen while I held pressure over a crimson wound just over the groin crease. With our heads nearly touching over the victim between us, Larimore gazed at me over his mask. "You OK?"

"Sure." I was curt, but it wasn't time for talking about the weather.

"Press firmer," he said, an edge to his voice, "he's bleeding around the wound."

Larimore looked at the resident. "Arensen! Scrub and assist."

After five minutes, my hand felt as if it might go into tetany.

I was fighting the urge to massage my hand when my fingers slipped a few centimeters from the top of the open wound. Blood sprayed my gown, prompting me to shift my fingers back into a better position. Larimore glared at me. "Careful, Camille!" He took a deep breath. "I thought you said you were OK."

"Just a little cramp. I'm OK. When Arensen comes, he can take over and I'll help you dissect the vessels."

He shook his head. "Rick can help me. Just keep holding pressure."

I looked at Derrick, who stood faithfully beside his scrub table filled with instruments. He didn't speak, but our eyes communicated enough. Larimore was acting like a jerk. He asked me to come help him, then relegated me to a job the intern could do, rather than allowing me to help with the delicate dissection.

I held pressure until Dave Larimore had the vessels clamped above the level of the injury, then he moved across from me and gently lifted my fingers from the wound. After another minute, Larimore suggested I allow Arensen the experience of assisting the vascular repair of the femoral vessels, and I slid to the side. When he'd been able to make sense of the bullet injury, he reclamped the blood vessels in the immediate proximity to the wound and removed the clamps up higher in the abdomen.

"Why don't you close the abdomen, Camille? Are you up to it?"

Up to it? I kept my comments to myself and held out my hand to Derrick, palm up. "Stitch."

I closed the fascia and stapled the skin, then watched as Larimore repaired the femoral artery in the groin, patching it with a segment of saphenous vein. When it was time for wound closure, he gave instructions to the resident and stepped back from the table.

I took that as my cue and stripped off my sterile gown, depositing the soiled garment in the laundry bin in the room's corner. I followed my colleague into the hall, where we stopped in front of the scrub sink. "Can you tell me what that was all about?"

"I shouldn't have asked you to scrub in."

"And why not?"

"You shouldn't have agreed to help me."

"You didn't answer my question. What are you talking about?"

"You've been drinking, Camille. I can smell the beer."

I felt my jaw slacken. "I had a beer at my own welcome reception, Dave. It was nothing."

"Your hands were shaking."

"Only because I was holding pressure in the same position for so long. I could have sped things up if you didn't have to instruct Arensen on every step."

"I couldn't take that risk."

"Risk? Dave! Really, I'm fine."

He looked at me with beady, judgmental eyes, gazing at me through his Lennon glasses.

I shook my head. "I don't believe this."

"Don't sweat it this time, Camille. Just don't ever let Gilles find out that you were operating under the influence."

"I wasn't—"

I stopped talking when the OR door swung open and a nurse called from the room. "He doesn't have a pulse in his foot, Dr. Larimore."

The attending groaned. I was about to follow him in, when he turned to face me. "Go home, Camille. Sleep it off. I'll take care of this myself."

I walked away in a state of disbelief. My first two days on a new job and I was setting records for offending the staff. Not only had I been misjudged by my chairman, I'd been falsely accused by a fellow trauma surgeon.

I padded on heavy feet toward the changing room, hoping against hope that Larimore would keep his mouth shut about his perceptions. My gut was in a knot.

How can things get any worse?

I AWOKE AT four with my heart pounding, a whispered phrase the only thing I could remember about the dream that vaulted me from slumber into a state of terror. I repeated it softly, as if by recounting the words I'd remember why the phrase seemed to carry such horror. "Everything's gonna be all right, baby. Everything's gonna be all right."

Rubbing sleep from my eyes, a memory pushed forward. The phrase was the identical one that Mark had whispered. My eyes opened, a minor revelation on the way. It was the same phrase that woman in the purple hat had spoken to her son in the ICU. It was the same phrase I'd heard as a child. From who?

I shivered, then wiggled deeper into my covers. This was crazy. I'd been upset over hitting the dog, and Mark was only trying to comfort me. My memory of the phrase must be tied to the panic I felt about running over the dog, that's all. So when Kendrick's mother spoke the phrase, it just made the memory surface again. And along with the memory, I reexperienced the emotion.

I thought about Pavlov's dogs and how Pavlov rang a bell before feeding the animals. Over time, ringing the bell alone made the dogs salivate. Maybe I'd just become a Pavlovian dog. I heard a phrase, I experienced terror. My theory was simplistic, but I was a surgeon, not a psychiatrist. Gallstones were so much easier to understand. They cause right upper quadrant pain after eating at Shoney's. You take out the gallbladder. End of story. Nice and tidy. That was the kind of problem I loved. That was the reason I was a surgeon.

I laid awake for an hour, telling myself over and over that I was fine and that the pressures of being a new trauma attending would subside in a few weeks. *I'll settle into a routine. The dreams will go away. They always have before.*

7

〰〰〰〰

S OMETIMES MY DADDY'S eyes smile when he talks, especially
when he's telling some crazy story about something he did
in the operating theatre. My mom hates it and stops him whenever he starts another story about some operation, 'cause she
says it will upset the dinner, but I just giggle and ask him to tell
me all about it after supper. Lately, Daddy's eyes have not been
smiling much, but look stern and worried all the time. I guess
it's the worry that the Simbas might try to hurt the hospital.
That's why we've stayed around, I think. We have to stay 'cause
there aren't any other surgeons trying to bring life to all the
bloody soldiers.

Daddy's eyes were the color of our Land Rover. He looked at
me and touched my shoulder. "I need you to take these down to
the leper house."

I nodded and lifted my sisal basket. I would do anything to
get to go outside for a little. More and more, because of the fighting, Mother makes me stay inside.

My basket holds a lot. My daddy loaded it down with rice,
bananas, papaya, and coffee for the lepers. Now, I walk with the
long handles looped around my forehead and the basket resting
on my back like the village women. Daddy tells me not to do it

much 'cause he takes care of the women's necks when they've been carrying their baskets this way.

I'm not sure why it has to be my job to feed the lepers. Dr. Rebert's wife always shopped for them before, but now the bad Simba men have taken them away—along with the Hansons and the New Zealand people—to Stanleyville. In fact, my daddy's the only doctor they've left behind. I think it's 'cause he treats the Simbas and the regular army all the same, and they need a doctor here in case the witchdoctor's spells on the bullets keep failing.

"Go quickly," my daddy said.

Everything I do has to be quick lately. Everyone worries about the war. I'm not allowed to go off the compound, even if I take Tumi with me. I walk slowly in spite of what my father said. It gets too boring in the house. I'd rather climb the loquat tree or follow Tumi as he chases the baboons.

I've made it only halfway and already the basket is getting heavy. I see a chameleon on the path and I let it crawl all over my arms for a few minutes while I rest. The Congolese children aren't allowed to touch them. I think they are afraid of curses or something, but my daddy says it doesn't work on Christians, so he doesn't care if I play with them. Lately I haven't played with them much because of the war and all.

The only good thing about the war is that my teacher was stolen by the Simbas, too, so the mission school closed. But my mother still makes me do the times tables every day. I think it's 'cause she's bored, too. She'd rather be out in the *shamba* hoeing the beans than cooped up all day in our little house.

I drop my basket with a thud on the concrete stoop of the little building where the lepers sleep. I don't even have to knock before Mrs. Mumbaya opens the door.

"Thank you, thank you," she says, smiling with her wide-gapped teeth.

I smile back 'cause she's so funny. This is the only English she knows. "You're welcome."

She lifts the basket with her good hand, and sticks her stumpy hand through the loops to hoist the treasures into the house.

Back when I was eight, I thought that she'd been attacked by the crocodiles. I'd seen her washing clothes in the river and thought she was the bravest woman. My mother won't let me go to the river since a village boy was eaten there. The village chief made some men kill the crocodile and asked my daddy to cut the boy out so they could bury him proper.

The river is just beyond the leper house, down the path between the palm trees. I walk down the hard-packed clay. I only want to see if Givan or one of the village boys is playing. But they are gone, too. It's quiet here so I sit on the bank and dream of the days when I could play with my friends before the war. I almost wish they'd bring back my teacher so I wouldn't be so bored.

The *rat-a-tat* of the machine guns startle me. I strain to see smoke rising back toward the center of town. Daddy says the national army are the good guys and he hopes they'll come to Wasolo soon.

"Camille!" My mother's voice. Urgent.

I groan. My mom wants me to come home. I've heard gunfire so many times and I've never seen anyone get dead except that Simba across the street from the hospital.

"Camille!"

I run up the path toward home. The air smells like smoke. By the time I reach the edge of the yard, I see a group of Simbas coming through the hospital gate.

That's trouble. But I don't get to watch 'cause my mother is motioning like crazy for me to get inside.

RICHMOND, 1984

TINA KINSER, MD, awoke with her lips being graced by her first-time lover. "I'm going to be late for rounds," he said. She watched his athletic form disappear through the door from the vantage point of their bed. She wanted to call his name, to tell him how special it had been, but he was gone with little warning, leaving her alone and naked, gathering a thin sheet around her.

She was a tenured psychiatry professor who rode the peak of her professional career. Her patients were committed to her counsel, her chairman was gleeful over her publications, and her retirement stock portfolio selection couldn't have been hotter. But that didn't ease the pain of a loveless marriage, or lift the resentment she carried for her husband's wanderings. She'd sought a healing balm in the excitement of forbidden fruit. Now, she held tight to a pillow in a downtown Richmond hotel room with her head full of images after a night of sex and puzzled over her boldness in directing a stranger in ways she'd never imagined with her husband of twenty years. Her mind swirled with emotions from the morning after. Guilt. Excitement. The exhilaration of new lust and the hollowness of revenge on a cheating husband.

Tina touched the empty space on the bed beside her before rising and walking to the bathroom. She told herself her actions were justified. She'd taken exactly what she needed.

What began as a shared round of drinks with a group of conference attendees had ended in a night of solace in another man's arms.

That delight contrasted with her mind fighting back a brand-new fear—not one of discovery of her indiscretion. As far as she was concerned, her husband had this coming. No, what worried her now was the look that crossed her lover's face in the midst of their delight. It was a brief flash of sobriety in an orgy of drunkenness. His hand had caressed her lovingly when suddenly, and only for a moment, his touch had turned clinical, exploring, defining. His eyes met hers and she recognized the look of a professional taking pains to hide a serious concern behind a poker face of calm. His eyes had closed and his lips searched for hers. He did not speak of it. He didn't have to. His eyes had communicated enough.

She touched her left breast. A mass lay just beneath the skin. It felt innocuous enough: lima bean in size, but firmer. She raised her hand above her head, observing a subtle dimple that appeared over the lump.

She frowned as her chest tightened. This was all too familiar.

Her mother had fought this battle.

And lost.

She returned to the bed and gathered the sheet around her. After a minute she reached for a small ID card on the edge on the bedside stand. Her lover had forgotten his badge.

She lifted the photograph for inspection. Despite the poor quality of the picture, there was no disputing the facts: her husband couldn't hold a candle to this man.

MY ALARM NUDGED me from sleep at six, but thanks to my hitting the snooze button three times, I was already late. I rose, feeling a low-level dread from my dreams. They were out of focus now, not as sharp as they were when they had jolted me from sleep in the early hours. I had the vague feeling that I was playing a dangerous game of looking beneath stones, ones Aunt Jeanine said should be left unturned.

I told myself a lie I didn't believe. The nightmares must have been due to the spicy hors d'oeuvres, the cigars, and the beer I drank with the boys of surgery. I plodded to the bathroom, where I opted for the essentials only: eyeliner and lipstick. The rest I'd reserve for Mark.

I dressed casually, knowing I'd change into scrubs when I got to the hospital. I poured my coffee into a large travel mug and dashed to MCV.

I needed to make social rounds so I stopped first on the peds ward, where I found Mark Lawson hovering over a patient chart at the nursing station.

Our eyes met. "Hey."

"Sorry about last night." He shook his head. "My conference ran late and—"

I squeezed his hand. "You hate stuffy parties."

He smiled.

He's so beautiful; I think I'll forgive him this time.

"What'd I miss?"

I shrugged. "A stuffy party." I dropped his hand. "My aunt Jeanine showed up."

"No way. Can I meet her?"

I shook my head. "She's already left. Turns out she was driving up to Martha's Vineyard. Stopped on the way to see if I've made good."

He stared into me. "You've made good, Camille."

"Every time she'd happen to visit me in Boston, she always had another agenda. Like yesterday, she was usually on her way to a vacation. She never stopped just to see me."

He leaned close to me and whispered, "She doesn't know you, Camille. She probably feels guilty." He seemed to hesitate, then added, "How was seeing Dr. Gilles?"

I smiled. "He didn't have the nerve to fire me at my welcome reception."

"Stop. You know he loves you. Like a daughter."

I raised my eyebrows. "That's scary."

He looked at his watch.

"I've got to run. Call me."

He nodded and I walked away. As I departed, I heard him ask, "Has anyone seen my ID badge?"

I smiled with the memory of him searching through my purse. Typical man. Can't keep track of anything.

I stopped next in the pediatric ICU to see if Kara was working. I waited until she finished starting an IV to approach. "Can we talk?"

Her eyes darted around the busy unit. She walked me to the side.

We both began in unison, "I'm sorry—" We giggled.

She reached for the sleeve of my white coat. "I *am* sorry."

I shook my head. "I've thought about what you said." I looked at her white shoes, which were spotted with old blood. "I count on you to say what I need to hear."

"I was harsh."

"You were right."

She wrinkled her freckled nose beneath her blond bangs.

"I went home last night and put a six-pack of Samuel Adams at my neighbor's door."

Her hand went to her mouth.

I shrugged. "I drank it to be one of the guys."

Her eyes dropped to the floor.

Kara and I had been friends a long time. She sensed I was going to talk about her addictions. I didn't even have to speak.

"It's not out of control for me," she said without lifting her eyes. "Not like before."

I touched her shoulder and stayed quiet for a moment. "Know anyone who likes Nicaraguan cigars?"

She smiled.

"Larimore is on trauma-call tonight. The BoSox are playing. Want to meet for the game?"

"Usual spot?"

I nodded. "No men."

"No Mark?"

"He skipped my party. I'm not inviting him."

"Good girl. Keep him wondering."

I walked away, happily leaving the buzz of the peds ICU behind. I found Ellis Hamilton looking slightly hungover. My welcome party must not have been so good for him. The last thing a trauma resident needed was to drink on his night off.

"Did the team admit anyone new last night?" I said this knowing at least part of the answer.

"GSW patient last night. Dr. Larimore repaired his femoral

artery. We took another hit at three," he began. "A thirty-year-old male with a fractured femur and brief loss of consciousness from a motor vehicle accident. Workup included negative head CT, C-spine, chest, and pelvis. I bedded him down for the orthopods to rod his femur this morning," Ellis whined in the quipped language of the trauma team. We called it "traumaese."

I nodded perfunctorily. "Nonoperative blunt trauma," I said, "reeks." I smiled. "But somebody's gotta do it, Ellis."

The general surgeon's role in trauma management is often clearing and managing sick patients for the subspecialists. Babysitting for the bone surgeons is the bane of existence for the trauma surgeon.

Ellis handed me a card with the name and number of my new patient. "We can see him on rounds. If he has no other injuries, we can turf him to ortho after they operate."

"Agreed."

This made Ellis smile. I could always count on lazy residents to whittle down the size of my service.

I stopped in the surgery ICU and examined the chart of the new GSW patient. Larimore had made no mention of my presence in the OR. I flipped a few pages to the OR record, a document I was sure Larimore had completed himself. Again, no mention of my name. Beside the "surgeon" slot, Larimore's name was printed. Beside "assistant" it read, "Rick Arensen." *Hmmm. Larimore is covering his tracks. It's as if I wasn't even there.* I felt my blood heating up. It was crazy to have to cover for something that wasn't even a real issue. But the fact that Larimore had adjusted the record meant he thought it *was* a real issue, and that made me furious.

I walked to the OR and changed in the newly labeled "Female" locker room. Afterward I slogged through two gallbladders, a hernia, and a colostomy reversal by 2:00 p.m., hardly private-practice pace, but I had to slow down to show the residents everything. After an emergency appendectomy, I was on my way out by four, all in all a short day for me.

And I did it without seeing Dr. Gilles. So far, so good, for flying below the radar—my new goal for staying out of sight and out
of mind of the chairman.

TINA KINSER, MD, spent the afternoon overseeing a resident-
run psychiatry clinic. It seemed all her patients were in crisis-
management mode. Everywhere she looked someone was paranoid,
suicidal, or psychotic. Others were passive-aggressive, noncompli-
ant in taking their medications, and overly demanding of a system
that groaned under the weight of too many patients.

In the midst of it all, she couldn't rid herself of the nagging
guilt about her unfaithfulness or the vague sense that her newly
discovered breast lump might be the payment that was due for
her indiscretion.

She shook her head at her own musings. *Keep thinking like that,
and you'll need to trade places with one of your patients.*

Last night was the culmination of a long downhill slide in a
marriage that was too far beyond CPR. Life had been tolerably
dull for too long. Exotic vacations, money, and a diversified in-
vestment portfolio had done little to spice up a relationship to
a man consumed with "taking care of Tina." At least that was
Dan's excuse. She'd long suspected that the extravagance he
showed in his gift giving was little more than a guilt offering to
salve a troubled heart. Last month, Dan had come to an uncom-
monly honest altar in their communication and confirmed her
fears, confessing an affair with a coworker that began in a New
York City hotel.

Could she forgive him? That had been the focus of her own
struggle.

Last night, she'd come to a turning point. She'd been hurt. So
why had exacting her revenge made her feel so bad?

After clinic, she walked to her private office. Kerri, her receptionist, smiled and hung up the phone. "How was clinic, Dr. Kinser?"

"I had to readmit Linda Jones. She said she'd swallowed a handful of nails."

"Do you believe her?"

Tina nodded. "Saw it on X-ray. Had to call a surgery consult."

Kerri shook her head.

"I need a favor," Tina said, lowering her voice. "I need a mammogram."

Kerri wrinkled her nose. "For you?"

Tina nodded.

"Who should I put down as the ordering physician?"

Tina picked up the MCV staff directory. She thumbed through the pages and pointed at a picture. "Her."

The receptionist frowned. "Dr. Weller? She's a trauma surgeon."

Tina didn't want to argue. "All the better. This is trauma for me."

Kerri nodded obediently and handed her boss an X-ray form. "Just show this at the radiology desk." She paused. "Dr. Kinser, is everything OK?"

Tina snatched the piece of paper from her hand, and told herself it was only a breast lump. She didn't know anything for sure. She looked at her assistant. "I'm sure it's nothing."

She sat at her desk and scribbled a quick note on a card: *You've helped me rethink a lot of things. Thank you for a wonderful evening.* She thought about the next line. Was it too soon to use the word "love"?

After a moment of deliberation, she decided: *It's only a card.* She signed the note, *with love, Tina.* She slid the ID badge along with the card into a small envelope to drop into the campus mail, allowing a smile to tease the corners of her mouth.

8

T HAT EVENING I gathered with my Boston buddies, Rachel Bell and Kara Schuller, at the Tobacco Company, one of Richmond's finest dining experiences. We ignored the niceties of the upper floors and gathered in the basement lounge to watch the BoSox on the TV. Normally they showed a variety of music videos, but I'd operated on the manager when I was a chief resident and he let me watch the Red Sox whenever they were on TV and I could break free.

Rachel leaned toward me across a small table. "Scuttlebutt around the hospital is that you're willing to take off a lot more than socks these days." She tried to withhold a giggle without success.

"I'm denying everything. Everything you've heard is a lie, designed with intentional ill will." I lowered my voice and looked at Kara. "What did you hear?"

"Just that you marched into the men's locker room to change."

I groaned and confessed, "That's pretty much it."

Rachel's jaw slackened. "You what?"

I winced. "It seemed like the right thing to do at the time. I went in, complained about the sexist sign on the door, and left," I said, waving my hand. "It wasn't really anything."

A waitress appeared. I traded looks with Kara, whose eyes told me not to say a word. Then she ordered a margarita.

I kept my voice low and said to her, "I'll have a Coke with you. It's OK with me."

Kara shook her head at me and repeated to the server, "A margarita. Strawberry." She looked at me and mouthed, "I'm OK."

I shrugged. "I'll take the same."

Rachel eyed me. "What? No amber beer for our BoSox?"

I winked at Kara. "I hate beer." I smiled. "I'm going to have a girlie drink."

Rachel was a second-year surgery resident. She ordered a beer and our waitress disappeared.

I raised my eyebrows at Rachel. "Still one of the guys, I see."

She stared back at me. "I learned from the best."

Touché. Maybe I hadn't been the awesome example I've always pictured myself to be. Or maybe I had—in the wrong direction.

Rachel tilted her head. "What did Mark say about your little locker room escapade?"

I smiled. "He was jealous."

Kara sat down her drink. "He's a man. Of course he was jealous."

We settled into superficial chat about baseball, men, our jobs, men, Boston, men, the outrageous dress on a woman seated at the bar, and men.

In the fifth inning, I yelled at the starting pitcher for throwing his fastball six times in a row. In the sixth, I turned down an offer to buy a Nicaraguan cigar from a woman in a short skirt. I wanted to tell her to get a real-woman job like laying bricks or surgery, but I could see by her figure that she was well suited to her present position. But then again, most of the men in the bar would have guessed that I was suited for little more than selling tobacco myself.

I smiled as she walked away. I'd just turned down a fine cigar. Maybe I could be my own person and still like myself.

It wasn't until after the seventh-inning stretch and Rachel's departure that I leaned forward and looked Kara in the eyes. "Have you ever been really afraid?"

She brushed her long blond bangs behind her right ear, which was graced by four earrings. She studied my face. "What's wrong, Camille?"

"I don't really know." I strained to keep my voice from breaking. "Ever had déjà vu?"

She shrugged. "I guess."

"This week I've had two episodes of, well, terror. I feel out of control, my heart races and—" I halted before continuing, "It's like I'm suddenly afraid, but I'm not sure why. I'm aware that something has frightened me, something beyond the reach of my mind."

She nodded. "What were the circumstances? What initiated them?"

"That's where the weird part is. Both times I'd just heard a phrase." I looked at my lap before I could finish. "This is embarrassing. Mark whispered in my ear, 'Everything's gonna be all right.'"

"What else was going on?"

I raised my eyebrows. *Wouldn't you like to know?* I almost said, but then the images flooded in.

"It was rainy and I—" My voice caught and I looked down.

"What?" Kara gently urged.

"I hit a dog, Kara."

Kara reached across the table and put her hand on my wrist. "Oh, Camille. That's horrible. I can see why that caused—"

"It was awful, but it wasn't that, really. It was later. Back at my apartment Mark tried to comfort me. He came up behind me and put his arms around me." I paused and smiled. "He started kissing me. Then he whispered in my ear. And suddenly, I thought I was going to lose it. My heart started pounding, and I just felt terrified . . . out of control."

She licked her lips. "I'd feel out of control if Mark started kissing me."

"Stop it. I'm serious."

"So am I."

I knew she was. Most of the nurses in the peds ICU had designs on him. Fortunately, I'd latched on to him first.

"Sounds like a panic attack to me."

I didn't want to hear it. "Panic?" I shook my head. "I'm a surgeon," I mumbled. "We don't panic."

She rolled her eyes. "You've been under stress. You just started a new job. You're breaking new ground, sis." She paused, her eyes intent on mine. "This started after your little episode in the men's locker room?"

I nodded. "Maybe I've got a pheo. They secrete adrenaline, you know."

"I don't need a physiology lesson." She paused. "And maybe when you hear hoofbeats, you should think of horses, not zebras."

"I'm from Africa. Zebras are common."

"Having panic attacks isn't a sign of personal weakness."

"I'm not afraid of anything." I sipped my margarita and wondered if she could tell I was lying. Of course she could. She was my best friend.

The truth was, I was afraid I wouldn't succeed in the world of surgery, dominated by testicles.

I was pacesetter.

The first African-American woman to ever finish the surgery program.

The first ever to be hired as a staff surgeon.

And suddenly I was afraid it had all been some weird twist of fate, that I wasn't really good enough all along. Someone was going to lift the lid and find out that I was a fraud.

"Having panic attacks has little to do with being afraid."

"What makes you the world's expert?"

"Hang out at the peds ICU as long as I have and you'll see a little of everything." She tapped the table. "You said that both times you heard a phrase that set you off. You told me what Mark said. When was the other time?"

"It was the same phrase. 'Everything's gonna be all right.' Except this time it was in the SICU and a mother said it to a patient."

She narrowed her eyes at me. "Everything's gonna be all right."

"Stop it. You can't make me freak out."

"It doesn't exactly work that way anyway. Panic attacks sneak up on you. Something in your subconscious was pricked by what you heard."

"It's not reasonable. How could something I'm not aware of make me panic?"

"Just because you don't understand it doesn't make it untrue."

"I'm a physician. We're trained to be skeptical of things that cannot be proven by the scientific method."

"Maybe you should talk to somebody."

I lifted my glass. "I'm talking to you. You're my friend, remember?"

"I mean somebody professional."

"I don't think so. It's probably just a conditioned response," I said, remembering my thoughts from early in the night. "I was anxious about hitting the dog when Mark whispered in my ear. I was conditioned to experience that emotion when I heard the phrase again, that's all." I wasn't sure I believed it, but I knew I wasn't going to see any shrink. I wished I hadn't even brought up the subject, but when I drink a little too much, my tongue always loosens.

"Whatever." She squinted at the TV screen, which was playing a Budweiser commercial featuring women with breast implants. Did guys really think they looked real?

Kara snapped her fingers. "You should see Dr. Tina Kinser. She gave pediatric grand rounds on using hypnosis to recover traumatic memories. It was fascinating."

"I don't believe it. Can't work."

"You're a surgeon. You think hypnosis is hokey."

I shrugged. "What's that have to do with being a surgeon?"

"It's the scientific bias." She paused. "What about faith? Your father was a missionary, right? Some of that must have worn off on you. You can't explain Christian faith by scientific theory."

"I agree. But I'm afraid you're grasping for straws here. I don't profess any religious belief."

"I know, I know. I'm just saying some of his beliefs had to transfer to you—even subconsciously."

"Well, they didn't. I didn't know my father well enough for his beliefs, whatever they were, to wear off on me."

Kara stared at the screen and shook her head as the third pitcher in the eighth inning took the mound.

"Dr. Gilles is giving me two months."

"What do you mean?"

"The last two guys they hired right out of residency busted within a few months. They couldn't handle the pressure. I heard Gilles tell Dr. Bransford that he thought I'd last two months."

"That's crazy. You're the best."

"Sometimes I want to quit. Go somewhere up north where my skin color and gender wouldn't mean so much."

"Don't you dare! You are exactly what MCV needs. Who else would care for the poor indigent souls of Richmond like you do? Not Gilles and Bransford." She reached for my hand. "I'm serious, Camille, the women of Richmond need you."

"Maybe I am needed. But I won't have a job unless I toe the line and act just like them. That's what they want, you know. They don't want a real black woman on the service. They want a black woman who thinks and acts like a white man."

"You're over that," she said, laughing. "No more stogies, remember."

Our laughter drifted into an awkward silence. We watched the game, finished our drinks, and I wondered whether there was any magic left in my red socks. Mostly, I was just thankful that Kara had dropped the therapy idea. Seeing a shrink was the last thing I needed.

In the bottom of the ninth, Boston overcame a 3–3 tie for the win. With my red socks on, rooting from the basement bar of the Tobacco Company, the BoSox were 6 and 0. That was good and bad for me. Good because I could gloat about it tomorrow, especially to Mark, who liked the Yankees and therefore hated the BoSox. Bad because my I'm-a-completely-rational-scientist foundation now had a small crack. And if I knew Kara, she'd hold on to this one like a pit bull. Maybe that's why I loved her.

We parted, rejoicing in our team, but I drove home somber, worrying about my mind. I told myself over and over not to worry, but a seed of doubt remained that these panic attacks, as Kara wanted to call them, could be the chink in my armor that would doom me to failure on the front line.

That night, I stood in front of the bathroom mirror wearing only one of Mark's old football jerseys, something I'd swiped from the bottom of his closet and refused to return. I told myself the truth: "You're in the Six-Liter Club. You are the first female trauma surgeon in Virginia. And you're the first African-American female to ever join the department of surgery at MCV."

"Everything's gonna be all right." The whisper rolled off my tongue as normally as any other encouraging statement I could throw at myself. But without planning, there it was, and I felt my gut tighten as soon as it was out.

As long as I could remember, I'd pushed myself to be the best. Why? Was I trying to prove my worth to an absent, dead father? Was I striving to prove to the men at MCV that I was worth so much more than a vision of me wearing black-lace panties?

What messages had I believed from my aunt Jeanine? *Am I really lovable?*

This all seemed so nebulous, so foggy, so just beyond my

reason. I smiled at the progress of my self-analysis. I made a pretty good psychiatrist for a surgeon.

I can deal with this crap on my own. I always have.

I nodded my head slowly as I realized that Dr. Gilles was not ultimately in charge of my fate. The stodgy surgical establishment that he represented would not be what crushed me. I had backbone enough to stand up to their inertia, that seemingly immoveable system that resisted change like an incumbent Democrat. I'd identified my own worst enemy. I had two months to prove I could last longer than my predecessors. If I didn't make it, it would be all her fault. The girl in the mirror. She was sabotaging me.

9

Darkness. Smothering heat. Arms around me, holding me against him. Quiet whispers in my ear.

Don't speak. Don't cry.

Kisses on my neck.

Everything's gonna be all right.

My first week as a real doctor and I was awake at four in the morning—again. Oh, right, I'd been a real doctor since graduation from medical school in Richmond. However, post-graduate training continues for up to a decade in some cases, and there was always someone else where the buck stopped. Now, it stopped with me. I got to make the final say.

I stared at the ceiling of my little apartment. I'd awoken moments ago, with Mark's jersey wet from sweat, as if I'd been running in the moist blanket this town calls summer. I knew only that I was afraid, but the dream's content was so vague that I could not pinpoint a source.

At five, I rose, showered, prepared for my day, and headed for MCV, arriving in time to see my ICU patients before my residents.

To my dismay, I found Kendrick Solomon had deteriorated. His oxygen saturation had been a constant challenge and his chest X-ray was worse. He was now on a constant drip of Norcuron, a paralyzing drug, to keep him from fighting the ventilator. He was sedated, unable even to blink because of the coma we'd induced in a final attempt to save his life. I checked all the numbers, studied the monitors above his bed, and inflated the balloon on his Swan-Ganz catheter to measure his pulmonary arterial wedge pressure.

This young brother laid in the center of a spaghetti tangle of intravenous lines, ECG monitors, urinary and stomach drains, and respiratory tubing. Days ago he was playing basketball with his friends, maybe skipping rocks on the James River, a young man without a significant care in the world. Did he have dreams of college and a career, of escaping the violent life of a street punk? That's what the mothering side of me believed—a side of me I'd been ignoring. The surgeon side of me had pulled away from such emotional musings. The surgeon in me saw a complex interrelationship of organ systems that were beginning a slow dance toward death. All we could do now was intensive support of each system and hope for the best. I turned to leave the room.

"Dr. Weller!"

It was Nadine Solomon, Kendrick's mother. She wore the same flowered dress as yesterday, but now it was creased from a night on the couch in the ICU waiting room. She was gastric-bypass-category fat, with most of her weight distributed around her generous waist. At least she'd lost the purple hat. Her hair was jet black—from a bottle.

"Good morning," I said, extending my hand.

We shook, and I resisted the desire to wipe the residual wetness on the side of my skirt.

"How's Kendrick?"

"Not good, Mrs. Solomon. His lungs are worse. We've had to medicate him to help him rest." I specifically avoided telling her we'd paralyzed him to keep him from fighting the ventilator. No one seemed to understand when I used those terms.

She nodded her head. Her eyes were moist.

"We're trying everything we can at this point. We're giving him antibiotics, nutrition, and supporting his respirations." I paused to see if she was following. "But he's continuing to decline. We need to start thinking realistically about the chance that Kendrick may not make it." I watched for a response. I avoided saying "die," but softening the word didn't help.

Nadine's eyes widened. She shook her head. "He will not die! That's my boy!"

I stood quietly, offering only my presence.

"He's a good boy. Never done nothin' to nobody. He's not gonna die!"

"Mrs. Solomon, I—"

She grasped my arm. "Let me call in the elders. We need to have a prayer meeting."

I nodded. "Praying will be a good idea." I kept the rest of the sentence to myself. *Nothing else is working.*

"The nurses wouldn't let me bring in the team."

I lowered my voice. "I asked you to call my office. I'll arrange to let the team in."

She looked pointedly at me. "Are you a believer, sister?"

I didn't want to disappoint her. But I couldn't just lie. "A believer?" I looked at the top of Nadine's shiny black shoes. "Not exactly."

"How can you do what you do, see the wonder of the human body every day, and not believe?"

This seemed to be an honest question rising out of curiosity. In her simple way of looking at the world, she undoubtedly thought this reasoning was black and white.

She deserved a response, but I wasn't sure how to tell her that what I saw every day, the suffering, the injustice, the inhumanity of man hurting man—the daily bread of the surgeon was exactly how I justified my doubts. Instead of spilling those words, I found myself falling back on a comfortable modus operandi. "I'm a scientist, Mrs. Solomon. I guess I have trouble believing things that can't be proven."

"God's going to raise up my boy, and he's going to do it to speak to you," she said, pointing at my chest.

Self-conscious, I stepped back and gathered my lab coat together.

"Do you believe Jesus loves you?"

Nadine Solomon looked as though she was warming up. Before she could take another deep breath, I held up my hands. "I believe you believe that, Mrs. Solomon, and that's great for you, but, well, I—" I stumbled. I didn't really feel like justifying myself to this steamroller. And I couldn't really tell her that sometimes I wondered if I was lovable at all, even to Jesus.

Her voice softened and she took my hand. "I know just what you are going to say, honey. You've never seen his love in action, so how could you believe? You're a Thomas. You need something practical and reasonable in order to believe in God's love."

"I, well—" I was completely incapacitated by her accuracy. This woman was looking right through my lab coat and into my soul. I drew my white coat tighter. "I really need to go." I hesitated. "Can you have your prayer team here at seven?"

She nodded.

"I'll meet you here."

I stepped away and accelerated quickly to normal surgical-attending pace. My heels clicked against the floor and echoed from the tiled walls, mingling with the clinical noise of breakfast trays, call bells, and interns shuffling in their short white coats to rounds.

Smiling, I stomped with a bit more purpose, happy to be escaping Nadine, and proud that no other surgeon could make this much noise when they walked.

THAT AFTERNOON, VANESSA greeted me in the clinic. She dropped a chart in the rack and whispered, "Private patient. She doesn't want to see a resident."

I raised my eyebrows in question.

Vanessa responded below the volume of the jazz she kept on as background music. I leaned close in time to hear, "A physician."

I picked up the chart in the rack outside room three. What physician would want to see me, the new kid in town? I glanced through Vanessa's interview report. The patient had a breast lump. Why was she here? She should be in Dr. Gilles's surgical oncology clinic. I knocked as I opened the door. The sight unnerved me. My patient, a thirty-eight-year-old Caucasian, was topless, sitting on the exam table reading a psychiatric journal. I scanned for the paper poncho she was to have been issued. It was folded, unused, on the top of the counter. "I'm Dr. Weller," I said, handing her the poncho. "My nurse must have forgotten—"

"Dr. Kinser," she said, lifting her hand to mine. "You can call me Tina. Your nurse explained the exam gown. I'm comfortable without it."

I tried not to stare. I wasn't used to beginning the interview with the patient undressed. I found myself hoping I'd look this good when I reached thirty-eight. "Uh, sure," I mumbled.

"I figure you're just going to see them soon anyway, and, well, frankly, I need a doctor who is as comfortable with my body as I am."

Different, I thought, but forward. I liked that. I sat on a rolling stool and tried to keep eye contact. Thank God she wasn't here for a pelvic or I'd bet she'd have been naked and spread.

"I found a breast lump. My family history isn't good. My mother died of breast cancer at age forty-four. I haven't used birth control pills in seven years since my tubes were tied."

I nodded, taking it all in. *Typical physician. She tells me everything before I ask.* I shifted the focus away from the problem for a moment. "You're a physician?"

"A psychiatrist."

The surprise must have registered on my face.

"I suppose you surgeons don't consider us real doctors."

I was taken aback. "Well, no. Just because I didn't choose to be a psychiatrist doesn't mean I don't think it's a valid occupation. It's just, well, I enjoy working with pathology that I can explain." I shrugged. "Appendicitis. Gallstones. Even breast cancer can be understood from a physiological standpoint. I'm a scientist."

"And I'm not?"

"No, I didn't mean that. It's just, well, I'm not so comfortable with things I can't see or explain."

"I see." She said it as if concluding an argument with a total imbecile.

"It doesn't really matter what I think of your occupation. What matters is what I think of your surgical problem."

"I think it matters. I want a surgeon who will care about the whole of me. Not just my breasts."

I sighed. I wanted to start all over. "Listen, I think we've gotten off on the wrong foot. Let me assure you that I respect you as a physician, and I'll do my best to treat your breast problem in light of your whole person."

"Fair enough." She seemed to relax a notch before launching at me again. "So are you uncomfortable with the treatment of mental illness?"

"Not at all."

"But you said you're uncomfortable with—"

"With things I can't explain. That includes anxiety and depression. I don't understand them physiologically, so I'm not comfortable with personally treating them."

"OK. Are you uncomfortable talking with me?"

I hesitated and kept my thoughts to myself. Yes. Definitely yes.

"Some people hate talking to psychiatrists because they fear being analyzed."

"I'm not afraid." *At least I don't think I am.* "Can we talk about your problem?" *Please get back on my turf. I'm tired of you controlling this interview.*

"This interaction is important to me. An adequate rapport between doctor and patient is essential to the healing equation."

The healing equation? This seemed like psycho-bull for sure. I smiled so as not to betray my thoughts, but feared this lady had me pegged. "Of course." I sensed my own need to be in control. "When did you first notice this lump?" I'm sure she'd told me this, but the conversation had twisted so far that I didn't remember.

"Yesterday."

"Any pain?"

"No."

"Nipple discharge?"

"None."

"Pregnancies?"

"None."

Good. I was on a roll. I sat in control again. "Any previous breast biopsies?"

"No."

I looked at the intake sheet. "I see you're on no medications. That's good. And your only previous surgery was an appendectomy?"

She nodded.

I stepped forward to begin my exam. I looked for symmetry. "Go like this." I placed my hands in front of me, waist high, and pressed the heels of my palms together to contract the chest muscles. She mimicked perfectly.

This move accentuated a fine dimple in the upper outer aspect of the left breast. Not a good sign, but my poker face was on.

"Now this," I said, raising my arms above my head. It's a simple move, but one that patients rarely take time to do at home. As she did so, the subtle dimple became more noticeable.

I moved through the exam mechanically, noting the presence

of a lump in the left breast. It seemed superficial, almost tethered to the skin. "When was your last mammogram?"

"This morning." She pointed to an X-ray folder leaning against the chair.

I took out the X-rays and placed them on the view box. Inwardly I groaned. There was a worrisome shadow in the left upper outer quadrant. It had small stellate arms reaching out like a hungry octopus. This wasn't good. Tina, the psychiatrist, was going to have to face the music. I was willing to bet my favorite Boston Red Sox hat that she had cancer.

"Well?"

"You need a fine needle aspiration. It's when we pull some cells out of this lump and see what the pathologist thinks."

"Today?"

"If you'll agree."

"Let's get on with it."

I summoned Vanessa, who prepared the patient for the minor procedure. Mechanically, I painted Tina's breast with Betadine to sterilize the skin. I poised a needle above the dimple. "You're going to feel a little sting." As I sliced the needle through the breast tissue, there was a gritty feel, another sign we were dealing with the big C.

Once I removed the needle, I held pressure against the stick site for a moment before Vanessa applied a little circle Band-Aid.

My patient began to dress. "When will we know the result?"

"Soon. I'll hand-carry the slides to the pathologist this afternoon. You can stop by my office tomorrow."

She nodded.

With my hand on the doorknob, I stopped. "I'm curious," I began. "Why did you come to my clinic instead of the oncology clinic? As a local physician, you have to be aware of his reputation."

"I'm aware. But you're a woman."

As if that will make me a better surgeon. I smiled. *Actually, it does.*

"A man cannot possibly understand what I'm going through." She paused. "Richmond needs more women surgeons."

My head told me to send this sensitive granola straight to Dr. Gilles for treatment. It was expected department behavior. My heart told me to help her myself. After all, I was Gilles-trained. I knew what he'd do.

I obeyed my heart. I handed her the exit sheet. "I'll see you soon."

THAT EVENING, I made four trips to escort the eight Colonial Heights Baptist Church elders two by two to their hiding place behind a curtain drawn around Kendrick Solomon's bed. Nadine cried. Kendrick Solomon had worsened. I was glad the team could gather, because tomorrow Kendrick might be singing with the angels. I stood back against the wall near the opening into the main ICU, where I could watch for Head Nurse Godzilla.

If I'd ever acted like an imposter by drinking beer and smoking stogies with the boys of surgery, I felt like a bigger one now. In spite of my father's apparent dedication to the faith, these things weren't passed through the genes, and I'd certainly put more effort into the study of medicine than any religion. I wasn't there to participate, but to facilitate what appeared to be a preburial anointing. I wanted to stand back, be invisible, and hope this came off fast so I could stop feeling like a hypocrite.

Nadine Solomon had other plans. The elders joined hands in a circle broken just to the left of Nadine. She waved me forward with her free hand. "Join us, Dr. Weller."

Feeling less than worthy, but unable to say no, I assumed my place between Nadine and a huge man with broad shoulders and bigger hands. I opened my hands to receive theirs and closed my eyes. For the first time in a long time, I wanted to pray. But sadly, my thoughts were focused more on hoping this group stayed quiet and in control than on the boy lying at the center of our circle. I hoped I wouldn't get caught, that the pastor would keep his voice down, and that Nadine's wailing wouldn't reach the nursing station.

I listened as the men prayed. Strangely, there was no pious posturing. No screaming or wailing in despair. Only the simple requests for God's will and for a healing touch. I found myself beginning to agree, with halting prayers of my own for Kendrick.

A man at the head of the bed broke the circle and tilted a little yellow bottle so that its contents touched his finger. He then rubbed the oil onto Kendrick's forehead and quietly said, "Amen."

I opened my eyes to see through my own tears. I wiped my eyes. *Tears? What is happening to me?* Tears were not part of my surgeon persona.

I hugged Nadine before realizing that I was again engaging in non-surgeon-like activity. When I blinked away my tears I was face-to-face with Tracy King, the unit's head nurse.

Her eyes were slits. "May I see you for a moment?"

I didn't feel like talking to Tracy. I'd done what was right regardless of the rules, and I didn't need to be reminded of protocol.

I looked back at Kendrick and watched his cardiac monitor for a few seconds. The group excused themselves and filed out, leaving Tracy and me alone. What I'd just seen, and in a small way, participated in, had warmed my heart unexpectedly. I was starting to open up in ways that were surprising . . . and a little scary.

"Do you mind explaining what is going on here? I thought we had an agreement."

I nodded my head toward the double doors at the entrance to the ICU, where an elder stood next to Nadine Solomon as she wiped her tears with a large white handkerchief. "Comforting the mother of a dying child," I said, narrowing my eyes to mirror hers. "Stuff that in your protocol manual."

I walked away, bypassing the group from Colonial Heights and hoping their prayers were more effective than mine.

10

THE CONGO, 1964

THE THREE SIMBAS kicked open our door and ordered my daddy, mother, and me to lay on the ground in the front yard while they searched our house.

"Show us your phone. You call on the American planes to come."

My father shook his head and spoke to them in Kiswahili. He always does that when he doesn't want me to understand. But I still understood. He keeps telling them over and over that he's here as a *daktari* and that he's not in favor of fighting anybody.

Now we hear glass breaking and crashing sounds from inside the house. I'm scared but I still want to see. Mom hugs me so tight against her dress that I can't breathe. I think the men are throwing things in the kitchen. Mom starts to cry. I think she knows they are breaking her favorite dishes.

A Simba points a gun at my daddy. "Get up. Walk!" He pulls my mother to her feet, and since I'm holding on to her, I come, too. Another Simba with a spear strikes my daddy with his fist and makes us walk behind him toward the *hospital*. They put us in the common room where the workers gather for tea breaks. Mr. Karanja is my father's assistant in the operating theatre. He is sitting on the concrete floor as another Simba towers over him, shouting.

We sit there for an hour on the hard floor. I don't understand what is going on until Mr. Karanja finally takes off his big hearing aid and hands it to the soldier. The soldiers look at it for a long time, passing it back and forth.

My dad leans down and whispers in my ear, "They think the hearing aid is a radio transmitter."

The Simbas are so stupid, I think. In a moment, one of the soldiers crushes Mr. Karanja's hearing aid under his shoe and kicks the little parts across the floor. I feel bad for Mr. Karanja, 'cause he couldn't even hear the cawing of the ibis before daddy got him that hearing aid.

Then the soldiers push my father ahead of them back out in the yard beside our house. I watch the whole thing from the hospital tea room. The men hit my father with their spears and then take his Land Rover away.

My father says the Simba's code doesn't allow them to steal, so they ask for the Land Rover first. If you don't let them have what they ask for, they will kill you, so you have to give it. But then they say, "Thank you, Daktari," like that's supposed to make it all right for stealing our Land Rover.

They put my daddy back in the room with us. His nose is bleeding pretty bad. We have to stay there until dark, when the machine gun fire finally stops.

Finally, after I've fallen asleep on the floor, my daddy wakes me. The Simbas tell us to go back to our houses. We aren't allowed to leave anymore.

Not that we could, since they have the Land Rover. My daddy still thinks we have it better than the missionaries down in Stanleyville. Some of them have been kidnapped now for months.

At least I think we're safe as long as Daddy agrees to help the wounded Simba soldiers. We're going to be in a lot of trouble when the supplies run out and he can't help them anymore.

I think that's why Daddy and Mother have been whispering at night again. Mother is afraid, and Daddy is getting desperate to have her go away to her family and be safe.

That's weird, I think. If it is safer away from here, why doesn't he want me to go, too?

RICHMOND, 1984

T INA CRIED FOR an hour after work. Dr. Weller hadn't said she had cancer, but she had the look, the same poker face of calm she'd seen on her lover. She walked from room to room, straightening, dusting, adjusting pictures, bringing order to her world, which seemed destined to remain in disarray. Her husband was due back from his business trip any time. What could she tell him? *I have bad news and worse news? I've been unfaithful and I have cancer?*

No, she knew better. She needed time to process both new problems before unloading on Daniel.

She blew her nose and stared at her puffy eyes before pressing them against her palms. It wouldn't take a scientist to tell she'd been crying. She'd better freshen up before he arrived home and began a million questions about what was wrong.

What *wasn't* wrong? Her marriage was a joke. Her husband gave her everything he thought she wanted, but gave her nothing of what she really needed. She looked around her exquisite home and wondered how she had thought all this stuff would make her happy.

She dusted the top of her bookshelf, replete with pictures of her parents. The thought of her mother's agony during her final days made Tina shiver. *Am I destined for the same fate?*

She shook off the thought and went to her bathroom to freshen up. *I'll put on the red dress Dan loves and offer to take him to Steak & Ale for dinner.*

She lowered her hands into the sink and pulled warm water

over her face. As she leaned forward, dripping, a cold sensation crawled across her stomach. *Now look who's planning guilt offerings.*

THAT NIGHT I sat on the couch at Mark's apartment, rubbing Max, his German shepherd, behind the ears. Max responded by lifting a large paw onto my lap and slurping the back of my hand with his rough, pink tongue.

"Max is kissing me," I called to the next room, where Mark was fixing a sandwich.

"Am I to be jealous of him?"

"Maybe he should be jealous of you," I responded. Then I scratched Max again. "That's OK, boy, you know I love you. I just came over here to see *you,* didn't I, boy?"

Mark joined me on the couch. "Why do you talk like that to him? Like a baby."

"He likes it." I reached over and scratched Mark behind the ear and used my cutesy-baby-doggie voice again: "What's the matter, Markie? Do you want me to talk to you this way, too?"

He took a large bite of ham sandwich, an act that muffled his response.

Max lifted his paw and dropped it in my lap again. Obviously, he wanted my attention.

"He loves you," Mark said through his sandwich.

"I'm glad I've been able to win over at least one occupant in this house."

"What's that supposed to mean?"

I stayed quiet. How could I explain that I'd waited nearly four months to hear the L-word from this guy's lips, and the first time I heard it, he used it to say that his German shepherd loves me? If I asked him to say it and he said it, it wouldn't count. I lifted my fingers from behind Mark's ear and caressed his face with my fingers. Somewhere inside I believed that if I had the love of this man, I'd be able to face anything. No sexist career barrier, not even a haunting ghost that threatened me from my past would matter in a world in which this man took me in his arms and pledged his undying love. I looked away and shook my head. "I think I care about you too much."

"You're afraid."

I nodded. I was transparent.

"I care about you, Camille."

"Where will you be next year?"

His eyes narrowed in a question.

"When I'm still slugging it out on the trauma service, and you've finished your fellowship, where will you go?"

"I—uh—"

"Out of my life?"

"I don't know the future."

I took his chin and turned it toward me. "We can make the future what we want." I hesitated. "After your training, will you want to be with me?"

"It's a year away."

I echoed his words. "You're afraid."

He nodded, then leaned forward to kiss me.

After a few moments, I pushed him away. How could I tell him, I'm thirty years old, that in spite of all my professional goals, I'm starting to realize I'm fighting maternal urges and watching the ticking of my biological clock? How could I admit that every time I looked at a man I didn't just look at the curve of his biceps, but I wondered if he'd be a good father?

Mark nibbled my ear.

I slapped his thigh playfully. "I've just figured something out."

"What's that?"

"Men can't spell."

Mark turned his attention back to his sandwich. "What?"

"Or perhaps they just use a different dictionary. Look up the word 'love' in my dictionary and it's spelled *c-o-m-m-i-t-m-e-n-t*. Look in any man's and it's spelled *s-e-x*."

ON THURSDAY, I stopped at my MCV mailbox on the way to a noon conference.

Today marked four months Mark and I had been dating, and on each of our previous month anniversaries, he'd left a little note in my box telling me how much he enjoyed our relationship. He never used the L-word, mind you, but I cherished them nonetheless. I quickly sorted through the junk mail and sighed. No Mark letter. Maybe the staff hadn't gone through all the mail in the back yet.

I filed two invitations for credit cards in a large blue trash can. I'd been an attending surgeon less than a week and already the banks presumed I was made of money. The only items of mild interest were the August trauma call schedule and a first-class letter with a return address emblem showing a miniature map of Africa and the initials CFW. I recognized it as the agency that sent my father to the Congo: Christ for the World. I knew little about them, short of my father's affiliation. All I understood came filtered through my aunt Jeanine. CFW helped sucker a young man who had high ideals and sent him to the Dark Continent to convert the natives with medicine and Jesus. To Aunt Jeanine, CFW left her with an unwanted child and a flimsy insurance pay-off of $5,000—not enough for one semester at my prep school in Boston.

Without CFW I wouldn't exist, so, naturally, I wasn't embittered like my aunt. But CFW had remained out of my life until this moment, so I was curious as I opened the letter. The note was handwritten, another rarity in modern business.

Dear Dr. Weller,

I'm writing to let you know that a generous supporter of CFW has named an endowment to honor your father, a faithful man who served with our ministry for twelve years. We are initiating some additional fund-raising to give the Weller Endowment a great start. We hope that you will join in our efforts to honor such a great man with a financial gift, as well as being present as a family representative at the public presentation of the endowment to take place August 30, 1984, at the Chicago Hilton and Towers. Please fill out the enclosed commitment card and RSVP.

Sincerely,
Jacob Richardson

I almost dropped the letter beside the credit applications. I'd never met Jacob Richardson. He might be a fine man, but as a representative of CFW, he should be mending fences with me before soliciting a contribution. I'd heard nothing from this mission agency for twenty years. No sympathy for my loss, no checking up on my progress, no communication whatsoever . . . until now, and it came with a palm open for a handout.

I turned the letter over, tensing my hand to crumple the request when suddenly I was staring at the face of my father. The man in the picture was a near stranger, wearing a white lab coat and holding a small African child. He stood on a dusty road in front of a door labeled HOSPITALI. It was a copy of an old photograph, one I hadn't seen until now. The image intrigued me, delighted me, and . . . unnerved me. If pictures like this existed, it was news to me. Aunt Jeanine had never let me even talk about my African past. It was a horror in Aunt Jeanine's eyes, something to be ignored and forgotten. Or perhaps ignored in order to be forgotten.

And so I had pushed forward in my life, taking counsel from Aunt Jeanine, and doing as she demanded. For the most part, my past had ignored me, too. And previously, when hints of terrors-gone-by rippled the surface of my life, I'd redoubled my efforts of maximizing today, working hard to improve my future. Yesterday was history, dust, a rumor.

So, instead of trashing the letter, I folded it carefully to preserve the image of my father and placed it gently into the breast pocket of my lab coat and sighed. No love note from Mark. A request for money. Not exactly a banner day at the post office.

As I entered the conference room in Sanger Hall an intern handed me a brown-bag lunch from a side table, and I began to look for a seat in the back of the auditorium. Most of these residents had worked with me when I was in their shoes, but my position had changed and they addressed me as Dr. Weller now.

The title may have changed, but the informality hadn't. Doug Givler slapped me a high five and shook his head. "Six-Liter Club!"

Inside, I gloated. Outside, I was cool. "He survived the surgery, but it looks like he's circling the drain now."

He nodded, understanding my lingo. "Once someone pulls the handle, you can't stop the flush."

I shrugged. "You'll probably hear about it at the morbidity and mortality conference."

I exchanged pleasantries with a few other residents and found a seat as Dr. Larimore cleared his throat to begin a sleepy slide show on thyroid disorders.

As the lights dimmed, I inspected the contents of the brown bag. An apple was the only redeemable item in a sea of quick carbs and fat. I ignored a roast beef sandwich, a bag of chips, and a chocolate chip cookie, opting for the fruit. I might be able to operate like the best of these boys, but if I was going to maintain this hourglass of mine, I couldn't eat like them, too—with the exception of Skull cheeseburgers, of course.

Ten minutes into the lecture, I tired of the noise of crunching potato chips and the crinkling of cellophane. The men were happily unsealing their cookies, oblivious to the thyroid lecture.

Hadn't whoever planned these lunchtime conferences learned that the male of this species cannot eat and pay attention at the same time? For most of these future surgeons, food, like sex, was taken whenever the opportunity to partake presented itself. The next opportunity might be insufferable hours away.

I leaned forward and tried to pay attention. A minute later, unable to concentrate, I snuck a look at the letter in my pocket.

There, in the darkness of the lecture hall, as the noises of hungry male residents rose around me, I studied the face of the man who gave me my name, and I sensed my heart quickening. His eyes carried a strange familiarity. Even in the dim light of this room, and looking at a picture, I saw the intensity of his gaze.

Aunt Jeanine was right. My father's eyes looked just like Dr. Gilles's. I glanced away, now more afraid that I was going to panic again than of what might be behind the attacks in the first place. No, not now. Not here! I tried desperately not to yield to whatever might be bringing this all on, but the only phrase I could think of to comfort myself carried even more anxiety. *Everything's gonna be all right.* I glanced right and left before dabbing the moisture from my forehead with my sleeve.

I closed my eyes, unable to stop the rising swell of fear. My chest tightened. I shifted in my seat, aware that I was feeling short of breath and longing to loosen my blouse to get more air. It seemed the closeness of the feeding bodies in the dark room triggered my tripping out again. I needed to get to a restroom to be alone.

This is crazy. I'll just close my eyes and pretend.

I started to hear my heart in my ears. If I didn't get some air, I was going to start gasping, or something else spectacular and weird right here in the conference room.

The beeper clipped to the edge of my skirt sounded: "Trauma alert, trauma alert." Two other beepers in the room sounded the same cry.

It was a common page sent out to the trauma service when

an incoming trauma victim was critical. The shrill beeping in the darkness gave me the chance I needed to escape. I shoved my nearly full brown sack onto the lap of the resident beside me and broke for the door, aware only that as I was hurrying toward the emergency room, my breathing was already beginning to slow. I was a trauma surgeon. I focused on the ABC's of resuscitation.

In three minutes, I stood in trauma bay number one with Ellis Hamilton, Rick Arensen, and Ellie Saunders, the residents on for the trauma service.

A minute later, the West End Rescue Squad joined us to unload our work for the afternoon.

TWO HOURS AND one splenectomy later, I sunk onto my desk chair to think. The very circumstances that would frighten the hell out of most people, standing in the OR with life and death in contest, blood on one's gloves . . . that's the place I found the most solace. In the OR, I was untouchable, in control. It occurred to me that the panic I'd felt just moments before entering the OR melted when I diverted my focus to saving a life.

Maybe that was the secret to beating this panic—stupidity. Just refocus. I looked up from my desk to soft knocking at my door. It couldn't be a surgeon. They open first, knock second. "Come in."

Tina Kinser poked her head through the small opening. "Camille?"

Her greeting lacked the professional distance that I enjoyed with routine patients. "Dr. Kinser, come in."

She sat in a chair opposite my desk. "Call me Tina."

"We need to talk."

She nodded. "I understand." She seemed to be studying the items around my office. "You've been to Africa?"

"I spent my first ten years there."

"That must have been fascinating."

I wasn't sure how to respond. Africa was small in my mind, a distant, vague child's memory. Fortunately, Dr. Kinser was off to another topic before I could formulate an answer.

"Why did you become a surgeon?"

I shrugged. How could a surgeon explain it? The need to cut, the chance to execute a mechanical cure, the trust that patients give—was powerfully addicting. I *needed* to do it. It was all I'd ever remembered wanting to do. I wasn't ready to share this with Tina. "It suits me."

"Why? How does it suit you?"

"I love working with my hands. I love medicine, the workings of the body. Surgery seemed like a natural pick."

"Does it bother you that most of your colleagues are men?"

"Sometimes, I guess."

"Do you think a woman brings something special to your field?"

I looked at the lecture notes in front of me. I wasn't sure why Tina was asking twenty questions while ignoring the elephant in the room. "Why do you ask?"

"I'm curious."

"Didn't you come here because you wanted to talk about your needle test?"

"Not yet."

"But I haven't even told you the result."

She frowned. "There will be time for that. I think we both have a sense of what is happening here." She hesitated. "I think it's more important now for me to find out a bit more about you."

I pointed to the new MCV directory. "I'm sure you've read my credentials."

"Those are academic. They don't tell me what I really want to know."

I leaned forward. "And just what is that?"

"I want to know what you think about surgery as a woman."

The surgeon in me was irritated at the psychiatrist in her. "I'm not sure my being a woman has much to do with being a surgeon. I'm a surgeon who happens to be a woman."

Her forehead wrinkled. It wasn't what she wanted to hear. "A woman has unique qualifications that suit her to caring professions like medicine." Her gaze met mine. "I want my surgeon to understand this."

My stomach tightened. Was that a threat? I'd spent most of my adult life trying to ignore my uniqueness as a woman and fit in with the boys. Now I was sitting across from a patient, a physician, who was insisting that being a woman was something that I should embrace? For the last five years, my womanhood had been nothing but a handicap. I'd had to work harder than my colleagues to gain equal respect. If I walked into a party with a man, I was "arm candy," not Dr. Weller. If I got tired, I was called a woman, a wimp. If I whined half as much as the men, I had PMS.

I leaned forward. I'd actually given this some thought lately, but I wasn't sure I was ready to open up to this psychiatrist. I thought about my encounter with the scared little patient on the elevator as he'd cowered behind me. He'd done that naturally, as if a woman would protect him.

I offered a plastic smile. "Of course."

"Women are often more intuitive than men. They are certainly more nurturing and mothering by nature. A medical world run only by men tends toward cool indifference. In fact, we were all instructed on the value of emotional detachment from our patients so that we could bring objectivity to our analysis."

I nodded. What she said was true. I knew from experience that it was too true in surgery. "Surgeons must be objective in the treatment of life-threatening illness. Emotional attachments can keep you from making the hard decisions to proceed with therapies which have significant side effects."

"Identifying with the emotions of your patients can make you a more effective healer," she responded.

I tried to keep my mouth from falling open. I wasn't sure whether to feel grateful or manipulated. At this moment, I was leaning toward irritated and manipulated. I felt like this psychiatrist was trying to mold me into the physician she wanted. Or else she was testing me. Regardless, I did not feel like being examined. As I remembered it, she was supposed to be the patient in this "healing equation," as she called it. "Look, I understand what you're saying, but certain fields lend themselves to emotional involvement and identification more than others. Psychiatry," I said, lifting my palm toward her, "for instance." I sighed. "But decisions in surgery are made based upon evidence. We know what is best for our patients because of research comparing various treatment outcomes. The hard decisions of surgery are often made on the spot, on your feet, so to speak. I have to be able to think fast and act fast based on what I feel is best for my patient." I smiled. "Fortunately, I'm very good at this." Shrugging, I added, "Getting tangled into the emotions of my patients could hamper proper judgment."

She smiled the smile of my ninth-grade geometry teacher, Ms. Wilson. It was the kind of condescending smile that dripped wax compassion, the I'll-just-have-to-give-you-more-homework-until-you-get-it kind of smile. Tina stood. "Did you have any women role models in surgery?"

Chuckling, I shook my head. "Women don't exactly flock to this field. I started with one other woman in training. She quit four months into our internship." I watched Tina's eyes scanning my desk. I had a sudden urge to hide my cigar humidor. Being one of the boys had always been a point of pride for me, but at that moment, with this woman wanting me to embrace my strengths as the bearer of two X chromosomes, I found myself hoping she wouldn't ask about my former penchant for Nicaraguan cigars. And I didn't think she'd believe me if I told her I'd come to my senses and I just hadn't given them away yet. Between Kara and Tina, I was destined to rethink all of my coping strategies.

She pulled the door open and stood silhouetted by the fluorescent light in the hallway. "I guess you'll just have to be the example for others to follow."

I nodded obediently. "I guess." I quickly thought of all of the female medical students at MCV. Without me, there would be no female surgeon role model. Tina was right. Maybe I should be concentrating on bringing something special to surgery instead of fitting Gilles's mold. Of course, if I didn't fit the mold, I'd forfeit my job.

She paused in the doorway, hesitating to leave. I looked at her, surprised she didn't seem to want to know what every other woman would be begging for. And then she said it.

"I've got breast cancer, don't I?"

Our eyes met. In a moment's time, this woman's voice had thickened and her hand lifted to her mouth as if holding back the words. Fear glistened in her eyes as tears threatened her mascara.

I was touched by the sudden transformation I'd witnessed: psychiatrist melted into a frightened child. She leaned forward, hugging herself across the breasts. Body language was heavy here. She was already protecting herself from my treatment.

I opened my hands toward her. "Do I need to say it?"

She closed the door, bit her lower lip, and nodded.

"It's cancer."

She paused before pulling her hand through her gray-streaked blond bangs. "You're going to work with me through this, aren't you?"

I'm not sure what she meant. Perhaps Tina, like most physicians, had a need to feel in control. So I nodded. "Yes. I'll work with you."

She brushed away a tear. "What's next?"

"We need to get a few tests. A chest X-ray, some labs."

She nodded her head rapidly before squeaking out her request: "Can we get on with it as soon as possible?"

"Sure." I paused, studying my patient. She was so vulnerable, appearing older than I remembered her in my exam room. But perhaps that's because then I was distracted by her nakedness. Aside from the gray hairs streaking the blond, she also had a fine spray of wrinkles at the corners of her eyes. Even so, she was youthful. Vigorous. And disarming in her ability to draw me in.

I tapped the Day Planner that lay open on my desk. "Can you meet me in the clinic on Tuesday?"

She nodded without speaking.

"Tina, would you like to have your husband present?"

"No. I'm not ready to tell him yet."

I had an impulse to walk to her, to wrap my arms around her shivering shoulders and again tell her I'd be with her through this. But the distant surgeon in me quickly deadened the urge. Instead, I spoke softly. "OK, I'll be there."

But then, in spite of the caution lights, I found myself standing and stepping out to be on the same side of the desk with her. I hesitated, then opened my arms and gave her my best Nadine Solomon imitation. I hugged her, not just to offer my comfort to another woman in medicine, but to thank her for helping me open up, even if it was just an initial baby step toward being who I was as a woman surgeon.

She collapsed in my arms and heaved a sigh. Then, sniffing, she pushed me to arms' length and spoke with a voice wavering with emotion: "You and I are going to work out just fine." She opened the door and stepped through.

I offered her a smile and looked down the hall. I couldn't imagine any of my male colleagues doing what I'd just done.

She folded her hands across her chest again and walked down the hall wrapped in her own embrace, not looking back once. I felt strangely warmed by touching her, and brushed back a tear of my own.

I returned to sit at my desk. The article in front of me predicted mortality in trauma patients based on the number of organs in failure, an attempt to quantify death based on numbers. I sighed. Trauma surgery was harsh business. A trauma surgeon can't think about children who die on prom night and miss out on college. Trauma surgeons can't worry about grade-school boys who won't play Little League baseball or girls who won't dance in ballet recitals because of drunk drivers. That's a mother's job. But lately that mother's heart within me seemed to be pushing its way to my emotional surface. I took a deep breath.

A surgeon couldn't worry about how cancer affected a patient's emotions, her marriage, or her family.

Could she?

11

I T WAS AFTER six when I made my final sweep through the ICU. I hugged Nadine Solomon, who kept vigil beside a dying boy who "ain' never done nothin' to no one."

She squeezed me back. "Keep the faith."

I didn't have the nerve to tell her that I didn't have any.

I thought about Tina Kinser on my way home. I'd been trained to keep a professional distance, but this woman was under my skin, worming her way toward my heart. Maybe because she was young, a woman, and a doctor like me. Or maybe she manipulated my emotions. She seemed to be in control one minute, suggesting the proper way for a woman physician to be present in the "healing equation." The next she presented herself in exposed vulnerability, fearful that her picture-perfect life was about to crash to a halt.

I'd never been prone to crying over a patient in the past. But when Dr. Kinser had walked away from me, suddenly it was me with breast cancer and I was facing removal of one of my finest features. I chalked it up to stress over my new job, or premenstrual tension, but I knew I was rationalizing. A crack was forming in my tough, be-a-man exterior. I could only hope that if it widened, I'd like what was underneath.

So why were my emotions on edge? I found myself afraid that I was on the verge of losing it totally, fighting panic I didn't understand. I thought about the hundreds of patients with life-threatening illness I'd treated in the past—I hadn't cried over them. So why Tina Kinser?

I grew fearful that whatever had tripped my flashbacks into high gear would freeze me while I performed in the operating theater. That would be my ticket out of MCV for sure.

I stopped at Ukrops for a six-pack of Diet Pepsi and a frozen pizza, and ended up throwing in a carton of Häagen-Dazs chocolate ice cream. It was definitely a night for comfort food.

I listed my woes.

Mark, the wonderful, unusually sensitive boyfriend, had forgotten our anniversary.

I hadn't exactly impressed the chairman in my first week as a surgery attending.

And, to add misery to my suffering, my concrete emotional constitution seemed to be on vacation.

I carried the groceries up the stairs to Kara's apartment. I needed her perspective on my love life. Besides, carbohydrates were meant to be shared by best friends. I knocked on the door and waited. I knocked again and frowned. When there was still no answer, I plodded back down to my car. I'd have to cry in my Häagen-Dazs alone.

I drove home too fast, but I certainly didn't want my ice cream to melt. At my door I paused, wrestling with my keys and a grocery bag, when I heard a knock on the door. From the inside! With my key in the doorknob, I felt the knob begin to move. I jumped back with my heart in my throat. In a moment, the door was open wide, and I stared at Mark, who stood open-armed and wearing a goofy grin.

"Happy anniversary."

I shoved the grocery sack at him. "Don't ever do that again!"

When I stepped into the front room and looked over to my small dining table, I realized I'd spoken too fast. There were candles on the table and an elegant setting for two. They were not my plates. I was more accustomed to eating mac and cheese out of a saucepan over the sink. A vase with four red roses decorated the table. I looked back at Mark as a wonderful aroma of fresh bread tickled my nose. "Mark!"

He looked in the bag. "We won't be needing this." He kissed me on the cheek before turning me toward my bathroom. "Go freshen up. Dinner will be ready in thirty minutes."

I smiled. This beat premium ice cream eaten alone any day. In the bathroom, another scent hit. Perfumed steam rose from my tub, which was filled with water to within two inches of the top. A goblet of something pale and sparkling sat on the edge. I shut the door, thought twice, and then turned the latch to lock Mark out. I hadn't shared everything with him yet, but treatment like this was definitely lowering my resistance. I shed my clothes into a clump that I kicked into the corner before dipping my toes beneath the first layer of white bubbles.

The water was deliciously hot, so much so that it took me two minutes to slip in up to my chin. I took a deep breath before sipping the champagne. I was in heaven and Mark was responsible.

I took the first taste slowly, savoring the tingling liquid. I'm not a cheap date, but if I drink fast the tingles hit my brain after one glass. I closed my eyes and soaked, trying to dissolve away the problems of the day in this tub and the champagne.

I opened my eyes, wondering if I'd slept. My eyes felt heavy. I stood and dried myself before stepping out and grabbing my robe from a hook by the tub. I cinched it tight and made a plan. I loved this man. I didn't have to cave to anxieties that lingered at the edge of sex. I winked my agreement with the woman in the mirror and snuck into the kitchen, where I stood silently behind Mark and parted my robe to form a narrow slit from my neck to my waist. I wasn't ready to give it all to Mark, but I wasn't opposed to teasing him either.

He was busy stirring something on the stove, singing along

with an oldies station playing Three Dog Night. I cleared my throat to make him turn.

This time I let him kiss me and I gave it back to him as forcefully as he came on to me. I pushed him backward, enjoying my aggressiveness as much as I imagined Mark would.

"Ahh!" He jerked away, shaking his hand.

He bent over and moaned, allowing me to see the saucepan pushed off the glowing-red burner.

"I'm sorry, I'm sorry, I'm sorry," I blubbered, watching with my hand to my mouth as the lateral portion of Mark's right palm turned bright red and began to blister.

I stepped back and gathered my robe tightly around me before grabbing a plastic bag and filling it with ice. "Here. Use this." I walked to my medicine cabinet, aware of the disappointing irony that hung between us. Our red-hot passion had been cooled by fiery heat.

I gave Mark four ibuprofen tablets and retreated to my bedroom to dress. When I returned to the kitchen, Mark laughed and smiled his apology. "Let's eat."

We sat, and he served me. Baked chicken with an herb sauce, green salad, baked potato, and fresh biscuits. I ate slowly and answered Mark's probing into my day. By the time I was eating a slice of a delicatessen carrot cake, I'd gained courage enough to tell him about my episodes of fear.

He looked at me while I stewed. I'd never been so vulnerable with him. Until Monday, when he witnessed my first real attack, I'd only let him see the confident surgeon in me. Opening up with Mark felt right. I thought I was on the path to figuring some of this out, but I wanted him to accept me, to tell me I wasn't crazy. It was scary but exhilarating, romantic, binding us like superficial discussions never would. He reached for my hand. "Welcome to the human race, Camille."

It wasn't the response I'd anticipated. "What?"

He shrugged. "You've had a very tough week. You're starting out in your first real job." He framed the words "real job" in quotes with his fingers. "You're fighting gender bias." He paused. "And this all started after you struck that dog. That was horrible for you. So give yourself some slack, Camille. So you've had some anxiety attacks. Who hasn't?"

"I hope you're right."

Mark let it fall, choosing not to explore any further. I expected him to try to draw me out, to help me sort through my symptoms, help me see things from a scientific perspective. But instead, he led me to the couch, where he obviously had other intentions, sore hand or not.

But I wasn't quite ready. I'd remembered the letter from CFW and I pulled it from my purse to show him. He sighed and read the letter. "Camille, this is great. You're going, aren't you?"

"I'm not sure." I had made up my mind not to go . . . until that moment.

"Camille, this is your father, a chance to get in touch with your roots."

I looked at the picture of my father. Even from the photo I understood what my aunt Jeanine saw. His eyes were piercing. I moved the picture to my right, then farther right again. He was still staring at me.

I wondered if my love-hate relationship with Dr. Gilles had something to do with my father. Maybe I trusted Dr. Gilles because he looked at me the way my father did.

Mark touched my arm. I handed him the picture.

"Your father?"

I nodded. "These people have ignored me all these years. And now they ask for money." I lifted my hands in surrender. "And I should go to support their cause?"

"Evidently your father thought it was worthy."

I shrugged. "That's obvious."

"You've told me you don't remember a lot about Africa. This

is a chance for you to talk to people who knew him." He hesitated. "This is who you are, Camille."

"Maybe it's not. I'm not even sure who I am. Except that I'm an orphan."

"So go find out."

"I've made it this far without roots. Maybe I don't want to know my father. What if I don't like him? Maybe having a snapshot of the past is better than being certain of having a bad one."

"Why do you think it was bad?"

The question gave me pause. It was hard to explain. At some level I understood that he could never be as perfect as the father I'd created in my fantasies. Recently I'd started wondering if he was, in truth, a far cry from being nice at all. It was the feeling of dread I had every time I started trying to remember the Congo. "I know a bit from my aunt Jeanine. She wasn't exactly enamored with my father." I took a deep breath. "She thinks he was an unbalanced fool with big ideas."

"He sounds like a hero to me."

"Why?"

"He died for what he believed, didn't he?"

"Not exactly."

"He died because he chose to go to stay in an unstable part of the world because he believed in what he was doing, right?"

I nodded my assent.

"Enough said. Your dad is a hero."

"Pardon me if I'm a little ambivalent. He may be a hero, and I've certainly had my share of fantasies of what I wish my father was like, but I know it was just a child's game. When I didn't like what my aunt Jeanine did, I imagined my father being perfect to make up for what I hated about her."

"So where's the ambivalence?"

"Maybe he put his faith in front of his family. Maybe if he'd have pulled out earlier, I wouldn't have grown up an orphan."

"You can't know that."

I felt my throat thickening. "I'm not even sure he really loved me at all."

"If you don't remember, how can you say that?"

I sniffed. "Just a feeling."

"I think you owe it to your father to go."

"I'll think about it."

Mark smiled. He moved closer and rubbed his nose against my ear. Evidently, he was ready for the next subject.

He started with his lips on my ear and neck, moving, searching, until I turned into him and opened my lips in response. He was so gentle with me, but I found myself frozen, unable to give in to his caress. The discussion about my father was fresh and I couldn't shift gears and move on. As Mark became more intense, my emotions wouldn't cooperate. Instead of passion, I found myself in the grip of fear. I was trapped in a repeat of Monday night. My boyfriend was ready for more and I felt a sudden need for air. My heart pounded and I pulled away. He resisted, moving his hand down my back.

"Stop."

His disappointment was immediate. "Camille!"

I couldn't look at him. I concentrated on slowing my breathing. I was sure he thought I was crazy.

His voice was softer, showing the strain of irritation, but also an attempt to understand. "Baby, what's wrong?"

I bit my lower lip. "I don't know what's wrong! It's not something I can explain."

"You can tell me."

I shook my head. "You don't understand. I can't tell you, not because I'm unwilling, but because it's not something *I* understand." I paused and looked at him. He had a serious case of puppy-dog eyes. "Mark, I hate it that I'm doing this. If I've ever wanted to give myself to someone, it's you. Don't think I'm pushing you away because I don't want you."

He sighed. "That's some consolation."

"I just need some time."

"You're not a kid anymore." He kissed my cheek. "What are you waiting for, Camille? Commitment? Is it me?"

"Mark, it's me! It's what I was explaining to you . . . this is one of those sudden episodic fears that attack me, grip me, and won't let me go." My voice rose and I put my fingers to his lips as I anticipated his attempt to comfort me. *Don't say it, Mark.*

He sat back and folded his hands in his lap, wearing the face of a teen who'd been denied the car keys for a date. We sat quietly for a few minutes while I tried to divert my thoughts elsewhere to calm the runaway train in my chest.

After a few minutes, I felt control returning and my mind drifted to Tina. Again.

"Would it affect the way you feel about me if I had a mastectomy?"

Mark straightened. "Camille, are you trying—"

"Relax," I interrupted. "I don't have cancer."

He slumped again and began to breathe.

"I'm just trying to imagine what one of my patients is going through. I'm treating a doctor who has breast cancer. She's absolutely beautiful, Mark. She hasn't told her husband, I'm sure. I suspect she fears his reaction."

"A doctor? Who?"

I looked at him, surprised at his question. We're both professionals. Confidentiality demands that we never ask for names. "You know I can't tell you that."

"Why did she come to you?"

"Thanks a lot."

"Camille, you know what I mean. I'm not saying you're not capable. But we both know how the system works. You're a trauma surgeon. The chairman of the department is an oncology surgeon with a worldwide reputation. Why did she come to you?"

I stared at him, offended by his question, but knowing I had the same first reaction. "I'm a woman."

"What's that got to do with it?"

"Apparently, a lot, to my patient."

"That's crazy."

"Careful," I warned. "I thought you were a sensitive man."

He kissed my cheek. "I am."

"There are strengths that a woman brings to medicine," I said as though I'd been thinking this way for a long time, and not just since Tina Kinser had challenged my paradigm.

"Such as?"

"Women are naturally more nurturing, gentler than men."

Mark raised his eyebrows higher. "This from a woman who smoked a cigar on our first date?"

"We were playing poker. I always smoke when I play poker." I halted. "Er—I used to."

He raised his eyebrows higher. "No more stogies?"

"I've made too many concessions along the way, Mark."

"Cigars were a concession?"

"Cigars, beer." I made a rolling motion with my hands. "Stuff I did, not because I liked it, but because I wanted to be in the boys' club."

"It made you unique. Hip."

"It made me just like every other good ol' boy who wants to be a cutter."

"And now you suddenly see that women have something special to bring to medicine?"

"You should be the last to question this. You chose a field that appeals to the mothering instinct many women have."

"I like working with patients who haven't spent a lifetime abusing their bodies, then coming to me for salvage."

"OK." I didn't feel like arguing.

Mark shifted in his seat and checked his watch. Apparently, he didn't feel much like only sitting and chatting on the couch.

I kissed his cheek. "You never answered my question."

"What?"

"Would it affect the way you thought of me if I had a mastectomy?"

He smiled. "You have other things to keep my interest."

I slapped him playfully before we fell silent. "I'm sorry about tonight." I hesitated, and then added, "I'm sure there will be plenty of time for this in the future." I pulled his face toward mine and kissed him slowly.

"OK." He was being strong, but I could read his disappointment.

"You've given me the nicest anniversary gift ever."

Mark sighed.

"Go home," I coaxed. "I've got to start early in the morning."

"Let me help with the dishes."

I shook my head and waved him off. Right then, I'd rather be alone. "I'll do them. You've done enough."

"They're my dishes."

I smiled. "It will be my excuse to make you come back."

I walked him to the door and kissed him good-bye, telling myself I was crazy for not asking him to stay. But something in me was terrified.

Am I afraid of intimacy? Or something more sinister from my past?

Two times panic had touched me when I'd been in Mark's arms. But each of those times I'd had a sense that something from locked-away memories was just out of reach. The first time it was the déjà vu of a bleeding dog. The second followed a discussion about my father.

From my bedroom window, I watched him. He didn't look up. He was in his car and gone, and I stood alone to blame myself for ruining another night.

12

THIRTY-EIGHT.

Too young to have cancer.

Too young to die.

Tina Kinser shook her head and wondered if she'd forever define her life into BC and AC, before and after cancer. Maybe she should look at it as a defining point. Maybe it was a clarion call to wake up and start living again.

She'd defined her marriage in a similar way. Before and after Dan's nine-month affair. For twenty years they'd been faithful to each other. One year ago, all of that had changed.

She looked across the dinner table to Dan, who seemed engrossed in his lasagna. Either he didn't care whether or not he could see her or he just enjoyed staring at the bouquet he'd brought home the night before. Tina could care less about another guilt offering. She pushed the flowers aside so she could see his face. She thought about blurting it out. *I have CANCER!* The word was always capitalized in her mind. *You were unfaithful to your adoring wife. Now she has CANCER.*

Dan would probably marry again a few months after her funeral. What would people say? That he must have been seeing her before Tina was dead? *Tsk, tsk.* Cancer *and* an unfaithful husband. And she was always such a good wife and such a great psychiatrist.

Dan looked up and smiled. "Pass the salt."

She didn't know how to tell him. She'd acted impulsively and slept with a resident? She'd wanted to hurt him, to let him know how much she had suffered, but now it all seemed dwarfed by her other news.

She pushed the shaker across the table and slowly rearranged the food on her plate.

Revenge was supposed to feel good.

She sighed and took her plate to the sink, feeding the disposal.

Dan raised his voice over the whirring sound of the disposal. "Any dessert tonight?"

She pulled a half-gallon container of Heavenly Hash ice cream from the freezer. She took it and a soup bowl to the table and set it in front of her husband.

She felt like screaming. And crying. She feared if she talked she might do both.

Where had they gone wrong? It hadn't begun in one night spent in search of acceptance in another's arms. They had strayed one step at a time until they were miles from the same location.

She silently cleared the table, then settled into a chair with a novel.

Dan plopped onto the couch and turned on the TV.

Tina left the room when a doctor on the screen put his hand on a woman's shoulder. "It's cancer." The woman began to cry.

At eleven, Dan slipped into bed beside his wife. He spoke the first words to her since dinner. "Do you think you'll ever forgive me?"

A NIGHTMARE STARTLED me from sleep in the dark hours of the morning. My eyes opened and I gasped for breath, but immediately the contents of the dream were beyond reach. All I knew was that I was in terror of something or someone causing imminent danger. I laid on my back, staring at the ceiling until my heart slowed and I convinced myself that dreams were only dreams, without a connection to reality.

My hand passed over the surface of my bed and I wondered what it would have been like if I'd have let Mark stay. I felt excitement at the thought. Excitement and fear mixed with the anxiety of what panic might erupt if I allowed him to love me like I knew he desired.

At five I rose, prepared for the day, and sighed as I looked at my Day Planner. A small red circle indicated the imminent start of my period. Prepare for flood day number one. Maybe that's why my emotions had been on edge last night. I shook my head, knowing it was wishful thinking.

I needed to begin outlining a study plan for my written board examinations. Although I'd successfully finished my residency training, I was officially listed as board eligible, not board certified, until I passed both a written and oral board examination. I sipped strong black coffee and sat at my desk to finalize the plan.

By 7:00 a.m. I was at MCV, my mood buoyed by the responsiveness of my new car. I walked with confidence, celebrating Friday and the milestone of almost completing week one at my first real job. Ellis called it POETS day. Piss On Everybody. Tomorrow's Saturday. Today, I felt the acronym fit. *Watch out team, I've got PMS.*

By seven-fifteen I began rounds with my team and tried to sneak past the ICU waiting room without disturbing Nadine Solomon. My efforts failed, and when I activated the automatic doors leading from the unit, the team was met head-on by the large woman. She wore a blue and gray polyester pantsuit, evidence that she'd been home to change, but the material was wrinkled from another night on a waiting room couch.

"Good morning, Dr. Weller," she said, corralling my team to the side of the hall. I met her gaze. At least Nadine had figured out who ran this team.

"Morning, Mrs. Solomon."

"How's Kendrick?"

I paused a moment, wondering how to phrase what I needed to say. "His liver function tests and creatinine are climbing."

"That's good."

"No, that's bad. It indicates his liver and kidneys have been shocked and are failing. I'm afraid if his kidneys shut down, we're going to lose him."

"I keep prayin' so you keep right on doctorin'. He's goin' to get better, Dr. Weller. You'll see."

This woman's optimism was going to cause a big problem when her son died. She was in denial, and it was my job to ease her gently back to earth. I reached for her hand. "Nadine, Kendrick is very, very sick. If his kidneys continue to shut down, he'll have a one in ten chance of surviving." I looked her in the eyes. "Do you understand this? Do you see what we're up against?"

She flashed a smile at me, the type you give to someone you pity for being so stupid. "You just keep doctorin'. Everything's gonna be all right."

My teeth clenched, and I winced at her statement, anticipating a rush of fear—relieved when it did not come.

I mirrored the smile she gave me.

I felt sorry for Nadine. I wanted her son to survive, perhaps almost as much as she did, but I was caught between feeling that I needed to get her to see reality and allowing her to have her tenacious optimism. "I certainly hope so." I squeezed her hand before letting go and directing my team toward the stairs.

"Let's get a move on, team," I chided. "We've got a full day ahead."

And night, I thought, knowing I was the trauma attending on call. Things always heated up in the city after the sun went down.

TINA SPENT THE morning in the MCV library doing a literature search on the latest in breast cancer treatment. After four hours she felt her outlook improving. Things had changed in the years since her mother was treated. A ray of hope pierced the clouds of her pessimism. Maybe life wasn't over. Maybe it was just time for some major adjustments.

She photocopied her selected articles and set out to find Mark Lawson. Perhaps what had begun as a one-night fling was another turning point for her. And maybe, just maybe, there was a chance to recapture joy in a new relationship.

She nodded her head to her own resolution. She was going to fight. Fight the cancer. Fight the dullness that had settled over her life and marriage like a cloud.

Breast cancer would prompt her to live again. There was no reason not to begin afresh in life . . . and love.

She found him in the pediatric oncology clinic, coming out of an exam room, his hand on the shoulder of a young patient.

He touched the boy's bald head. "It will grow back, sport. I promise."

Mark Lawson looked up. His eyes met Tina's, then quickly darted up and down the hall. He walked over, his voice quiet. "Tina. I—"

She shook her head. "I shouldn't have come." She searched his face for clues as to how he felt about her. "I just . . . well . . . I can't get you off my mind," she whispered.

"We had a good time, Tina, but—"

She looked down. "I know, I know," she said, suddenly embarrassed by her boldness in coming to see him here. *What was I thinking?* She didn't want to hear him say it. *It was only a one-night stand.*

Their eyes met for a moment before she looked away. She could lose her soul looking in his eyes. She inhaled the scent of Drakkar Noir. His scent. She felt her cheeks flush.

"I've got to go," she said, turning away. She halted when she felt his hand on her arm.

"I wish things were different."

She implored him with a look. "Don't say it, Mark. I shouldn't have come." She squeezed his hand. "Bye."

She walked away holding back tears, wondering how she could have been such a fool.

13

D R. TINA KINSER sat on the exam table in front of me. It had been a typical clinic day until then, with hernia and gallbladder patients, and the follow-ups on people assaulted by what the residents affectionately call the Richmond knife and gun club.

She came at the end of my morning clinic so I would not have to race through her visit. As customary, since she was my private patient, I excused the residents from examining her first. This was her official pre-op visit prior to surgery.

In her lap she held a stack of photocopied articles she'd pulled from our medical library. "I want your opinion. What's the appropriate next step?"

I thumbed through the chart. Everything seemed in order. Her chest X-ray was clear. I was ready to proceed. "Let's talk about your surgery."

Fine lines in her forehead deepened. "To remove my breast?"

"The operation is a modified radical mastectomy, a removal of the breast and the lymph nodes under the arm."

"I'm familiar with it."

"Is that what your mother had?"

"She had the old radical operation." She frowned. "It was awful. She went into the operating room for a biopsy, not even knowing if she had breast cancer, and woke up with a crisscrossed skin graft where her breast used to be."

"We've come a long way since those days."

"Not far enough." Tina chose an article from the stack in her lap.

I shifted in my seat uncomfortably. I had the feeling that Dr. Kinser was going to take over her visit. Again.

"Are you familiar with the work of Bernard Fisher?"

"Of course. He leads the NSABP." Since Tina brought it up, I threw out the initials, suspecting she was familiar with the National Surgical Adjuvant Breast and Bowel Project.

"There is evidence that the choice of local treatment has little to do with survival."

I leaned forward, bracing myself so I didn't roll around on my moveable stool. "Are you suggesting we do something other than remove the breast?"

She froze for a moment before answering. "Yes."

I paused to let her explain, but she waited for my reaction. I held back from my initial emphatic, no-way response. "What are you suggesting?"

"Remove just the tumor and the axillary nodes. Then I'll get radiation therapy."

I let my breath out slowly. What she was suggesting was a radical departure from current thinking. "What you are asking may be appropriate for some small breast cancers, but the data from the NSABP is not in. Removing only the tumor in your case may result in a recurrence, and ultimately the cancer gaining the upper hand."

"Don't dance around with me. You can say it, Camille. I could die, right? That's what you're telling me."

I looked her in the eye. "You are playing with your life, Tina. We should plan this according to what we know will work."

She lifted another paper from her stack. "Trials comparing

mastectomy with lumpectomy and radiation have been done in Italy," she began. "Look at this. *World Journal of Surgery*, 1977."

I glanced through the article, which was now nearly ten years old. It was from the cancer institute in Milan. She'd done her homework. Fortunately, for the past five years, so had I. "Look, breast conservation trials have been going on since the early sixties. At Guy's Hospital in London, modified radical mastectomy was compared to lumpectomy, removal of lymph nodes, and radiation. The outcomes for radiation patients were disappointing."

"But they used lower doses of radiation in those trials. The higher doses used in Italy and the ongoing trials in the United States may be better."

We shouldn't have been arguing about this. I slid my stool away so that I could lean against the wall. I wasn't used to finding my way with such an educated patient. All I could think of was what Dr. Gilles would do to me if I deviated from current standard practice. "I—"

"People are doing lumpectomies for cancer all the time, Camille."

"Sure they are, but at this point, it's appropriate only within a controlled trial. There is no national consensus on this issue."

She crossed her arms across her breasts. "I'm not ready for a mastectomy." She hesitated. "I'm willing to take the risk."

"Have you talked to the radiation oncologists? Do you think you can find one who is willing to treat you?"

"I've already spoken to Dr. Chadaury in hypothetical terms. He said he would treat a patient who refused conventional therapy."

"I'm not sure I can do this. I'm just starting out in this department. If Dr. Gilles knew I intentionally treated a patient with an experimental therapy outside the NSABP trial, I could lose my job."

Her eyes narrowed. "Dr. Gilles can't understand what it means for a woman to have a breast removed. A breast is for mothering, for nurturing our children. In our culture, breasts are also celebrated for beauty and sex." She locked eyes with me. "What would you do?"

"I—" I stopped before giving the quick answer, the one I'd been trained to give for the board exam. "I—" I couldn't quite get it out. "Honestly, I guess I've never thought about it in that way."

Tina's voice softened. "Think about the last time you were caressed by your lover."

I blushed.

She continued. "Would sex be the same?"

"I don't know, I—"

"What about the joy you have in wearing a swimsuit or dress that accentuates your cleavage? Are you ready to do without that?"

I took a deep breath to speak, but Tina rolled forward with arguments she'd had a week to prepare.

"Are you ready for what it will do to your self-image? Are you ready to look in the mirror?"

Finally, I found my voice. "Are you ready to die?"

She didn't hesitate. "Yes."

"Dr. Gilles may fire me." I paused. "Why not go to a center where the trials comparing therapy are ongoing?"

"They won't enroll patients who are not willing to be randomized to either therapy arm. Besides, I know you have the training to do what I need. And you are a woman who can identify with me." She tapped the stack of papers with perfect nails, the kind a female surgeon only dreamed of. "At least I can identify with you, and that's important to me."

"Dr. Kinser," I said, shaking my head. "Certainly your husband will still love you with only one breast. Many patients have healthy self-images and wonderful sex lives after mastectomy." I said this, but even as the encouraging words rolled from my tongue, I knew I'd never asked a patient if this was true.

"My husband has lost interest in me."

I tried to keep my mouth closed. I was a bit dumbfounded.

As a surgeon, I was ready to talk about surgical risks, options, and outcomes. But Tina had sucked me into her life beyond her physical illness. Fortunately she rescued me from my inability to respond.

"You've felt the mass. It's not exactly subtle. You would hope a husband would notice something this obvious." She hung her head. "It's been months since he held me."

"I, I'm sorry."

"Look, I know what I'm asking. And I'm ready to take the risk. If I really thought it would significantly decrease my chances for a cure, I wouldn't ask you to do it. But we really don't know that, do we?"

"The evidence isn't all in and—"

"Camille, I'm not just a breast cancer. If I was, you could speak of the studies, the evidence, and the rational facts. However, since I am a woman with emotions, a failing marriage, a career, and a desire to fill out my little black cocktail dress, the evidence isn't all that you need to consider."

What she said made complete sense. But my training wasn't exactly rich in compassion. In fact, I could quote survival statistics for every stage of breast cancer, and I knew it wouldn't impress Tina a bit. The humbling thing was that she had chosen me not because I was a competent surgeon who knew all the board answers. She'd chosen me because I was a young woman, and she thought I could be trusted to identify with her pain and treat her accordingly.

After a few moments of silence, I formulated a plan. Basically I wanted to buy some time before I agreed to detonate another blast at my career. "I want to talk to Dr. Gilles. He—"

"He's old school, Camille."

"I respect him. I have to talk to him about it." I tried not to think about what rocking the boat again in my first two months might do to my career.

She shrugged. "Fair enough." She extended her hand, which

instead of shaking, I held for a few moments, making a conscious effort to put myself in her shoes.

I offered a smile—a real one—because I had a sense that the patient would become my teacher. Dr. Gilles may have taught me how to be a surgeon, but Tina Kinser was teaching me how to be a physician.

THE WEEK HAD not been easy on Kendrick Solomon. His kidneys had shut down, and I had to consult the nephrologists for hemodialysis. Now he was barely hanging on, and I'd begun to feel the subtle pressure from the nurses to pull the plug. Nobody enjoyed prolonging death, but sometimes we pushed so hard for a win that we couldn't see the inevitable.

In front of Nadine, I hung black crepe. I'd determined not to let her feel false optimism.

Concerning Kendrick's care, I'd not pulled back a notch. He was my ticket into the Six-Liter Club and I wasn't going to let him go gracefully. I used every resource available to push for a save. At home, mostly after the sun went down, I wondered if I was torturing Kendrick just so I could prove my worth to Dr. Gilles. Or maybe because I was afraid the chairman would call me to task for using so much blood on one patient and I'd inch closer to the precipice of losing my job.

I stood at Kendrick's bedside late in the night after pulling another gunshot victim back from the brink. Attending to Kendrick first thing in the morning and again right before heading for home had become my routine.

I looked at his numbers and frowned. He was hot. His core temperature was over 102. The stuff they suctioned from his endotracheal tube was thick and nasty. He suffered from one of the other problems associated with being in the hospital too long: hospital-acquired pneumonia.

The curtain at the entrance to the ICU cubicle moved to reveal Nadine. I'd give one thing to this woman: she had the stamina of a beaver trying to dam the Mississippi. If I had a living mother, I'd hope she'd stick with me the way this woman was glued to Kendrick.

"It's after midnight, Mrs. Solomon. You should be getting some sleep."

Her eyes were moist. "I can't sleep. I need to pray for my son."

"OK," I said and patted her arm. This time I couldn't bear to tell her any more bad news.

She stilled her trembling hand by gripping the bed railing until her brown knuckles blanched. "I've been prayin' for this boy for fifteen years." She wagged her head slowly, then looked at me. "He don't know the Savior, Dr. Weller. He needs another chance."

The unspoken message was clear. She didn't fear death as much as hell beyond the veil. The thought chilled me in a way I didn't understand. I thought I was a rational woman. I didn't believe in torture other than what I saw man inflict upon himself. I cleared my throat. "We're doing everything we can."

She looked at me intensely. "It's not up to you."

I took a deep breath. I wanted to remind her of the countless hours I'd spent paying attention to every detail of her son's care. I wanted to tell her how remarkable it was that I was able to get her son off the operating table alive, but I held my tongue because Kendrick was still likely to die soon, and the words about my great efforts would seem shallow. Instead, I reached for Nadine's hand and held it while I watched her son's chest rise and fall with the ventilator.

"Is it OK if I stay with him for a while longer?"

"Sure," I whispered, tentatively gathering Nadine into my arms. I didn't care if visiting hours were over or if the head nurse found me breaking the rules. What was best for Nadine Solomon was that I let her son receive prayer before he died.

"Thanks, Dr. Weller," she said, her voice thick with emotion. "Everything's gonna be all right."

MARK LAWSON HAD been waiting for a woman like Camille Weller for a long time. He'd had his share of dates. In fact, medical school had added more than just initials to his signature. It seemed the MD brought with it a whole new breed of willing women who wanted nothing more than to share in his dreams for a successful pediatric oncology practice and the rewards that came with it.

Camille Weller was different. She wasn't impressed with his degree. He was sure her accomplishments in medicine would eventually overshadow his. What struck him about Camille was her complete lack of the normal accessories that tagged along with academic surgeons like ornaments on a Christmas tree. Pomp and aggrandizement were found infrequently in her, if at all. She actually cared about the down-and-outers that Richmond cast at the doorstep of the trauma service. And best of all, she seemed to appreciate Mark Lawson as a person, not for his degree.

He wanted to take the next step in commitment with Camille. He knew she was ready. But along came Tina Kinser and in one day, he'd been swept into a relationship more intense than any he'd ever known.

He picked up the phone. He needed to talk to Camille. He wanted to tell her the words she wanted to hear. But now, if things were going to work, instead of confessing his love, he needed to get honest . . . with himself and with Camille. He'd made a desperate mistake. Could she ever forgive him?

He set down the phone. He couldn't unveil his mistake that way. Sitting in the solitude of his study, he dropped his head into his hands. Maybe he shouldn't tell her at all. It would risk destroying the trust she had in him. Besides, it wasn't like they were married or anything.

Tina Kinser. What had intrigued him so? The girlish way she giggled at the end of a serious comment? The way she listened— really listened—when they talked together about common problems they had in helping families cope with kids with cancer? The excitement he felt when she brushed the back of his hand with hers as they sat side by side? She was mature. Yet so alive. Experienced, yet her eyes wide with wonder like a child seeing everything fresh and new. The memories of her being in his arms excited him . . . and frightened him.

She was married.

He'd fallen to a depth he'd never experienced. And she'd taken him to heights he'd not known before.

He paced his apartment and told himself to get a grip. He'd held fire in his breast, and the risk of a significant heart scorch increased with every second he entertained her image in his mind.

It was a mistake. *She* was a mistake. Now he needed to focus on being right for Camille or risk losing everything they had.

He baked a frozen pizza and ate alone in front of the TV. At nine, he was jarred awake by the doorbell. He got up from the couch and went to the door, peering through the peephole. It was her. Tina Kinser had found his apartment.

14

WHEN THE SIMBAS finally let us go back into our house, all our things were everywhere. They had broken the dishes and knocked the pictures off the walls. When we first got in, Mother started crying, and Daddy was busy quieting her, so I just went to my bedroom. I didn't feel much like cleaning, but I picked up a little picture frame with a photograph of my mother. She didn't like it because it was taken before she came and lived with us and she doesn't have all her clothes on. Mother says she covers up now because Daddy says it is Christian. I like the picture. My mother is pretty and she shouldn't be ashamed. She won't let Daddy display the picture in the front room, but she said I could keep it in my bedroom if I wanted.

But now the stupid Simbas have messed it up, and the frame is twisted and the glass broken. I slid the little picture out and hid it in my math book.

Tumi, my dog, must know something bad has happened because he is slinking around like he is guilty or something. I guess most of the time when there's glass on the floor it's been 'cause his happy tail knocked something down. I bet he's waiting for my mother to scream at him or send him outside for being bad.

I stayed quiet while my parents cleaned up, and then I went

to sleep under my mosquito net. When I woke up, Mother was making chai. I guess the Simbas must not have broken all the cups because Mother and Daddy have their tea in cups, but Mother brought some to me in a plastic glass.

I didn't get to go out for the rest of the day.

I looked out the window and it looked like the Simbas were burning the school. Daddy says that is because the regular army has been using the schools to sleep in.

I watched from the front room until Mother made me get away from the window.

I wish Daddy would take us all to his home in America, but he says we've waited too long and we're going to have to stay put.

That makes me scared, 'cause every time the Simba men bring in another wounded soldier, they look at me and point, and I hear them talking about my skin. One man asked if he could touch me, but my mother yelled at him and grabbed my arm, telling me to get myself into the house.

RICHMOND, 1984

DRIVING HOME WITH my window down, I felt the languid, moist Richmond air. Something about the closeness of the night lifted Africa to my consciousness. I remembered dusty roads during the dry season, and riding on the roof of my father's Land Rover. I remembered playing in puddles during the rainy season, and building a mud hut for a family in our village. I remembered climbing the loquat trees and sucking sweet fruit while hiding in the haven of thick branches. I remembered chasing baboons away from our garbage pit and the roaches that lived in our latrine. I let the few and fleeting memories flood my mind for a moment. I felt a twinge of guilt, as if I peered into something forbidden. But I had a sense that I needed to remember, that it was time to face whatever had been bubbling to the surface and interrupting my life.

Past Henrico High School, all was quiet except for the barking of a lonely dog. This stimulus quickened my heart. I concentrated to remember. I had a dog in the Congo. Yellow with thick fur that would tangle with tan blobs of mud. We called him Tumi; short for a longer Kiswahili word I couldn't recall. I couldn't go beyond the hospital compound without him.

Tumi is barking, snarling. A high-pitched yelp cut short. A gurgle, then silence. The acrid smell of burning kerosene hangs thick in the air.

It is dark. Close. Very close and hot. His breath is heavy on my neck. His fingers are clutching me, silencing my cries, muffling my desire to scream. He is holding me against him, his hand moist. Sticky fluid. Blood. He whispers in my ear. Kisses on my neck. "Everything's gonna be all right."

I looked at my speedometer. I had rocketed my Prelude to over ninety miles per hour. I braked hard and pulled to the side of the road, gasping, aware that my memories had pulled me from the present, and that I'd been driving—reacting and not aware. I was an ocean away in my mind, here only in body, responding to the naked emotion of repressed memory.

My hands trembled. I was sweating and my heart pounded. I dropped my head against the steering wheel, fighting the terror that pulsed within my veins.

I waited for my heart to slow and concentrated on controlling my breath, taking two counts in and four counts out. One, two . . . one, two, three, four.

After a few minutes' rest, I began driving again, concentrating on every detail of driving to take my mind away from the Congo. I inhaled the new-car smell. I shifted from first to second—paying attention to things I did mindlessly to gain a sense of control. I braked with my right foot. I downshifted from third to second. I turned into my apartment complex, slowing, stopping, unlocking my door.

This mental game was likely to push me to the verge of insanity faster than the panic that had driven me to try it.

I walked into my apartment and turned on every light. Although it was late, I did not want to sleep, for I feared the time between alertness and slumber, that when I let down my guard, thoughts of terror would invade. I knew on one level that this was irrational, but the feeling of stark fear that had gripped me in the car still clawed at the door.

Something, somewhere was incredibly wrong. It was like the dread I'd experienced as a child when waking from a dream that I'd gone to school in my underwear. Except after a minute, this one hadn't gone away.

Calling Kara, I let the phone ring six times before she picked up. I feigned nonchalance. "Feel like watching a movie?"

"I'm gonna crash. I've got an early shift tomorrow."

I took a deep breath. "It happened to me again, Kara."

"What—"

"An attack." I felt silly for admitting it. "A panic attack."

"Tell me what happened."

I gave the *Reader's Digest* version.

After a pause, I heard a snicker on the other end.

"What? Why are you laughing? This isn't easy telling you this, and you're going to laugh?"

"I can't help it, Camille. It just started to tickle me, that's all. Here you are, the most together woman I know, and you're telling me your problems. You should take a look in my closet." She giggled again.

"You've been drinking."

The silence on the other end was all the answer I needed.

"Kara, you swore off—"

"I'm OK, Camille," she huffed. "How did you turn the focus on me? I thought we were talking about your problems."

"I'm over it. I'm worried about you now."

She laughed at my ploy. "Glad I could be of service. All I need to do is show you how screwed up my life is and you'll feel better about yours."

"Kara, that's not what I meant!"

She sighed. "I know."

"Should I come over?"

"I really need to crash."

I nodded my head, even though she couldn't see. I hesitated. "Thanks for listening."

"I still think you're the most together woman I know."

"Good night, Kara."

I sat up studying for my board exams, refocusing on the textbook in front of me anytime my thoughts attempted to slide away. At midnight, I stared at a page that was half highlighted in yellow. I held the marker, but I didn't remember anything I'd just marked.

I crawled into bed, too tired to shed my clothes, and not about to turn off the light. The feel of the covers on my clothes brought me another memory, one I was too exhausted to stave off.

I remembered sleeping in my clothes in Africa.

TINA SAT ON the couch and wiped her eyes with the back of her hand. "I have cancer."

Mark handed her a Coke and sat forward in a leather chair opposite her. "What? How long? When—"

"You found it."

"Me? I didn't—"

She stayed quiet as the revelation dawned.

He stared at the floor. "Breast?"

She nodded.

"Tina, I'm so sorry."

"Don't be sorry for me. Be happy," she said, her smile forced. "Already this whole whirlwind has made me look at my life differently."

Mark watched as the confident physician in front of him

started to unravel in spite of her strong words. She lowered her head. "I've been lulled to sleep, Mark. My marriage is dead. I've been living without love for too long." She lifted her eyes to his. Her cheeks were moist with tears.

He moved to her side, touched by the sincerity of her emotion. He wiped her tears with his hand. "Tina, I—"

She buried her face in his neck. "What you gave me was so special," she whispered.

Red lights flashed, then turned to yellow. Mark's resolve weakened.

In another minute, consolation quickened into passion. Fortitude fractured into compromise. Their lips brushed. He tasted her tears.

Mark pushed a warning from his mind. There would be time for confession later.

15

TINA WOKE TO the sound of Mark's alarm. She looked up as he walked into his bedroom fully clothed, sans tie, ready for work. "I've got to go." He looked around. "Can you lock up when you leave?"

She propped herself on one elbow. "Just like that? You're going to leave me in your apartment?"

He walked to the side of the bed. He leaned over and kissed her forehead. It was a kiss you give your sister when your parents force you to make up. No passion. Pure mechanics.

She frowned. "Not a morning person?"

"I'm going to be late."

His attitude dampened her initial excitement of waking up in his bed.

"Are you mad?"

He paused. "I don't know what I am."

"Come here," she coaxed.

He sighed and obeyed.

She tapped the side of the bed. "Sit for just a minute."

He obeyed and she spoke again. "You need space to adjust."

"You're married."

She nodded. "For now."

"Tina, what's going to happen? We—"

She pressed her fingers against his lips. "What is happening between us has been very beautiful. That's all I know right now."

He took a deep breath. "Tell me about your cancer."

"I'm going to meet with my surgeon to make some final plans."

"Dr. Gilles?"

She smiled. "Heaven's no. Someone young. A woman. Camille Weller."

She watched his lips tighten. He hesitated. "You should see someone with experience. She's too fresh out of training."

"She's wonderful, Mark. She won't treat me as just a breast cancer." Tina reached out and touched his shoulder. "She'll treat me as a woman." She smiled. "Why don't I meet you in your clinic for a cup of coffee. Say, around three?"

He ran his fingers through his hair. "I'd rather you didn't come around the clinic to see me."

She felt her throat thicken.

"It's just, well, for now, you know . . . people will talk. I don't want you getting hurt. People respect you."

She nodded. She didn't like it. But she understood.

"Do me a favor. Go see Dr. Gilles. Weller is a trauma surgeon. You need an oncologist."

Tina appreciated his concern. She stayed quiet. She wanted Dr. Weller.

She pulled his hand to her mouth, and pressed her lips to his open palm. "I'll lock up."

I awoke with a start, gasping. Something, someone was there. A small place. A closet. Darkness. Unspeakable horror.

I looked at my alarm clock and rubbed the sleep from my eyes. Six-thirty. I'd overslept.

I was weary of stupid dreams. If there was something scary

in my past, I wished it would stay quiet. But for some reason, it seemed to want to come in uninvited and threaten my peace. I started to wonder if the stress of being an attending surgeon was bringing this on. Nightmares had dogged me throughout my life at intervals, but never with the pit-bull persistence that they were showing now.

I made coffee, strong and black, and savored the rich aroma while standing over my Mr. Coffee. When just enough had dripped out for a large mug, I pulled the pot away and shoved a mug under the spout so as not to spill precious drips while I poured the steaming brew. Perhaps my job was my biggest obstacle and salvation all at once. The stress might be playing tricks with my subconscious. But then, what if it wasn't a trick? What if there were hideous secrets in my past? If so, I wanted them to stay secret.

Thankfully, patients like Tina provided me with plenty of work to occupy my mind, staving off invading terrors that could slip unnoticed into a vacant mind.

Closing my eyes, I sipped the coffee across happy taste buds. Each teaspoon pulled me closer to a functional state. Caffeine nudged my cerebral cortex like an elbow in the side of a sleeping spouse.

It was then that it occurred to me that Mark might be playing the same role in my life that my occupation did. His desire for intimacy seemed to bring excitement, but also terror. Yet his willingness to listen had been the encouragement for me to carry on. Mark. My job. Both must be stimulating unseen horror . . . and providing a way of escape.

I checked the time and decided to call him. Perhaps we could meet for lunch. I was thirsty for his attention and I needed his perspective on my problems.

I dialed his number, my fingers moving over the pad without thinking.

A woman's voice startled me. "Hello."

I froze for a moment. "I'm sorry. I've got the wrong number." I put the phone back in the cradle and redialed, paying attention to each number.

The phone rang eight times before I gave up. He must have left for the hospital.

Maybe I'd catch up with him at lunch.

BY ELEVEN I was finished with two hernias and hunched over my desk reviewing what I had found concerning the status of breast-conserving therapy for breast cancer. The current American literature didn't hold a definitive answer. I found plenty of invited commentaries by experts on both sides of the issue, but there were no absolute answers because the data from the NSABP was not complete. There were educated guesses about the future: fewer women would need mastectomies. More women would get radiation.

I tried wearing Tina's shoes. What would I want? If I knew that a lumpectomy and radiation would likely cure my cancer, wouldn't I want that chance? Wouldn't I at least want the opportunity to take that chance? Would I take the risk if I knew the chances for a cure were the same as if I had a mastectomy? Certainly.

What if a small doubt remained? Would I take the chance to save my breast if the evidence was strong, but a definitive answer wasn't in?

Several good studies suggested that lumpectomies and radiation were equivalent to mastectomy for cancer survival. But large numbers were needed to prove a benefit of one therapy over another, or even that two therapies were equivalent. And that was the data the NSABP trials would provide. In the ongoing trials, thousands of women were being randomly placed into one of two treatment arms; some received mastectomies, some were able to save their breasts. Could it be wrong for me to offer Tina a lumpectomy outside of a controlled trial?

I knew the department's mantra: unless a surgery was taking place within a randomized trial, we didn't do it until it was proven. And until now, I'd had to do exactly what the attending surgeon on the service wanted to do. Since I was the attending on the service, I was responsible for making the right decision.

I paged Mark and asked him if he'd like to have lunch with me. He sounded depressed. Probably from a tough morning in his pediatric cancer clinic. The cases he saw were enough to depress Jolly Old Saint Nick. He accepted my invitation to the Skull and Bones—MCV dining at its finest.

I checked my watch. With an hour before my lunch date, I walked down the hall to the chairman's door, pushing it open with my gentle knock.

I heard Dr. Gilles grunt and took that as an invitation. The door opened into the lair of a king, the decoration a style I'd call classical intimidation. I didn't think Dr. Gilles intended it to be that way, but nearly forty years of academic surgery had left little room on his walls for more awards and certificates. The largest wall was opposite me, and contained pictures of Dr. Gilles with famous politicians, framed academic certifications, diplomas and the like starting six inches from the floor and lined up all the way to the ceiling. If wall space was a determinate of career length, his retirement was past due.

He looked up from his desk, an early bird happy with a worm. He put down a manuscript, no doubt a surgical volume he'd edited. He had a wrinkled, grandfatherly face with a sprinkling of salt white hair over a tanned scalp. He was trim, probably because he had little time to devote to eating in his efficient pursuits, not because he was given to exercise—other than kicking the backsides of lazy residents.

He led by example. He expected hard work because he exuded it himself. I counted it an honor to have trained under him, but I'd never been cozy with him. He was a father figure in that stern, guiding, disciplinarian sort of way. Dr. Gilles had my awe, not my friendship.

"Camille." He pointed to a black wooden chair emblazoned with the emblem of his alma mater.

"I need your advice."

"Good. You're on time."

I didn't understand. Evidently he read my puzzlement with his laser eyes.

"You're in your first month as an attending. I never feel good about a new attending if they never ask for help. Just because you're running your own service doesn't mean you stop learning."

I relaxed a notch. A good start. He pointed to the chair again. I sat. "What's on your mind?"

"One of our female psychiatrists has come to me. She has a breast cancer. She wants me to do a lumpectomy instead of a mastectomy."

He stared at me with those eyes penetrating my brain. I looked away, as if interested in a photo of someone who looked familiar, but whom I couldn't quite place.

"What do you want to know?" he asked.

"What would you do?"

"You know the answer to that. You trained under me." He paused, his eyes focused on mine. "You didn't answer my question."

"What question?"

"I asked, 'What do you want to know?'"

I was confused.

He spoke again. "You answered me, but that's not really what you're asking."

"I'm not?"

He shook his head. "What you want to know is what will happen if you do something in this department that I wouldn't do."

He'd seen right through me, as usual. "I . . . uh. . . ." I halted. "I guess I wouldn't be in a quandary otherwise."

"You know the board answer, Camille. I wouldn't have hired you otherwise." He paused and leaned toward me. "Your job is not to do what the patient requests. Your job is to guide them into accepting what is right."

"What if the accepted cancer treatment doesn't align with the treatment that seems better for the person with the cancer?"

"Camille, if you do something unproven outside a research protocol, you're going to take heat." He held up a finger. "From me? Perhaps. You will have to defend yourself at the tumor board conference." He held up a second finger. "From a malpractice standpoint, if you have complications, you'd better be sure what you did met the state's standard of care. If it doesn't, you have no grounds for a defense." He seemed to hesitate, then added, "Both of those things are very important to me in determining a long-term fit for an attending in this department."

I nodded.

"I'm not the type of chairman who will tell you what to do, but I will expect you to stand up and take responsibility for your actions."

There was the Gilles message again, I thought: Stand up and take it like a man. I wished he would do the fatherly thing, comfort me, and tell me exactly what to do. But he wouldn't.

He wouldn't hang me if I did something other than a mastectomy, but he'd give me a rope and let me hang myself.

"Who is this woman?"

"Tina Kinser."

His hand went to his chin and his head shook back and forth in a tremor. "Tina has breast cancer?"

"You know her?"

"She and her husband are members at Pinewood Country Club." He tapped his fingers on his desk. "She knows my reputation," he said. "Perhaps she came to you because she knew I couldn't be manipulated."

I wasn't sure how to respond. Tina Kinser came to me because I was a woman. I supposed the boss was offended because she'd selected me over him. What an ego blow that would be.

He appeared put off by the knowledge that someone he knew would choose someone other than him. He shook his head as if dismissing the idea as preposterous. He looked at me again. "So other than this challenging patient, how are you doing?"

He studied me as I formulated an answer, then continued before I could speak. "Making the right decision isn't always easy when the buck stops with you. The first year out of residency is the most difficult of your professional life."

I thought about my first days as an attending. "I believe it."

He stood and put his hand on my shoulder. Suddenly, I felt like unraveling. I felt like telling him about the terror that stalked my nights and kept me running all day just to stay out of reach of the tentacles that tickled the edge of my thoughts. I felt like telling him that I was failing at love, that I couldn't seem to respond to the man who loved me. I wanted to cry out the pressure I felt trying to save the life of a teenager whose mother couldn't seem to grasp reality. And I wanted to tell him that I wanted to be the best surgeon I could be without denying who I was as a woman, that in fact, I could be better than any man at meeting my female patients on a heart level. I wanted to stand up for who I was—different from any of the men I trained with. And I felt like melting at the same time.

He gave my shoulder a gentle squeeze. "Hang in there, Doctor, everything's gonna be all right."

I closed my eyes for a long blink, willing my heart not to respond. When I opened them again, Dr. Gilles was staring into my face.

Perhaps my eyes had been closed longer than I'd realized. At any rate, there was alarm in his eyes.

"Camille?"

His eyes. My father's.

"Camille?"

I spoke through clenched teeth. "I'm fine."

I scanned the room, searching for anything to captivate my busy mind, to keep it from spinning into fear.

That stupid phrase! It was as if a pebble were launched into a pond every time I heard it, and I desperately tried to prevent the inevitable circle of ripples from disturbing the water's surface.

I needed to get out before I self-destructed in front of my boss. I offered a smile—an implant—and mumbled, "I'd better let you get back to your work." I pivoted on my heels and managed to escape to his outer office, where I paused to take a deep breath.

My eyes met his secretary's. I must have looked like I'd run a hundred-yard dash.

Her mouth was agape.

What are you thinking? That he chewed me out? Or that something this man has done has left me breathless? It's not what you think!

I stomped out of the office, down the hall, and hid in my little office. There I willed myself to read from an article I'd pulled on treatment of breast cancer. In a few minutes, my heart quieted and my thoughts turned again to my dilemma about Tina Kinser. Did my struggle over what to do about Tina have anything to do with my newness as a surgical attending? Did I dare step out of the rank and file to do something that Gilles wouldn't do? Or should I just be a good little attending and not upset the boss so I could survive on this hallway and have a happy life?

The sad fact was that my struggle had a lot to do with my newness as an attending. If I were well established in the department like the old-school men around me, I wouldn't have to watch my steps.

I slumped over my desk, at odds with the male establishment that ruled this medical college. I was swimming against the current, feeling the tug of a dangerous undertow. I felt out of place, just as I had hiding in the men's locker room.

I pulled open my desk drawer and extracted a small mirror. I asked myself a simple question in a whisper, an encouragement technique I'd used over and over during my medical training years. When I was in need of a little psyching up, I looked at myself and asked, "Who are you?"

The answer I usually gave didn't come to my lips this time. Instead of saying, "A surgeon," the title I'd come to associate with the ability to make tough decisions, I forced myself to give the answer that Tina would have wanted to hear: "A woman." The answer made me smile. I nodded. It made perfect sense to me now.

16

I GROWLED THROUGH THE afternoon because Mark begged off on our lunch date at the last minute. His clinic ran over and he needed to prepare for a conference. I told him it was OK, but I did mind missing the date because I needed a fix of staring into his dark eyes, of having him probe my heart and nourish my soul with words about how much he loved just a moment with me in the middle of the day. The fact that his cancellation bothered me so much told me I was falling for him hard. Since I hadn't allowed much room for romance during my training, and because I'd basically been in training forever, my love life had been on hold as long as I could remember.

In fact, the list of those males who would fall into the category of "boyfriend" was microscopic. This was a surprise to most, who claimed I had a charming personality, beautiful face, and great figure. I didn't know about the first, but the latter two could be true if one gauged such things by the number of male heads turning as I walked by. How the males of the species viewed my physical attributes had been a blessing and a curse—as most women know. We want men to find us attractive, we just don't want that to be the only basis of our acceptance.

I developed early, and when I was thirteen and in the eighth grade at prep school, Troy Johnson, a senior, thought he'd teach me a thing or three in the custodian's closet at school. The smell of floor wax did little for my mood, but I was intrigued by his invitation, and receptive to his first kiss until he forced his tongue through my incisors. I blackened his eye and forever gained the reputation as a stuck-up half-breed.

Aunt Jeanine said that I intimidated the boys by my intelligence, and advised that I dumb down my conversation to get a date, but I wasn't inclined to talk about *Gilligan's Island* reruns to boys who thought Ginger and Mary Ann were hot and that Big Mac combos constituted a square meal. College wasn't much better, except I learned that a flirtatious giggle could get me just about anything I wanted, and that the curves most of my male profs enjoyed weren't bell-shaped; my intelligence didn't win dates. Although nerdy boys weren't put off by my smarts, it seemed that what intrigued them most wasn't my brain. Also in college I'd come to hate men who wanted me only to serve as an arm dressing . . . or for undressing. I found what I did enjoy, however, was the control I felt when I kept them at arm's length. By my junior year, with my heart and mind set on a medical career, I felt relief at having a pursuit outside the marriage chase that occupied the time and thoughts of so many of my girlfriends.

All in all, I came away turned off by men interested in only a physical relationship. I wasn't sure why, even back in college, I couldn't get comfortable with physical intimacy. While some of my other college girlfriends were celebrating their freedom, I retreated to the library, where safer territory didn't carry the suggestion of dark memories.

In medical school, keeping away dates was as easy as mentioning my career aspirations. It seemed that around Richmond, a female medical student made a good one-night stand, but a lousy long-term prospect. I wasn't interested in the former. Surgical residency was essentially a date-free environment. I didn't have time to breathe, much less get naked and breathless.

That's how I ended up a thirty-year-old virgin, pouting that my love life was in disarray, feeling the pull of desire to intimacy, but scared at the thought of the same.

Mark seemed destined to change all that, and I sensed my protective shields breaking down. I thought about calling him to see if tonight would work, but I didn't want to appear too pushy. I would not grovel, or show him my hurt, at least not yet, so instead of asking him for supper, I called Kara Schuller. I was overdue for a fix of her Boston practicality, and for someone in the South who didn't think I was crazy for being a BoSox fan. I only hoped she had forgotten her idea that I talk to Tina Kinser about my emotional issues. I wanted to have a fun evening without thinking about terrors from my subconscious. And I was definitely not the type to open up to a shrink. Especially one I was treating.

We met at my apartment, played oldies music on the radio, and ate take-out lasagna from the Robin Inn.

That was when Kara lifted flowers and a bottle of wine from a paper grocery sack.

"Kara, we shouldn't." I paused, meeting her gaze. "You shouldn't."

She laughed and waved me off. "Believe me, you need this."

"But you—"

"I can drink a glass." She put her hands on her hips. "I won't be a hypocrite," she said. "I'll drink right in front of you."

I began to protest, but Kara was already looking for my corkscrew. I would watch her, I thought, to make sure she stayed in a safe zone. With reluctance, I let her pour me a glass, and watched nervously as she topped off her glass twice just as I started to sip.

By ten, I'd had enough red wine to loosen my tongue. I told Kara all about my dilemma. Could I offer cutting-edge therapy before it was considered the standard of care by the surgical establishment? Did I dare resist the inertia of an old-school, male department?

"I've always been one of the guys," I said. "I don't know if I can really do this."

Kara laughed out loud, whether from my statement or the wine, I'm not sure. "You've never been one of the guys. You've acted like it to get what you want."

"I can survive if I stay in formation, if I toe the line." I paused. "I can do that. I've been doing it since I got here."

"Making no waves."

"The key to survival," I said.

She scoffed. "You might have stayed in formation in residency, but since the day you were handed your own service as an attending, you've been marching to the beat of your own rhythm." She looked at me, her eyes soft. "You want to know what I think? Sometimes stepping out of formation is the right thing to do."

I couldn't respond. I thought for a moment before deciding she was right. I shrugged. There was no use trying to argue with a girlfriend who had intuition.

Kara set down her glass. "Is there good evidence that the procedure you propose will cure breast cancer?"

I nodded. "Sure. But the studies haven't been large enough to change everyone's opinion."

"Everyone in the largely male surgical establishment."

I hesitated. "Well, yeah, but—"

"What's best for your patient?"

I paused, and then found myself defending the establishment that I was bucking. "A mastectomy is the proven standard of care. It will offer her a known probability of cure."

Kara shook her blond bangs. "You're giving me the department line. You and I both know what's best for treating the cancer." She pointed at me. "What's best for your patient?"

Leave it to Kara to focus the issue. "Well, I—"

"What would Dr. Bransford do?"

"The standard." I shook my head. "This department is conservative with a capital *C*. Everyone follows established practice. It's safe."

Kara gulped the rest of her wine then filled her glass and mine. We were both on our way to silliness. I mumbled a weak protest and knew I was going to regret not being firm.

Before long, we'd decided that a conspiracy was on, and that male surgeons were uncaring and unsympathetic to women's needs. They were geeks who invariably got their thrills by looking at the naked bodies of their female patients.

We drained the bottle. Kara was destined to sleep the night on my couch.

"I'm not a heavy drinker," I said. "You are so bad for me."

She smiled. "Surgeons are wound too tight." She stabbed her finger into the air as if a new revelation had appeared. "This reminds me of Passover."

I missed the connection, except that Kara almost always talked about religion when she drank too much. The question on my face must have prompted her to continue.

"My family always had a special meal, then sat around drinking and talking."

"Passover?" I repeated. "You're a Jew? We've been friends for how long and you've never happened to mention it?"

She held up one hand. "My father was a Jew." She held up her other hand. "I'm a Jew."

"If you're a Jew, I'm a Christian." I lifted up one hand to imitate my friend. "My father was a Christian." I held up my other hand, but I couldn't complete my imitation. I was stuck on my father. I backtracked. "I think he was a Christian."

Kara laughed. I wasn't sure what was funny, except for her laughing. "He was a missionary, for God's sake."

I shrugged.

"You stole Passover from us."

"I did?"

"Christians." She giggled.

Listening to her made me giggle, too. I held up the empty bottle and found it hard to focus on Kara's words.

"It was our celebration. You know, lamb's blood on the doorpost protecting the household from the angel of death."

My lips felt large and slow. "I've heard the story. But how did Christians ssssteal it?"

Kara looked annoyed. "Christians call Christ the Passover lamb. You should know this stuff. His blood sacrifice protects you from death."

I thought I should be serious, but all I could say was "ooooh" and even that came out like molasses.

She waved her fingers at me, holding them in front of her face. "Ooooh," she mimicked, sounding spooky.

"How do you know this stuff?"

"Joel Bryan," she said, the corners of her mouth turning up in a little smile. "Every time he comes in to visit one of the children in the ICU, he stops by the station."

All of the young women on the pediatric staff knew Joel. He was the youth director at St. Giles Presbyterian Church. He was so easy on the eyes that most of us could listen to him for an hour before we'd get irritated at his conservative viewpoint. And most of us paid more attention to his brown curls than his message. Apparently, Kara had been paying attention to both. I wiggled my fingers back at her. She'd been holding out secrets from me. "Ooooooh," I said. "He brings a smile to your face, does he?" I could hardly get the words out. My lips didn't want to cooperate. Kara thought it was funny. I wanted to know all the details about Joel. Her smile hinted at hidden hope, stuff I wanted to know but was too drunk to process. Instead, I just giggled.

We both laughed until I thought I'd pee in my black-lace undies. I stumbled to the bathroom to address the urgency. When I got there, I somehow got my underwear snagged on my shoe when I lowered them much farther than needed to do my business. I cursed, something I never did when I was sober. I peeled

off my black pumps and my bikini bottoms got hopelessly tangled on the right heel. I tried to remove them but they seemed
stuck. I tossed them on the bathroom floor, got dressed without
them, and walked back out to my favorite chair.

I must have look toasted, because one look at me and Kara
was giggling again. I wasn't sure what was funny, but I couldn't
keep from laughing with her.

Kara had scoured my kitchen for more alcohol. She'd come
back with a four-pack of wine coolers, something I'd bought in
planning a barbecue with Mark. In the back of my mind, I knew I
was going to have regrets, but the buzzing in the front of my skull
had taken over. I told myself that one more for me couldn't hurt,
though I already felt guilty for letting her go this far.

"Tell me about Mark Lawson," she said, propping her elbows
on the couch and holding up her chin.

"I love him." The words tumbled out before I could stop
them.

"Oooh." She giggled.

"He's smart. He's cute. He adores me . . . I think. He likes
baseball." I paused, feeling my emotions riding a roller-coaster. I'd
hit the top, and I'd started down. Something struck me as terribly
sad. I sniffed. "He's afraid of commitment. He doesn't tell me he
loves me."

Kara reached for my hand. "He's a man. A man will never
love you the way you want." She spoke from experience. She laid
her head on the couch pillow and sighed. "A dad is the only one
who loves you even when you're bad."

"I wish I could remember."

"Oh, Camille, I didn't mean to—"

"Forget it."

She stayed quiet for a moment. "Maybe that's why you are
still looking for the perfect love," she responded, sniffing. "You
don't remember love from your father?"

I shook my head. I wasn't sure what to say. My memories of

my father were spotty. I looked through blurry tears. The wine had made everything very sad or very funny.

"Mark Lawson can't give you the love you have in your dreams."

"Maybe I still believe in fairy tales." I smiled. Love without conditions. Then I confessed what she probably knew anyway. "Kara. I'm a virgin."

Obviously not. This tickled Kara more than anything in our history. She held her sides and rolled off the couch.

Her reaction embarrassed me.

She looked up from the floor, trying to stifle her giggles. "I'm sssorry." She crawled over and grabbed my hand. "You're serious, aren't you?"

I nodded, feeling a sudden urge to cry. A thirty-year-old virgin. How sad. Hopeless. Unloved.

Kara patted my hand and her eyes met mine. For a moment, I thought we might share a tear. Instead, a smile broke across her face and she let fly with a raucous belly laugh.

I responded by a raspberry spray of halting snort-laughs, which caused us to laugh even more. I slid off my chair, dropping my butt with a thud on the carpet. We fell into a giggling embrace, holding each other as we shook with a fresh wave of hilarity.

We lay on the floor together, our hysterics slowing to an occasional chuckle, then a random giggle-gasp, and then the heavy breathing of someone who had sprinted the last few feet to summit a mountain.

It was an exhilaration of sorts, an emotional uncorking that soothed my soul and left me with a hunger for some lasting satiety untainted by the threat of hangover.

There I lay, staring at my apartment ceiling, listening as Kara's breathing became deep and regular—the rhythm of slumber.

I desired to make that moment of peace a lasting one, but a sense of longing seemed to hang heavy above me. The love I desired with Mark, the intimacy I'd yet to experience, floated just beyond my grasp. When I closed my eyes to regain an illusion of calm, the terror stared full into my soul. This time, I remembered a dark place, a musty, wet smell.

Our hiding place.

His arms are around me. He's kissing my neck.

"Don't make a sound. No one can know we are here."

I feel the shudder of his body against mine.

"Everything's gonna be all right."

I tried to divert my thoughts. My eyes were fully wide, searching the room for any object to catch my attention and guide me to a safer place.

Kara awakened. Did I wake her? I was unaware of my own tears until she reached for me. I felt the moisture against my cheeks as she brushed them away.

She held me for a few minutes longer, her breath mingled with wine, warm against my neck. This was the embrace of a friend who loved me in spite of my brokenness.

She is my best friend. This present terror cannot overcome me as long as I have a friend like her.

I didn't remember making it to bed, or helping Kara to the couch. Or did she help me?

All I knew was my alarm going off at seven-thirty and a pain behind my temples that told me I'd been a bad, bad girl.

17

Tina sat at the breakfast table opposite her husband, who was drinking black coffee and reading the *Richmond Times-Dispatch*. She'd practiced her line a dozen times, imagining his reaction.

"Dan."

She could barely see his forehead over the morning paper. "Uuh."

"Daniel."

The paper lowered an inch. "It's raining in Chicago. Do you know where my umbrella is?"

"We need to talk, Daniel. Our marriage is a joke."

"I want that little tote umbrella. It will fit in my carry-on."

"I want a divorce."

The paper came down, the corner of the sports page dipping into his coffee cup. The look on his face said he thought she was joking. In a moment, his brow furrowed. "What?"

"You're never home, Daniel."

"What?"

"I said I want a divorce."

He stared at her. "You're serious?"

"This isn't a marriage." She didn't want to look at him. "It hasn't been for a long time."

"Tina!"

"Dan! You don't get it. We live in the same house." She paused. "Some of the time."

"So what's next? You want out? Just like that?"

"It's not 'just like that,' Dan."

He dropped the paper to the table. "This is about Mary, isn't it? I told you she means nothing to me."

"Mary was just a symptom."

"Tina, I—"

"Are you so naive? You knew this was coming." She slapped the calendar on the wall. "How many days have you been out of town this month? And how about next month? I'm tired of waiting alone."

"I'll change."

"It's a broken promise, Dan. I've heard it too many times." She imitated his excuses. " 'Let's just get our feet on the ground. Let's just pay down the mortgage. Let me just put away a little for retirement.' "

He looked at his watch.

That infuriated her even more. She knew he had a plane to catch. Obviously that was more important than his crumbling marriage.

"Be reasonable. These were our dreams—"

"Your dreams."

"Let's talk when I get back from Chicago. I'll take a few days off."

"This marriage is beyond resuscitation. I want out."

"Tina, let's talk this through. I've been away so much, I know, but—" His eyes met hers. He halted, then began again as reality dawned. "There's someone else, isn't there?"

She hesitated. "This isn't easy, Dan. You're away all the time," she began, her eyes on the floor. "Emotionally, physically, you've been absent for months."

"That's life."

"That's pathetic."

"Tina, I'm not ready for this."

"Dan, we're no good together anymore. What is there be-tween us?"

"How about twenty years?"

She looked at him without averting her gaze. "You're wel-come to pack your things yourself. If you're not willing, I'll pack them for you while you're away."

"You want *me* to leave?"

"The house is mine, Dan. You can refresh your memory with our attorney. Not only did we use my mutual funds for the down payment, the mortgage comes straight out of my paycheck."

He stepped back, loosening his tie. "This is too quick."

"This is overdue."

"Let's talk it out."

"Talk to my attorney." She unfolded a little business card from her hand and set it on the table in front of him.

He ran his hand through his graying hair. "Tina, I know I haven't been perfect, but—"

She put her hand on his. "I'm sorry," she said. "I'm so sorry."

She turned away and strode out the front door.

She would tell him about the cancer after he was out of her life.

THE NUMBERS ON the clock were green and blurry. It was seven-thirty and someone was pounding a stake into my right temple. I slipped my feet onto the floor and padded off to the bathroom in search of ibuprofen. I swallowed four tablets and looked at myself in the mirror. Thank God I didn't have an early case. I rubbed my eyelids, hoping to massage out some of the puffiness. I felt terrible. I thought back to last night. My final memory was of sil-liness and terror, of being held by my friend. Kara would be upset if I let her sleep too late.

Poking my head out the bathroom door, I called, "Kara, the sun's up."

I undressed and showered. I let the water run for a full fifteen minutes and thought about what to say to my friend. I'd let her down. I'd needed to be the strong one for her last night, and I'd let her and myself get out of hand. Over the years of our long-term friendship, we'd had tough discussions about addictions. As I let the shower massage my neck, I strengthened my resolve for a confrontation. She needed my tough love. After all she'd done for me, I promised myself that I'd not give in again.

After my shower, I felt human. Almost. I still heard no noise from the den. "Kara. Rise and shine, girl."

I threw on a robe and headed for the kitchen to start some coffee. In the dim light, I saw Kara faceup on the couch. Her mouth was open, her skin ashen. Immediately, the surgeon in me was on full alarm. The smell of death was heavy. "Kara!" I snapped on a lamp by the couch. Certainly, my instincts were wrong. "Kara!"

Instantly, I dropped to my knees. Her skin was cold. Her lips were parted and deep purple, her chest still. I pulled her face toward me. Already her neck was stiff. There was vomit on her cheek, the couch, and the carpet. Her eyes were partly open, unblinking. "No! God, no!" I put my face up to hers to begin giving mouth-to-mouth, but her eyes stopped me. I pushed back the lids and grabbed the lamp, pulling it over her face. Her pupils were dilated. Nonreactive.

Kara was room-temperature dead on my couch. Her corpse was hours beyond resuscitation.

"No!"

This isn't happening. My closest friend cannot be dead.

I pulled her onto the floor where I could begin CPR. I tilted her head back and lay my lips against hers, pinching her nose. I blew hard into her lungs. The breath that belched back at me was sour and cool. I gave another breath, then moved over her chest and began compressions.

I cycled through compressions and respirations, spilling my tears onto her lifeless face. After five cycles, I ran to the kitchen and dialed 911.

"Nine-one-one emergency. May I help you?"

"My friend isn't breathing. I need an ambulance at three-two-two Kirkland Drive. Colonial Apartments, off of Azalea Avenue."

"Do you know CPR?"

"Yes. I've initiated resuscitation. I just need some help."

"Can you stay on the line?"

"I'll lay the phone down, but I need to get back to CPR."

"A team is on the way."

I dropped the phone and ran back to Kara. I gave one breath, five compressions, one breath, five compressions, one breath, five compressions. Over and over.

In five minutes, I heard the warble of an approaching siren. In two more, I heard a knock at the door.

"Come in," I shouted, before realizing it was locked. I dashed to unlock the door.

I swung open the door to see Tony Perry and Del Williamson.

"Dr. Weller!"

I pointed to the floor where Kara was sprawled.

Del moved to a kneeling position and laid his hand on her neck. "How long has she been down?"

"I found her this morning."

Tony set down his supplies. "Oh man," he groaned. His hand went to his mouth. "Kara?"

I started to cry. I'd kept it together until now. I slumped into a chair and held my head.

Del took out a flashlight and shone it in her eyes. "There's nothing here, Dr. Weller. She's cold."

"Oh God, oh God, oh God," I cried. "This can't be happening."

Tony lifted her shirt. I saw deep purple discolorations on her sides near her back. They were postmortem changes as blood settled in the lowest dependent parts.

I opened Tony's large supply bag. "Entubate her. Resume CPR!"

Del Williamson took me by the hand. "She's dead, Dr. Weller. We can't bring her back."

I stared into his eyes, knowing that what he said was true. I'd known it from the instant I'd seen her lying there, eyes and mouth agape. The surgeon in me knew she was gone. The friend in me was in agony. Denial. "No."

Del opened his arms and I collapsed into him, wailing. He was a brother, large as a linebacker, with the heart of Mother Teresa. When he was not volunteering on the rescue squad, he ran a local children's museum.

Tears found their way around my tightly pinched lids. The atmosphere was surreal.

Death was a common acquaintance of the trauma surgeon, but the experience could not penetrate the emotional armor I wore to work. I usually stood, unflinching, looking death in the face before moving on to my next task. Death was merely the cessation of cardiac and brain function, a consequence of some explainable pathology.

But that day, death slipped in the back door when my guard was down. This was unfair. Kara was my best friend. She was going to help me through. I pounded Del's chest before pulling back to see that he was crying, too.

18

THE CONGO, 1964

I SPENT THE DAY playing checkers in the house, mostly against myself or Tumi, but that's really the same thing, 'cause he just lays there and slobbers and I have to move the checkers for him. I kept totals and Tumi won six times and I beat him fourteen. I did manage to run to the banana grove to hide a few times and sneak a look down the street at the burned-out school, but Mother caught me and made me come inside 'cause the fighting got closer and they brought three wounded men for Daddy to help.

Daddy said they came into the theatre and held a gun the whole time he operated.

After nighttime, my daddy just slipped in the back door. His forehead was wrinkled almost all the time. "What's in the bag?" I said.

Daddy talked in a whisper. I'm not sure why, 'cause the Simbas were all the way out by the front gate. "Radio parts."

"What are you doing?"

"I've taken apart the hospital radio."

My mother came into the kitchen. "Jack! Our radio is the only way we can—"

My father shook his head. "Everyone we talk to has already been captured by the Simbas. So now the radio is only a risk. If the Simbas find it . . ." He stopped and looked at my mother. He gave her a look that said, *I can't say it in front of Camille.* That meant the Simbas would kill him.

I edged closer to him and wrapped my arms around his waist.

"I've dismantled it into twelve parts. I'll hide them in different places in the stuff we have boxed in the attic."

My mother followed him up the little ladder into the attic. I stood at the opening so I could hear them talk.

"We have to leave," my mother pleaded.

"If I leave, they will kill the African staff."

RICHMOND, 1984

FOUR HOURS LATER, after marathon interviews with the medical examiner, two police detectives, and tearful conversations with Rachel Bell, Mark Lawson, and finally with Kara's father, I'd successfully retreated to the surgical intensive care unit and gathered my team for attending rounds.

We'd seen three patients. I was back in my element, coping by working. I was quizzing my residents, probing for deficiencies. The medical students took notes on small pads extracted from overstuffed pockets. I'd covered management of chest trauma, common causes of hospital-acquired pneumonia, and surgical treatment of bowel obstructions when I spied Nadine Solomon peering from between two of my medical students. I could see her purple hat bobbing up and down as she attempted to get a better view of the proceedings. Her son was in the next bed. I ignored her, and went on asking questions of my entourage. We'd get to Kendrick and his multisystem organ failure in a minute.

"Worldwide, what is the most common cause of bowel obstruction?" I looked for my answer from a med student wearing a short, white coat and who sported a day's growth of beard.

The student shifted his feet and cleared his throat. I felt a touch on my arm and looked to see Dr. Gilles. He leaned forward and whispered to the medical student, intending for all of us to hear, "Inguinal hernias." He winked at the student and tightened his grip on my arm, motioning me away.

We stepped toward the counter in the center of the ICU. His face was etched with concern. "Camille, I'm so sorry."

The grapevine had worked faster than I expected. If Gilles already knew about my morning, the cafeteria workers would know before night.

I didn't want to talk about Kara here. His comment was enough to make my throat tighten. I didn't want to cry.

"How are you?"

I feigned a smile. "I'm OK."

He scrutinized me, deepening the wrinkles above his brow. I knew his eyes well. As a resident, I'd spent endless hours across from this man, someone's abdomen open between us. I'd look up to see his masked face, only his eyes and a slice of his forehead, and learned to discern his thoughts from a subtle change in his eyes or the wrinkles in his forehead. The look he gave me now was concern, a bit of alarm, but short of the expression he showed when a patient's blood pressure was bottoming out. "What are you doing here?" he asked.

I sniffed. "I didn't know what else to do." I paused. "I couldn't stay in my apartment." I looked down. "I've got a service to run."

"It's OK to take some time away. I'll arrange for Dr. Larimore to cover for a few days."

"Really. I'm better if I'm working." I pulled my white coat around me. "This is what I do. I'm a surgeon. My identity is here."

I saw a subtle shaking of his head. He wasn't buying into my need to be here.

His voice was soft, showing a side of the chairman that residents rarely saw. "Is this what I've done to you? You're shut down, Camille."

"What you've done . . ."

He looked away. "We train surgeons to remain emotionally

distant so they can do what is right for their patients." He turned, and his eyes bore in on mine. "But that doesn't mean shutting out caring. Kara was your best friend. You owe her some time to grieve."

I stared at the floor pondering his words. *Shut down emotionally. Has this career path that I've chosen done this? Am I really that closed to feeling pain . . . or even feeling love?*

He spoke again. "I need you healthy, Camille. You are a cornerstone of our ICU care right now."

I knew what I'd done was a bit dysfunctional, but it had been a standby defense mechanism for me: lose myself in work so I couldn't feel pain. "I am healthy."

Dr. Gilles frowned. "But if you don't take care of yourself, things will break down."

"Working keeps me healthy."

"I admire your dedication, but get out of here for a few days." He placed his hand on my sleeve again.

I glanced at my team in the distance. I'd overheard enough hushed comments and a few gasps to know that they knew as well. They stared at me with wide eyes.

"Look, I don't really think—"

His expression stopped me. "I insist." He nodded to my team. "Fill Larimore in on your service. He's covering trauma tonight anyway." He paused and took a deep breath. "Kara was a great gal."

I nodded. I wasn't allowed to argue.

He walked away. The issue was closed. Now I needed to face my team with the news. I walked toward them and they fell silent. They were all eyes and ears, focused on me, and not because they expected me to impart some tasty morsel of surgical knowledge. It was the solemn attention you gave to someone who has just buried a child or walked out of a burning building alive. "It appears the MCV grapevine is alive and well," I began. "I'll be taking a few days away." I tossed my head in the direction of Dr. Gilles's disappearance. "Boss's orders, you know?" I looked at Ellis. "Dr. Larimore will be covering."

Ellis nodded.

"Anything new with Kendrick?"

"Nah. The renal guys actually skipped dialyzing him today. They seem to think he might be a little better."

I looked around, but Nadine seemed to have disappeared from behind my team. "Amazing. That's the first good news we've had about him in a while."

The team nodded in unison. No one was making the usual jovial comments. Everyone treated me as though I were fragile. It made me uncomfortable. I touched Ellis's sleeve. "Finish rounds, would you? I'll be on my pager today." I lowered my voice and spoke only to him. "I think there will be a memorial service Saturday or Sunday. I'll be back here on Monday for sure."

I walked toward the door of the ICU and heard someone call my name just as I pressed the pad to activate the automatic door. I turned to see Nadine Solomon. I thought I'd lost her, but she could track me like a bloodhound.

I took a breath and anticipated her daily inquiry. *How's Kendrick doing?* I gave her my best attempt at a smile. "Hi, Mrs. Solomon."

"I heard what's going on," she said. "And I wanted you to know that I'll be prayin' for you."

Coming from Nadine Solomon, I knew her statement was more than the polite gestures I'd heard from Christians before. She caught me off guard. I stuttered, "I . . . I . . . thank you."

I turned, hoping to avoid being enveloped by this prayer warrior. I imagined her grabbing me and dropping to her knees right in the doorway to contact the Almighty. Instead, she touched my hand gently with hers and caught my eye. "This is a tough time for you, isn't it?"

I looked away numbly. I didn't want to open up to this woman. "It is hard," she continued. "But I know God loves you."

My reply tumbled out in bitterness before I could keep it back. I didn't particularly want to dump on this woman, but it'd been an exceptionally bad day. "He has a funny way of showing it."

She squeezed my hand and exclaimed, "He sure do!"

It wasn't the pat answer I expected.

She shook her head back and forth as if she was musing over an amazing truth. "He sure do," she repeated. She stopped and a little smile broke onto her broad face. "Kendrick is getting better. The kidney doctor told me so."

I nodded, but stayed quiet. Her son was a long, long way from being out of the woods. In fact, the trees were so thick, the edge of the woods was impossible to see.

Nadine stepped through the doorway along beside me. "I know you need some evidence to believe it."

"If I didn't believe boys like Kendrick could recover, I wouldn't be in this business."

"I wasn't talkin' 'bout Kendrick. I was talkin' 'bout believin' that God could really love you."

"Oh." I didn't have anything else to say.

"The evidence is coming. You need some practical proof. He let Doubtin' Thomas touch his side, didn't he? He'll let you see, just you wait."

I wanted to ask her why, if God loved me, did he let my best friend die, but I stayed quiet. My eyes met hers one more time before she headed back into the ICU to continue her bedside vigil.

I plodded toward my office. I passed my secretary Linda's desk, and noticed a blond man in a golf shirt sitting in the reception area. Linda followed me inside my office. She closed the door and gave me a look that irritated me. I was tired of sympathetic gazes.

"I'm so sorry, Dr. Weller." She stood and stared at me with such tension on her face that I thought she would burst into hysterics.

I wanted to tell her to leave me alone, but I said a quiet thank you instead.

"I hate to bug you with this, especially now, but I wasn't sure what to do. He insisted on staying."

"What are you talking about?"

"That man in the reception area is here to see you. He doesn't have an appointment, but he's from out of town and really wants to talk to you." She handed me a business card.

His name, Jacob Richardson, was printed beside a CFW logo and a miniature outline of Africa. I muttered to myself, "Impeccable timing, Mr. Richardson. I lost my best friend this morning and I'll bet you're here to ask for a donation for starving African children."

Linda's face turned to steel. "Shall I tell him to leave?"

I doubted whether timid Linda could toss out a stray cat. I shook my head. "I'll take care of him. Send him in."

In a moment, he stood in my open doorway, a tall man looking a bit like a young version of the golfer Jack Nicklaus. "Dr. Weller?"

Offering my hand, I nodded. "Hello."

His cheeks flushed as he took my hand. "Jacob Richardson. I apologize for barging in on you this way. I'm sure your secretary gave you my card. I was in Richmond doing a candidate interview for CFW, and I thought I'd chance a visit with you as well."

I pointed to the chair opposite my desk. "Why don't you have a seat and tell me what's on your mind?"

He sat on the edge of the chair. "I hope you received my letter. I—"

"I did," I interrupted, looking away from his clear blue eyes. "But I've not sent in my RSVP yet."

He cleared his voice. "I wanted to make a personal invitation." He halted. "We'd really like someone there to represent the Weller family."

This man looked as if he'd just come straight from a golf game. He had no idea what I was about. Somewhere, somehow, I knew this had to do with the bottom line: money. I looked him in the eyes again. He seemed taken with me. I could tell by the adoring way he met my gaze.

"Have you contacted my aunt Jeanine?"

"Your father's sister?"

"The one and only."

A smile threatened to turn up the corners of his mouth. "She was . . ." He coughed nervously. "Well, shall we say she wasn't very receptive to the idea." He brightened. "But she did help me find you."

"She did." I feigned nonchalance, but I wondered why Aunt Jeanine would sic these money grubbers on me. Maybe to get me back for costing her so much money to educate me. "So tell me about this endowment."

"Dr. Francis Solfelt worked with your father for a brief time in the Congo. He returned to the States and built a remarkable orthopedic spine practice. He approached us a few months ago offering a large donation to set up a fund to help sponsor new medical missionaries to the African continent." He shrugged. "Dr. Solfelt insists on naming the endowment after your father. Our board unanimously agrees."

I tapped my ballpoint pen on the desk and leaned back. "How much was the donation?"

"Two million. We're hoping to increase it over the next few months so we can launch the endowment at two point five million by the time we go public at the celebration dinner."

I studied the man in front of me. I'd guessed he was forty, maybe forty-five. I saw early changes on his thinning scalp from too much sun exposure. He had a fine spray of wrinkles extending from the corners of his eyes from frequent smiles or squinting into the wind, I could not tell. He looked fit, like a man infatuated with exercise. "Did you know my father?"

The look of admiration flashed across his face again. "I met him once." He hesitated. "He was a great man."

I looked down. "I don't remember him much." I kept the rest to myself. *What I do remember frightens me.*

"He had an old Land Rover. He took me into Stanleyville when things were getting hot with the rebellion."

"You were there?"

He nodded. "I worked with an agriculture development team." He hesitated. "You must be very proud of him."

I didn't know what to say. He had placed my father on a pedestal, and I couldn't add to his adoration.

"We would like for you to come to the dinner to honor your father."

"I . . . I don't know," I said, shaking my head. "My memory of the Congo is very conflicted, Mr. Richardson. I'm not sure I can add much—"

"Just having you there will be addition enough."

I looked up, trying to hide my suspicion. "I won't have to speak?"

"No." He laughed. "If you're like your father, you're a better surgeon than you are a speaker. The work of his hands was message enough for many of us."

I nodded, as if I knew firsthand what he said were true.

He folded his hands and leaned forward. "Do you remember Tumi?"

The name carried anxiety for me. "My dog," I said. I could see him in my mind, walking around the hospital perimeter. "You remember Tumi?"

"He rode with me and your father in the Land Rover." Mr. Richardson's eyes glazed over and he seemed to be looking far

away to my right. "I think of your father every year at Passover."
He spoke quietly. "What a picture."

The mention of Passover brought Kara's comments of last
night to my mind. I felt my throat tighten. I pressed my fist
against my upper lip. I didn't want to cry in front of a stranger.
I forced myself to concentrate on his comment about my father.

He appeared to be romanticizing my father's death. Honestly,
I couldn't think of anything romantic or glorious about it. My parents were civilian casualties of war. It was not a pretty picture to me.
I couldn't get misty-eyed comparing my father's death to the sacrifice of a lamb. In fact, the whole concept of glorifying my father's
death rather than recognizing it as anything but a tragedy was distasteful. He hadn't died to save anyone. His death had made me
an orphan and dropped me on an aunt who didn't care. I thought
Mr. Richardson was a sincere man, but he obviously hadn't been
touched by my father's death like I had. I didn't feel like sharing
my feelings with this stranger, so I smiled demurely and hoped he
would leave soon and let me get out of there like I'd been instructed.
I needed to grieve, and it wasn't over a man I barely remembered.

He cleared his throat, trying hard to contain his emotions.
"I shouldn't take more of your time." He stood and extended his
hand. "Please come. For everyone who knew him, seeing how you
turned out would mean so much."

How I turned out?

I took his hand. "I'll give it some thought." I smiled in front
of my negative thoughts. I thought I'd rather not relive my Congo
nightmare.

I watched him disappear through a door at the end of the hall
and then followed, stopping at Dave Larimore's open door. "May
I come in?"

"Sure, Camille," he said, lifting his head. "Sit." He cleared
his throat. "I talked to Del Williamson. He told me about Kara."

I nodded. "Dr. Gilles has asked me to take a few days." I
winced. "That means extra duty for you. I'm sorry."

"Don't be. You need some time." He hesitated and touched the corner of his Lennon wire-rimmed glasses. "Ellis can tell me about the patients. You don't need to worry about the service."

"Thanks. I should be back on Monday."

"That's too soon." He pulled off his glasses and began chewing on an earpiece.

"I cope by working, Dave."

He cleared his throat and shifted in his seat. "You . . . I . . ." He paused. "How do I say this? I've never been very good at confrontation."

My gut tightened. "What? What do you want to say?"

"Del told me that you'd been drinking."

I didn't like his tone. "Kara and I had some wine last night." I stood up. I didn't want to face his accusations. He was already biased against me for smelling alcohol on my breath the night I helped him after my reception.

"You're not the first surgeon to need some help with addictions, Camille."

"I don't believe this. You don't know anything about me."

"Oh, I think I know enough." He leaned forward. "Just because you're the cute little woman in the department, don't think you're everyone's little darling."

I was aghast. The man was jealous. He'd been in the department for a long time and was still fighting for tenure, so maybe he had a chip on his shoulder. Maybe he expected everyone to stop referring to him as inexperienced and now that I had shown up it still hadn't happened. I didn't know and frankly didn't care. For him to accuse me right after my best friend had died was heartless. I stared him down. "You have no idea what I've been through. I'm no one's darling. And I'm not an addict!"

I backed into the hall and into the line of sight of at least three secretaries who were looking in my direction. I'd been speaking too loudly. I felt naked. And I felt like cursing. Instead, I practically ran down the hall to escape.

TINA KINSER KNEW the hospital grapevine well enough to know it should be called the megaphone or the electronic speedway. A grapevine didn't seem to be the appropriate metaphor for something that moved so fast. Personal affairs must be kept discreet to keep them from being discussed over the daily breakfast special at the Skull and Bones. She'd found that certain news traveled faster than others. And, as always, the female attendings, particularly those with an ounce of lipsticked femininity, stood out above the rest as juicy fertilizer for the vine.

A good reason to be appropriately secretive about her affair with Dr. Lawson. After all, she was a married woman, a woman of commitment and standards.

Her heart quickened as she ventured toward his oncology clinic during her lunch break. Mark Lawson was her first taste of love away from the arms of her husband, and the flavor lingered on her tongue with an aching hunger for more. Today marked a new level of openness for her, a willingness to risk being the subject of dark rumor and secrecy. She knew Mark had shown a bit of ambivalence toward her, and had even expressed concern about their being seen in public, but had always responded when she took the lead. That emboldened her to try to curl another finger around his heart by taking this step—her second purposeful contact with him in public.

She lingered in the hall, feigning interest in the crayon drawings that brightened the clinic walls, the work of bald children with cancer, still naive enough to draw rainbows instead of hospital beds.

He came out smiling, winking at a young boy with one leg.

"Hi," she said quietly.

His eyes darted beyond her and back. "Hey."

She pressed a key into his hand, and spoke with her voice just above a whisper. "I asked him to leave, Mark. My husband is gone."

His eyes widened. "Tina, I—"

"I had the locks rekeyed this morning." She lingered with her hand against him for a moment before letting him go. "This one is yours."

He spoke in a low volume etched with tension. "This is too fast. I didn't ask you to leave your husband."

She shook her head. "Mark, this was way overdue."

"But I didn't mean to—"

She touched his arm. "You didn't cause anything. You only helped me see the inevitable with more clarity. I'd stopped living, Mark. I was existing on automatic."

Mark ushered her to the end of the hall next to a door leading into the waiting room. The look in his eye caused a knot to rise in her stomach. Maybe the key *was* too much. She should have known. "I'm not asking for a life commitment. I just thought . . . well, after the other night . . . the way you held me, I thought that you felt . . ."

Her voice began to thicken. She pinched her eyes closed. This wasn't turning out the way she'd imagined. "I'd better go."

"Tina," he whispered. "I loved the time we had. It's just, I—" He stopped and looked away.

She didn't dare speak for fear she would cry. She turned and fled, his words echoing in her ears. *I loved the* time *we had. Not I love* you.

She pressed her hand to her lips. He'd said "had." Past tense. She shook her head. *I'm too young for a midlife crisis!*

MARK LAWSON LOOKED at his watch. One o'clock. He had four hours to finish clinic in time to take dinner to Camille. He turned his hand over, alarmed to see he still had Tina's key.

He lifted it up and down in his hand, weighing it in his mind.

Then he slipped it into his pocket and went to the next occupied exam room.

19

MARK SHOWED UP with pizza and flowers at six. He lifted his nose as he came through the door. The room was thick with a chemical smell thanks to an emergency call I'd put in to a carpet specialist this morning. I knew if I was to ever sleep in that place again, the stains had to come out of the carpet.

He put the pizza and flowers on the kitchen table, and I fell into his embrace. He held me for a minute while my emotions flooded my eyes for the umpteenth time since that morning.

I didn't wait for him to release me before I started unloading my guilt. "It's my fault, Mark. It's my fault. She passed out drunk and vomited. She aspirated, Mark. I should have heard her. But I was passed out in my bedroom."

As I verbalized this confession, I began to feel the impact of my irresponsibility for the first time. It was a crushing weight. I felt like vomiting. "I let her drink, Mark."

I pulled away from his arms, needing air and space. I saw his blurred face through my tears.

"You couldn't have known."

I leaned against the sink, willing the ocean in my gut to be still. I took slow, deep breaths.

After a few moments, I sat in a kitchen chair. "What's bad is that Dave Larimore seems to think that I might be an addict and that my drinking may have played a part in Kara's death." I sighed. "I'm afraid he's right about the last part."

Mark took the chair across from mine. "Tell me what happened."

I pushed the weight of guilt to the back burner and replayed the evening's events. "We got takeout from the Robin Inn. Kara brought a bottle of wine. I told her we didn't need it." I saw the scene in my mind as I related it to him. "She told me she would drink just one glass."

I stared into Mark's eyes. They were deep, uncondemning.

"I knew she wasn't telling the truth, Mark. I knew she wouldn't stop. I wanted a drink. So I went along even when I knew she wasn't in control."

"You couldn't have known how it would turn out," he said again. He paused, taking my hand. "What happened next?"

"We ate. We talked. We drank the bottle of wine, then I had a wine cooler. I fell asleep." I paused, skipping the part about the terror I'd felt and the comfort I had knowing Kara would be with me in my present trouble. "When I got up the next morning, she was dead."

"You didn't make her take a drink. You discouraged her."

"I could have stopped her."

He shook his head. "Kara has always had a mind of her own. How many times has your relationship been on the outs because you confronted her about her drinking?"

"A few."

"More than a few." He opened the pizza box. "That's reason enough to make you reluctant to fight the same old battle again, particularly if you find yourself wanting a glass of wine." He nudged my hand. "Look at me."

I lifted my gaze from my shoes.

"All of us—all of her friends—would have done exactly what you did."

I absorbed what he said, unable to speak. After a few moments, I found my voice. "I'm afraid that Larimore might make trouble for me. I think he will be delighted to have attention shift off him for a change and on to the new guy."

He shook his head. "I know Dave. He may be a bit slow in the OR, but he's not the jealous type."

"Mark, the night of my reception, I stopped by the ICU to check on Kendrick. Larimore asked me to scrub a case with him, then basically didn't let me do anything. When I questioned him, he said he smelled alcohol on my breath and that I shouldn't have agreed to scrub." I folded my arms across my chest and sighed. "I'd had a beer at the reception. I wasn't drunk. It wasn't like I knew I was going to be scrubbing, and I didn't think the alcohol was affecting me. Now he's biased. He thinks I have a drinking problem and may make trouble for me."

"Listen, that's a distraction. Kara didn't die because you have a drinking problem. Kara died because *she* had a drinking problem."

I wished I could make my heart believe that.

I watched Mark eat. Now that Kara was gone, he had assumed the role of my best friend—whether he knew it or not, whether he wanted it or not. Maybe it was long overdue for me to have a guy for a best friend. I knew he was going to be a good one. He was already helping me cope.

I thought about what Kara had said about men—Mark in particular. Her words to me were framed in gold, now that they were her last. Was I looking for a love that didn't exist because I couldn't remember receiving it from my father?

I retreated from that idea. My father loved me. At least that's what I imagined.

I just didn't remember. But my gut seemed to be telling me something different.

Mark finished his second piece of pizza, wiped his hands and his mouth on a napkin, then went over to my bookshelves to pull out a photo album of my school days in Boston. He paged through it, looking at old pictures of Kara, forcing me to remember good times.

We shared stories about setting Kara up for dates that bombed, and laughed about her cooking. We talked about her skill as a nurse and her ability to make a hurting child smile.

I leaned my head on his shoulder. "I love you," I whispered. There, I'd said it.

He turned to me and kissed my lips.

When he pulled away, I saw a flash of something in his eyes that made me afraid. It was as if he was on the verge of telling me something very painful.

It was an intuition I couldn't explain. I put my fingers on his lips. "Not tonight," I whispered. If he didn't love me, he'd better not tell me tonight.

I'd had a rough enough day. And for now, I still believed in fairy-tale love.

For the next three days of my forced vacation, I fumbled my way through grief, spending hours crying over picture albums and wishing they made Kleenex in a larger size. At some level, I knew what Dr. Gilles said was true. I was shut down emotionally. I suspected I'd been like that a long, long time, maybe since my days on the Dark Continent. I found myself hoping that Kara's death would open a crack in the hard facade that protected me. But after a few day of tears, I turned to my routine modus operandi and made myself busy with other thoughts so I couldn't be sad. I outlined twenty chapters in Sabiston's textbook of surgery in preparation for my board exam, went jogging, and shopped for a funeral dress. I think I tried on ten dresses before finding the perfect one at Thalheimer's downtown. It was conservative enough, falling just below my knees, but had a slit up the side for spice. Kara would have liked it, so I shed another tear in the dressing room when I found it.

I did another weird thing in Thalheimer's. I found myself in the children's department looking at baby clothes, cute little frilly pink infant dresses and little boy coveralls. And again I found that part of me I thought I'd pushed aside. Maternal urges were a surprise to me. But the more I began to look past my professional goals, the more I found myself thinking of marriage. Naturally, after that, I'd have to think about whether the equation included children. Mark would make a great dad.

Mark Lawson seemed to have a knack for knowing when I needed space, a quality I adored. The night after bringing pizza, he brought flowers again, and a large box of Kleenex. My tears had run dry for the day, so I didn't open the box until just before Kara's funeral.

Again, Mark left early in the evening, this time to return to MCV to see a sick kid. Loving a doctor wasn't easy. You had to share him with so many others. Being a physician myself helped me understand. He promised me dinner over the weekend to make up for leaving early. He was either falling hard or feeling guilty. Either way, I appreciated the attention.

On the day of the funeral my phone rang, and I recognized the voice of my mentor, Dr. Bransford. "Camille, I wanted to find out how you are."

I sniffed. "I'm OK. The funeral is this afternoon. I should be back to work on Monday."

I listened as Dr. Bransford's breath whistled into the phone. "You need to know, Dr. Larimore has been raising concern with the department staff. He thinks you may have a problem that you're not admitting."

"What do you think?"

"I think I need to hear from you straight. I've never known you to have a problem with alcohol. Has the stress been getting to you?"

"I don't have a problem with alcohol. I have a problem with Dr. Larimore," I began. "The night of my reception, I stopped by the ICU to see a sick patient and he asked me to scrub and help him on a gunshot patient. I was happy to help, but after I scrubbed, he barely let me participate. Afterward he told me he smelled beer on my breath and that he was uncomfortable letting me get too involved." I huffed. "Dr. Bransford, I was fine. Sure, I had a beer at my own reception, but if I'd have been on call, I wouldn't have had anything. I scrubbed in the case because I thought I was fine. There may have been a remnant of alcohol on my breath, but I was not impaired."

Dr. Bransford grunted. "What about Kara's death?"

"She's been fighting a battle with alcohol for some time. Yes, I drank with her the night before she died, but I discouraged her from drinking." I sighed. "She has a mind of her own. I fell asleep. She may have drank more by herself after I went to bed. I do feel horrible, even guilty, but Kara was ultimately an adult. She made her own bad choices."

"OK, Camille. Try not to worry about this too much."

"I'm not sure what Dr. Larimore has against me. He certainly seems to want to point the finger in my direction."

"He hasn't always had an easy go of it himself, Camille. Maybe he's just happy the negative attention is off him."

"He didn't even record my name on the operative record when I came and helped him that night. It's as if he wanted it covered up."

Another sharp breath into the phone. "OK, listen, Dr. Gilles will have to make the final call on this one, but as far as I'm concerned, I'm satisfied. I'll talk to Gilles, tell him to be sure Larimore backs off."

"Dr. Gilles likes Larimore."

"Yes." There was silence over the phone as we let the sober fact hang between us. Gilles liked Larimore and Larimore didn't like me.

I broke the silence. "Thanks."

I hung up and put on my new black dress for the funeral service.

I attended the funeral with Mark on one arm and Rachel Bell on the other. Kara's father must have been less Jewish than I suspected, because the memorial service was held in a large room at McCall's Funeral Home and nowhere close to a temple. Joel Bryan, the youth pastor at St. Giles Presbyterian Church, led the service. I wasn't sure how the Schullers had found out about Joel, unless Kara had something deeper going on with him than I knew.

The Reverend Bryan, as he was listed on the program, talked about Kara like she was an old friend. I'd always been a bit skeptical of emotional preachers, but when Joel Bryan's voice choked up, I had no doubt of his sincerity.

I listened as Joel recounted memories from Kara's family and friends, but when he opened his Bible, I started feeling pretty guilty for my role in the whole affair. If only I hadn't been drinking with her. If only I had stopped her. If only I hadn't been so consumed with my own problems, maybe I could have helped. By the time Joel wrapped up his little speech, tears were pouring down my face again, either from my own guilt, or sorrow at Kara's death, or a jumble of both, I wasn't sure.

After the service, Rachel suggested we crash in the basement of the Tobacco Company, and drink to our lost friend.

"I can't."

Mark understood. I was beginning to think my emotions were an open book to him. He took my hand. "Swearing off having a drink won't bring her back. Kara was the kind of friend you could cry in your beer with. She wouldn't want you to blame yourself."

I nodded and stayed quiet.

Mark drove my Prelude to my apartment, where he'd parked his '78 Datsun. He kissed me tenderly on the cheek before moving to my mouth, allowing me to taste my own tears.

He held me for a few minutes before saying good-bye.

He hadn't pushed to stay over since our anniversary dinner. He sensed our time would come and was being patient. That alone made me love him more.

From my bedroom window I watched him go, and I tried to ignore a fear that my baby steps toward intimacy would drive him away. Mark knew I wanted him. And he knew our love would find a vent in passion soon. I'd promised him as much.

I just needed a little time to make sense of the terror that seemed to linger at the edge of sex.

20

ON MONDAY MORNING, I sat in front of Tina Kinser in my clinic. "I talked it over with Dr. Gilles."

"Well?"

"I'll do what you request."

"Dr. Gilles agreed?"

I wrinkled my nose. "Not exactly." I closed her file and placed it across my lap. "He won't tell me what to do, but he makes it clear what he would do."

"Are you going to be in trouble?"

I reached for her hand. "This is right for you. As far as I'm concerned, this is an issue between you and me. What's right for someone else or for everyone else, for that matter, may not be what is best for Tina." I shrugged. "If someone has a problem with that, I'm ready to defend myself."

"When do we operate?"

"I've got space on my schedule the day after tomorrow."

She took a deep breath and exhaled slowly. "OK."

"Have you told your husband?"

She pulled her fingers through her hair and shook her head. She laughed nervously.

"We've separated."

"I'm sorry."

"It was overdue."

"He doesn't know?"

She shook her head. "He's not in the equation."

"How long have you been married?"

"Twenty years."

I pushed my rolling stool away from the table. "How much of this is due to your diagnosis?"

She stared at the wall. "Cancer has nothing to do with my failed marriage."

"Facing cancer makes people do crazy things. I know a seventy-year-old woman who went bungee jumping as soon as she found out she had colon cancer."

"What are you saying?"

"I'm just exploring a possibility with you. I want to make sure you aren't making rash decisions because you've had a serious threat to your health." I paused. "Decisions you may regret."

She looked down at her hands. "Cancer has made me wake up a bit." She sighed. "OK, so I'm entitled to my own little midlife crisis. Psychiatrists aren't exempt."

I settled into a very nonsurgical mode, one that felt good. Relaxed. "Do you want to talk about it?"

Her shoulders slumped. Lines appeared at the edges of her full lips. "I had an affair with a resident."

I stayed quiet.

"At first, I think I did it to get back at my husband."

"He's hurt you?"

She nodded. "Then this happened."

"Your cancer?"

Another nod. She pressed her fist against her upper lip. "At first I thought it was what I deserved because of . . . the way I'd be-haved." She sniffed and looked at me with wet eyes. "Then I started realizing that this apparent curse could be a blessing of sorts."

"A blessing?"

"A wake-up call. It helped me see that I'd fallen into a boring routine with a man I no longer loved."

"You said he hurt you. Did he have an affair?"

She bit her bottom lip. "Yes."

"But you stayed with him."

"I didn't know what else to do. I wasn't brave enough to leave." She paused. "Until now."

"What does he want?"

"What do most men who have an affair to stroke their ego want when they come to their senses?"

I shrugged. "Forgiveness."

"He'd be a fool to leave me. I've supported him in the lifestyle he wanted."

"Forgiveness is tougher than leaving."

"Are you married?"

I almost laughed. "No."

"You have an idea about love."

I felt myself blushing. I had taken an emotional step toward my patient. A heart step of honesty. "I'm looking for a man who will love me in spite of my faults."

"Have you found him?"

I couldn't keep from smiling. "I think so." I looked at my patient as she responded, smiling with me. She needed a man like Mark Lawson. A professional who would understand the pressures she was under as a physician. Someone articulate, smart, handsome, and funny. Someone who loved children and would make a great dad. Like Mark.

We kept each other in our gaze for a few moments, with a new level of comfort between us. Finally, I broke the silence. "I think your husband would want to know about your surgery."

She shook her head slowly. "I don't want his sympathy right now. It will just complicate things."

I disagreed, but I couldn't force the issue. "Is there someone else close that you'd like me to talk to?"

Tina lifted her head as if a name were about to bounce off her tongue. Instead, she halted. "No."

I picked up her chart. I toyed with the idea of asking her opinion of my nightmares and the anxiety that had stalked me since I started this job. After a moment, I decided I'd better not risk letting Tina lose confidence in her surgeon before her procedure. Maybe later. I touched her shoulder. "Very well. I'll see you before your surgery on Wednesday."

MY FIRST DAY back, people treated me nicely. Too nicely. The kind of nice you use to treat someone fragile. I specifically avoided Dr. Gilles. And Dr. Larimore. If either of them had a bone to pick with me, I would face him and fight. If not, all the better. I wanted to be in and out without undue attention from the boss or any of his minions.

That afternoon Nadine Solomon was convinced a miracle had occurred. I, being a scientific skeptic, wasn't so fast to credit any deity, only my team and their intensive-care efforts. Regardless of who was credited, Kendrick Solomon had taken a definite upward turn. I stood at his bedside and talked with Kendrick as his mother stood by.

"Kendrick," I said, "do you know this woman?"

His eyes made contact with his mother and he gave a definite little nod of his head.

Nadine beamed. "I told ya, Doc. He knows me!" Hope filled her eyes. "Will he come off the ventilator soon?"

"Let's see how strong he is." I turned to Kendrick. "Lift your head up, Kendrick. Lift it off the pillow."

He strained. He was able to lift his head only for a moment before letting it down again. I looked at Nadine. "I'll leave the tube in his windpipe until he's strong enough to breathe on his own. If he keeps improving, we'll have him off in a day or two."

"Praise the Lord." She touched my arm, giving me a squeeze. "Maybe this will help you believe."

I smiled politely.

"You know God loves you, Dr. Weller. Just like a father. He's your heavenly father, he is."

I suppressed the urge to tell her I wasn't sure that I knew the first thing about a father's love. How was I to believe in a heavenly father's love if I didn't have a clear earthly father's example? I cleared my throat instead of telling her I was an orphan.

I stepped away and she followed, her expression suddenly changing. Sober. "Dr. Weller," she said, "with Kendrick getting better, I just wanted to make sure you didn't, well—" She halted. "I jus' don't want you to send him home too soon."

"He's not going anywhere soon."

Nadine brightened.

I leaned toward her. "Why Nadine? Why wouldn't you want your son at home again?"

"It's just, well . . ."

I watched as she searched for the words. This normally chatty woman was finally hesitant to speak. "I just don't want him at home before he's strong."

"We'll be sure of that."

"His father and him don't get along."

"What are you saying, Nadine?"

Her face tensed up. "Nothing," she said. "I'm not saying anything. I just want my boy to get better." She nodded and stepped back.

I slipped away as Nadine resumed chatting with her son. It must have been torture for him, I thought, a fifteen-year-old boy too sick to get away from his mother.

I walked away musing about what Kendrick might understand about a father's love. Was his father abusive? Why had Nadine brought up their relationship? I hadn't seen hide nor hair of a masculine figure around Kendrick, unless you counted the elders from his church. The thought gave me pause. Maybe I *should* count the elders from his church. Role models were hard to come by.

THAT NIGHT I met Mark at Strawberry Street Café in the Fan—
the streets that stretch westward away from VCU like spokes on a
wheel. I loved the café and ordered the salad bar, which was laid
out in an old porcelain bathtub.

Mark concentrated on his steak while I pushed the greens
around on my plate.

"Kara advised me to talk to a psychiatrist."

He paused. "What brought this up?"

I shrugged. "Us."

"What?"

"I keep thinking about us. Our future."

He looked at me, intent on my face and my words.

"It's this panic stuff, Mark. I'm afraid it's getting in the way
of us. . . ."

"Of us?"

"You know."

He smiled. Tender. Understanding. "This isn't easy for you, is
it? Surgeons aren't used to being needy."

"Surgeons like to be in control."

"That's what makes you afraid, isn't it?" He pushed his plate
away. "Being out of control."

He understood.

"Yes."

I sipped sweet iced tea and stared at the man I loved. "So what
do you think? Should I do it?"

"It doesn't mean you're weak, Camille. Asking for a little support from a doctor doesn't mean you're crazy."

"I know." I looked down. "I just wanted your opinion. It's
important to know you're supporting me."

He reached over and took my hand. "If it will help you sort
out why panic is nipping at your heels . . . and if it will help

us . . . you know . . ." The corners of his mouth turned up. "Then I'm all for it."

I nodded. "Kara recommended Tina Kinser."

Mark's head popped up.

"What's wrong?"

He shook his head. "I . . . I think you should see someone outside MCV. You know how the grapevine sings."

"No one's going to know."

"You know how people talk."

I felt like telling him I was treating Tina for breast cancer and I wasn't spreading that all over the hospital. But I held my tongue. Confidentiality between patient and doctor was sacred and I wouldn't stoop in order to toot my own horn. Besides, if I told him I was seeing her as a patient and not revealing that information to anyone, I would instantly be a liar because I would have just given the information to him.

I let it drop.

I skipped dessert. Mark ate cheesecake. He let me pay the bill, his concession to women's liberation. After all, I had a salary easily quadruple his. I was an attending, he, alas, a lowly fellow in training.

We talked in the parking lot for a few more minutes before he embraced me against my Prelude. "Come to my place."

I felt a twinge of excitement and guilt. He kissed my neck and pulled the small of my back toward him. He nudged my earlobe with his nose, then gripped it gently in his teeth. I shivered, and then wondered if he was going to suck off my earring. He was going to aspirate my pearls and I'd have to resuscitate him right there in the parking lot of the Strawberry Street Café.

I kissed him back, then buried my face in his neck. His hand moved lower and he whispered in my ear. He leaned forward. My back pressed against my car mirror.

I sensed my gut tightening. Now I seemed to be afraid that

I was going to be afraid. The beginnings of panic played off the idea that I might have another attack. This was stupid. I loved this man. I wanted to accept what he wanted to give. Being fearful of becoming fearful was a circle of despair that was new to me, not part of the surgeon persona I exuded. I would concentrate on the now, the tenderness that was offered.

I fought the rising tide of anxiety. I bit my lower lip until I felt pain, trying to control my runaway thoughts. I turned my face full toward his to disguise my panic. I grabbed his thick curls and directed his lips to my mouth. If I was in control, I couldn't panic.

Mark pulled back, his eyes reflecting the streetlamp. I sensed his readiness for more. Fortunately, we both had small cars or he might have been tempted to consummate his urgency right there in public. "Let's go," he said, his voice nearly breathless.

My eyes betrayed my terror.

He kissed my forehead. "Camille, everything's gonna be all right."

That was exactly what I didn't want to hear. Even if the words carried no magical significance to deliver me into a web of fright, the fact that I was afraid they would tripped me into alarm.

"I . . . I can't, Mark. Not tonight."

"What is it, Camille?"

I was frozen. Unable to respond.

His eyes flashed with anger and frustration. "Do you love me?"

"Mark, you know I do."

He released me and stepped back.

"Mark," I protested. "I need some time."

He shook his head. "Maybe Kara is right."

My eyes returned daggers. "What are you saying?"

He sighed. "I don't know, Camille. I'm just frustrated."

Moving toward him, I softened the look I had just given him. "I know, I know. I'm frustrated, too. There will be time for love to blossom," I said, touching his chest. "For us."

"You're driving me mad, Camille. You know I want you."

"I know, and rest assured, I want you, too. It's just . . ." I hesitated and sighed. "Do you love me?"

He stared at me for a moment, searching for the answer. "Yes."

My heart soared. He hadn't exactly said the L-word, but he'd said yes to my question!

He kissed me again.

I pushed him away. "So we're in this together?"

He nodded and spoke softly. "Sure."

I felt stupid and awkward, almost like I'd just come out of the janitor's closet with Troy Johnson at prep school. I was allured by his kisses, but not quite ready to be groped among the disinfectants. "Be patient," I whispered. "When it happens, it will be special."

He puffed up his upper lip, something I'd noticed him doing more and more when he was resolved, but not quite on board. "OK."

He kissed me one more time. This time on the cheek, a brotherly peck that said, "bye-bye."

THAT NIGHT, I laid awake wondering what it would have been like if I had yielded to Mark's urging. What would it be like to hold Mark in an intimate tangle?

He definitely had what it took to get me going. Passion rose in me, in the darkness of my room, as I fantasized about his touch.

My feelings both delighted and frustrated me. I'd waited long years to find a man who could love me, not be intimidated by my success, and who had the gut-level sex appeal to paralyze my desire to wander. And now that I was on the verge of falling into his arms, I found myself unable to surrender. Fear haunted me, toyed with the corners of my mind, whispering of events long suppressed.

I stroked the empty sheet beside me and whispered his name into the silence.

And then I began to weep.

MARK LAWSON PACED his small apartment, unable to sleep. He felt stretched, torn between two women. Camille was young, vibrant, innocent, smart, and so adored him. Tina was vulnerable, taken with the newness of relationship with him, but so open, ready to revel in life. Like so many physicians who put their education first, he'd delayed the gratification of a serious relationship with a woman. And just when he had started to think of Camille as the one, Tina had sprung into his life. Unexpected, but full of life and possibilities.

Camille needed him, more now that Kara was dead and she faced the pressures of her new position alone.

Tina needed him, more now that she faced cancer without the support of a loving husband.

Camille was reliable, faithful, and witty.

Tina was easy to talk to.

Camille struggled to find her way in a man's world.

Tina was established, comfortable with who she was as a doctor and a woman.

Camille was fatherless, not yet comfortable receiving the love he longed to give her, but believed in fairy-tale love. For sometime in the future.

Tina was perched, ready to experience new love with all the trimmings, emotional and physical.

He was falling in love with Camille. But the temptation of sex with Tina grew with each day he avoided her grasp.

Mark took a deep breath and walked to the bathroom. It was the memories of the hours spent enjoying the unexpected offering of Tina's nakedness that both titillated and tortured him. She was married!

But she said her marriage was over.

He splashed cold water on his face, willing the replay of their pleasure to melt from his mind.

As he brushed his teeth to prepare for sleep, he remembered her kisses.

As he slipped off his shirt, he recalled the desperation in which she tore his clothes from him.

As he laid on his bed, his heart pounded with the memory of her scent, her touch, her kiss.

In a few minutes, he rose, dressed, and lifted a key from the top of his dresser.

The memory was too sweet.

And he was too weak.

In a moment, he was in his car, pushing back regrets, driven by a lust for passion. Hopefully, he thought, she will be receptive to a night visitor.

21

THE MORNING OF Tina Kinser's surgery was heavy with Virginia humidity. Within seconds of exiting my Prelude's AC heaven, I was perspiring, wishing for a summer storm that would wash away some of the miserable downtown heat.

When I arrived in the pre-op holding area a few minutes later, I had shed my civvies and donned typical surgical scrubs, a pair of size-medium men's pants, and a large shirt pinned at the neckline to preserve my modesty. Tina was behind a curtain in cubicle three. There, in contrast to the outside weather, the air was decidedly icy. I pulled back the curtain to see a man sitting on the side of the bed next to Tina, whose eyes were darts aiming right at me.

"Good morning," I said.

The man stood and held out his hand. "I'm Daniel Kinser, Tina's husband."

I traded glances with Tina, who returned a glare. "I'm Dr. Weller," I said, shaking hands with Daniel. I touched Tina's shoulder and kept my voice low. "How are you? All ready?"

She nodded without speaking.

I studied the couple for a moment.

Daniel broke the awkward silence. "Dr. Weller, I have some concerns about Tina and her treatment."

I raised my eyebrows.

He continued, "First, let me express my thanks for caring for her up to this point." He paused, and looked at me with the expression a principal might give a naughty student. "I'm going to ask that you remove yourself from Tina's care."

"Excuse me?"

Tina shook her head. "Absolutely not. Dr. Weller is my surgeon. It's my choice." She looked at me. "Why did you have to tell him?"

"I did nothing of the—"

"You were the one who thought he should know."

Dan held up his hands. "Tina, I have never talked to this doctor before. James Gilles called me to see how you were doing."

Tina and I stared at each other for a moment until she looked away.

I nodded. "Remember, I asked your permission to run your case by him? I had no idea he would share our discussion with—"

"All the better," Dan interrupted, before folding his arms across his chest. "Now, as difficult as this may be, I'd really like to insist that Tina see Dr. Gilles for another opinion."

"I don't want another opinion."

I cleared my throat. "Mr. Kinser, I know you are concerned for Tina, but you must know that she has the ultimate right to make her own decisions."

He looked at his wife, who continued to stare at the wall. "Tina, Dr. Gilles is a world expert in cancer treatment. I discussed your case with him." He looked up at me. "His recommendations are not the same as Dr. Weller's. According to Dr. Gilles, what Dr. Weller is proposing may endanger your life." He paused and locked eyes with me. "And from what he tells me, Dr. Weller may not even be here to follow up your care if she follows through on this reckless plan."

I took a deep breath. It wasn't time to lose my cool. I did not want to rehash the surgical debate with this man.

I heard the curtain move behind me. The transporter was there to take Tina into the OR. A teenaged boy cracked a smile through a face dotted with acne. "Excuse me, Dr. Weller. I can wait."

"I'm ready," Tina said. "Let's go."

Dan stepped forward. "I really will have to insist on stopping you. I want my wife to see Dr. Gilles."

I glanced at the nurses' station behind Mr. Kinser. I gave a signal to the nurse manager, who had obviously been listening to the interchange. I crossed my arms in an X, tapping my wrists together.

She picked up the phone, while I did my best to think of what to say.

I sat on the bed next to Tina, to show I was clearly on her side.

Tina began to cry. "Dan, please don't do this. Please just go away!"

He shook his head. "I'm concerned about you, Tina. Imagine how I felt learning about this last night."

She huffed. "Imagine how I feel."

"I want the best for you."

"You don't know what's best."

I looked at Mr. Kinser. "I'm going to ask you calmly, and only once, to step out of the way and not obstruct this young man from taking your wife to the OR."

As he took a breath to protest, I interrupted him, "Or these men will escort you out of the hospital." I nodded my head toward the nurses' station, where two men in security uniforms now stood. The duo, looking like they'd be comfortable anchoring the front line for a Nebraska football team, tilted their heads at me without smiling.

Daniel Kinser glanced over his shoulder, looked back at Tina, then took a longer look at the linemen as he contemplated his options. He stepped back to allow the transporter to come forward.

Mr. Kinser shot another glare at me. "Nothing, I mean nothing, had better happen to her."

I didn't appreciate being threatened. "Have a nice day, Mr.

Kinser," I said before squeezing Tina's hand and standing up. "I'll see you in a few minutes."

BY EIGHT, MY team was assembled around the sleeping form of Tina Kinser. Derrick stood to my left to pass instruments. Rich Arensen stood across to assist me. Normally, this would be a resident case, but any time one of our own in the medical community came under the knife, the understanding was that the attending would hold the scalpel.

"Knife," I said, holding out my right hand.

Derrick laid the instrument gently in my fingers.

I made an elliptical curvilinear incision around the dimpled skin in the upper outer quadrant of the breast. I could feel the firmness of the tissue I'd set out to eradicate. Breast cancer is not stupid. Although the center of the tumor was hard and unable to hide, there were microscopic fingers that reached into the surrounding tissue, making discovery by the finger or the naked eye impossible. For this reason, I stayed well away from the palpable firmness and cut away the tissue at least a centimeter back from the edge of the indiscrete margin.

After I closed the breast, I turned my attention to the axillary dissection. This was the time-consuming portion of the operation. Nerves supplying movement of the shoulder needed to be meticulously dissected and preserved. Tributaries along the large, blue axillary vein were divided between thin silk ligatures. After an hour, I'd cleaned out all the fatty tissue from the axilla containing the necessary lymph nodes. I breathed a sigh of relief and began to close.

Smiling behind my mask, I said, "Closin' music."

Derrick bobbed his head. "All right."

My circulating nurse turned up the volume on my favorite local pop station. The mood lightened.

Thirty minutes later, I gripped Tina's hand in the recovery room. She stared at me with bleary eyes, still thick from anesthesia.

The words slipped from my lips before I could stop them. "Everything's gonna be all right."

22

ONE OF MY favoritist things of all is getting to watch my daddy operate. His fingers move so fast when he is tying knots that you can't follow him. Sometimes he brings me the extra suture thread left over after a case so I can practice tying knots. My mother thinks this is funny because she's never heard of a woman becoming a surgeon.

The best part is getting to dress up in the surgical scrub stuff. I get to wear a hat and mask and even a special pair of shoes. My dad lets me change in the little room outside the operating theatre after chasing out the men. There is only one place to change, and the assistants who help my daddy are all men, so he does this for me to make me feel special.

In the operating theatre, Mr. Karanja is the boss. He makes sure I wear all the stuff correctly so I don't cause any infections or anything.

The Simbas brought another wounded man in today; I think he's someone important, 'cause they said they couldn't let him out of their sight.

Mr. Karanja always follows the rules. "You can't go in there dressed like that!" he said, standing to block their way.

One of the Simbas—he looked like a teenager—hit Mr.

Karanja on the head with the end of his gun. Mr. Karanja fell over. His head was really bleeding. When he stood up and got in their way again, the Simba teenager shot him in the chest.

I saw the whole thing from inside the theatre where I was waiting 'cause I had on all the right scrub stuff that Mr. Karanja wanted.

I'm not sure what is wrong with me. I was so scared, but I didn't even cry. I ran home and hid in my bed beneath the mosquito net.

It was two hours before my daddy came home and found me and told my mother what had happened to Mr. Karanja.

My mother is typical African, I think. She cried so loud for Mr. Karanja that the neighbors two doors down came to see what was wrong.

I wonder what is wrong with me. I loved Mr. Karanja, too, but my tears were shut off.

RICHMOND, 1984

W HEN I VISITED Tina's room that evening, I found her resting, and apparently at peace.

"Hi, Doc," she said, taking my hand.

"Hi." I looked at a bouquet of roses and raised my eyebrows. "Your husband?" I was meddling, but I knew her well enough to know she didn't care.

But this time she hesitated. Her mouth hung open for a moment while her brain formulated a response. "Secret admirer," she said.

I let it drop. Obviously there were secrets between us. The doctor-patient relationship hadn't broken all barriers.

"How'd we do today?" she asked, still holding my hand.

"Great. The size of the lymph nodes isn't a reliable indicator of whether they contain cancer, but at least none were large and suspicious."

"Good."

"How do you feel?"

She lifted her left arm slowly out to her side. "Bad if I do this."

I smiled. "Don't do that yet." Sage advice from a seasoned surgeon.

She laughed before sobering. "When will I find out the results from the pathologists?"

"A couple of days."

She nodded.

I checked the reservoir bulb of a drain that exited under Tina's arm. The contents were bloody, but not significant in amount. "This is fine," I explained. "I'll pull the drain in a few days." I paused. "You can go home with it if you're comfortable."

"OK."

She caught my eyes and held them. "Thank you."

My voice tightened, and my words came out in a whisper. "Sure." I broke her gaze because I didn't want to cry.

"Really," she added, "I'm so sorry about this morning. I had no idea that Dan—"

"Forget it," I said. "It's over."

She tilted her head. "Your job—"

I raised my hand. "Hush." She knew I'd skated on thin ice for her. But I was learning that some things were more important than job security. And those things I was learning from Tina. I didn't want her indebtedness, but her appreciation was touching.

For a moment I thought about how it would feel to be on the other side of the stethoscope. What would it be like if I were the patient? It was odd, I thought. Two weeks ago, talking to her would have been the farthest thing down my to-do list, somewhere in the next century. But Kara thought I should talk to her. Nightmares were haunting me, threatening to destroy my love life, and now, on top of it, I was a bit concerned Tina's husband might hunt me down.

I took a deep breath. I couldn't burden Tina with my problems now. She needed space to recover. "I need to get going. I'll see you in the morning."

She waved good-bye with her right hand as I closed her door.

At the nurses' station, I paged Mark. I picked up the phone after the first ring. "Hello."

"Dr. Lawson, I was paged."

"It's me. I'm done. Hungry?"

"Sure," he said. "Give me forty-five minutes, OK? I've got one more patient to see and some paperwork to do."

"Fine. I need to freshen up anyway." I always liked to shower after a day in the OR. "How about takeout at my place? I'm beat."

"Cool with me. See you." He hung up the phone without a romantic salutation. Typical male, I thought. Other guys must be nearby. He must hate the gossip grapevine even more than I did.

I looked at the receiver, now dead. "Bye to you, too."

MARK SLIPPED INTO Tina's room and shut the door quietly. Her eyes were closed. He nudged her shoulder.

"Hi," she whispered. "I thought you were a nurse. I was going to feign sleep and hope they didn't bother me."

"Sorry, it's only me."

She wiped a tear from the corner of her eye. "I'm glad you came by."

"It's been a crazy day." He sat on the side of her bed. "How do you feel?"

"Not so bad if I'm still." She offered a little shrug. "It hurts when I move my arm."

"Then don't move it."

She smiled. "That's what my surgeon said."

"Smart surgeon . . . for a woman."

"Careful."

He held up his hands. "I'm kidding."

"Don't make fun of my doctor. She's great. She just left me, Mark. She had tears in her eyes."

He shifted on the bed and looked at his hands. "So when will you be released?"

"Tomorrow." She touched his hand. "Thanks for the flowers."

He looked at the bouquet on the bedside table. "Sure."

After a moment of silence, she asked, "What are you doing, Mark? I'm getting confused."

"You think you're confused?"

"I'm serious. You make me think you were just a fling. You act like you're not ready for something long-term. So I adjust my thinking, tell myself you're just part of my midlife crisis." She paused, her voice thickening. "But you keep showing up and we keep—"

"I know, I know." He shook his head. "What do you want?"

She bit her lower lip. "I'm trying to keep my expectations low." Her eyes met his. "But I'm having trouble getting you off my mind."

"Me, too," he whispered. He took a deep breath. "It's just, well—"

She brought her hand to her mouth. "You have a girlfriend."

He looked away. "Are psychiatrists trained to read minds?"

"It's not hard, Mark. You're indecisive. Why else wouldn't you embrace what we have?"

"You're married."

"Touché." She touched the back of his hand. "I told you that was over."

He couldn't look at her. "I was in a relationship when we met."

"Were?"

"Were . . . am . . . Things happened so fast with you that . . ." He hesitated, then added, "that I haven't been able to untangle my other relationship."

Tina pulled his hand to her mouth and kissed it. "Things did happen fast with us, didn't they?" She smiled. "I'll give you some time."

"You're not mad?"

She stared at him for a moment before answering. "I was in a relationship when we met, too, remember?" She laid his hand on the bed beside her. "So I might need some time as well."

He stood to leave. She was so beautiful lying there. She wore a green hospital gown and her hair fell onto her shoulders in a tangle of blond and gray. He leaned down until their foreheads touched. She smelled of clinical antiseptic. Yet, seeing her in that state of vulnerability and openness, he could not remember a time that he felt a stronger attraction. He kissed her forehead and pulled away breathless, puzzled by the power she had over him. "We must be careful around here," he said before opening the door. "The walls have ears."

"Go away," she said playfully. "My lips are sealed."

I STOPPED IN Kendrick Solomon's room before I left, bringing a small bouquet of flowers to celebrate his move out of the ICU. I set the flowers on his bedside table. He was watching TV, a rerun of *I Love Lucy*. "Hi, sport."

He lifted his head.

"Where's your mom?" This was the first time I'd seen them separated.

He shrugged. "Don't know."

I lifted a can of a nutritional supplement from the tray table in front of him. "You like this stuff?"

"It's OK."

Typical talkative fifteen-year-old, I thought. "If you keep improving, I'll let you go home in a few days."

He looked toward the wall and stayed quiet.

"What's up, Kendrick? You want to go home, don't you?"

He kept his eyes on the wall.

"Kendrick?"

Eventually he turned and spoke, his eyes alight with fear. "Don't send me home."

I was stunned. Most boys his age couldn't wait to get out of this place. "What's going on?"

"My daddy's the one who shot me."

23

THAT NIGHT, MARK and I ate take-out pizza from Pizza Hut in my apartment. However, Kendrick Solomon's revelation cast a somber shadow on my mood and robbed me of my appetite.

Mark tried his best to pull me out of the blues. He looked at his watch. "Want to catch the last few innings of the Braves? They're at home tonight." He lifted his eyebrows. "I'll even pay."

"It's free admission at the Diamond after the seventh-inning stretch."

"I'm not stupid."

"Just cheap."

"Just a resident trying hard to impress an attending."

I pushed my half-eaten pizza slice around my plate and sipped my Diet Coke. "I'm not up for baseball tonight."

"What's up, Camille? You love baseball."

I shrugged. "I'm worried about Kendrick."

Mark slid his hand across the table to mine. "Are you going to talk to the police?"

"I'll talk to the social worker tomorrow."

Mark reached for another slice of deep-dish pizza. We ate in silence for a few minutes before I spoke again. "I've made a decision to see Dr. Kinser."

Mark swirled his glass and set it down. "So you're going through with this, huh?"

"I thought you'd be happy."

He ran his fingers through his hair. "Oh, I'm ecstatic."

"Mark!"

"What do you expect me to say? You are doing what you want to do, regardless of my advice."

"You happen to be the only one who doesn't approve of Tina. Remember, Kara wanted me to see her."

He sighed heavily.

"What difference does it make to you? I'm the one who has to talk to her." I studied him for a moment. It wasn't like him to sulk. "What is it? You're offended because I went against your advice?"

He gulped the last of his beer. "It's not just that. You should see her if you want to. It's . . . well . . . I don't like the idea of my name being talked about in her office." His eyes met mine. "I see Tina on the wards all the time. I'd feel funny knowing you'd con-fided in her about us . . . the problems we're having."

"So let me get this straight. You're not that upset about me seeing Tina. But you're worried that your reputation might be tarnished in some way?"

"It's not that," he said, pleading. He spoke with a gentle tone. "It's just that there are certain things that belong only to us right now. Our relationship is special, Camille. If you and I are strug-gling with the physical part of our relationship, I want that to remain between us."

I softened. Intimacy was a private issue. I could understand Mark not wanting me to discuss our sex life with a therapist. I backed down. "OK, baby, I spoke too soon."

"Can't you just talk about your past? I think if you come to peace about those issues, the present will be fine." He stroked the back of my hand. "Very fine."

His brown eyes melted me every time. I reorganized myself so I could speak. "It's all mixed up together. The past, the present. Something in the present triggers my panic, Mark. She's bound to question me."

"Why don't you call me your boyfriend? How about that?" He lifted my hand to his mouth and kissed my fingers. "That could work."

"You're distracting me," I said, pulling my fingers away from him. "Why can't I brag about my doctor boyfriend?"

He pulled his chair close to mine and started kissing my neck. "You're a surgeon. No one cares if your boyfriend is a pediatrician."

"OK."

He pulled back. "OK what? You will keep our secret between us? You won't mention my name?"

"I said OK." I glared at him.

He smiled. "You mean this is all I have to do to get my way?"

"Careful, cowboy, I might drop your name just to impress her."

"Don't tease me."

"This is really important to you?"

His face was immediately sober. "Our love life is no one else's business. I want to be the only one to know certain things about you."

I held up my hands. "I'll keep your name in my heart, but not on my lips." I paused. "What about you? Don't you like to brag about me in the locker room? I heard guys do that, you know."

"And what would I brag about?"

"That I'm willing to be seen with you."

He laughed. "Be serious. I'll give you the space you need. But I need to know a ballpark figure here. How much time do you think you'll need?"

I smiled. "Two, maybe three years' intensive psychotherapy."

He frowned. "Real funny."

"A few weeks, Mark. I have a hope that things will be right for us very soon."

"I'm counting the hours." He stood to leave.

I stood with him and kissed his forehead. "I'm counting, too."

He gave me a sweet kiss on the lips and slipped out the door.

I closed it behind him, hoping he could be patient enough to wait.

As a trauma surgeon I'd seen just about all the blood and gore that cruel people and circumstances can dish onto the plate of humanity. Nothing turned my stomach anymore. Nothing except the thought of a parent abusing a child.

Just when I thought I was about to untangle my life from Kendrick Solomon's, he dropped anchor hoping to stay.

The next afternoon I worked at my desk until Dale Stiner appeared in the doorway. Dale was a social worker, a veteran of sorts, having worked in and around a complex system protecting Richmond's children for over twenty years.

I pointed to the chair opposite my desk, eager to learn what he'd discovered.

Dale was an unpretentious, open-collar type of guy. His home was Houston, Texas, and if you didn't learn something about how things in Texas were bigger or better than in Virginia during your first visit with him, you were fortunate. He sat with his legs crossed, so I could see his rattlesnake-skinned cowboy boots. He leaned forward over a large shiny belt buckle. "Kendrick's family is a piece of work," he began. "His father, Clive, has been busted a half dozen times on petty drug charges. The scoop around the neighborhood is that he's dealing, something that Clive and Nadine both swear is a thing of the past. I searched the police records filed after Kendrick's shooting and the official version is that it was all an accident. Kendrick was on the wrong side of a wooden door during target practice."

"Target practice—in a house?" I leaned forward against my desk. "That's ridiculous! Kendrick said his father is paranoid about the cops, said he's going to the penitentiary for sure if he gets convicted again. Kendrick's version was that his father was making a deal when Kendrick arrived home with an older cousin who is wise to his uncle's dealings. The cousin pounded on the door and yelled, 'Police.' The next thing Kendrick knew he was in the ICU at MCV."

"Nadine is supportive of Clive."

"Tell me about it."

"Clive's got a job at a local body shop."

"Clive drinks too much."

Dale sighed. "Kendrick's mother wants him home."

"Nadine is afraid that if we make too much of this, she's going to end up with a husband in the pen and she'll be without his income."

He held up his hands. "All your reports are from a troubled child who was shot in a terrible accident."

"Kendrick says his father is a violent drunk."

"Nadine says, 'He drinks a little, but don't every man?'"

"It's not a safe environment for my patient. How can I send Kendrick back to a home where Daddy gets drunk, makes drug deals, and plays with guns?"

Dale Stiner sighed. "Hey, I'm with you on this, but when the parents are both telling the same story, there's nothing much I can do. The authorities haven't even pressed charges against Clive for dangerous use of a firearm within the city limits."

"They should."

"The docket's too full." He pushed back his chair and set his booted feet on the floor. "Besides, I have it on authority from a beat cop that they are tightening the grip on a drug ring in Colonial Heights. They suspect Clive's going down soon."

"Meanwhile, I save a boy who shed six liters of blood, just to send him back to the father who nearly killed him?"

"Ask Nadine to let him recover at a relative's."

"Dale, a relative? His smart-ass cousin got him into this, remember?"

"My hands are tied, Dr. Weller. You know I'd initiate a custody hearing if Nadine wasn't so supportive of her husband. But the law will be on her side."

"I don't get it. How could she talk so much about trusting God to heal her son, and not trust him to protect her if she left her husband?"

Dale clasped his hands on his lap. "My take on Nadine is that she is positive about everything. She sees everything through rose-colored glasses. She believed God would help her son. She believes there's good in her husband."

It didn't feel right. I needed to talk to Nadine myself. I suspected behind that praise-the-Lord smile was a woman afraid of her husband.

THE NEXT EVENING, I returned to MCV to operate on a twelve-year-old boy who'd fallen out of a magnolia tree while trying to climb from it to his bedroom window. He fractured his left arm, broke three ribs, and split his spleen like a ripe tomato dropped from a kitchen counter. I tried all the maneuvers to save it, even wrapping it in an absorbable mesh, but I finally excised it because it wouldn't stop bleeding.

I finished at eight and checked the phone book for an address. D. and T. Kinser lived in the southwest corner of Richmond in a gated community off Midlothian Turnpike. I thought it was time to pay my patient a surprise visit. Tina and I had come a long way in our relationship, and knowing Tina, I thought she'd relish a little spontaneity.

I stopped for a frozen yogurt on my way. Chocolate, it seemed, had a way of soothing my soul. Besides, I hadn't eaten since breakfast and I needed a little time to think.

After my frozen supper, I drove thirty minutes to Tina's place.

At the gate, a large brother in a uniform looked at me with eyes that lingered too long in the name of a security inspection. "Hello, ma'am," he said, his voice deep.

"I'm here to visit Dr. Kinser."

"She expecting you?"

I flashed him a smile. "Not exactly. I'm just dropping by."

"Name?"

"Camille Weller."

He returned a smile, showing me an even row of white teeth that stood out against his dark skin. "I'll have to make a call."

He disappeared into his little booth, reappeared, and waved me on. I found her house with little trouble. A minute later, I stood on her front porch wondering what I was doing. Could I confess the terror that followed me?

I rang the doorbell and inspected the lawn. It was gardener-perfect with crisp edging and the smell of a recent cut. Tina answered the door wearing a robe drawn tight across her chest.

"I hope I'm not too out of line dropping in on you like this."

Tina smiled. "Not at all. This is really a pleasant surprise. Really."

I followed her in, admiring the contemporary flavor of the decor. A white leather couch was framed with two plants, trees I couldn't identify, but green, leafy, and full. A glass tabletop held two glasses and a wine bottle was nearby. I smiled. The wine was Mark's favorite.

"Sit, sit," she said.

I obeyed and cleared my throat.

"It's bad news, isn't it?" she began, gathering her robe even tighter under her chin. "Is it in my lymph nodes?"

I shook my head. "No!" I reached for her and squeezed her

arm. "I'm not here to give you bad news. In fact, I just talked to the pathologist about your lymph nodes. They're all negative."

"Negative," she gushed. "All negative."

I shared a smile with her before taking a deep breath. "Listen, I've never taken the initiative to visit a patient at home, but you're, well, you—" The words stuck in my throat. What was I trying to say?

She leaned forward. "What's wrong, Camille?" She'd read my anxiety.

"What am I, an open book?"

She shrugged. "Maybe half open. Or open to page one, but it's a mystery."

I picked up a little frame on the glass coffee table in front of me. It held a saying attributable to some long-dead world leader, Philo of Alexandria: *Be kind, for everyone you meet is fighting a great battle.* I looked at the woman in front of me. Since I'd met her I'd practiced seeing patients as complex humans with desires, needs, and dreams, not just cases.

I offered her a weak smile. She no longer clutched the neck of her robe. She turned her concern to me, her physician. I decided to let down. "There's been something I need to share." I halted.

She looked at me and stayed quiet.

"Something I haven't wanted to share with a professional. Something I haven't wanted to share with you especially because you were my patient."

She twisted her mouth like she tasted lemon candy. "I'm not following you."

"Something is haunting me. Haunting my mind," I clarified, already wishing I'd chosen a different word to describe my feelings. I held my hands out, palms up. "Kara called them panic attacks." I looked up. "She wanted me to see you." I hesitated. "You know, professionally."

She nodded and stayed quiet. I could see she was good at drawing her patients out. She didn't interrupt.

"I've never seen a psychiatrist." I tapped my leg nervously. "I guess you know from our talks that surgeons aren't so quick to ask for help, you know . . . emotionally. We take pride in handling things ourselves."

She nodded again.

I glared at her for a moment. *Come on, Tina, say something.*

"Anyway, Kara died. So now I feel guilty on top of all the other anxieties. I've never been like this before. Little things seem to set me off. The terror comes at me and I feel so out of control because it comes at me from nowhere and now I find myself just being panicky about being panicky and—"

She held up her hand. "Whoa, Camille." She smiled and clasped my hands in hers.

My speech stuck in my throat, but the cork was out of my bottle of tears. I felt the moisture on my cheeks, but Tina had a lock on my hands and I couldn't wipe the tears away. I had been afraid of this. I admitted I had a problem, and that very act broke the top off an emotional volcano.

In a moment, I pulled my hand away and wiped my cheeks with my palm. "I'm finally at the place professionally that I've been striving toward for so many years and now it's all threatened by this . . ." I didn't have the word to explain what I felt, so I just circled my hand in the air as my voice choked up again. "I'm sorry."

"Don't be," she responded, pulling a tissue from a big pocket in her robe.

"Do you think you can help me?" I hesitated. "Will it matter that I'm *your* doctor?"

"Not a bit." She smiled. "It will make it easier for both of us. We already have the basis for a great professional relationship." She paused and took my hand again. "Trust," she whispered. "And *yes*, I can help you."

Suddenly, I wanted to put my arms around her and sob. I wanted to blubber and tell her everything right then, but somehow I held back and just smiled. She could help me. She'd said it with enough confidence that I drank it in like cold water on a Richmond summer day. I curled my fingers around it and wouldn't let go. For the first time in weeks I recognized what I'd let slip away, something I'd always kept in front of me as I trained, but dropped sometime in my first days as a real surgeon. Hope.

Then as abruptly as the hope had dropped in on my heart, Tina lifted her hand to my shoulder and spoke the words softly into my ear. I knew they were coming and started to flinch before she had them out: "Everything's gonna be all right."

24

TINA SET MY first official visit as a patient for ten days later. She needed time to heal and get back on the job.

In the meantime, the only assignment she'd given me was to summon the courage to remember. Whatever horror had come my way in the past was over. I was in a safe place now, she said. Whatever evil surfaced couldn't hurt me in the here and now.

So I spent time trying to remember Africa. I thought about my mother, staring at her picture that I carried in my wallet. She loved me. I remembered her spending hours braiding my hair, adorning rows of woven hair with small beads, telling me I was a queen. I remember eating finger bananas and mangos, cabbage and stew. These were comforting memories. I looked at my beautiful mother and felt profound loss. I wished she could see me now.

I remembered the small, rock-block house with a corrugated tin roof we called home. I remembered heat, the unforgiving sun of the Congo, deeply rutted roads that were crusty-dry or river-wet depending on the rains. I remembered walking the hospital grounds, playing with Tumi, and Sunday services that lasted long into the afternoon. I remembered sneaking down to the river and sitting on the bank, even though my mother warned me about crocodiles.

Remembering my father was the hardest part of my assignment. There was something dark and hurtful about my recollections of him. Whenever I thought of him I remembered Tumi's growl. I didn't understand the link. Every time I consciously brought my father to mind, he seemed to drag along oppressive emotions, invisible chains that sought to link me to a heavy dread. He was not in clear focus yet, but he was not the father that I'd built in my fantasies.

It was a week into my focus on the Dark Continent of my past when I finally vocalized a feeling I'd carried around with me for a long time.

It happened on a joyful day for Nadine Solomon. We had moved Kendrick to a regular ward bed seven days before. He'd continued improving every day, and it was time to push him from the nest and see if he could fly at home. Each of those seven days I'd been dragging my heels, reluctant to send him back to a troubled and possibly dangerous home. But every time I brought up my concerns to Nadine, she'd just say that I needn't worry. Her husband wasn't a perfect man, but she could take care of herself and her son with the Lord's help.

The only other time I caught Kendrick without his mother, he pleaded with me to allow him to stay. "Take me home with you," he said, his eyes dead serious.

My heart tore. Part of me wanted to do just that. I put my hand on his shoulder and smiled in an attempt to lighten the mood as his mother appeared in the doorway. "I'm always here," I whispered as Nadine walked in. "Besides, my house is no fun."

So, against a nagging check in my spirit, I decided to discharge him the following day. Mom wanted him home, and if Dale Stiner said it was OK, I had no other recourse. But that wouldn't make me stop worrying about my six-liter boy.

In the hall outside his room, Ellis shook his head in amazement. "I thought he was a TOBAS for sure."

I nodded and smiled, in spite of my dislike for the acronym he used. Crass surgical residents often classified hopeless cases as

"Take out Back and Shoot." They pronounced it "toe-bass," like the fish.

Nadine appeared in Kendrick's doorway and held her arms wide. I surrendered to the hug she wanted to give me. "My boy goin' home's the picture of the father's love you needed, isn't it, Dr. Weller?"

"A father's love isn't something I'm familiar with." I looked at Kendrick. From what he'd told me, he wasn't familiar with it either.

Nadine stepped back, held me at arms' length, and stared.

"I'm an orphan, Mrs. Solomon. And all I remember of my father brings me pain." I shook my head. "I don't know that he loved me at all."

My whole resident and student team fell quiet. They looked at the floor, the ceiling, anywhere but at me. It was as if I was sharing something so personal, so painful, it was akin to admitting I had a yeast infection.

Nadine, however, didn't flinch. "Ain' nothin' too hard for God," she said, drawing me back into her arms. "God showed you he can answer prayers by raisin' up my boy." She squeezed my chest while my eyes made contact with Ellis, who obviously enjoyed seeing me at the mercy of this love machine. Nadine continued, "He's going to show you, child."

As Nadine released me, I felt my cheeks blush. I should have kept my mouth shut. If my past hadn't been on my mind so much lately, I think I'd have maintained the standard practice of keeping my private life shielded in mystery.

I nodded at Mrs. Solomon. I was the most educated woman in the crowd, yet I felt like a first-grader. In her simple way, I knew Mrs. Solomon believed she was dispensing wisdom like the old king whose name she bore.

She quieted her voice and spoke directly to me. "Kendrick don't have a good earthly example of the way a father should be either," she said, patting my hand. "But God can still show him his love, and he can show you, too."

I tried to smile, and after a moment of eye contact with Nadine, I slipped away with my team. I gave instructions to the intern whose job it would be to discharge Kendrick. "I want to see him in my clinic next Thursday. Send him home with a prescription for enough antibiotic so he can finish treatment for his pneumonia."

My team's last patient was Jeremy Douglass, the boy who'd fallen out of the magnolia tree. He, too, was ready for discharge. "I made something for you," he said, handing me a pencil drawing of a Boston Red Sox baseball cap. I'd been giving him grief because he was a Yankees fan.

I tousled his blond bangs. "Thanks. Now I know you have some style."

He beamed. I looked at his mom. "How's he eating?"

"He eats everything they bring him."

"Good." I looked at my second intern. "Discharge him. Bring him back to my clinic in two weeks."

I glanced back at Jeremy when I reached the doorway. "And as for you, whenever you want to get in your house for the next six weeks, use the front door, not the second-floor window."

He smiled.

So did I.

If only my own problems could be fixed so easily.

TWO DAYS LATER Tina suggested I bring whatever supplies I needed for her post-op visit to her office for my first therapy session. I think it was her way of helping me feel a sense of control over my situation.

I walked slowly through the halls of the hospital to her office, still unsure, in spite of all the talk, that I was going to be able to follow through and find the peace of mind I needed. A scalpel's work is crisp, mechanical, results exact, understood as a physical rearrangement or removal of tissue. Medicine was like surgery in my mind, only the scalpels were smaller, ingested to do their work in the cells, molecule reshaping molecule, killing an invading bacteria or modifying the body's response to injury. These were the things that I lived by. The work of psychiatry, plumbing the depths of the human soul, scared me because I couldn't explain the molecular basis for mood, memory, or in my case, terror.

So after today, I would officially be "in therapy." I'd always hated the term as it'd floated past me in social settings. It seemed a preppy phrase for rich women coming to grip with lives and relationships that hadn't lived up to their expectations. I'd heard it from some of the attendings' wives as they chatted at department Christmas parties, referring to being "in therapy" as if it were a rite of passage. I'd always listened with a private scorn, an orphan overhearing the whining of privileged white women with nothing better to do than explore their inner child or blame their fathers for the rage they felt toward Y chromosomes.

Why had we reserved that stupid phrase for people in counseling? Weren't all my patients "in therapy"? It seemed to me that the term itself was an attempt to give credence to theory based less on science than on the touchy-feely hypotheses of men who found the discipline of double-blind studies abhorrent.

Part of me wanted to cancel the whole deal, return to the ER or my office, where I could concentrate on things I understood. But I'd waded in too deep to turn back to shore. I'd told Tina and Mark that I'd do it. I'd even promised Kara in the week after she died that I'd follow through. But now I wished I hadn't whispered the stupid promise to the ceiling in my sorrow.

I'd done so well so far. I was a surgeon, the first woman to lead a trauma service at a busy Southeastern university hospital. I could handle a few bad dreams on my own. I—

I looked up. My feet had taken me to the door of the psychiatry department. I sighed. I wished I were wearing sunglasses.

I took a deep breath and walked to the receptionist. She said my name before I could speak. "Dr. Weller? Right this way," she said, standing. "Dr. Kinser is expecting you."

The secretary appeared twenty, maybe twenty-five max. She was better dressed than the receptionist we had in the surgery department. Maybe money flowing to the psychiatry department was better than I knew. "Wow, our patients always have to wait."

The receptionist kept her voice low. "Dr. Kinser never lets her physician private patients wait in the waiting room."

Oh good, I thought. I'm just a number in the crowd. I'm not sure if I'm supposed to feel better or worse. Tina was treating the whole staff.

The receptionist, wearing a name tag that labeled her "Kerri," opened the door to Dr. Kinser's office. "You can wait for her in here. She'll be right in."

"Right in" turned out to be fifteen minutes. But in that time, I got to know Tina from a whole new angle.

The office was a blend of academia and home. Deeply stained bookshelves behind a small desk held bound psychiatry periodicals. The desk was empty, save for a banker's lamp—nothing like mine, which overflowed with works in progress. Around the room were more shelves containing less rigorous fare. Novels, plants, and pictures of friends dominated, rimming a white carpet and a setting of overstuffed, brown leather furniture. The office was big enough for a couch, two chairs, and a stereo stack. I searched the room for speakers and saw them hanging from the ceiling in opposite diagonal corners. Centered on the one wall without bookshelves was a seascape oil painting. Smaller pictures, double-matted and framed with antiqued wood, complemented the larger one. The wall itself was sponge-painted in blue hues so evenly that at first I thought it was wallpaper, but when I picked at the wall with my fingernail it proved to be authentic.

Conspicuous by its absence was the ego wall—the display of diplomas and awards that was common fare in academic surgery. I liked the atmosphere. I didn't miss the certification of her credentials. I knew Tina had them. Better for them to catch dust in some closet than to cover the artsy sponge-painting.

I settled into one of the leather chairs and began to dream about changing my own office. This was nice, I thought. I could be at home in an office with a woman's touch. I smiled. I'd spent so much time trying to fit in with the guys that my office looked just like theirs. A small gold-colored wood frame sat on a shelf at eye level. I leaned forward and squinted to read the Old English font, a saying attributed to Dr. Francis Peabody, 1927: *The secret of the care of the patient is in caring for the patient.* The place was so Tina, just like her home, adorned with little sayings that helped frame her existence.

She entered quietly, and laid a stethoscope on the coffee table in front of me. "Sorry I'm late."

The instrument took me by surprise. She must have followed my eyes to it.

"Yes, psychiatrists use stethoscopes, Camille. In fact I want to schedule a complete physical exam as part of your workup. There are many emotional difficulties that are rooted in physical problems, ones we can easily define. Anxiety, for example, can be the presenting complaint for hyperthyroidism, Cushing's disease, pheochromocytoma, or hypercalcemia. Depression can be the first symptom of hypothyroidism. I'll have you talk to my receptionist on your way out. I do my own physical examinations and I want you on my schedule."

I nodded obediently. She certainly was taking charge. That was good. I liked that.

She walked to the stereo and pushed a button. A tenor saxophone lilted through the system. "Is jazz OK?"

I cleared my throat. "Sure."

She disappeared through the door again, only to return a few moments later carrying a tea serving for two. She set it on the table in front of me. "I have a friend from East Africa," she explained. "She taught me how to make authentic chai. It may not be exactly what you drank in the Congo, but I thought it might be close."

"Thanks." I reached for a cup steaming with tea steeped in milk. I sipped the liquid and held it in my mouth, letting my tongue savor the warm, sweet taste. "It's been a long, long time since I drank tea this way."

"Good," she said. "I thought it might help stir up some memories that may give us some insight. Taste and smell have powerful links to our memory and emotions."

I felt nervous. I didn't like being the focus of attention in this way. Examine my performance in surgery, yes. Examine the deep recesses of my past and motives, no.

"Camille, let me assure you, like I did during your visit to my house, that whatever has been causing your panic attacks can be dealt with. If it is something from your past, something you've repressed for some reason, remembering can be painful." She picked up her own cup of tea. "But whatever happened in the past, *if* something bad happened to you, or was done to you, that event is long gone. If a person hurt you, they are long gone. If Africa held a situation for you that set up your harm, it is far, far away. Memories can hurt you only if you don't face them, put them in proper context, learn from them, and move on. Memories can haunt you only if you let them."

I felt timid, nothing like the control I felt when I was in the OR with someone's intestines in front of me. I found myself nodding quickly, partly from agreement, and partly because I wanted to get the process over as quickly as possible.

She set down her tea and took my hand. "Are you with me? You are in a safe place now. You are a long way from the pain that may be precipitating your anxieties."

"OK."

"But first," she said, "I want you to look under my arm. I think I'm accumulating fluid or something."

I smiled. Good. Something I could control.

"Let's go next door to an exam room."

I picked up my little bag that I'd packed with alcohol swabs, gauze, tape, and a syringe and needles. I was ready for this. Post-op lymph collections were very common after axillary dissection.

In the exam room, Tina unsnapped her brassiere and slipped off her top. I focused first on the breast. The scar felt firm, normal for her stage. There was no redness, no drainage. She raised her left arm to ninety degrees and stopped.

"Easy now," I said. "How high can you go?"

She winced and raised it another inch.

I smiled. "We can do better than that." I put my hand out to the side until my fingers touched the wall. I started walking my index and long fingers up the wall like two little legs. "Do it with me," I coached.

She put her arm out to the side and extended her fingers like mine.

"OK," I said. "Walk up slowly until you feel pain from the scar stretching. Then stop and rest. Then go two more tiny steps."

She followed my instructions, but bent sideways at the waist away from the wall to make the last two finger steps.

I laughed with her. "You're cheating." I gently coaxed her back to upright with my other hand. "The whole idea is to increase the angle between your left arm and your chest."

"It's sore."

"You've got some fluid here," I said, palpating the area beneath her axillary incision. "I'll draw it off and you will feel better."

"OK."

"I want you working hard with the exercises. It will keep you from having problems down the road with reduced mobility."

She nodded. I smiled again because it was so nice not to slow down to explain everything to a patient, for a change. I turned to my leather case and removed an alcohol swab, a 60cc syringe, and a 20-gauge needle. "You'd better sit for this."

I swabbed the area just inferior to her axillary scar knowing it would be unlikely that she would feel a needle prick there because of normal post-operative numbness. I swiftly passed the needle through the skin into the swollen area under her arm and was rewarded by a flash of deep yellow liquid. I emptied two syringes of the fluid, removed the needle, and held pressure with a small gauze. "All done."

She looked down and examined the area with her right hand. "Feels better already."

I put a Band-Aid over the puncture site and stood outside while she dressed. In a moment, Tina joined me in the hall and held her hand up toward the door to her office. "Your turn."

We sat opposite each other on the leather furniture and I picked up my tea, which was still warm. I thought Tina had planned it all this way. She had wanted me to see her first, to honor me with her ongoing confidence as her surgeon. Now, I had to change hats.

Personally, I'd rather be the caregiver. I swished the tea in my mouth and swallowed slowly, as if my throat refused to cooperate.

She picked up a yellow legal pad and a silver ballpoint pen. "Tell me about the very first time you had an experience of un-controlled anxiety." She paused. "At my house, I believe you said Kara called it a panic attack."

Here goes.

I took a deep breath.

I was in therapy.

"My aunt Jeanine said I had nightmares for months after arriving here from the Congo. I don't remember. All I know is what she told me. My parents were killed by the rebels during the Simba rebellion."

"Nightmares?"

I nodded. "She said I'd wake up screaming. I was pretty much OK during the day, but nighttime was bad."

"What happened?"

I shrugged. "They disappeared with time, I guess. My aunt took the shove-it-under-the-carpet approach. Discussions about the Congo became pretty much off-limits. I think she resented my father for dumping me on her. My aunt wasn't silent about her dislike for my father. She said he was an idealistic fool who got himself killed so he could be a hero for Jesus."

"She told you that?"

"Not when I was a child. That was later. In college, when I started asking questions about him."

"The nightmares lasted . . . ?"

"A few months, I guess." I fidgeted with my empty teacup.

Tina scribbled notes. "You were an orphan. Your aunt took care of you?"

"I came to live with Aunt Jeanine in Alabama when I was ten. I started school there, but things didn't really work out, so she put me in a prep school in Boston."

"Things didn't work out . . . ?" Again she drew out the question for me to continue.

I shrugged. "Kids in Alabama can be cruel to little black nigger girls." I hated the N-word, but that's what they had called me. It didn't matter that my father was white. Any African blood was enough to contaminate me in their minds.

She nodded. "How was prep school? A better experience?"

"Mostly my days in Boston were great. Going to school there opened a lot of doors for me."

My face must have betrayed me. Tina prodded again. "But? You said 'mostly.'"

"I had nightmares again for a while after starting school there, but after a few months, they seemed to fade." I shrugged and looked back at Tina's searching eyes. "I've had a few since, a few times a year, I guess."

"What did you do?"

"Do?"

"How did you deal with them?"

I winced. "Pretty much the Aunt Jeanine approach, I guess. I ignored them, worked harder, and concentrated on my goals. When I focus on the dreams, I get anxious." I shrugged. "So I don't."

"What happened the first time you had a full-blown panic attack? What were the circumstances? If you can remember, tell me what was happening that day." She paused and sipped her tea. "You've only had them since becoming an attending surgeon?"

"Right. Is there a connection?" I asked, wondering if my assumptions were correct.

"Maybe. You're under tremendous stress as a trauma attending. The buck stops with you now, not with anyone else. Times of increased stress can do funny things to our psyche. Sometimes old things that we've repressed come out under stress."

I nodded.

She picked up her pen.

"My first day as a surgery attending, I made a big save. A kid came in with multiple gunshot wounds. He almost bled to death, but we brought him back." I smiled at the memory. "We have an informal prestigious group in surgery called the Six-Liter Club. You become a member when a patient sheds six liters of blood during a case, and you're still able to save them. I joined the club on the first day."

"That's good, right?"

"I thought so. I figured the guys would respect me for it. But Gilles rebuked me in front of everyone just because I didn't call for help during such a big case."

"Did you panic there in front of Gilles?"

"No. I walked away. I went out to dinner with a friend to rehash my day. It was raining while I was driving home and I hit a dog. The dog died in front of me." I paused as the painful memory replayed. "The dog reminded me of Tumi. That was the name of my dog in the Congo. It was the first sensation of déjà vu, I think. Something about seeing that gasping, dying dog kind of freaked me out. I got real anxious, but I was able to push it out of my mind until I got home."

"What happened there?"

"I was standing at the sink. Mar—uh, my boyfriend came up to me from behind. He wrapped his arms around me and started kissing me." I looked at her. "Is this too much detail?"

"No. I want to know exactly what was happening when you had your first attack."

"OK. So then he whispered a phrase in my ear. It's just a little phrase, so common."

"Don't tell me. 'Everything's gonna be all right.'"

"Exactly. But how—"

"I saw the fear in your eyes the other night when I said it to you."

"That's it. That's all he said. My heart started racing. I thought for a minute that I was having a heart attack or something. I was hyperventilating. The whole thing seems quite stupid now. I can say the phrase and it means nothing. 'Everything's gonna be all right.'"

"But the setting was that his arms were around you, and he whispered in your ear."

"That's right."

"Has anyone ever said that to you before?"

"It's such a common phrase. I'm sure they must have."

"Has anyone ever held you like that? Kissed you and whispered that phrase?"

I closed my eyes. I felt my chest tightening again.

Tina spoke to me softly, "You are safe here, Camille. A memory cannot hurt you."

"I think so." I shifted in my seat. "I'm not sure."

I closed my eyes tight, not wanting to say the words. Tina said nothing. Waiting for me to offer what I would.

I took a deep breath and dove in. "Maybe my father."

"What makes you say that?"

"Because several times since that night, the nightmares have returned. I wake up conscious of a man holding me, whispering to me. And I'm afraid."

"What makes you think it was your father?"

"Something I can't pinpoint. A feeling."

"Trust your instinct. Does the man say anything else to you?"

"I don't know. I can't remember."

"Does talking about this make you anxious?"

I looked at the teacup, which I held upside down. I let go a nervous laugh. "Yes."

"Good," she said, smiling. "Then we're scratching the right itch."

25

THE NIGHT AFTER Mr. Karanja was killed by the Simbas I listened to my parents' whispers at their bedroom door. My mother actually got louder than usual so I could have probably heard them all the way from my bed, but I was up and my bedroom was too hot. So I knelt in the hall and listened.

My mother was crying. "We have to go, Jack. At least let me take Camille. We will use Dr. Rebert's canoe. We can cross the river and—"

"You cannot take Camille!" His voice was hushed. "Her skin is a curse. They will know she has the white man's blood."

I looked down at my arms. I wasn't white, more like the color of the crust on the bread when Mommy takes it out of the oven.

I started to feel like crying, but no tears would form. I didn't understand. My skin was a curse?

"I'm afraid for her here. I've heard of the evil the Simba soldiers commit when they go on rampages through the villages."

I heard my father's sigh. "They will leave her alone here. Because of me. I've helped their soldiers."

"But I have seen how they look at her. They are captivated, Jack."

"God will protect us," he said. "Just keep her inside."

THE NEXT DAY, after I'd spent two hours helping Ellis snip adhesions in a patient with a bowel obstruction, I retreated to my desk only to find a summons to the chairman's office. The hand-scratched sticky note was plastered to my door where I, and the rest of the department, could see. It was brief: *See me*. The signature was recognizable as a *G* followed by a line with two dots that looked more like hash marks.

As I was still in my scrubs, and wearing a white lab coat, I returned to the OR to change. Gilles was a stickler about wearing street clothes outside the OR for professionalism. Although many residents and attendings wore scrubs up on the wards, more formal attire was advisable for a meeting with the boss. I spent an extra few minutes applying fresh lipstick and eyeliner, the bare essentials for an appointment with Gilles.

As I passed Libby, Mr. Gilles's young secretary, I raised my eyebrows in a silent question. She nodded and pressed an intercom. "Dr. Gilles? Dr. Weller is here to see you."

Libby met my gaze as we heard the snap reply from the boss: "Send her in."

Libby seemed to be trying not to frown. Her neck muscles were tense, like small cords wrinkling her skin. "Have fun," she whispered.

I pushed the door open to see Dr. Gilles running his hand through his thinning hair. He took a deep breath and blew it out through pursed lips.

Not a good sign.

He pointed to a chair. "Morning, Camille. Have a seat."

I tried nonchalance. Inside, I was uneasy. "What's up?"

He sighed again. "Tina Kinser," he responded bluntly. "Her husband called me again this morning. He's quite upset."

"Upset?"

"Tina is refusing to talk to him. She's locked him out of their home."

I nodded knowingly.

"And he's a bit fixated on you."

"Me?"

He shook his head and winced. "Did you really have security throw him out of the hospital?"

"Is that what he said?"

"Basically."

"It's not true," I responded. "But he was threatening to physically stop the transporter from taking his wife into the OR." I shrugged. "The security boys came up and stood by in case things got out of hand, but once ol' Dan saw them, he let us go."

"I've known Dan for a long time. He can be bullheaded."

"Why are you telling me this?"

"It's just that, well—" He halted and looked up from his desk and stared at me with those piercing eyes. "You did a lumpectomy, not a mastectomy."

"Yes." My throat tightened.

"Dan asked me what I thought Tina needed." He held his hand in the air. "I answered him honestly. I told him what the current standard is: mastectomy."

"The decision was between Tina and me."

"I know, I know, but Dan can be a bit of a pitbull. He's completely out of control in his relationship with Tina. She's cut him out of communication altogether, so he's riled up about that. Now he's fixated on caring for her from a distance. He wants some control back in his relationship, so I think this is how he's attempting to do it."

"What is he doing?"

"Not much. Yet. Mostly he's standing back and criticizing the way his wife is being cared for."

"What else would he do?"

"He's threatening a lawsuit, but I don't think he'll get too far. His wife would have to be the one to initiate such foolery."

"I'm sorry that you've had to get into the middle of this." I shifted in my seat. The last thing I wanted was to be a thorn in his side, but so far, I wasn't being the good little toe-the-line department member he'd anticipated.

"If he calls again, I'll try to put a damper on him." He pushed his chair away from his desk. "I want you to put Tina's case on for discussion for the morbidity and mortality conference this week."

Inwardly, I groaned. The M and M conference was a weekly rehashing of surgical mistakes. It was supposed to be a benign learning event, but to the residents who presented the problems, it felt malignant. "But there were no complications."

"It's a learning case." He paused. "I told you that you would have to defend your decision, Camille."

I nodded. I'd seen this conference for the past six years as a resident. I'd seen Dr. Gilles get red-in-the-face mad as he laid a resident or a junior attending bare for preventable complications.

"I'll be ready, sir."

"You'd better." His expression was dead serious. "I really wish you'd follow established protocols. It doesn't look good on your record."

"Established protocols don't always take everything into account."

"Save it for the conference, Camille. You know how it works."

I nodded. "Sure." I turned and left.

Dr. Gilles could be compassionate and encouraging, yet demanding and furious. His eyes warmed me . . . and scared me.

Eyes just like my father's. Maybe that's why I love him . . . and hate him.

I walked away with a familiar sense of foreboding. Something just beyond the edge of my mind. Teasing me. Threatening.

I shook away the thought. Silly me. It was only because I'd been concentrating on these issues that they nipped at my heels. *Every lioness is a bit conflicted over the dominant male in the herd. Isn't she?*

FROM ELEVEN TO twelve, I gave a lecture to the first-year medical students, a canned talk on chest trauma that I'd given for the past three years. The subject intrigued me because such trauma could be deadly so fast, and a save was very rewarding. The lecture was part of their education on emergency medicine, an attempt to dangle a carrot in front of the new medical students, and probably the most practical information they had received in the midst of an ocean of biochemistry, pharmacology, physiology, and anatomy.

As I left the auditorium in Sanger Hall, I parted a group of students fresh from the cadaver lab. The aroma of formaldehyde clung to their clothes and identified them as M-1s, MCV lingo for first-year med students.

On my way back to my office, I strolled through the ER. As the trauma attending on call, I liked to keep my finger on the pulse of activity in the pit. Things were quiet from my standpoint. The trauma bays were empty. Two patients were sleeping off a drunk, their IV bags yellow from the added B vitamins they neglected in their daily pursuit of liquid refreshment. As I passed a stretcher, I heard my name.

"Dr. Weller."

I looked to see Joel Bryan. He sat beside a young girl in a hospital gown. His smile was perfect. Men of the cloth weren't supposed to look this heavenly. I understood why Kara was apparently interested. "Hi," I said, extending my hand. "What brings you to our turf?"

He leaned his head toward the girl beside him. "Christy here is one of the St. Giles kids. When they're here, I'm here."

He followed me away from the bedside a few steps before asking, "How are *you* doing? I know you were close to Kara Schuller."

"She was a good friend," I said. "The best."

"She told me you are a BoSox fan."

"Is that OK?"

"You must be a woman with great faith."

I laughed.

He shrugged.

Our eyes met for a moment before he looked away. Body language for attraction, I thought.

I cleared my throat. "I got a letter from the medical examiner's office this week. About Kara."

He sobered. "Oh."

"Kara and I had been up crying in our beer," I said. "Actually, I was doing the cryin' and she the encouraging. We both drank too much that night."

His eyes seemed to search my face. This time, I looked away, another sure sign of attraction.

"She got sick to her stomach, Joel. She vomited, but was too intoxicated to keep from sucking it into her lungs."

He wrinkled his nose.

He probably already knew most of this. But I needed to say it. I looked at the top of my shoes. "It was my fault. I should have heard her, but I was passed out, dead to the world."

Joel stayed quiet, listening.

"The sad fact is, I'd been friends with Kara long enough to know where she was weak. I knew I should have insisted that she not take a drink. I shouldn't have been drinking so I could have heard her when she got in trouble."

My shoes needed polish. I scuffed them along the linoleum floor. "Listen, I'm sorry to unload on you. I hate it when people show me their moles in the checkout line at the grocery store. So here I am, dumping my guilt off on a preacher."

He smiled. "It's fine. Really."

"I . . . I don't really know you. I shouldn't—"

"It's OK. I'm used to it." He smiled. Man, what a beautiful smile.

He reached for my hand. "Too often I live my life by the 'if onlys.'" He shook his head. "It makes for a miserable time."

"So what's your answer?"

"I have a father who is in charge of everything. And he forgives my failures."

I nodded as though I agreed. I wished I did, but the father thing tended to trip me up. I pointed my head toward the curtain. "You'd better get back."

He was still holding my hand. He gave me a little squeeze. "Forgive yourself, Camille. You never intended Kara any harm." He let his hand slip off mine.

I felt a rush a faithful woman shouldn't feel. I smiled with my lips and my heart. "Thanks."

Kendrick rested on a couch in the den of the Solomon house downtown. He kept one eye on his comic book and one eye on Clive, who slurped Budweiser and stared at the TV. It was there Kendrick formulated a plan. His mother didn't seem to get it, so he was going to have to be the one to protect them from this monster he knew as "Father."

Clive grunted, "Get me another beer." It wasn't a request. Kendrick had lived with his father long enough to know the consequences of ignoring his demands.

Kendrick sat up slowly, testing for pain in his abdomen. Easy, he told himself. Every day was a little better. Hopefully Dr. Weller would let him start exercising soon. He was just getting old enough to have a good abdominal six-pack when surgery ruined his workout routine.

He plodded from the couch to the refrigerator, where he retrieved two Budweiser beers. He glanced back at the den, where the television blared. Unless his father needed to relieve himself, he wouldn't stir until unconsciousness carried him away.

Kendrick opened a small medicine container, the strong painkiller Dr. Weller had prescribed. How many would it take? Too many would be a disaster. Too few, and his plan would fail. He popped the tab on the first Budweiser, then opened a red capsule, emptying its contents into the beer. Foam bubbled from the beer can. He sniffed the can and withdrew at the smell of the bitter mixture. He waited until the foam disappeared, then emptied the contents of three more capsules into the beer. He shoved the empty capsule halves into his pocket. Then he pulled back the tab on the second beer walked back to his father's side, handed him the beer, and set the tainted can on a table a few feet away.

Clive looked at the second beer and nodded. "Smart boy."

Kendrick eased back onto the couch and prayed his father would be too drunk to notice a difference in the taste of the next brew.

TINA PULLED INTO the driveway and looked over to see Dan sitting on the front steps. She opened the garage door, hoping to slip in before he came around, but he was too quick. He stepped into the garage behind her car just as she pressed the button to lower the door.

She stepped outside her car.

"Hi, Tina."

"You aren't supposed to be here."

"This is our house, remember?"

"I'd appreciate it if you'd leave." She pressed the button to raise the garage door.

"I want to talk. You can't just end our relationship and not talk to me."

"I need space. Time alone to think."

"Or time with your new boyfriend?"

She shut her door and stepped away from Dan to put the car between them. "How did you—"

"I asked Ms. Trenton, across the street." He sighed. "I never thought I'd stoop to talking to the neighborhood gossip to find out what's happening with my own wife."

"Dan, we're not—"

"Who is he, one of your residents? A medical student, perhaps?"

"That's none of your business."

"Tina, I still care about you. About us."

She reached for the door to the house. "Our relationship died a long time ago, Dan. Take joy in what we had." She opened the door. "But it's over. Now go away."

"Can't we talk about it?"

She sighed. "Talk to my attorney."

"I need to talk to you."

"I don't want to do this. Not now. We need time away from each other, Dan." She held up her hands. "We were stagnate, Dan. We're not good for each other anymore."

"We made mistakes. I made mistakes, Tina. Don't throw this away."

"I don't love you anymore."

He hung his head. "We can get some help. Lots of couples go through low times."

"I don't want help. I want out."

Dan took a step toward her. Tina jumped into the house and slammed the door, locking it as Dan turned the knob.

"Tina! Don't shut me out. I'll just keep calling!"

She heard a thump on the door.

"Tina, open up. Just talk to me!"

Tina laid her hand against the door. She felt the door move with the sound of two more thumps. "Dan, stop it. Dan, you're scaring me!"

"Tina, don't act like this. You don't need to be afraid."

"I'll call the police and tell them you've forced your way into my garage."

"Tina, just tell me how you are. Just tell me about your cancer." He paused as his voice cracked. "Just tell me you're going to be OK."

She listened for a quiet moment as she stared at the door. Was he really concerned?

She opened the door and looked at him. He made no attempt to enter. It was the first time she noticed he was wearing running shoes along with a shirt and tie. She wanted to roll her eyes. He dressed like an orphan. "I'll give you five minutes."

He nodded and walked in behind her.

She pointed to the kitchen chairs. "You might as well sit down," she said. She sat opposite him. "I've started radiation treatments."

"Does it hurt?"

"It's painless. I lay on a special table while they shoot me with X-rays."

"Will you be OK?"

"Probably. I saw a medical oncologist today. They want me to take some chemotherapy."

"Oh God," he said, gripping the table. "Do whatever they suggest, Tina. You've got to fight this thing."

"I am fighting."

"Why didn't you tell me?"

"I didn't want you to stay with me because of cancer."

His eyes narrowed. He always did that when he didn't understand.

"I didn't want your sympathy."

"This would be easier to fight together."

"I'm OK."

He spoke softly, his voice edged with pain. "You have all the help you need."

"Dan," she said. "I'm really sorry."

His body slumped. He got up from the chair and walked to

the door before turning around. "The stupidest thing I ever did was taking what we had for granted."

"And sleeping with Mary Newbie."

He gaze was fixed on the carpet. "I was such a fool."

She wasn't going to disagree. "We had some good times, Dan. Let's focus on that. Maybe this split won't be so painful that way." She took a step toward him. "We need to move on, Dan."

His eyes pleaded with her. "How about forgiveness?"

She opened the door for him. "It's too late for that."

"Let's talk to a counselor. We can make a fresh start."

She cocked her head. "A fresh start?"

I'm making one, she thought, without you.

AT MY PLACE that evening, Mark and I ate Chinese takeout and talked about how our days had been. I told him about working with Ellis, and my fears that he'd need extra time in the program before his skills could be unleashed safely on an unsuspecting public. Mark talked about sick kids and complained about needing to take extra call while one of the residents below him was on vacation. It wasn't until we were finishing the last bit of shrimp lo mein that I broached the subject of visiting Kendrick. I lifted a shrimp with my chopsticks and popped it in my mouth. I smiled at Mark, hoping he'd be warm to my suggestion.

Mark rolled his eyes and stabbed a shrimp with his fork. "Why do you insist on using those things?"

"I'm a surgeon. It's good dexterity practice." I cleared my throat. "Let's go see Kendrick."

He looked at me for a moment, perhaps questioning my sanity. "You've discharged him, Camille. Let it rest. Your responsibility is over."

I pulled my hand over my hair. "It's just a visit. I want to check on him, see how he's doing."

"You're losing your emotional distance."

"And that's a problem?"

He sighed. "You really care about this kid, don't you?"

I hesitated before answering. *Why do I care? Is it pride in my six-liter save? Is it guilt for discharging him to a troubled home? Or do I really care?*

I knew the answer.

I was changing. Kendrick had started out as my ticket into the club but ended up with a grip on my heartstrings. I wanted to be different. I didn't want to treat illnesses anymore. I wanted to treat people. "I . . . I just want to see how he's doing, OK?"

Mark took my hand. "You know what I think?"

I shook my head.

"I think some mothering instinct has kicked in since you lost Kara. Women who experience significant losses often want children. It's their way of finding connections with people who love them."

I smiled to soften my reply. "I think you're full of psychological bull." He smiled at my sudden brazenness as I continued, "I didn't say I wanted to have children. I said I wanted to visit a teenage boy, a patient."

He pointed at me. "You're changing, Camille. You were looking at infant clothes at Thalheimer's. Now you want to do a pediatric home visit. You tell me. Is it the same urge?"

"No."

He looked away. Maybe he didn't believe me. Maybe I didn't either. "Where is the emotionally distant surgeon I once knew?"

"I'm going. Are you in or out?"

"If it's the only way to spend time with you, I'm in."

I kissed his cheek as I picked up my car keys. "I knew you'd see it my way."

KENDRICK WATCHED AND waited until his father's breathing was deep and regular before he carefully unclipped Clive's key ring from his belt. Then with a swiftness that belied his recent surgery, he slipped down the hall and into his parents' bedroom. He pulled open the closet door and unlocked the metal filing cabinet. He slid open the top drawer. There it was, in the back, in a Nike shoe box.

Kendrick lifted the nine-millimeter pistol from its hiding place and weighed it in his hand. He admired the shine and held it up to see his reflection. *Dad will never torture me again.* He slid the drawer shut, locked it, and closed the closet door.

He tiptoed up the hallway listening to Clive's snoring. He snapped a loaded clip into place and imagined what it must feel like to fire. He held it up at arm's length and sighted down the barrel.

26

"K ENDRICK?"

I rapped my knuckles on the door again.

The door opened against a chain lock. Kendrick's face appeared. "Dr. Weller?"

The door shut and opened again without the chain.

"Hi, Kendrick. I stopped by to check up on you."

He stood framed by the doorway to the little house and stared.

I wasn't sure what to say. He didn't seem too interested in inviting me in. I nodded my head toward Mark. "This is Mark Lawson. He's a pediatrician." That sounded stupid. Too formal. "A friend."

"Oh." He glanced over his shoulder.

I could hear the blare of a sports announcer and see the flicker of a reflection of a TV in the glass door of a hutch against the wall.

"Are you alone?" I hesitated. "Is your mom around?" I couldn't imagine that Nadine wouldn't make a huge deal out of my visiting. It's so great that you came, she would say, extending her arms to hug me and pull me in.

But not Kendrick. He stood there like a stray pup, wondering if he could trust a stranger. "Mom's not here."

"Your father?" I said, feeling a bit foolish for thinking I should come. I looked down at the boards under my feet. They were a few years overdue for a gray paint job.

Kendrick backed into the house and pointed. I followed him in and stood for a moment to let my eyes adjust to the dim light. The room smelled of beer and sweat. In the corner, silhouetted by the light of a large TV, was a man in a recliner, a half dozen beer cans cluttering a table beside him. The man's mouth was agape, his chin pointed to the ceiling.

I studied him for a moment, as alarm grew within me. Was he breathing?

Just then the man gasped for air. I watched as he paused. I counted to ten before his chest lifted again.

I looked at Mark. The guy was barely breathing.

Mark spoke quietly, "He's plastered."

I wrinkled my nose as the aroma of something less than fresh emanated from the sleeping man's body.

Kendrick held up a hand toward the recliner and whispered, "Dr. Weller, meet Clive Solomon, my father."

I turned to face Kendrick, turning my back on Clive. I felt out of place, like I'd just been shown something private. I was a schoolgirl peeking into the teachers' lounge. "I really wanted to know how you are doing."

I watched as Kendrick flinched. The chair creaked behind me. I turned to see Clive Solomon stir into consciousness. "Kendrick!"

"Right here."

Clive squinted toward us, stretched, then leaned forward to stand. He managed to get mostly upright to assume a wobbly stance before grabbing the back of a second chair. He pushed his fingers onto his eyelids and shook his head. "Must've dozed off."

"Dad, this is Dr. Weller, the surgeon who saved my life."

I wasn't sure if I was comfortable with that being my sole identity, but for a man the size of Clive Solomon, maybe it wasn't so bad.

The man's head jerked up. I was about to say hello when he began to speak just above a whisper: "You the one who sent out the social services people to check me out?"

My surprised expression must have been answer enough.

He stumbled toward me, pointing and cursing.

Kendrick stepped in his father's path. "Dad, no!"

Clive swatted his son aside. "I'm the boy's father. He belongs with me!"

"Sir, I never—"

Clive took a wild swing over my head and connected with the side of Mark's. Mark fell backward against the hutch, sending dishes crashing. Clive stepped toward Mark. "Get out of my house," he yelled before looking at me. "Who's this beauty? She with you, Doc?"

I realized Clive's confusion. He thought Mark was Dr. Weller. I took a step back. I wasn't sure admitting to being a surgeon he hated was such a good idea. I glanced at Mark, who held the side of his head, and Kendrick, who was lying on a couch holding his stomach. "Go," he coughed. "Go."

I moved to Kendrick's side and pulled up his T-shirt. His incision looked fine.

Mark grabbed my arm. "Let's go."

"Smart man," Clive said.

THE NEXT DAY, Tina lifted the single yellow rose from her desktop and inhaled the fragrance. She'd found it in her mailbox with the *Richmond-Times Dispatch*. Mark caught on fast. It had taken Dan months to figure out her favorite flower.

She let the rose touch her upper lip and closed her eyes. She was nearing midlife. A decision to leave her husband and begin a new life was gut-wrenching but necessary. How slow she had been to realize that happiness could not be purchased with money! True joy came from shared love, the giving and reception of acceptance that grew from tender commitments.

She knew the break from a twenty-year routine with Dan carried pain in abundance. Their relationship was one of inertia, continuing down a chosen path long after the stimulus to do so had ceased. Her decision to cut off communication was calculated and purposeful. They needed space to sharpen the focus on a relationship blurred by the boredom of material pursuit. Talking to Dan now would bring harsh words and resentment. There would be time to talk later. It would be best if they separated clean and fast, having time only to themselves.

But the notes in front of her indicated how frustrated Dan was growing with her tactics. She lifted the phone messages one by one, each punctuated with more exclamation points than the one before.

She crumpled the notes and wrote one of her own: *Tell Dan I need a few weeks to think. I will call him when I am ready to talk.* She signed it "Dr. Kinser," as she did all communication coming from her office.

She set the note in her out box and picked up Camille's chart. Tina wanted to review it before Camille's visit later that morning. She read all her handwritten notes and then her dictated entry. At the bottom, she'd written two thoughts, both circled with question marks beside them: *Post-traumatic stress disorder? Sexual abuse?*

A knock interrupted her thoughts. She checked her watch. The surgeon was right on time.

I PUSHED THE door open a few inches and peered in. "Knock, knock."

Tina's smile greeted me. "Come in, Camille." She held up her hand, gesturing toward the leather chair. "Sorry, no chai today."

"No problem." I settled into the chair and inhaled the leather fragrance. It was a comfortable smell. I reminded myself that I was loved here. This was a safe place.

Tina sat on the couch and opened the familiar yellow legal

pad and pulled the top off her silver ballpoint pen. "Anything new since we last talked? Any anxiety attacks? Any new memories or insights?"

"Nothing really new. I've had a few nightmares—the same as before. So many times throughout the day I'm aware of a feeling of dread." I halted, unsure how to explain.

"Dread?"

"A low-level feeling that something's not right, like a guilt feeling almost, but not exactly that either. It's like I'm walking around trying not to become afraid, and it's gotten to the point where I'm afraid I'll have an attack. And that in itself makes me feel like I'm about to have an attack."

She laughed. Laughed at me.

I looked up, a little incensed at first, but her gentle expression diffused it.

"That's so common! It's a cyclical problem. We're anxious about being anxious."

"Exactly."

"The nightmares. Same as before? Anything new?"

"Same memory. Darkness. Being held. Being afraid. Whispers in my ear."

She scribbled a note on her pad. "Can you remember the dark place?"

I concentrated. "Africa," I said. "And I say that because it's the only place I had Tumi."

"The man in your dream. You said you believe it's your father. You're sure it's him?"

My instinct told me yes. "I'm not sure, but I think so."

"This whole thing is pretty upsetting to your image as a surgeon, isn't it?"

I felt naked. How did she see right in? "Sure."

"You're not a typical surgeon, Camille. You care. You're still human and in touch with your patients. Don't lose that."

I shifted in my seat. "OK."

"Last time you mentioned kisses. You even told me about feelings you had." She paged back through her legal pad and explained. "Sometimes we remember feelings, emotions, smells, even physical pain, other sensations . . . some people refer to this as body memories. Are there feelings or sensations that accompany the memory of the whispers?"

I tried to concentrate.

"Close your eyes for a moment." Her voice was soft, instructing, prompting. "Now go back to that time. You are in a small place, a dark place. You are being held. Your *father* whispers in your ear. 'Everything's gonna be all right.'"

My gut tightened.

"What do you feel? Can you smell anything? Taste anything? Are you having pain?"

I shifted in my seat uncomfortably. "I smell kerosene burning. We used kerosene lamps when the power failed."

Tina waited without speaking. My eyes remained closed.

"I'm scared."

"Are you in danger?"

"I don't know."

"What are you feeling?"

"Hot. My father is holding me close. His breath is on my neck."

"How is he holding you?"

"I'm on his lap. He is holding me from behind."

"Are you enjoying being in his arms?"

I started to shake my head, paused, and then shook it with confidence. "I want to get away."

"Any other sensations? Can you feel anything else?"

"I remember sticky fluid on my hands. Blood maybe. I wipe them on my dress."

My pulse quickened. I opened my eyes to find that this office was suddenly too small.

"Camille." Tina tried to hold my gaze. I didn't want to look at her. I felt dirty. I rubbed my hands on my skirt.

"Camille, you're OK. Try to slow down your breathing." She leaned forward. She took my hand, reached out to touch my face.

I shook my head and blocked her approach. I didn't want to be touched.

"Camille, you are OK, girl. I'm here with you. No one is here to hurt you."

I stood up to pace away some of the energy I felt. This was embarrassing and frightening. I felt like sprinting a mile, yet at the same time, I was winded, like I'd just finished a run.

I looked at Tina. "I don't like this."

"You feel afraid?"

I nodded, not wanting to cry. "Terrified."

"Do you want to sit?"

"Let me walk for a bit." I paced the room, willing my heart to slow down. "I feel so stupid."

"This is not your fault, Camille. Your mind has responded to some event in your past in a way that has helped you cope for a long time."

After a couple minutes, I sat again. Tina offered me water. I sipped and wiped my upper lip. "My dream, for the longest time, was to be where I am today." I lifted up my hands, palms open, and started to cry. "But this," I waved my hands, "whatever it is, is threatening to ruin everything!"

Tina shook her head. "You are an incredible woman. What you are experiencing is very normal for the type of trauma you endured."

"But why now? Now that I'm on the verge of accomplishing everything I wanted?"

Tina touched her pen to her lips. "I'm not sure about that. Something in your recent experience triggered it. Perhaps it's the increased stress of becoming a surgical attending." She shrugged. "Or maybe the threat of losing your dream job."

She hesitated, then continued, "I want you to consider something."

"I'm listening."

"We may be able to unlock some of your memories if you undergo hypnosis."

All I knew of that was what I'd seen on TV. Hocus-pocus. "No way."

"I think the memory of your father and the whisper may be the key. If we can bring that back, we can deal with it, close the door, and go on."

"It's what's behind the door that scares the hell out of me." I paused to see her response. She was staring at the legal pad. "Do we have to do this?"

She nodded. "You know we do."

She was right. I knew it. Something was down there, hidden, working away at me like an unseen cancer. In this way Tina and I were alike. Maybe if I thought of it like that, I could stomach this psychological chemotherapy of sorts. It was a cancer. It needed to be exposed and dealt with.

"Something is behind the door. But every time I peer inside, I sense the terror in the darkness."

"Like a child peering down the basement steps. They just need a parent to flip on the light to guide the way."

I wasn't sure I liked the simile she'd borrowed from me.

Like a child, I was peering into the darkness.

But most of a child's fears are make-believe.

27

D ANIEL KINSER SAT at a conference table across from Lawrence Stein, his attorney. He watched as he opened a
folder.

"Give me the scoop. Can you get any information from Tina's
attorney?" Dan tapped his hand on his thigh. "Tina won't tell me
anything. She won't return calls. I camped on my own doorstep
for two hours just to talk to her for a few minutes."

Lawrence folded his hands and laid them on the open folder.
"Tina's on blackout. She wants communication between the at-
torneys only at this point. I'm not sure, but this may be on advice
of Ms. Peterson, your wife's attorney."

"But why? Why won't she talk to me?"

"Several reasons may explain her actions. Sometimes early
communication is filled with verbal concessions from the spouse
who is seeking divorce. They can be hard to overcome later when
the settlement is drawn up. For that reason, Ms. Peterson may be
telling Tina to be tight-lipped."

"What else?"

He shrugged. "Sometimes turning your back and walking
away is less painful than working things out face-to-face."

"I think she's snapped," Dan responded. "She's always been
so keen on helping others through communication. Now, we
have a problem and she won't talk. It doesn't make sense."

The attorney raised his eyebrows. "You know her better than I do."

Dan frowned. "I don't think I know her at all."

Mark Lawson looked at his watch. "My afternoon clinic starts in fifteen minutes. I'd better get going."

"Not yet," Tina whispered. "Lay here with me five more minutes." She touched his hand. "Watch me," she said, stretching her arm out to her side and above her head.

"Farther every time."

They lay quietly staring at their hotel room ceiling for a moment before Tina spoke again. "You saved my life."

"You'd have found the cancer without me."

"I don't mean the cancer, silly." She smiled. "That was only a side benefit."

He turned on his side to face her. "What do you mean?"

"You make me want to live every day. I don't ever want to go back to a life without love."

"Do you miss him?"

"Him?"

He cleared his throat. "Mr. Kinser."

She paused. "He was never home."

"Do you miss him?"

She rolled toward him and brushed his hair away from his forehead. "There is a certain element of sameness that is comfortable in life. I suppose I miss the security that I had with Dan. But we took each other for granted. We concerned ourselves with career and money until we were strangers living in the same house. We reached our goals, but sacrificed our relationship."

He sighed.

"Do you feel guilty because I'm married?"

"Not really." He kissed her forehead. "You said your marriage was over before I came along." He touched her hair. "What about you? Regrets?"

She pressed her finger over his mouth. "I've told you how I feel. I have thankfulness, not regrets, that you came along when you did."

They laid side by side in the silence for a minute before Tina touched his shoulder. "Do you sleep with her?"

His eyes widened.

"You'd have told me if you'd made a clean break. Your silence means you are having a hard time saying good-bye."

Mark kissed her again before slipping out of bed and walking to the window. "Richmond's a busy place during the lunch hour."

"Lucky us the Jefferson is walking distance from MCV."

He stretched, silhouetting his torso against the window light. "I don't sleep with her."

Tina started dressing. "Make a decision, Mark. I'm not going to share you with another woman."

"I've got to get back to the clinic."

I PICKED UP my patient list and wondered. After Kendrick Solomon, my next three patients were listed in order as breast cancer, abnormal mammogram, and nipple discharge. I looked up to see Vanessa, my clinic nurse, smile. She'd changed her fingernail color again. Now she sported a little sunset of orange and purple on the end of each fingernail. "What's up with this?" I asked, waving the patient list.

"It seems your reputation is getting around."

"What are you talking about?"

"Like it or not, the word is out. Dr. Weller is a 'woman doctor.'" She framed the words in finger quotation marks. "The word on the streets of downtown Richmond is that you may offer another option besides what Dr. Gilles is doing."

I held up my hand. "Wait a minute. The word is out? People know what I did to Dr. Kinser? How?"

She shook her head. "They don't know who you treated." She sat in a rolling desk chair and scooted toward me to keep her voice low. "I wanted to know the same thing, so I asked a few questions."

I knew I could count on her. "And?"

She held up a painted nail to slow my questions, or drive me crazy. Either way, she succeeded. "The transporter who moved Dr. Kinser to the recovery room goes to church with these women."

"Great," I said, sighing. So much for my secret treatment.

"There's more."

"Stab me again."

"Nadine Solomon has been in the waiting room for an hour priming these women. She thinks you walk on water and these women believe her." Vanessa smiled and rolled her chair away.

"What's so amazing about that?" I threw my shoulders back and gave her a wicked grin. "I do."

"It's time to start your clinic, Dr. Weller."

I flipped her off. Vanessa stuck her tongue out at me. We'd enjoyed this same rude banter since my internship. Vanessa helped keep my sanity.

I looked at my watch. I had three hours until the morbidity and mortality conference, where I'd be expected to defend Tina Kinser's unusual surgery. Gilles had already given me fair warning of the upcoming heat. I needed to get working or I wouldn't make it to my own roast.

The chart in the door rack of exam room one beckoned. Kendrick Solomon. My six-liter boy. Maybe I could put that on my résumé to get a job in another trauma center when Gilles gave me the heave-ho.

I pushed open the door to see Kendrick sitting on the exam table. Nadine sat beside him wearing a flowered dress. Her hands were folded across her purse. On her left ring finger, a large diamond caught my eye. "Hello, Kendrick," I said, then reached for Nadine's hand. I held it for a second while I inspected her ring. It was breathtaking. Either cubic zirconia or the Solomons had inherited a mint from a rich uncle. Or worse. Maybe old Clive had scored a major street contract. I searched her eyes. "What a nice ring."

Nadine smiled. "Clive gave it to me."

Kendrick stayed silent.

Nadine touched my arm as I turned my attention to her son. "I'm sorry about your visit." Her eyes searched the wall beyond me. "Is your friend OK?"

"He's bruised. Pride mostly. He'll be OK."

I looked at Kendrick. It was confrontation time. "Has your father ever struck you like that before?"

Kendrick traded glances with Nadine and stayed quiet.

I let the silence hang, hoping it would work to my advantage. Nadine rose from the exam table where she had perched beside her son and sat in a chair, her hands fumbling over her purse.

I looked at Nadine. "Has he ever hit you?"

She cleared her throat and twisted the diamond ring around her finger until the stone had done three laps.

There were tears in her eyes, answer enough for me.

"You shouldn't stay with a man who hits you."

Nadine touched her nose with the back of her hand and sniffed. "I love him," she said quietly.

I didn't understand. How could she love a man who raised his hand to hit her? And what of her faith? I'd seen this woman's tenacity. She'd seen God practically raise her son from the dead, believing every minute that he would do it. So why didn't she believe that God would care for her if she left her husband? "How can—"

She shook her head and raised her hand to stop me. "He's OK unless he drinks. When he sobers up he apologizes. He makes it up to us." She stared at me as if daring me to go on. "I saw God raise up my son. Certainly he can change my husband."

I looked at the ring and understood. I also realized I wasn't going to change things for Nadine in one post-op visit. I'd planted a seed. It had to be enough for now.

I turned my attention to Kendrick and went through the litany of post-op questions about pain, eating, bowel movements, and general recovery. I examined his abdomen. His incision had healed nicely. Kendrick was bored, perhaps a little embarrassed, and tried not to smile when I commented on his washboard abs.

Nadine sniffed. "He's doin' good. He's been eatin' and sleepin' mostly."

"When can I go swimmin'?"

"Now."

He glared at his mother. "See?"

Nadine shook her head. "He wants to go off the diving board."

I started counting days since his operation. "I'll tell you what. You can swim now. Ride a bike. But no diving, football, or wrestling for two more weeks."

Nadine glared back at her son.

I moved away from the table and folded my arms over his clinic file. I was about to step over the line, but I'd been so far over it with Kendrick before that I doubted it would matter. My head said remain distant and professional. My heart told me to go ahead.

"I've been thinking about something. Have you ever been to King's Dominion?"

Kendrick's fifteen-year-old eyes sparkled. "No."

"How'd you like to go with me?" I hesitated, and looked at Nadine. "If it's OK with your mother."

"Can he do that now?" she asked.

"Sure. His incision has healed enough. If he gets tired of walking we can grab a bite to eat and rest."

I watched as his eyes did the talking. *Come on, Mom!*

"It can be our secret," I said. "Maybe you can bring him down to MCV. Saturday morning, say around nine o'clock?"

Nadine smiled. "I guess so."

"Meet me at the Skull and Bones." I took Nadine's hand. "I'll have him home by ten p.m."

She bit her lower lip. "Clive won't like it."

"I'll drop him at the curb. Clive doesn't need to know I've taken him." I teased her. "If he sees me, it will be fine. I think he likes me. He thinks I'm Dr. Weller's girlfriend."

"OK," she said. "It's a date."

As I exited the room, I listened as Kendrick exploded to his mother, "It's not a date, Mom. Why'd you have to say that? She'll think—"

I smiled. Kendrick needed a little taste of happy teenage life and I might be just the ticket to get it.

M AND M conferences—the weekly conferences where residents presented the prior week's complications and took the bitter pill of criticism that followed—were a horror I thought I'd seen the last of as a chief resident. I'd learned well the secrets of survival— the casual introduction of a controversial topic that was certain to turn shark attendings to snapping at each other instead of devouring me. If blood was in the water, the safest place for the resident was onshore, staying out of the conversation, venturing back into danger only if directly summoned by an attending. It was never a time to offer an opinion. Opinions came from experience. And residents, even if they'd been in training for most of a decade, were not thought to be experienced.

Attendings rarely presented cases for discussion, hiding behind the resident staff to take the first blows of criticism by the other professors. But today was different. I was expected to present Tina Kinser's case because Gilles wanted the staff to understand the controversies. I kept the residents away from her because she was one of us, a professor, and deserved not to be treated as a teaching case. As a result, I had no one to hide behind. I was the first line and would have to take my hits.

I cleared my throat as I stood behind the little podium in a lecture auditorium in Sanger Hall. In the audience, the surgical attendings, residents, interns, and medical students rotating through surgery were in varying states of alertness or slumber, depending on the relative state of sleep deprivation that we knew during surgery training.

"The next case is a thirty-eight-year-old female who presented with a palpable left breast lump, found only several days before I saw her in clinic. Her past medical history is unremarkable. Her family history is positive for a mother who developed premenopausal breast cancer and was treated with the old radical mastectomy procedure, and subsequently died of metastatic breast cancer."

I knew I was adding more information than is typical for these brief presentations, but I needed to prime the pump to justify why I'd selected the operation I had, and why Tina was so against a mastectomy. I watched as Dr. Gilles shifted in his seat, so I knew I needed to keep moving. "She brought this mammogram to her clinic visit," I continued, slapping the X-rays on a portable view box. I listened as several groans grew up from those residents still awake. The ugly crab in the left upper outer quadrant was visible even to those on the third row.

I added her chest X-ray. "Her other studies, including this chest X-ray, were normal." I paused. "After considerable discussion, my patient refused a modified radical mastectomy. I proceeded with a lumpectomy and axillary dissection. Her axillary lymph nodes were negative. She is currently undergoing radiation therapy as an alternative to mastectomy."

I hesitated. I wasn't going any further unless I had to. I held my breath. No one commented. I'd pulled the X-rays off the box and moved a step toward the front row, when Dr. Gilles took the first bite. As per usual protocol, he questioned an upper-level resident first. "Dr. Hamilton, how would you have managed this case?"

Ellis was in trouble. He was on my service, so he couldn't disagree with what I'd done, but he couldn't agree with me either, knowing I'd stepped outside the standard care. "If the patient refuses appropriate therapy, I think you're bound to do what you can."

Dr. Gilles wasn't satisfied. The scent of blood was in the water. He stepped up to his own department, the surgical oncology attendings. "Dr. Jacobs, how would you handle this? If a patient wanted an operation that you felt was inappropriate, what would you do?"

Evan Jacobs hadn't done a breast operation in years. His sole interest was biliary and pancreas surgery, and liver transplant. "I think we are obligated to educate our patients to make the proper decisions, not bend over backwards being nice, when we know it can be to the patient's detriment."

Dr. Gilles trolled the water for more supportive sharks. He looked at another white hair in the oncology department. Sam Harrison sat on his left. Dr. Gilles slapped Sam's knee. "Sam? Comments?"

"I know of this case. What Dr. Weller didn't tell us, in preservation of patient confidentiality, was that this patient is a professor of psychiatry, which puts the surgeon in a greater obligation to do the right thing."

I started keeping score. So far, Gilles and the old school were lining up on one side, opposing me. I started to feel lonely. I searched the audience for support. I met Dr. Bransford's eyes, but he looked away. Although he'd mentored me, he wasn't going to cross Gilles on this one. So far, I'd managed to listen and stay out of the fray, rule one for swimming with sharks.

"Dr. Weller," Gilles said, gesticulating with his right hand. "Enlighten us. Why did you choose to behave in this way?"

"There is growing literature on both sides of this issue," I began. "I can expound on the foundation for the ongoing studies of lumpectomy and radiation if you like."

He nodded and I gave the *Reader's Digest* version of the current controversy. "In the end, I concluded that neither camp had enough evidence to prove that standard mastectomy had any advantage over lumpectomy and radiation."

"This has not been proven conclusively, has it?"

"No."

"Then why did you step outside a research protocol and perform an operation which has not been conclusively shown to be of equivalent value?"

I sighed. I'd just expounded on the literature supporting what I'd done. He was leading me down a pathway that I wanted to avoid. But I opened my mouth anyway. "I did the operation that I'd want performed on me."

The audience fell silent. This was a new, unheard-of argument for academic surgeons. Especially male, old-school types like Dr. Gilles. It was as if I'd admitted to surgery option A over B just because it was reimbursed at a higher rate by an insurance carrier. It might influence us, but we're not supposed to admit it. I looked at their blank stares. Maybe they were aghast that someone would admit to such a nonscientific approach.

They sat there staring at me like I was a delicious meal that just got away. The sharks were hungry, but I'd ridden my surfboard onto the beach.

I edged toward my seat. I thought I'd gotten off easy, but Gilles wasn't letting go.

"We've heard your evidence, Dr. Weller. And what you've done may well be an appropriate option. But the proper place to do experimental surgery is within a controlled trial. Otherwise, in this department, we follow the standard operation until it's been proven to be substandard behind another procedure. We don't perform surgery just because of emotional sentimentality. Is that understood?" His eyes glared at me. Those eyes, which seemed to care about me or catapult me into orbits of fear.

I stood transfixed, anxiety rising. Suddenly I found myself in the stupid swirl of feeling panic that I might feel panic.

"Dr. Weller?"

Words lodged in my throat. "Yes, sir?"

"I can't have the residents believing that we choose surgery on the basis of what we would want done to ourselves. We are scientists first. I'll not have you making decisions based on fluffy emotion!"

I nodded numbly. I edged to my chair and sat on the first row. Dr. Gilles continued expounding on the stupidity of basing a surgical decision on personal feelings rather than science.

I sat in my seat with my temperature rising. Finally, when Dr. Gilles's voice of criticism faded, and against my better judgment, I stood and raised my own voice in protest. "With all due respect for you and for science, sir, what I did was not based on fluffy emotion. Every part of the scientific controversy was completely discussed with the patient. She knew she might be risking a recurrence and she was willing to take that risk."

Eyebrows went up across the crowd. No one ever spoke up after Dr. Gilles gave his conclusion. They now sat silently, perhaps wondering if Gilles would explode at my arrogance.

I was on a roll. If I was going down, it wasn't going to be without at least making them rethink the status quo. "It is time that we begin to treat patients not as bags of chemicals that can be manipulated by science. We are treating fellow human beings with complex emotions. The breast in our society is celebrated as an object of beauty and sex. When my patient came to me, I gave her the party-line option. But she convinced me that because she was a woman with emotions, a woman with a career, a failing marriage, and who still desired to fill out her little black cocktail dress, the scientific evidence was not all I needed to consider. In all, I decided I wasn't interested in treating cancer. I was interested in treating my patient."

With that, I glared at the crowd, daring the men to speak. One at a time, I locked eyes with the old guard. When they didn't speak, I tipped my head toward Dr. Gilles and walked out of the room.

28

I STOPPED AT MARK'S apartment on my way home to find him preparing a lecture for pediatric grand rounds. I gently touched the dark rim under his left eye and winced. "Sorry."

"It was a lucky shot. I'd have ducked if I thought he was aiming for me." He smiled. "Have you eaten?"

"Not yet. Want to grab a bite somewhere?"

"I really can't."

"Let's go to Kings Dominion Saturday."

He moaned. "Too hot. Let's go to Virginia Beach and walk the sand in the moonlight."

"Sounds romantic. But I can't." I cringed. "I invited Kendrick to go with us to Kings Dominion."

"Us?"

"Go with me. It will be fun."

"With Kendrick? Didn't you hear his father? He wants you to stay away from his kid."

I frowned. "I feel sorry for him. He needs someone to show him some fun."

"Why are you doing this? He's not your responsibility."

"You saw where he lives. His father is a violent alcoholic."

"What are you going to do? Mother every kid you pull back from the brink of death?"

"Maybe." I paused. "No." I shook my head. "I don't know. I don't want to rescue them all. I just want to help this one."

"What are you trying to prove?"

I was incensed. I wasn't trying to prove anything. Was I?

"You know what happened when we visited him."

"Nadine said she'd bring him down to MCV to meet me. That way I won't risk running into Clive."

"I've got to work on my lecture for grand rounds."

"You can work on it Sunday," I said, taking Mark's hand. "Kendrick needs a positive male role model, you know."

"Is it the only way I can spend time with you this weekend?"

I smiled and kissed his mouth. "I knew you'd help me." I stood and walked toward his door.

"Hey, this was just getting good."

"You need to work on your lecture. Besides, you've just shown me the love I wanted to see."

"I only agreed to go to an amusement park with an abused kid."

"Exactly," I said, opening the door. "And that spells *L-O-V-E.*"

KENDRICK SOLOMON CLOSED and locked his bedroom door, but the hollow wooden door did little to shut out the noise of his father in the den below. He heard a slap and his mother's cry.

He slipped his hand under his mattress and retrieved his father's gun.

"You will never, ever use this to hurt me again," he whispered. He held the pistol and took aim at a poster on his wall, a basketball star transformed into a helpless enemy who threatened his family's peace. He quoted a line from a western he'd seen at the theater. "Twitch and you're dead," he said in his best sinister voice.

TWO DAYS LATER I forced myself to keep an appointment with Tina Kinser. After peering into the darkness during the last visit, I wasn't sure I ever wanted to bust down the door holding back my past.

But I knew Tina was right. I had to do this so I could move on. I was afraid something would set off a panic attack while I was in the OR, the one place I felt in total control.

I sat and watched Tina open the yellow legal pad. The silver ballpoint pen was balanced against her lower lip. A single yellow rose sat a vase on the table between us.

She followed my eyes to the flower. "A secret admirer," she said, winking.

"Again?" I leaned forward, my curiosity pricked. "You can tell me. That's what we're here to uncover," I said. "Secrets."

She smiled. I could see her cheeks were flushing just thinking about this guy. Whoever he was, she'd fallen hard. "We're here to uncover your secrets," she said.

I felt my smile fade. I could see she wasn't ready to talk about men with me. At least not about her men.

"I've been thinking about something you told me during our first visit. You mentioned that one of your attacks, the first one, I believe, occurred when you were being kissed."

I nodded.

"Have you ever had problems like that before?"

I shifted in my seat.

"What I mean is, have sexual relationships been hard for you? Could this be a stimulus for anxiety?"

"I wouldn't exactly say that sexual relationships have been hard for me. I'd pretty much say I've never had any."

She tilted her head to the left and stared at me, the kind of look you give someone when you think you haven't heard them correctly. "Hmmm."

She flipped a few pages of her yellow pad and slid her finger over the surface to rest on her notes. "Tell me about your boyfriends in medical school and residency."

"Tina, you've been through medical school and residency. There's not exactly an abundance of time for surgeons in training to develop serious relationships. Besides, I'd pretty much vowed to make any physical experience I had to be on my terms, when and where I decided it was right."

"I was married in college."

"So you never really had to think about dating." I shrugged. "I didn't have time." I looked away. "And I was still a little scared."

"A little?" Her eyes narrowed like she didn't believe the line. "So what about now? How are you handling intimacy with your boyfriend?"

I met her gaze. I suppose I'd known I'd have to have this discussion sooner or later. "I'm a virgin."

"Is that a problem?"

"Maybe. I mean, I guess so. I have a boyfriend. I love him. But we haven't been active, you know, sexually."

"Is that a problem?" she asked again.

I nodded. "Ever since the first attack, whenever my boyfriend begins to get physical, I get very, very anxious."

"So you're talking about . . ."

"Kissing. Holding me."

"It reminds you of something in the Congo."

I looked at my hands. I'd been clenching my fists without realizing it. I slowly relaxed. "I guess so. I don't know. This sounds so crazy." I sighed. "I think that's the only way I wound up this old and so inexperienced."

"It's not crazy at all."

"He's the first man that I've really wanted to be with."

"He feels the same?"

I smiled. "Yes."

"He's a very lucky man. He's found a wonderful woman in you, Camille."

I looked down. Tina's openness was disarming.

"When he kisses you, do you find yourself troubled with the memory you told me about?"

"Yes. But now, even if I'm not thinking about anything in my past, I find myself afraid when he starts to kiss me, that I'll soon be panicked. The whole thing pretty much destroys the mood of the moment."

"Is it stressing your relationship? Does your boyfriend understand?"

"Yes, and yes, I think."

She paused and turned the page on her legal pad. She scribbled herself a note I wished I could read. Then she looked up and asked, "Do you have any happy memories with your father?"

"I remember riding in an old Jeep. I think that was fun. I remember being given a puppy for Christmas one year."

She flipped the pages on the legal pad. "Was that Tumi?"

I nodded my affirmation.

"What else do you remember about your father?"

"Everybody loved him."

"Did you love him?"

That was a tough one. "I think so."

"Did he ever hurt you?"

I checked my right hand. My knuckles were blanching again. I uncurled my fingers. "I think so."

"How did he hurt you?"

I closed my eyes to think. "I don't know."

"Are you thinking about the dark memory you told me about?"

"Yes."

She made a note again. This was driving me crazy. I wanted to know what she'd written.

"What other things bring memories of Africa back to you? You've told me about the whispered phrase, intimacy with your boyfriend, and about the time you hit the dog that reminded you of Tumi. Have there been other things recently that seemed to bring Africa to your mind?"

In a moment, it came back to me. "The other night I stayed up late studying for my board exams. I was so exhausted that I crawled into bed with my clothes on. It was something about the feel of the covers on my clothing. . . ." I looked at Tina. "I remembered sleeping in my clothes in Africa."

She wrote that down. I couldn't imagine why that would be significant. Perhaps everyone who goes crazy at age thirty wore their clothes to bed when they were a kid.

"Do you have any idea why?"

"Maybe I was cold."

"In the Congo?"

"I don't really know."

She tapped her silver pen against her upper lip again. "Have you thought any more about trying hypnosis to bring some of this back?"

I inhaled a big breath and blew it out through pursed lips. "I'm not ready."

Tina reached over and picked up the yellow rose and put it beneath her nose. She was obviously in love.

She was where I wanted to be. Maybe if hypnosis could get me there, I ought to try it.

I thought about a watch dangling before my eyes and a voice telling me my eyelids were getting heavy.

There was no way on earth the scientist in me could stomach that.

29

I SAT IN THE second row of the hospital chapel between my parents. I wanted to lay down, 'cause I was so tired, but it seemed everyone in the hospital had to say something good about Mr. Karanja before we put him in the hole they dug at the top of the hill by the church. My mother was afraid the Simbas wouldn't let us out of the hospital compound, but Mr. Dickson and Mr. Barnett told them the funeral was going to be at the church and that was that.

Well, when they saw all the Simbas guarding the church, I guess they changed their mind, so we all had to crowd into the hospital chapel. It was worse than how they crowd on one of the town buses and the smell of sweat was just as bad, so I kept sticking my nose against Daddy's armpit 'cause he's wearing deodorant and it kind of covers the smell.

After about fifteen men told how wonderful Mr. Karanja was, my daddy got up and told a story of how Mr. Karanja brought over a fish net 'cause my dad had said he wanted to talk about the mission. And here poor Mr. Karanja had thought he'd said fishin'. That was before Daddy got him that big hearing aid the bad Simba busted. All the Africans laughed real big. They all knew stories of Mr. Karanja not hearing too good.

After about four hours on the hard bench between my parents, even Daddy's armpits weren't smelling too fresh. I couldn't keep my mind on the sermon. I stretched out my arms to see if my plan to darken up had worked. I had stretched out on the grass with just a T-shirt and shorts and laid there till I thought I'd just bake. But my mom caught me and made me come back inside. I don't think I'm any darker. Maybe I can borrow some of Lilly Barnett's makeup. It seems to make her face darker. I don't want my skin to be a curse.

RICHMOND, 1984

I STOOD BACK AND watched as Kendrick leveled the gun at the targets in the arcade at Kings Dominion. I leaned over to Mark. "Scary," I said. "He's a natural with guns."

Mark laughed. "He should be. What's this, his tenth time?"

"I thought we'd never get him away from Rebel's Yell."

"Or the ice cream shop."

I smiled. "He's having fun."

Mark nodded. "Me, too."

"So maybe it wasn't so bad sharing me with Kendrick after all."

He sighed. "Hey, at least he'll ride a roller-coaster with me."

"Hey, I rode it."

"Once."

Mark put his arm around my shoulder and whispered in my ear, "You're changing, Camille."

I turned to face him, wrinkling my brow.

"There was a time when you would have ridden all of these fast rides to prove you're one of the guys."

I shrugged. "Maybe it's about time I started acting like who I am." A woman.

I leaned my head against Mark's shoulder and lost myself as the *plink, plink, plink* of Kendrick's gun mesmerized me. Was I really changing? Was the shedding of my tough-guy exterior responsible for some of the terror that'd bubbled its way through a softer surface?

I was jarred from my trance by a request. "Just one more time? I almost had them all that time!"

I nodded my head and pulled out a dollar. "Sure, hotshot. One more round."

SUNDAY NIGHT DANIEL Kinser sipped a cup of lukewarm coffee and hunkered down in his seat behind the steering wheel. How had it come to this? He had staked his position down the street from his own house to size up the competition. With his car concealed by a row of azaleas near the curb, he contemplated both his happy life and his current remorse. He'd married young. He had been twenty, Tina only a year out of high school. In his mind, the marriage was sorted into neat time slots of Tina's training: college, medical school, and psychiatry residency. He worked construction so she could attend college and borrowed heavily so she could study in medical school while he finished a BA in business. By residency, they were in debt, but very much in love. Dan landed a job as a sales representative for Ethicon, selling suture products to Virginia hospitals. His travel and Tina's internship created unique stressors. Her hospital obligations demanded she stay "in house" every third night, covering medicine services at MCV and the VA. With some ingenuity, they kept their marriage vows sparkling. Dan saw her most evenings, often sharing a home-cooked meal with her or takeout from their favorite Richmond restaurants in the house staff on-call quarters. Some nights, they searched for a vacant hospital bed on the private ward to share secret delicacies other than food.

In the years since residency, money flowed freer. Tina's attending salary allowed luxury vacations, a few investments, and a house in the suburbs away from downtown. Dan moved up the corporate ladder, traveled more often, and delayed a desire to have a family until Tina could be tenured in her job as a professor.

Now, with a marriage apparently falling over the precipice toward divorce, Dan wanted desperately to reclaim the years they'd spent on their careers.

In the days since Tina had asked him to leave, he'd thought long and hard about the past. He had not been perfect. He had neglected her, substituting pursuit of their financial security in place of intimacy. They slipped out of love with a thousand little steps, each falling on the heels of the other. Finally, a year ago, what had begun as an innocent drink with a coworker continued beyond their night in a New York City hotel. He'd fallen into the cliché: traveling on imaginary business trips in order to be with the excitement of his new love.

In the days, weeks, and months that followed the end of his affair, Dan had wrapped himself in a blanket of guilt that muffled his attempts to reach his wife again.

Now, with Tina's declaration of her independence, all communication had ceased. This was the worst thing of all. What had once been the strength of their union was now the biggest stumbling block. He'd called. Talked to their answering machine. Left messages with her receptionist at work. All had gone unanswered. He was reduced to playing the voyeur, desperate for a window onto her life again.

He'd been such a fool!

A plan seemed just beyond the horizon. If she wouldn't talk to him, how could he try to make amends?

This whole event made little sense. Had cancer, this unwelcome visitor, prompted her to such change? Had passion emboldened her to execute a secret wish for a different life? Had her comfortable life been too routine? How had he missed her growing discontent in their life?

There were no answers to his difficult questions. All he had were inquiries and regret.

Movement in front of their house drew his eyes. A young man with dark curls and a white coat folded over his arm stood beside the porch light and kissed Tina before walking briskly across the lawn, coming straight toward Dan's position.

Dan pushed back against his seat. The darkness should conceal him if he did not move. He dared to follow the man with his eyes as he passed his car. This man, the *other* man in Tina's life, appeared so young. Could it be a resident she was training?

Dan felt his anger rising.

The man passed Dan's car and got into an old-model Japanese car parked fifty feet beyond him. Perhaps the man had something to hide. There was plenty of room in the driveway for his car.

The man started his car and rolled down his windows. Deep throbbing bass cut through the languid night. The man passed without looking at Dan, who scribbled down the Virginia license plate number.

Dan felt a stab of inferiority. How could he compete with *him*?

He knew one thing. He wasn't going to let her go without a fight.

THE NEXT AFTERNOON Tina flipped the yellow legal pad open and poised her hand for taking notes. "Talk to me about Tumi. That's an interesting name."

"Tumi was a Kiswahili name short for something that I can't quite grasp out of my memory."

Tina nodded and scribbled.

I tried to think of details. "He had thick, yellow fur. A face like a Labrador retriever. Always slobbered when he said hello." I smiled. "His nose was wet. He slept by my bed."

"Do you remember his death?"

I closed my eyes. The image of Tumi gasping was one I'd not thought about for years, but one that had resurfaced when I struck the dog on Chamberlain Avenue. I strained to remember. "I remember a dog gasping, spitting blood. I think it was Tumi."

"Think again of the dark memory. Your father is holding you, whispering to you. Warning you?"

I nodded. "Yes. He didn't want me to leave him."

"You wanted to get away, didn't you?"

"Yes."

"Is there a link to your memories of Tumi?"

I searched. "Yes. I remember wanting Tumi."

"OK. You've told me some of your body sensations. Do you remember saying anything?"

I shook my head.

"Think this through. It's dark. He's holding you on his lap, is that right?"

"Yes."

"Close your eyes again, Camille. He's keeping you from getting away. Did you cry out? What did you say?"

I could only whisper. "Tumi." The revelation hit hard. Yes, I remembered calling out. "I do remember! I was calling for my dog!" My voice broke. "Tu-mi. Tu-mi!"

"Where did you want to go?"

"I wanted to see my dog."

"He slept by your bed?"

"Protected me."

"Where is your mother in the memory? Is she there?"

I tried. I thought. "I don't remember her there. She wasn't there. Only my father."

Tina smiled. "You're making progress. It's all in there, Camille," she said, taking my hand. "And it's coming back, so we can sort it out. That way it won't hurt you anymore."

"I'll try to remember more. I think I've hit a wall. I can't bring anything else back."

"I want to use trance induction. I think we're right on the edge of some real understanding here."

"Hypnosis? Why don't you just call it hypnosis?"

"Because you'll only think of what you see on TV."

I squirmed and wrinkled my nose.

"Just because you don't understand it doesn't mean it isn't grounded in science."

I sighed. "I know."

"Let me try."

I checked my watch.

"I don't mean now. We've covered enough ground for today. Go home and think about yellow dogs and see what you remember. We'll use a little trance tomorrow, if you agree."

THAT EVENING WHEN I'd finally separated myself from the OR, the western sky over the James River downtown was already beginning to color. I walked to my Prelude, looking forward to a hot bath and a bed. As I slid the key in the door, I heard my name.

"Dr. Weller."

I looked to see Kendrick astraddle an old bicycle with a banana seat.

"Kendrick! What are you doing here?"

He shrugged. "I like riding in the parking deck."

I knew for a fact that security guards chased bikers and skateboarders out on a regular basis. I frowned. "How'd you get in here past the guard?"

He pointed to a low section of brick wall on the opposite side of the lot. "It's not hard."

"Shouldn't you be at home?"

"Mom doesn't care."

"Have you eaten?"

His eyes brightened. "No."

I was getting suspicious. "Have you been waiting for me?"

He wrinkled his nose and stayed quiet.

"How long have you been hanging around?"

He didn't flinch. He was steel. A cool man. "Two, maybe three hours."

This boy needed something to do. "Ever eat at the Skull?"

"No."

I put my arm around the shoulders of my six-liter boy and nudged him toward MCV's diner. He pushed his bike along, still sitting on the banana seat. He let me keep my hand on his shoulder until we approached the street, where he wiggled free.

"They have great chocolate shakes."

He smiled.

"My treat."

I reached for the swinging glass door leading into the Skull and Bones.

Kendrick had saved me from going home and thinking about the Congo.

30

THAT NIGHT, I awoke at 3:00 a.m. to a palpable terror. I heard my father's voice. Whispers from the Dark Continent.

I remembered crying, fighting against his strong arms. Something had been taken from me. Something precious. It was hot, very hot, and he was sweating. His hands muffled my cries.

"Tumi, Tu-mi."

He came for me when I slept, with Tumi on the floor by my bed.

There was an odor I remembered, too. The odor of blood. Moisture. Sweat. Blood on my clothing.

Rising from my bed, I was aware only that I had touched the edge of memory, an event that refused to reveal its colors, and hidden in the dull shades of night. It was a nocturnal animal lurking in the blackness, unwilling or unable to stand the scrutiny of my eye.

I filled my coffeemaker and let the first cup drip straight into a mug emblazoned with the Boston Red Sox logo. Then I sat at the kitchen table and concentrated to remember, but found the door to my past sealed tight. The creature, this memory of darkness, refused to cooperate.

I rolled the caffeine across my tongue, savoring the flavor. I sipped coffee until five, then showered and prepared for my day. As I drove to MCV, I thought about the futility of my quest. Were there things too dark, too horrible for a child to know, so that any remembrance was forever locked away?

Did I really want to know? I'd often heard of being blissfully naive.

Could it be that the naivete I carried was the only bliss I'd ever know?

I imagined a hoard of drumming demons sitting, waiting to invade the moment I unlocked the door to my African past.

Once in the hospital, I made quick rounds alone, and wrote short attending notes to convince Medicaid and Medicare that I was really doing something worthy of sending them a bill. After that I helped a third-year resident remove the gallbladder from a sister who made Nadine Solomon look small.

An hour later I sat on Tina Kinser's couch.

Tina sat across from me, prodding with a soft voice, rhythmic, almost as if she had identified my breathing. She spoke when I exhaled, halting her speech each time I took a breath. "Relax, Camille." She paused. "Close your eyes." Pause. "With every breath you will feel more relaxed."

She spoke at intervals without me interrupting, describing in quiet tones the darkness of the closet, the warmth of my father against me, and the sensation of blood on my hand. With the skill of a surgeon dissecting away the overlying tissue, she laid a memory bare.

Suddenly, I am awake. Daddy's hands are on my shoulders.

"Wake up, Camille."

I open my eyes to his face, my father's face next to mine. His eyes are wide. There is sweat on his brow.

He yanks down the covers. He is moving quickly, almost frantic.

"Why Camille? Why did he do that?"

"He came to get me."

He lifts me in his arms, apparently ignoring or not hearing my question.

"Where is Tumi?"

I twist about, squinting in the dim light of the room.

Daddy carries me into his bedroom.

"Where's Tumi?"

"Don't worry about Tumi, honey." He opens the closet door.

"What's that smell?"

Daddy is acting strange. He won't answer.

He sets me down.

"Do you know what the smell is?"

"Blood."

"You're sure?"

I nodded. "I know the smell."

"We need to get into the closet. No one will see us there."

I am standing by the closet door, but I am very afraid.

"Why, Camille? Why are you afraid?"

Tumi always sleeps by my bed. Something has happened to Tumi.

Daddy has set me down by the closet in his bedroom. I run to the hall to get Tumi.

"Camille, no!"

I step on something wet. I am kneeling to see when Daddy pulls me away, his strong hands around my waist.

In a moment, he has pulled me with him into the small closet.

I begin to speak, but stop, cut off by his hand over my lips. His hands are wet, sticky. With blood?

"Be very quiet, Camille, and everything will be all right."

He holds me tight, but in the darkness, my right hand reaches out and grazes against something soft. Fur?

I pull back the blanket that is covering . . .

Daddy pins my hand against my chest.

"Tumi!" I scream before Daddy clamps his hand over my mouth. I begin to cry.

"Shhh, baby. Everything's gonna be all right."

Tina's hands were behind my head as I sobbed into her shoulder. I heard her calling to me as in a tunnel, but I could not stop the tears.

"Camille. It's OK. No one is hurting you now. Camille!"

The moment was surreal. I had touched something long buried, something horrible, and the terror was as fresh to me as it was when I was ten. I clutched Tina's arms with my hands and pulled them away, burying my face in my own hands and shivering with naked fear. Something very bad had happened in that closet. Something very, very bad. I was on the verge of full discovery when Tina called me back. I felt as if she had lifted me just before I looked full in the face of something evil. There was still terror lurking in my past. I whispered a prayer to a God I wished I believed in. "Don't let me see this all at once. I'm not sure I can handle this."

TINA KINSER PUSHED open the door to Ed Cowen's office. Ed, at fifty-two and pushing forty, ran the psychiatry department at MCV with the inefficiency of someone in love with medicine and at odds with business.

Ed looked up.

"Can I bother you?"

He smiled, showing an even row of teeth within a Sigmund Freud beard. "Not a chance."

"I need a curbside."

He lay down his pen. "Shoot."

"I'm seeing a young woman who is troubled with painful flashbacks of some pretty dark stuff." Tina sat in a chair opposite his desk. "Today I used hypnosis to bring out some of it. She started reexperiencing an event in front of me, just like it happened twenty years ago. She started crying out, screaming." Tina shook her head. "It scared me. It was so real to her that I had to bring her out again. She was shaking for a good thirty minutes after the trance."

"Sounds like you're uncovering some serious pain."

Tina nodded.

"So what's your concern? How can I help?"

"Do you think there are some things so bad that we shouldn't try to overcome the mind's defense to keep them buried?"

He stroked his beard. "What do you think?"

Just like a psychiatrist. Answer a question with a question. Tina waited for a moment while she considered and formulated her response. "Turn over the rock of a person's greatest pain and you will often find their point of greatest fear . . . or greatest trust."

Ed nodded. "And likely a bit of both." He leaned back in his desk chair. "What do you think is going on?"

"I'm not entirely sure. Child abuse of some sort. Possibly sexual."

"What makes you think it was sexual?"

"Some memories she has of her father holding her. She slept in her clothes."

"Typical for sexual abuse."

Tina nodded. "But today, she uncovered something else. She remembered her father's hands being bloody."

"Bloody?"

"She remembers blood in a closet, perhaps on the floor, somehow related to her pet dog." She sighed. "I'm not sure how it relates to her other problems. She has some real hang-ups now when her boyfriend wants to get physical. She panics, but doesn't know why."

"Sounds like you're turning over the right rocks."

Tina sighed. "Thanks."

"You answered your own question."

She stood to leave.

"Just be sure that when you uncover the greatest pain, you're confident she has the tools to deal with it." He paused. "Otherwise, she'll be worse off than if you'd left the stone undisturbed."

THAT NIGHT, MARK Lawson was jarred awake by the phone. He peered at the eerie green glow of his clock. One o'clock. *Who is calling at this hour?* He started running the list of his ICU patients. Maybe someone was in trouble.

He lifted the receiver. "Hello, Dr. Lawson."

Silence.

"Hello?"

Click.

Mark grumbled and rolled back over.

In thirty minutes, the phone rang again.

"Hello."

Breathing. Silence.

"Hello!"

Click.

Mark slammed down the phone. This wasn't funny. He pulled a pillow over his head.

He had just fallen into slumber when the phone rang again. Two o'clock.

"Hello."

Heavy breathing into the phone. "Stay away from Tina." Click.

31

A WEEK LATER, I left the OR and changed into my street clothes, dreading my scheduled appointment with Tina. I spent twenty minutes psyching myself up for a good cry before heading to her office.

At one, I found Tina sitting in a leather chair, reviewing the notes from my last visit. What I wouldn't give to read the scribbles on her yellow legal pad.

Tina looked at me, tapped her cheek with her silver pen. "Ready?"

I shook my head. "I can't do this yet."

"You're afraid?"

"Yes." I looked at my physician. "I need a breather. I don't think I stopped shaking after our last session until I went to bed."

"That means we're on the right track."

"And maybe the track leads out of hell and I don't want to look back anymore."

"Then why are you here?"

I thought about Mark and my desire to take our relationship to the next level. I didn't exactly want to explain this to Tina. I shrugged. "This whole experience is so not me. I'll admit, I'm a control freak. I don't like feeling like there is something that can flip me out at a moment's notice."

"How's your love life?"

I huffed. "What is it with you? How do you know what's going on in my head?"

"I'm a woman."

"OK. My love life or my sex life? I still get panicky at the thought of intimacy."

Tina shifted in her chair and leaned forward. "I want you to think about something."

"I'm listening."

"I think you were sexually abused as a child."

I caught my breath and looked away.

"It all fits, Camille. Your present troubles surfaced just as you and your boyfriend started heading to second base." She paused. "You remember your father holding you on his lap in a dark closet, a place he took you so you wouldn't be discovered."

As I listened, my gut tightened. Because it was the truth, or because I couldn't stand the thought, I couldn't tell.

"Little girls who are abused by their fathers commonly sleep in their clothes."

I shook my head. "I don't know. What about Tumi? This all started when I hit that dog. What about the blood in my memories?"

"I don't know how Tumi fits. If your father really killed your pet, as you suspect, could he have done it because Tumi always made noise when he came to you in your bed?"

The thought chilled me. I was a virgin. At least I thought I was. The thought that my own father could have . . . it seemed unthinkable. "I don't have any direct memory of . . . sex with my father."

"Many don't. It's such a violation of trust that you may have shut it away."

"So why dig it up now?"

"You know the answer. It's affecting your life. It's starting to interfere with your relationships with men." She raised a finger. "Your boss." Another finger. "Your boyfriend."

I knew she was right. But the process was too painful. I sat quietly, studying my fingernails.

"Camille, you are a beautiful woman. And you're beginning to open up in so many areas where you've been shut down, emotionally, physically, maybe even spiritually."

Shut down. The same words used by Dr. Gilles. Everyone seemed to think I was so closed. I nodded slowly, really starting to understand.

"How's work?"

"Dr. Gilles hasn't fired me yet."

"Be serious."

"I am. Dr. Gilles was none too pleased about what I did for you."

"But I was very pleased."

"You didn't hire me."

"Follow your heart, Camille. You won't be happy doing less."

I smiled. "But I might be jobless." I leaned forward, hugging my knees.

"You are a very driven woman." She made the statement as if it was fact.

"I—"

"Don't even protest this one."

I sighed and sat back, waiting for the evidence.

"You have outperformed every male in your residency, becoming the only one hired by Dr. Gilles. Over and over through your education, you have risen to be the one who was praised above your peers."

I nodded. What she said was correct. Unfortunately, I hadn't found being the best to be enough.

"Look at the choice of your career. You didn't just go into medicine. You had to take the hard route and select surgery. And then you go and choose one of the most macho areas to concentrate upon: trauma."

She stared at me, waiting for a response. I had nothing to say.

"Why are you so driven?"

I shrugged. "Why does anyone strive to do their best?"

"Doing your best and having to be the best may be different, Camille."

"What are you driving at?"

"Sometimes we operate out of our own sense of inferiority. We are searching for acceptance. Love. Pats on the back. So we can feel good about ourselves."

I looked at the floor. I knew what she was trying to do, softening her message about me by saying "we." "Don't we all do that?"

"Sure. To an extent." She paused. "But what about you? Why do you do it?"

"Obviously you have an opinion," I sulked. "You tell me."

"Maybe you need to prove to everyone that you aren't the little nigger that the Alabama children said you were. Maybe you have issues with men, stemming from Troy Johnson at the prep school, or from competing with men in surgery training, or God knows what else." She paused and softened her voice to continue, "And maybe, just maybe you're seeking the kind of love you never had from your father."

Tears filled my eyes. I had always hoped my father loved me, and certainly wanted him to be the perfect father I invented when Aunt Jeanine didn't measure up. "You think he didn't love me?"

"Maybe he did, in his own way. And maybe he didn't know how to show you. And maybe he hurt you very badly, Camille. Maybe something he did is behind all this terror."

She tapped her silver pen on her cheek again. "Let's make a plan. I won't probe deeper with hypnosis just now at your request. I want to proceed with a pace you are comfortable with. Let's let things simmer for a while. Maybe more will come to you over the next few weeks."

I nodded, relieved. We sat quietly for a few moments, letting the heaviness of our conversation settle.

"It may be helpful," she said, "to be the one controlling any sex between you and your boyfriend."

I tilted my head, not understanding.

"If I'm correct, and you were abused as a child, then having a man be the aggressor may be the thing that scares the memories into interfering with your present pleasure."

I thought about taking control of Mark. My cheeks flushed.

Tina stood, signaling our time was going to be shortened.

"I've been meaning to ask you something," I said. "I've been invited to a dinner by the agency that sent my father to the Congo. They are beginning an endowment in honor of my father. They want me to come to represent the family."

"Has this invitation brought back some memories for you?"

"Some." I shrugged. "Mostly, I think about how little I know about who my father was."

"When did the invitation come in relation to your flash-backs?"

"Soon after they began, I suppose."

"So at least it was not the initial stimulus. It still may be your adjustment to the stress of becoming a surgical attending."

"So do you think I should attend?"

She thought for a moment. "Yes. Being around others who may have known your father may help you remember."

Her opinion resonated with me. "Maybe I'll go then."

She gave me a reassuring hug.

It was a good plan, I thought. I'd go to the dinner. It was ironic, in a way. They wanted to honor my father's ghost. I just wanted to confront him.

THAT AFTERNOON, TINA lay quietly on the padded table while invisible beams of radiation sliced through her left breast. The process was painless and took no more than a few minutes out of each weekday. So far, the only thing she'd noticed was a faint pink color to the irradiated skin.

She'd fallen into a routine. She went for radiation each afternoon before going home. And while she was on the table getting her treatment, she held a yellow rose in her right hand. She smiled as she lifted the rose to her nose at the completion of her day's therapy. Mark sure knew how to make a woman feel supported.

I MET KENDRICK at the Skull for supper and sat amazed at how much he consumed. It had become a comfortable routine for us: a chocolate milkshake, large fries, and a double cheeseburger with bacon for him and a chef's salad for me. I shook my head. The guy ate like a surgery resident: quick, without pausing for conversation that might inhibit getting the calories in before the next disaster.

I hadn't been such a good influence on his food choices, but at least he saw what I ate. Maybe he'd get the idea from example.

He wore a baseball cap pulled down over his forehead. He ate so fast and close to his plate that the bill nearly tipped his milkshake.

"Slow down, sport. You act like that burger might get away." I reached over and tapped his hat. "And take that off. Gentlemen take off their hats when they enter a fine dining establishment."

He looked around the room. "Those guys are wearing caps."

I followed his gaze to two men sitting on bar stools at the counter. I whispered, "They must not be gentlemen."

He shook his head. "This must not be a fine dining establishment."

I smiled. "The Skull and Bones? It's a classic."

I started to lift his cap, but he resisted, putting his hand over mine. We struggled for a second, until he huffed and yanked off the cap.

He had a tennis-ball-sized bruise, puffy and red, right at his hairline. He glared at me.

"Kendrick!"

He stared down at the table, his eyes cold steel.

"I'm sorry." I paused. "Your father?" I whispered.

He hesitated, then nodded.

"I had hoped things were getting better."

He huffed again. "He mostly drinks on Saturdays now, 'cause he has a job at a body shop." He hesitated. "He apologized."

"How's your mother?"

"Her head looks worse than mine. But she likes big hats, too."

My heart sank. I wanted to barge right up the hill to Colonial Heights and tell Nadine to move out, that she didn't need to take that kind of abuse, but the reasons she stayed were complex. It was a decision she'd have to make on her own.

Kendrick looked vulnerable. He was young—so full of fun and potential when given the opportunity to laugh or dream. I thought about my own childhood. Was I bonded to this boy by more than the empathy I felt for his plight? Was I also hurt by a parent who was supposed to protect? I reached for his hand across the table and enveloped it in mine, feeling a moment of solidarity that I couldn't explain. Kendrick was unknowing and didn't return the squeeze I gave him. I supposed it wasn't cool for a fifteen-year-old to hold hands with a woman old enough to be his own . . . well, big sister. I wasn't ready to admit that I was old enough to be his mother, but I'd been through MCV's obstetric ward and I knew the truth whether I'd confess to it or not.

"Let me live with you."

I stared at him, my heart caught in a tangle of emotions. There was a mom inside me. She wanted to take Kendrick home and protect him. I felt like killing his father. I was afraid for him, but I couldn't care for a teenager. "I . . . I can't do that, Kendrick. I'm never home. You know that. You've got a mother who loves you. She barely left your side the whole time you were in the hospital."

"You would fight back."

I shook my head. "Fighting back is not the answer either."

Our waitress appeared and set two sodas on the table, a Coke in front of Kendrick and a Tab in front of me.

"I didn't order these."

A smile broke across her face. "I know." She tilted her head toward the bar. "He's paying for it."

I looked over to see Joel Bryan. My eyes narrowed and met his. He expression was serious, but his eyes were alight with mischief. I watched as he strained to keep from smiling. He didn't hold back long. After a few seconds he broke into a beautiful grin.

He sat next to a teen, about the same age as Kendrick. Perhaps we were both in the rescue business that evening.

I gave Joel a thank-you wave then turned my attention back to Kendrick. "There are shelters for women who—"

"No. My mom will never leave him. He cries and says he's sorry. Then he gives her jewelry."

"I can talk to a social worker and—"

"No!" Kendrick's voice was loud enough to embarrass me. Perhaps he was beyond that himself, as he didn't seem to mind the looks of the other patrons.

I stared at him and whispered, "Lower your voice."

He glared at me. "Don't ever send a social worker. That will make him mad."

I was stuck. What could I do if Nadine was unwilling to make a move?

We sipped our drinks silently for a few minutes. After we finished, Kendrick headed to a magazine rack to browse while I settled the bill.

I stopped by Joel Bryan. He looked up.

"You didn't have to—"

His raised hand stopped my protest. "Accept a gift, Camille. You guys looked like you could use a lift over there. And that's what I hope I can be about."

"I—" I hesitated and sighed. "You were right," I said quietly. "And thanks."

His smile was disarming. The way he looked at me made me want to gather my white coat around my neck. I felt he saw into my soul.

Our hands touched. He held mine for a second, just long enough to tell me he cared.

He wanted to give me a cold drink to give me a lift?

I smiled. He'd done just that.

32

B Y LUNCH ON the day after Mr. Karanja's funeral, my parents had reached a compromise. It was agreed that my mother would leave. She was Congolese and could mix with the people in the village and be safe. I would stay with my daddy and he would stay on at the hospital. It was weird, thinking about being around here with just Daddy. Mother said I'd have to be the woman of the house and take care of him.

Daddy was around the house more lately 'cause the rebellion had ended most of his work at the hospital—all except the emergency work on the soldiers.

Daddy told Mother that anything that would identify her with the white man might draw attention from the Simbas. He wanted her to dress like everyone else.

They sat at the kitchen table and discussed it while I pretended to sip my chai, but really I was listening.

"I've talked to Margaret. I promised her one of your dresses. You can use her clothes."

My mother whispered back, "She doesn't even cover her breasts. I can't go out like that."

My father gave her a desperate look.

"I haven't dressed that way in a long time. It's not Christian," she said.

"I don't want you to look like a Christian."

It was the first time I'd heard Daddy say anything like that.

"You have to look like you are simply visiting a patient. You can't walk past the Simbas wearing that, you know."

My mother wasn't happy.

"You have to do this. I can't go. You can blend in."

"I don't want to leave you."

My daddy looked over his shoulder at me, and then started to talk in Kiswahili. It didn't bother me. Kiswahili. French. English. I understood them all.

I couldn't imagine my mother baring her breasts like the village women. Maybe she can't either.

I told myself that's why she was crying.

RICHMOND, 1984

F RIDAY NIGHT I sat between Mark and Kendrick high above the third-base line at the Diamond, home of the Richmond Braves, eating hot dogs and sipping overpriced soda. We stood for the national anthem, and were on the last line, "home of the brave," when Mark, Kendrick, and the rest of the stadium erupted in a shout on the last word, screaming the name of their home team.

I participated in their revelry, but my mind was elsewhere, stuck on my last conversation with Tina Kinser.

The boys cheered the opening lineup as I snuck a look at Mark Lawson. Was my desire for his love related in some way to an unfulfilled need I'd experienced as an orphan? Was my driven behavior somehow tied to my need to be recognized and applauded? Was all of this a reflection of the unconditional acceptance I'd lacked as a child?

Kendrick made it through the first inning before going back to the snack bar to refuel. Mark handed him a five. "Bring back some popcorn."

Five minutes later, I was crowded between two animals competing for the bucket of popcorn. "Hold on," I said, smacking their hands. I stood up. "Here," I said to Mark, "switch seats with me." I sat back down in Mark's seat. "Now you two can enjoy your popcorn without me being the coffee table."

The men munched happily.

I cuddled Mark's right arm in mine and leaned my head on his shoulder. I was comfy for five seconds until he attempted to snag a fly ball that landed two rows in front of us.

A moment later I resumed my position and my musings. Since our trip to Kings Dominion, Mark had settled naturally into the role of big brother to Kendrick. Maybe I shouldn't have been surprised. He was a pediatrician. He was supposed to love kids. It was a quality I'd always thought important to me, another reason I believed my relationship with Mark might be the real thing.

I sighed. Tina had confirmed what I had previously thought. The panic that had been stalking me had affected my relationship with Mark. I sensed that he had been holding back, waiting for the signal from me that this love I had was for real.

I thought ahead to the CFW endowment dinner in honor of my father. Maybe getting out of town could be the change our relationship needed.

Was he the one? Was I ready to make the kind of commitment I expected from him . . . undying devotion through richer and poorer, sickness and health, till death do us part?

After the game, Mark pointed to an area next to the field where Richmond players were known to gather to sign autographs. "Why don't you go?" he said to Kendrick. "Some of these guys will be playing in the majors some day. A signature could be valuable."

Kendrick wrinkled his nose. "I don't have anything for them to sign."

Mark reached into his backpack and pulled out a small square box. "Here."

Kendrick slid a new baseball from the box. "Oh, wow." He looked at me as if to ask if it was OK.

"It's a gift," Mark said. "Go ahead."

"We'll wait right here," I said to his back.

Kendrick scampered down the steps, two at a time, rushing for the fence. I looked at Mark. That little act of kindness was enough to convince my heart. "I want you to go to Chicago with me."

He raised his eyebrows, and a smile lifted the corners of his mouth. "What's up?"

"Remember the fancy dinner I was invited to? It's to commemorate the endowment and honor my father?"

"You're going?"

"I thought you wanted me to."

He shrugged. "I do."

"Go with me," I whispered. "Getting away from Richmond in a nice hotel may be just what we need."

He looked at me from the corner of his eye. "You're serious."

I leaned in and kissed his neck. He turned to me and we shared a kiss that tasted like popcorn. "Of course I'm serious."

"OK." He kissed me again and turned back toward the field. "I'll go to Chicago with you."

I sat a minute watching for Kendrick in the crowd of fans in line for an autograph. "Tina has some interesting insights into some of my problems with intimacy."

Mark shifted in his seat. His lips looked like he'd just tasted something sour. "You don't talk about us, do you?"

"Sure," I said, cuddling his left arm in my hands and grazing his elbow across my breasts.

"But—"

I squeezed his arm. "I don't use your name," I said. "But it wouldn't really be a crime if I did. She's a professional, Mark. She knows about confidentiality."

"I'd rather keep what is intimate between us private," he whispered.

"This doesn't reflect negatively on you, stupid." I giggled nervously. "This is about me."

"Well?" He shifted in his seat. "Aren't you going to tell me what insights Tina has?"

"Maybe the ballpark isn't the place."

"We're alone up here."

"OK," I said, trying not to seem alarmed. "Tina thinks I was abused by my father."

"Abused?"

I nodded.

"As in sexually? Physically?"

"Sexually," I said, mustering as much of a matter-of-fact tone as I could.

"But you don't remember?"

"I remember enough."

"Do you believe her?"

I sighed. "I don't know. Sometimes it seems she's reaching for the easiest solution. But some things are consistent with that diagnosis. The dark-closet nightmare, my panic when we get close . . . it's all getting clearer."

"So what's to be done? How can you know for sure?"

"Maybe more hypnosis. Maybe going to hang out with people who knew my father will help bring out some memories."

"Why dwell on it?"

"I'm not dwelling on it. I'm trying to make sense of a nightmare that keeps interfering with my waking hours."

"So is that the plan in Chicago? Hang out with people who knew your father to see if your memory will return?"

"That's only part of it," I said, trying to sound sexy. "The other is that we will be alone, in our own room together. We'll have all the time we need to . . . get to know each other. No pressures. No beepers. Just you, me, and a king-sized bed," I whispered.

"And how do we know that when it comes down to the time, you'll be OK with it?"

I took a deep breath. "Good question. It will be on my terms. My speed. I get to be in control."

He raised his eyebrows. "When is the dinner?"

"Next Saturday, but we should go up on Friday so we can have an extra night together."

"I'll have to trade call."

"I'll make it worthwhile."

He smiled. I joined him. This felt right. Mark Lawson would be mine at last.

33

SATURDAY MORNING MARK Lawson pulled into Tina's driveway and took a deep breath. This wasn't going to be easy.

He found her on the back deck, bending over a bed of raised flowers. She wore a pair of dark running shorts and an old white tank top that didn't reach all the way to her shorts. He watched her from the corner of the yard. She was beautiful.

He cleared his throat.

Startled, she whirled around. "Oh," she said, breaking into a relieved grin. "You scared me."

He approached and forced a smile.

She read him right away. She closed her eyes and looked away.

"Tina, we've got to talk."

He waited for her to turn. He took a step toward her. He could see her fist clenched around a small digging tool. When she turned, she had tears in her eyes. "I lost, didn't I?"

"Lost?"

"Why are you looking at me that way? You've come to say good-bye."

He stepped closer, his arms out, palms up. "This isn't easy. I don't want to hurt you."

"Too late," she said, pressing her hand to her upper lip. "I should be smarter than this." She looked away. "I've seen this in other women. I've had to hold their hands when their hearts were broken."

"You're married."

She glared at him. "That's not why we're having this conversation."

"Tina—"

"You've never made a break from your other relationship, have you?"

He sighed and looked down. "No."

"I'm such a fool."

"You're not a fool. You're a beautiful woman, Tina."

She dropped the tool to the deck and stepped toward his open arms. She buried her head against his chest. "Then why don't you want me?"

He encircled her sobbing frame with his arms, his heart breaking. "You aren't a fool, Tina. I am," he whispered. "This is my fault."

He released his grip as she pounded his chest with her fists, each blow driving a stake through his heart.

"It's not that I don't want you. If things were different—"

She pushed him away. "Go."

"I'm sorry."

"I'm sorry I met you."

SATURDAY AFTERNOON MARK, Kendrick, and I launched out onto the James River for a lazy float on three truck inner tubes. With the way midsummer had settled on Richmond, it was the perfect escape, and for Kendrick, whose head danced with visions of Huck Finn on the mighty Mississippi, it was an adventure just this side of paradise.

It had all been Mark's idea. He showed up at my place midmorning, with the trunk of his little car tied shut over the inner tubes and with a spark of excitement in his eyes I hadn't seen for weeks. "Let's call Kendrick," he said. "We can put in behind Dr. Rawlings's house and float down to Dr. Lawrence's place."

I called Nadine. She sounded unusually stressed and talked to me in hushed tones. She was glad to send Kendrick off on his bicycle to meet me at MCV.

We floated with the current, lazily letting the river have its way. Kendrick and Mark water-battled their way along the shore. I was content to rest my neck against the squishy tube and gaze at the blue sky.

Watching Mark with Kendrick brought me joy in double portions. Something was different about Mark today. He seemed freer, more at peace than usual. Perhaps getting away on the river was the medicine he needed to cool the pressures of dealing with kids with cancer.

We'd been in the water two hours before stopping for lunch along the north shore. Thanks to Tupperware, we ate dry sandwiches. Mark opened a Budweiser.

Kendrick frowned as he watched Mark drink. "Doctors should know better," he said.

Mark laughed it off, but I could tell Kendrick was upset. When Mark's attention was on me, I looked to see Kendrick pouring the beer onto the shore and filling the can with James River water.

I stayed quiet. I was not thrilled about that particular example Mark was setting for this teen.

"I shouldn't stay out too late," Kendrick said.

"Plans for the night?"

"It's Saturday night. I try to be home for my mom."

I traded glances with Mark. Kendrick was trying to protect her.

"Dr. Lawrence's place is just a few miles down the river."

Kendrick studied the sky. "Maybe we should set out again."

"I can take your bike up to your place in my car," I suggested. "That will save you some time."

Kendrick nodded. We watched as Mark lifted the beer can to his lips and took a large swig of the river.

"Yeauuk!" He spewed the liquid back onto the bank. He glared at Kendrick. "Why, you—"

Kendrick dashed away, pushing his inner tube. "Hey, I warned you." He laughed.

I tried hard not to laugh, but it was funny. I handed Mark my Diet Coke. "Here."

He wiped his mouth with the back of his hand. He shouted at Kendrick, "Scar belly!"

Kendrick patted his incision. "Better than being a beer belly!"

Mark looked at me. "Whose idea was it to bring him along?"

I smiled and pushed out toward Kendrick. "Yours."

Two hours later, with the Richmond sky beginning to color, we stashed the tubes in my car, which we'd parked at Dr. Lawrence's place. He was a pediatric attending with a heart of gold. I slipped on a pair of running shorts over my bikini bottoms and jumped in the driver's seat of my Prelude.

I drove while Mark and Kendrick argued over which of the Richmond Braves was going to get called up to Atlanta.

When we reached his car, Mark kissed me and whispered, "Can I come back to your place?"

I took a deep breath. The day had been so nice. I searched his eyes. I was afraid of what would happen. I could tell by his kiss that he was feeling amorous, probably because he'd been staring at my little bathing suit for half the day. "Maybe we'd better wait."

He looked away, but I saw his eyes glass over just for a second. "Let's save it for next weekend."

His eyes met mine. He was hungry. He looked down and opened his car door, nodding consent with his head, but not with his heart. He got in his car as I stood by, hoping he understood.

I leaned down and kissed his open mouth, hoping he'd take it as a deposit, but not a frustrating tease.

"Bye."

"Wait!"

I turned back and leaned into his open window again.

His eyes danced over my face. "I wanted to tell you something."

I waited. He just kept looking at me. "What?" I asked.

"I love you."

I shut my eyes for a long blink. I was dreaming. Did he actually use the L-word? *Be still my heart! He said he loved me!* I looked at him, studying his face for a moment. He was desperate for a response from me, but I wanted to appear cool.

"I know," I said. I straightened up, feigning a move to walk away, but my emotions were supersized by his confession. I turned back and gave him one more kiss, this one just shy of an R rating.

I looked back to see Kendrick staring. As soon as he saw me, he looked away. I guess I should have figured that a fifteen-year-old might be a bit too interested in learning about passionate good-byes. "Come on, sport. Let's go get your bike and get back to Colonial Heights."

He sat silently beside me, staring straight ahead. I turned on my headlights. Night was descending on the Richmond skyline, but it was morning in my heart. *Mark said he loved me!*

"Take me home with you."

I sighed. "I thought you wanted to be home early."

"Maybe it's better if I don't go at all."

"What about your mother?"

"She's a big girl."

I glanced at him. It sounded funny coming from him, talking about his mother like he was the one trying to let her grow up. "She relies on you?"

He kept his eyes straight ahead. "We rely on each other."

"That's the way it should be in a family, Kendrick."

He sat quietly for a moment. "I told her to leave him."

I wasn't sure what to say. Breaking up a family, even for something as bad as physical abuse, was such a waste.

"I told her that you thought she should leave."

I listened to the wail of a siren heading for MCV. It was appropriate, mirroring the warning I sensed in my soul. I wanted to comfort him, take him in my arms, and tell him it would be OK, but I wasn't about to tell him what my gut told me was a lie. I felt a sudden tightness in my throat. When I finally found my voice, we were sitting at a red light. I hoped I'd speak without crying. "What did your mother say?"

He put his hands on his hips. I saw Nadine. " 'You shouldn't talk such foolishness, boy.' "

His imitation was enough to lighten my mood. Maybe his sense of humor would help keep his head above troubled water.

We stopped at MCV, where we unchained his bike and placed it in my trunk. It wouldn't quite fit so I tied the trunk of my Prelude shut with a handlebar sticking out. In a few minutes, we were approaching his little house in Colonial Heights.

"Let me off at the corner. Dad won't want to see you."

I tried to keep the mood light. "He thinks Mark's Dr. Weller, remember?" I paused. "I think he liked me."

"He doesn't like anyone when he drinks."

"How do you know he's drinking?"

"It's the weekend. He'll be drinking."

It was a sad thing to be so predictable. I slowed the car as we approached the Solomon house. Lamps were on in the den, spraying light through worn curtains onto the covered porch. The image was peaceful, but it belied hidden unrest. My window was down so I could enjoy the evening as Richmond's heat melted away. As we passed, I heard Nadine scream. It was a note that cut the night like a knife.

I saw Kendrick shrink. There was no mistaking the sound. Nadine wasn't shrieking for joy. Hers was a cry of imminent terror. "Let me out now," he said, his voice etched with strain.

I pulled over, my heart pounding. I heard glass breaking. Another scream. I looked around the neighborhood where houses were as close as they could be, stuffed on the little lots. No one was out enjoying the night. I could see the flicker of a TV set through a neighbor's window and hear the pulse of a bass guitar resonating from another.

Kendrick was in the house before I could slow him down. I stepped out of the car onto a small sidewalk leading to the house. I was torn. I should investigate. But what could I do?

And then, in a moment, I saw Nadine, standing behind the screen door, fear gripping her mouth into a gross contortion. Even from my position at the road's edge, I could see the sweat glistening on her forehead, hear the wind whistling into her chest. In a moment, she disappeared, jerked backward by her hair. She didn't scream this time. I heard only a sickening groan and the crash of her bulk hitting the floor.

The image was all I needed to propel me into action. I was on the porch and in the den before I could think of my own safety. Clive was an animal standing over his prey, his hand entangled in Nadine's Afro. Kendrick was nowhere. Nadine's eyes were wide. "Help."

"Clive!" I yelled as loudly as I could. "Let her go!"

His eyes locked on me. Eyes that were glazed, unfocused, and wild. "You're that surgeon's girl."

I felt immediately underdressed, wishing I'd pulled a top on over my bikini. Clive stared at me, his eyes alight with interest.

"Let her go!" I repeated.

He dropped Nadine's head to the floor and stepped toward me.

"No," Nadine yelled, flailing her arm out at his leg. In a moment, she was leeched to his leg with both arms, slowing his progress toward me. "Clive, don't!"

Clive raised his fist over Nadine's face.

Kendrick's voice interrupted Clive's strike: "Touch her and you're dead!"

Kendrick stood at the foot of a wooden staircase holding a pistol leveled at his father's chest.

"Kendrick," I gasped.

Nadine released Clive's leg. "Kendrick!"

"No," he cried, moving toward his father.

Clive cursed and took a step toward his son.

"Stop right there!"

"You stole my gun!" Clive staggered forward, his eyes fixed on his son.

Kendrick began to cry, the gun weaving in his two hands. "Get out."

Clive laughed and grabbed his son's wrist just behind the gun. "Give me the gun, son."

"Daddy," he cried. "Please go."

Clive's hand closed over his son's as the gun fired.

The sharp explosion from the pistol was followed by an eerie silence.

Clive stumbled back and the handgun tumbled to the floor.

Nadine, Kendrick, and I stared without speaking, while reality dawned. Clive had been shot.

Everything around me seemed to slow. Kendrick froze, his face caught in the same expression of terror that he'd revealed on our first day together.

Then Nadine started to scream.

34

CLIVE JERKED UPRIGHT as a red circle expanded over his left chest. Then his eyes froze as he dropped backward to the floor.

Kendrick's face contorted with pain. "Daddy! No!"

I spoke through my horror, willing my heart to be calm. I looked at Nadine. "Call nine-one-one."

Nadine crawled toward her husband from her place on the floor. "Clive!" she wailed. An eerie moan erupted through her lips as she grabbed her husband's face.

Clive gasped. "N-Nadine."

"Hold on, baby," she cried.

Kendrick fell to his knees over his father. "I didn't mean to shoot him! I was just trying to scare him." His voice dissolved into tears. "Daddy, no! Daddy, no!"

I grabbed Nadine's arm. "Call nine-one-one. Now!"

She stumbled off, screaming as she went.

I pulled up Clive's shirt to see an entrance wound to the left of the sternum. His chest was a red fountain. I pushed my hand against the wound but the blood quickly seeped through my fingers. "Bring me a towel."

Kendrick ran.

I felt for a pulse in the neck. Nothing. Clive's chest rose one more time in a hungry gasp for air and then stopped. He was in full exsanguination and there wasn't a thing I could do about it.

In desperation I began mouth-to-mouth resuscitation and chest compressions. Nadine and Kendrick looked on, both crying. I was onstage trying to resurrect Lazarus.

The rescue squad arrived ten minutes into my futile attempts. I was doing what I could for the sake of Kendrick and for Nadine. And maybe because if I stopped I'd be crying, too.

I rode with the squad to MCV, coding Clive Solomon, and placing a chest tube en route. It seemed his entire blood volume, at least what wasn't on the floor back in his den, was in his left chest cavity.

We did CPR until the chief trauma surgery resident could open his chest in the ER. The hole in Clive's left ventricle was as big as a quarter. His heart was flat. His pupils were fixed. We called the code at 9:59. Clive Solomon was dead.

I stepped away from the stretcher, the clinical noise of the trauma bay and the ER beyond clamoring in my ears. I felt a chill, and suddenly I became aware of the blood on my hands, and that I'd been running a trauma code in my bathing suit.

The trauma bay was scarlet red. Blood covering Clive's body. More on the floor. Nurses and residents were cleaning up and starting the busy work of charting. I was numb.

With my heart in my throat, I grabbed a patient gown from a portable laundry rack and headed for the female changing room outside the OR. I needed to clean up before I faced the Solomons.

What could I tell them? Nadine would expect the same miraculous performance that had snatched her six-liter boy from the cold fingers of the grave.

But Clive was beyond salvage, a father accidentally downed with the same weapon that had come razor-blade close to stealing the life of his only son.

I stripped, tossing my bloody swimsuit and shorts in the trash. I chose a pair of scrubs and headed for the showers.

There, my tears flowed unchecked and indistinguishable from

the water that showered the bloodstains away. I am a hero, I told myself. I am a surgeon who cannot always win the fight against suffering and death.

But how will I explain that to Nadine?

Or to my miracle boy?

TINA PICKED UP the vase of yellow roses and tossed the whole thing in the trash.

She had only herself to blame. She walked to the bathroom and splashed water on her face. She felt nauseated. She calmed herself with slow, deep breaths.

It didn't work. In a moment, she was clutching the porcelain and emptying her gut.

She spat in disgust, trying to rid her mouth of the bitter taste. She'd spent the afternoon first brooding in anger, then slithering in self-pity. Now, to top her misery, she had to deal with a sick stomach.

She leaned back and let the tears flow again. Breast cancer. An unfaithful spouse. A failed marriage. A young boyfriend who'd been all too willing to take what she gave and treat her with contempt. The last month had been a whirlwind of pain, realization, and . . . stolen delight.

Suddenly, a new apprehension dawned. It couldn't be! She reassured herself that she was nauseated because of her anxiety over Mark. Still, she rushed to her purse and pulled out a small calendar and searched for a notation she'd made charting her last menses. She stared in disbelief. She was a week late.

She pulled her hand through her hair and felt a sudden rush of perspiration. *No. I'm just getting a little irregular as I age. Or maybe it's the stress of surgery and radiation. Certainly I can't be . . .*

She couldn't think of it. She wouldn't. She paced her spacious bedroom as worry after worry assaulted her. Wouldn't radiation be damaging to a baby? How would Mark Lawson respond to the news?

I'm overreacting.

She felt as if her stomach were doing gymnastics. She ran to the bathroom for relief.

I'd better get a pregnancy test before I continue with my cancer therapy.

BY THE TIME I'd showered and called Mark, it appeared that half of Colonial Heights Baptist Church had gathered in the ER waiting room. I found Nadine praying and Kendrick sitting expressionless at her side.

I touched her shoulder. "Nadine."

She stood and searched my face. Kendrick gripped the edge of her dress. I shook my head. "I'm so sorry. We did everything we could."

I opened my arms to hug the woman who so often had opened her arms to comfort me. As we hugged, Kendrick slumped in his chair and began to sob.

I felt helpless. I released Nadine into the arms of her friends and sat beside Kendrick. Our eyes met. He buried his head against my chest as I encircled his shoulders with my arms. He might be a man tomorrow but today he was a lost boy without a father.

I could not stop my tears. Clive was an abusive father and I would not cry for him. I cried for the boy in my arms who would have to live forever with the tortured memory of that night. A beautiful day on the river had turned into hell.

We cried together, my tears falling into his hair. When I finally found my voice, the words tumbled from my lips before I could stop them. "Everything's gonna be all right, baby. Everything's gonna be all right."

35

I FINALLY GOT TO bed at 2:00 a.m. after returning to the Solomons' and going over the gory details of the evening with Police Detective Reynolds. He was a veteran of Richmond's force and allayed my fears about what would happen to Kendrick. With my testimony, he doubted anyone would look deeper than his report, never question if Clive's death was anything but an accident.

I shut my eyes but I could not shut out the image of Clive's face as his eyes went dull.

I tossed and turned until my mind drifted to Mark Lawson. In the turmoil of the night, I'd almost forgotten what he'd said as we parted.

I held the memory close to my heart, cuddling it as carefully as I would a precious gem, not daring to let it fall away. I chose not to think of anything else, warming my heart with the one word I'd longed to hear him say. *Love.* With that, I slept until my alarm sounded at seven.

THAT MORNING TINA arose with the same queasiness that she'd carried to bed. She sipped hot tea and ate crackers in hopes of easing the nausea, but headed back to the bathroom for another round of what Dan had always called hugging the porcelain Buick.

When nine o'clock arrived and she still felt lousy, she called her receptionist.

The voice on the other end of the line was typical Kerri: cheerful, clear, and dripping with femininity. "MCV psychiatry department, may I help you?"

"Kerri, this is Dr. Kinser. Look, I'm sorry about the late notice, but I'm fighting some sort of stomach bug here. I'm going to have to get you to reschedule my patients. Are there any urgent matters?"

Kerri sighed. "The surgery team called. They wanted to discharge Linda Jones, but she drank a cup of Betadine that she swiped from a supply closet."

She groaned. "Tell them I'll talk to her. In the meantime, let our chief resident know that I won't be in."

"Sip some ginger ale. My grandma always made me do that when I was sick."

"Thanks, Kerri." Tina hung up and took a deep, cleansing breath. *If only Grandma's ginger ale could solve the problem this time.*

THE NEXT MORNING, I hibernated in my office catching up on paperwork and making plans for my weekend. I called Jacob Richardson from CFW and accepted his invitation, informing him that I would be attending with a guest. I then made flight and hotel reservations. When I hung up the phone, my heart was pounding.

I could do this. I was thirty years old. I loved this man. I'd tell him the truth on the plane flight up. I had no experience and he was going to have to be gentle. I stared at the wall thinking about what it would be like. I was scared and excited at the same time.

I wasn't sure how long I'd been lost in my fantasy when a knock on my door jarred me to alertness. My hand flew to my lips to check for drool. William Bransford stepped in. "Hi, Camille. Mind if I sit down?"

I nodded toward the chair across from my desk. "Sure. What's up?"

He held up a computer printout. I recognized it as the appointment roster for the general surgery clinic. "We hired you as a trauma surgeon, Camille."

I nodded, but felt immediate alarm. Where was he going with this? He had stopped talking, perhaps to get my attention. Finally, I questioned, "The point is?"

"You saw six breast patients last week alone. It seems the word is getting out that we have a new breast cancer doctor at MCV."

I held up my hands. "I'm doing my job as a trauma surgeon. I can't help it if these ladies want to see a woman."

"Dr. Gilles watches this, Camille."

"I thought I was allowed to do anything he trained me to do."

"Gilles trained you to be a scientist."

"I'm still a scientist." I smiled. "A scientist with heart."

"After your little speech in the mortality conference, Gilles is vowing to review every case of yours that falls outside your specialty area."

"I didn't ask these women to come to me."

"I know, but you aren't supposed to be developing a specific interest in an area outside your chosen subspecialty."

"I'm not choosing these women. They are choosing me. What am I to do?"

He sighed. "I can't make you toe the line, Camille. Nor can I protect you if you color outside the lines. Stay in established protocol or you will be asked to move on."

"Everything I have done has a scientific justification."

"I'm not asking for a defense. We heard that in M and M."

This was unfair. I hadn't asked to be put in this position.

"OK." I paused. "Now that you've brought it up, I've been thinking about something. Why is it that we aren't participating in the NSABP trials to determine whether lumpectomy is just as good as the old-school therapy?"

Dr. Bransford glanced over his shoulder and shut my door. He took a deep breath. "Look, Camille, I know you love Dr. Gilles. He's a great surgeon. And he likes you, but there are certain areas you should know not to push."

I shook my head. "What? What are you talking about?"

He spoke in a quiet tone. "You didn't hear this from me. Gilles was overlooked for the top job overseeing the NSABP trials a few years back. It's a sore spot for him." Bransford shrugged. "So MCV hasn't been participating in the trials."

"That's unethical."

"Careful, Camille. That's politics, an all too common distraction in academic medicine."

Pushing back from my desk, I questioned, "So what are you saying?"

"Only that you should understand the undertow below the surface of what you see. If you push the envelope in the treatment of breast cancer patients, you will only be scratching at one of the boss's old wounds." He lifted his eyebrows. "And new attendings need to stay in good graces."

I nodded resolutely. "Thanks." I hesitated. "I think."

Bransford left without saying good-bye. I was sure he thought he was doing me a favor, but I'd have rather not known this about Dr. Gilles. He had always been above this sort of pettiness in my mind. The patient came first, not our egos. I sighed. I suspected there was a depth of mystery behind those piercing eyes I'd rather not uncover all at once. This week had been bad enough without having to double my efforts at not offending the boss.

One thing I knew. I wasn't advertising for specific business. But whoever came my way in need of a general surgeon, I was their woman.

THAT NIGHT, MARK and I dropped by the Solomons' place to find the same crowd that had filled the MCV emergency room. I only managed to say "I'm sorry" to Nadine and Kendrick before they were whisked away by comforters. There was food everywhere. Plates of ham biscuits, cheese balls with crackers, and buckets of Popeyes fried chicken seemed to cover everything with a flat surface. I didn't have an appetite, but Mark easily ate what I normally consumed in two days.

On Wednesday afternoon, we attended the funeral service at Colonial Heights Baptist Church. Mark sat to my right, the only white face in the sanctuary. To say that the crowd was colorful would have been an understatement. Everyone was in black, for sure, but double-breasted suits, sharkskin, hats, and sunglasses were vogue.

Mark seemed uncomfortable. He leaned to my ear and whispered, "Just think what a bomb in this place could do to the Richmond drug traffic."

What? I looked at him like he'd just passed gas in church, but I didn't have time for his foolishness. I shushed him with my elbow and strained my eyes to see a fifteen-year-old boy on the front row beside Nadine.

Kendrick had a lock on my heart, which ran cross-grain to my training. I didn't know if I could follow through with my plans to spend the weekend with Mark. I was torn. I glanced at Mark. He wasn't going to like it if I backed out.

We sat through a ninety-minute service that ended at four. I doubted if we'd have been out before dark if Clive had actually been a member there.

I finally got to talk to Kendrick as he stood in the parking lot before the procession to the burial site.

"How're you doing?"

He stayed quiet and looked away.

I sighed, feeling stupid. "It was a dumb question, Kendrick. I didn't know what else to say."

He kept his eyes on the hearse a few yards away. "I'm going to northern Virginia tomorrow. I've got cousins there."

I nodded. "How long?"

He shrugged. "A few weeks, maybe longer."

"Will you call me when you get back?" I hesitated. "There will still be some time for summer fun before school begins."

"Sure."

I cleared my throat, wondering what was in his mind. "Don't blame yourself for this, Kendrick. I was there, remember? Remind yourself why you were doing what you were doing."

He looked at me, then quickly away again. He wiped at his nose with the back of his hand. He wanted to be a man. He didn't want to cry. His chin quivered. When he found his voice, it rushed out with a sob. "I hated him."

The admission seemed to crack the veneer of manliness to let his tears flow.

I gathered him into my arms. I pressed my lips into his hair and whispered, "You remember something, Kendrick. You were acting out of love for your mother and for me. Don't you believe otherwise."

Kendrick pulled himself away and pressed his fists into his eyes. I turned to see that Mark had appeared. It may have been OK for Kendrick to cry in front of me, but not in front of a man.

A few of the elders ushered Nadine past and into a car. She motioned for her son.

I hugged him quickly again. "Remember to call me, OK?"

He nodded.

Mark gripped Kendrick's shoulder to say good-bye before he hopped into a large silver Cadillac.

When my eyes met Mark's, he was smiling. "What?" I asked.

"You're changing, that's all."

"Changing good or changing bad?" I intertwined my fingers with his.

He whispered into my hair, "Changing good." It made me smile. I knew he was right. Two months ago, I'd have never gotten emotionally invested in a patient.

We watched as the caravan began moving, lights on, into the street. "He's going away to his cousins'."

Without looking at me, Mark asked, "Are we still going to Chicago?"

"Sure." I looked down. My heart was half filled with doubts about my plans, fears that I would freak out again and ruin everything, and half filled with excitement to explore the unknown with a man who had dared to use the L-word on me. "I guess I have business with my father to deal with." I smiled and elbowed his gut. "Among other things."

I thought about being shut down, and how right Tina was about me opening up more emotionally. There were still other rooms in my life with doors locked tight, but I sensed I was about to unlock one of them for Mark. We stared as the hearse disappeared, carrying Clive Solomon's body toward its resting place. Mark put his arm around me. "Kendrick is laying his father to rest. Now it's time for you to do the same."

36

NIGHTTIME WAS SUPPOSED to be a respite from the day's hassles. But lately it seemed the day wasn't large enough to contain my anxieties, and the day's troubles bulged into the night.

Tonight was no different. I laid awake waffling over the rightness of asking Mark to share the weekend with me. One moment I was convinced that confronting my father's memory was a good idea; the next, I thought I'd better leave sleeping dogs lie. At least asking Mark to go with me had created an interesting diversion from my fears of facing memories of the Congo. Now, in the little time I found to look ahead to the weekend, my focus had changed. So, instead of worrying about memories of an abusive father, my worries were centered on sex.

My first time. It was so common a phrase. I'd been in on scads of conversations over the years where my friends filled me in on their first experiences. I'd listened with a quiet fascination, mostly glad that it wasn't me, but also curious about their bravado over their own conquests.

I was glad I'd waited this long. If Troy Johnson had taught me anything in the janitor's closet back in prep school, it was that physical affection divorced from love was about as romantic as a broom closet. Maybe I should thank him for that. Conversely, maybe I should blame him that I couldn't stand to mop floors.

Perhaps it had something to do with my association of ammonia-laden floor wax with having my tonsils licked by his tongue.

I rehearsed what I liked about my man to quiet my pounding heart. Finally I surrendered to the slumber that called, my fears no longer able to fight the exhaustion.

AT THREE I awoke to the full experience of fear I'd faced in Tina's office during my hypnosis.

I run my hand along the corner of the blanket and pull it back to reveal the fur that I'd felt moments before. In spite of the darkness, I know it is Tumi.

I scream, "Daddy!"

His hand clamps over my mouth. "You must be quiet."

I can hardly get my breath to speak. "What happened to Tumi?"

"Be quiet, Camille! Tumi had to die."

Stale air from the closet comes to me in gasps between my father's fingers. Something terrible is happening. I don't understand why he is holding me this way. Did Daddy kill Tumi?

My hand searches for signs of life but Tumi's fur is lifeless, matted, and sticky.

I am afraid to make noise, so my tears roll down on my father's hands without sound.

"Everything's gonna be all right."

After a minute, his grip loosens, but I understand that I'd better not speak again.

Daddy holds me in the darkness stroking my hair. He kisses my neck, my cheek. He holds me for a long time until his body trembles against mine.

I pulled back my covers, which were saturated with my sweat. I gasped for air, sucking wind like I'd just run a hundred-yard sprint. I stared wide-eyed at the wall, as the realization of who and where I was dawned. *It's 1984. I'm in my apartment.*

"Daddy," I whispered to the ceiling. "Who were you?" A hero? A missionary surgeon. A loving father or not? An optimistic fool intent on saving Africa for Jesus?

I remembered riding next to him in the Land Rover. I hadn't felt scared then.

So why did my heart squeeze with fear at the mention of his name? I reminded myself of Tina's words. *No one was here to hurt me now.*

I plodded to my study and retrieved a copy of a fat surgical text. I sat at my desk glancing over the next chapter I needed to outline for my board review. I reminded myself who I was. "A woman," I whispered.

I opened the text and attempted to concentrate on a chapter on esophageal tumors.

After ten minutes, I gave up. I paced my little study for a minute and thought about calling Tina Kinser. I looked at the clock. I couldn't call her at this hour.

My thoughts shifted to the upcoming weekend in Chicago with Mark. What if I couldn't follow through? What if he whispered in my ear and I began to freak?

This was crazy. I was on the edge of a weekend I'd remember for the rest of my life and I was letting a twenty-year-old experience threaten it.

I could do this.

I was in control.

I retreated to my couch and grabbed a magazine, but worried about my weekend performance. What if I froze up the minute he took me in his arms?

I resisted following the same rabbit trail of anxieties. I clenched my fists in silent resolution. I could face the ghost of my past.

But I thought I'd call Tina in the morning just to make sure.

The following morning, with a large mug of black coffee in my hand, I did just that.

She answered after the first ring. "Hello."

"Tina, it's me, Camille. I'm sorry to bother you so early, but I wanted to catch you before I let this go much further."

"No bother, Camille. Let what go?"

"I've made plans to go to Chicago to attend the dinner honoring my father this weekend."

"That's good. We talked about that. I think you should go."

"That's not my question." I hesitated. "I invited my boyfriend. I—"

"You're having second thoughts?"

"Sort of. I had another nightmare last night. I'm just imagining the worst, I guess. What if I freak when he comes on to me?" I hesitated, then went on, "I feel stupid even bringing it up."

"Camille, chill, honey. I think inviting your boyfriend with you is a great idea. From what I gather, you really love this man."

I sighed. "Yes."

"And you're ready for a physical relationship?"

"I think so, er, I thought so."

"Don't let the past, or fears of the past, ruin what you've got today. I think this relationship may be a key ingredient in restoring you to a healthy image of men."

"I thought getting away with him, away from Richmond, away from the pressures of my job, may be just the thing. But then I thought about how intense my feelings about my father may be after the ceremony, and I started thinking all of this might be a very bad idea. I just wanted your feedback."

"Of course I don't know this man, Camille, but I would think the more loving support you have around you when you confront the demons from your past, the better." She cleared her throat. "But don't put so much pressure on yourself to have the perfect weekend getaway. Just realize you're taking him along for support. If the physical relationship blooms, great, but don't put all your expectations at the highest level. This is going to be an intense time for you."

"I guess."

"And remember what I said in our last session. It may be easier for you if for a time you took the aggressor role. Don't be passive. It may be best if he understands the ground rules before you go, so he doesn't have unrealistic expectations." She paused. "I take it he's expecting to sleep with you?"

Duh, Tina. "Yes."

"You may want to talk this out up front. Men with sex on the brain can get pretty bent out of shape if they think conquest is near and the prey gets away."

I laughed. "Thanks for the warning."

"Sure. Where will you be staying?"

"Chicago Hilton and Towers."

"Ooh, that's nice. I've been to a psychiatry meeting there once."

"Thanks, Tina. I guess I just needed a little shot of courage."

"Don't worry, Camille, everything's gonna be all right." She fell silent for a moment before she added, "Oh, Camille, I didn't mean to say that, I—"

"Forget it. It only works if you whisper it in my ear."

She laughed. "You are going to be fine."

TINA KINSER HUNG up the phone. She hadn't been to work in three days. And each day she had skipped her radiation treatment. Dr. Chadaury had called her yesterday to see if she was OK. She told him she was nauseated. He said it was an infrequent side effect of radiation. She was afraid to tell him about her real fears.

But today, she felt amazingly good. She lay still on her bed for a moment, taking inventory. No headache. No nausea. Maybe she wasn't pregnant after all.

She bought a home pregnancy test and used it in the women's restroom down the hall from her office.

She stared at the little test strip and sighed. Relief! The test was negative.

She saw ten patients before lunch. Six were quick follow-up patients for medication adjustments. Three were old patients with ongoing needs for psychotherapy. One was a new-patient evaluation for a man with obsessive-compulsive disorder, whose hoarding of newspapers, magazines, and junk mail filled his house from floor to ceiling. As she left for lunch, she paused at her receptionist's desk.

"Could you look into flights to Chicago for this weekend?"

"Business?"

Tina nodded. "I can't get Camille Weller off my mind. She's going to Chicago to a dinner in honor of her father."

Kerri smiled. "When do you want to leave?"

"Saturday. Back on Sunday."

"That'll cost you."

"I know, but I'll put it on my travel expense account. I hardly ever use it."

"And this is business?"

"You already asked me that," she responded, positioning her hands on her hips. "I'm going to support a patient."

Kerri lifted her plucked eyebrows. "Whatever."

Tina walked away, irked at her secretary's comment. The truth was she had wanted to get out of town, and since she needed to get Mark Lawson off her mind, this seemed the perfect solution.

Camille was poised on the verge of recapturing some intense memories. Facing people who were honoring the very man who abused her could be the spark that initiated an emotional healing . . . or the stimulus that could tip her over the edge.

As she walked toward the Skull, Tina wondered about the counsel she had given Camille. Facing her father's ghost might be hard enough without adding the stress of her sex life on top of it. She shook her head. *Camille will be all right. She's a big girl.*

Then Tina remembered the horror on Camille's face as she came out of hypnosis. The face of someone who had touched evil and recoiled in pure fright.

Camille is teetering on the edge. I'd better be there for her after the ceremony . . . just in case she doesn't fall the right way.

37

MOMMA LEFT THIS morning. My daddy made her go. I heard him whispering again last night that we would have a better chance of surviving if we split up.

She practically squeezed me for an hour before she left.

Then Daddy took her over to the hospital in her regular clothes and had her switch out into the ragged clothing of one of the village women. I watched her walk out the gate right by the Simba guards. I had to squint my eyes 'cause it didn't look much like my momma.

Daddy said she will walk through the forest to her brother's house. It's really more of a hut, but my uncle wasn't much for what Momma called modern living. But then again, my father says not much of the Congo understands that sort of thing.

She's carrying letters my dad says may help us since the radio doesn't work in twelve separate pieces.

He won't say it, but I can read his face, especially his eyes. He kissed Momma like he wasn't going to get to kiss her again.

I ran down to the river after she left. I didn't care if a crocodile ate me. I needed to be by myself.

RICHMOND, 1984

THURSDAY I WAS so busy with trauma call that I had little time to obsess over my upcoming weekend with Mark. After my nightmare flashback, I supposed work was a good thing, otherwise I'd have been tempted to call the whole thing off.

By Thursday night I hadn't packed, except to lay out a little black dress for the endowment dinner. Now I stood in front of my underwear drawer wondering what the appropriate lingerie was supposed to be. I'd never bought a sexy negligee. I certainly didn't have time to buy one now. Should I wear anything to bed at all? Should I wear an old T-shirt like I did at home?

I picked up a pair of black lace bikini undies and smiled. Whatever else I packed, they seemed like a good addition. They certainly had caused a flare of testosterone when the guys talked about them in the doctors' locker room.

My beeper sounded, interrupting my fantasies and my packing. I plodded to the phone and dialed the number I recognized as the ER. "Dr. Weller. I was paged."

"Dr. Weller. It's me, Ellis. We've got a trauma lap to do."

"Give me the bullet version."

"Twenty-eight-year-old male, victim of a knife wound to the mid-abdomen. Hypotensive en route. Currently on his second unit of blood and second liter of crystalloid with a blood pressure of ninety. I've notified the OR."

"I'll meet you there. I'm on my way."

I threw aside the black lace and headed for the door. Packing for Chicago would have to wait.

THE NEXT MORNING Tina heard the phone just as she stepped out of the shower. *I should pick it up. Camille is leaving for Chicago today.*

She's probably in a last-minute panic. Tina tucked a towel around her waist and hurried to the phone. "Hello."

As soon as she heard Dan's voice, she regretted not letting her answering machine pick up. "Morning, Tina."

She sighed. "What? You know I'm not ready to talk."

"I can't handle talking to your attorney. I can't get anything out of Ms. Peterson. What's going on? How are you doing?"

That's why I hired her, Tina thought. "Dan, number one, I'm trying to get ready for work. You want to know what's going on? We're getting a divorce, remember? These things take time. Ms. Peterson will be contacting you soon with a request for a list of items to which you feel entitled."

"I don't want items. I want you."

"You want who I was when I married you, Dan. Things have changed."

"How is your treatment going?"

"I really don't have time for chatting. I need to run."

"Meet me for dinner tomorrow night. We'll meet on neutral terms and just talk."

She stood dripping on the carpet. "I can't. I'm going to Chicago."

"With Dr. Lawson?"

Tina jerked her head upright. "Where did you get his name?"

"I didn't know it was a secret."

"Don't be evasive."

"It doesn't really matter how I know."

Tina paused. "For your information, I'm going to support a friend and I'm traveling alone, Dan. There is an endowment dinner at the Chicago Hilton and Towers in honor of Camille Weller's father. I'm going to support her."

"Tina, I . . . I—"

"You're jealous."

He sighed. "Yeah."

"This will be easier if you don't call."

His voice quivered. "I want to talk to you."

"I can't."

The phone was almost in the cradle when she heard his voice crack.

"Tina, I miss you."

IT WAS 8:00 a.m. before I finished with the previous night's trauma victims, and 2:30 p.m. before I finished my elective operating schedule. With my eye on catching a six o'clock flight from Dulles to O'Hare, I called Dr. Larimore and gave him my patient list.

I left the hospital and strode at a surgeon's pace toward the parking lot and my darling Prelude. With every step, I gained confidence that I was doing the right thing. So why did doubt have to nip at my mind's edge?

In the driver's seat I fought back a twinge of anxiety.

When I arrived at my apartment at three-thirty, I found Mark waiting.

He was leaning against his car. I kissed his cheek as I brushed by and ran up the stairs to my apartment. "I've got to pack."

"What happened to last night?"

"It was buried under the Richmond knife and gun club."

Mark understood my trauma service lingo by now. He smiled and said, "Better hurry."

I went through my bathroom and slid the contents of the countertop into my suitcase. Then I added socks, underwear, a pair of jeans, black pants, two blouses, and my little black dress. After a moment's extra thought, I added a small jewelry case with a solitary pearl necklace and a small evening purse to accessorize my dress.

"At least surgeons pack fast," he muttered.

"We're trained to think on our feet." I shut the suitcase and motioned for Mark. "Do you mind?" I said sweetly, offering my suitcase to him.

He groaned, but I could see he was only acting put out over my request. As soon as he disappeared from view, I dashed through the house looking for last-second add-ins. I paused, eyeing the dental floss, and tossed it in my purse. You should never forget to floss, even when you're away from home.

I locked the door and walked down the stairs. I looked at Mark. "Can you drive? I didn't sleep at all last night."

He held up his hands to catch my keys.

I settled into the passenger seat in my Prelude. I watched Mark for a few minutes and started to dream about our first night together. How would it feel? Would he enjoy what I did?

Snuggling against Mark's shoulder allowed me to sample his cologne. He smelled heaven-sent. I kissed his cheek as we accelerated onto I-95 heading toward D.C.

I reclined the seat as far as it would go and allowed my eyelids to droop. I could see Mark through the streaks of my eyelashes. He looked content. I let his image blur. Within a few minutes, I yielded to the sleep that had been calling me by name since I'd left for MCV yesterday evening.

AFTER RUSHING TO get to Dulles on time, Mark and I spent two hours walking the airport and catnapping in the chairs because of a delayed flight. Finally, when we were allowed to board our United flight to O'Hare, we spent another hour on the plane before we were allowed to take off. Wind shear or some such effect that I didn't understand was the only explanation forwarded from the cockpit.

When we finally settled in, I must have looked road weary, because a stewardess handed me a sleeping mask to keep out the light.

"Do I look that bad?" I whispered to Mark after the stewardess passed.

"I think she thought it'd be a mercy to keep you from having to see me."

I leaned my head against his shoulder. "Your problem," I began, "is that you know you're handsome."

He grunted and pulled a flight magazine out of the seat pocket in front of him.

I'd been wondering how to bring up the issue of my anxiety over our first night together, and how to be sure his expectations were kept in check. After talking with Tina, my week had fallen apart, and I never had a chance to talk to Mark as she had suggested.

I looked around the crowded airplane. It didn't seem like the place for such a private conversation. Too bad I couldn't have stayed awake on the drive up to Dulles.

Darkness smothered out the light as I pulled the mask over my eyes and reclined my seatback. Maybe we could have a nice late dinner out and talk before we got too cozy on the king-sized bed I'd reserved.

I fell into that wonderland between alertness and sleep, stumbling over thoughts of how silly I was for my concerns. Thousands of college coeds had more experience than I did. Why should I worry? Certainly, I had the physical and mental maturity to perform at a higher level than they.

I snuggled my head against Mark's neck and held his arm in my hands. There, I slept until we touched down in O'Hare.

BY THE TIME we opened the door to our room at the Chicago Hilton, it was eleven-thirty and my thoughts of a private dinner out where I could explain my fears had evaporated in our delays.

The room was beautiful, spacious beyond my dreams. The bed was turned down and a small chocolate mint rested on each of two pillows. Mark dropped the suitcases with a thud on the padded carpet behind me. In another moment, he pressed his lips against the back of my neck and whispered, "Ahh. Finally."

I wasn't ready. I hadn't laid down the ground rules yet. And as he encircled me with his arms and began to hold me in the dim light of the room, I felt the first stirring of panic.

"Just you and me," he said, turning my shoulders to face him. He pushed his face forward into mine and I received the first of his kisses, but as he lingered and grew more passionate, I pushed him back with my fingers on his searching lips.

"Slow down, Mark. I've been thinking about this for a long, long time. We need everything to be just right."

He sighed, but cooperated, diverting his attention to a mini-bar beneath a TV console. There, he retrieved a small bottle of wine. "Here," he said. "This will help to set the mood."

It wasn't exactly the type of preparation I needed, but I consented as he handed me a glass. I kicked off my shoes and sat, leaning against the wall at the head of the bed. Mark followed suit, shedding both his shirt and his shoes before taking his place beside me.

After a few sips of wine, Mark was on me again, caressing, stroking my hair, and moving quickly to undo the buttons on my blouse.

"Excuse me," I responded meekly. "You're going to spill my drink."

He pulled away, smiling. "So?"

I took a deep breath. "We need to talk."

He sat up with a blank expression on his face. I think testosterone had taken his brain captive. This was probably past the point that I should have taken him before having this conversation. I wasn't sure he was capable of hearing me now. Drooling, yes. Meaningful communication, I was having doubts.

"I told you about what Dr. Kinser thought about my childhood."

He nodded with a faraway look.

"You're going to have to work with me here," I said softly as I planted a kiss on his forehead. "I'm a grown woman."

"I know."

"But I'm a virgin." I watched for subtle signs of surprise. I saw only an almost imperceptible rise of his eyebrows.

"That's cool." A café au lait virgin. Mark's thoughts of heaven were transparent.

I lifted his hand from my blouse. "I need you to understand something."

He nodded. His eyes met mine. I thought he was really with me, listening now.

"I'm scared."

"Everyone's scared." He touched my hair. "I'm a little scared, too. Every time you open up your heart there's risk."

Opening up. I smiled. "That's what makes love exciting."

He leaned forward to kiss me. I yielded once, but stopped short again.

"You don't understand. I'm scared to death."

"We'll go slow."

"It's not just speed, Mark. I talked this through with Tina. One of the reasons I've been having these panic attacks has to do with the possible abuse I suffered as a child."

I watched as Mark's expression changed. His eyes flashed with a hint of impatience. "So what are you saying?"

"This is an important weekend for me. For us," I added. "This weekend isn't just about us taking our relationship to new heights. It's about me confronting the man responsible for a lot of my present pain."

Mark sat up and sighed. He picked up his glass. "So tell me what to do."

"Let me set the pace. I get to be in charge. I get to be the one being the aggressor."

The corner of his mouth turned up. "I'd like that."

I slid off the bed and headed for the bathroom.

"Hey, where're you going? Things were just getting good."

"I've been traveling for six hours, Mark. I'm not exactly feeling sexy."

I retreated to the bathroom behind the locked door and sat on the commode to take my pulse. I was still below ninety, not bad considering I was on the edge of my first time.

I took a shower and ignored Mark's soft knocking. As the water ran over me, I washed and explored the parts of me that I had never voluntarily shared with anyone else beyond my routine visits with a gynecologist. No one else had touched me there. Or had I locked away that memory as well? As I gently probed, a shiver of excitement and warmth seemed to envelop me.

I wondered: Just as his whisper has called out ghostly memories from a life long buried, will Mark's caress be the key to open a door barred to protect me from secret horror?

My fingers lingered for a moment, before tingles spread across my back and I quickly withdrew my hand.

I shut off the water and grabbed a towel. I stepped from the shower and rubbed a small circle in the fog on the mirror. I could see only my face, and I realized I was on the verge of tears.

I stared at my reflection, steeling my gaze. How could I be a rock in the operating theater, unmoved as life and death delicately battled for the upper hand, while terror tore at my heart at the thought of falling into the arms of a man who loved me? Less than twenty-four hours ago, I had looked in the face of death without flinching. So how could love threaten to bring me down?

"Camille, open the door."

I lifted a thick terry-cloth robe from a towel rack and draped it around me, cinching the belt around my slender waist. I opened the door. I could do this.

Mark exchanged places with me without speaking. In the silence I heard his disappointment.

I looked around the room. Now two little empty wine bottles

were sitting on the desk. I must have been in the shower longer than I thought.

Let yourself go, I told myself. You love him. Let your feelings find expression without fear. No one is here to hurt you.

I propped myself up on the bed and loosened the robe to my waist. After a few minutes, I shed the robe and put on a T-shirt and a pair of my black lace underwear.

Mark stayed in the bathroom longer than I expected. When he appeared, he wore only a pair of boxer shorts.

I looked over, trying to appear dreamy, sexy, and ready for everything he desired.

My face must have betrayed me.

He slid into the bed and pulled the covers over my shoulders. Then he nuzzled against me, side by side, with his hand resting on the outside of my shirt.

His voice was soft, barely above a whisper. "Don't be afraid of me, Camille. I'm not your father."

I nodded, unable to speak. Someone had stolen my voice and replaced it with dry crackers.

"I tell you what," he whispered. "Let's get some sleep. Face the demon of your father tomorrow evening. Make your peace with the memories that come." He paused, lifting his face so that his lips could brush my cheek. "Then tomorrow night, we'll find our fill of love."

I closed my eyes and smiled. The pressure was off. I relaxed against his strong arms.

"This is heaven enough for tonight."

I turned into him and kissed him softly, and he brushed away the tears welling in my eyes.

I loved this man.

I turned and wrapped his arm over me as if I were rolling into a blanket.

We slept as one until morning.

38

W E SPENT THE morning lazily strolling along South Michigan Avenue, looking in store windows and eventually ending at the Art Institute of Chicago, where Mark's patience was stretched as I looked at a large East African exhibit.

I, however, was connecting to my roots and in no particular hurry.

"Look at this," I said, pointing at a display of Masai necklaces and bracelets. "There must be ten thousand little beads in this one piece alone."

"Cool. Do you want to get Chicago-style pizza for lunch?"

"The Masai are the tribe holding most closely to their old ways. The women build the huts while men watch the cattle."

"Ron Taylor told me about a place where the slices are over an inch thick."

I smiled at my boyfriend. I gripped his arm and laughed. "OK," I said. "But let me look in the gift shop for a minute."

He indulged me. I purchased a coffee-table book on African art before we headed back arm in arm.

TINA KINSER OPENED the door to her spacious room at the Hilton and rolled her suitcase in between the two double beds. She smiled. This was a good idea. Escaping from the pressures of Richmond, her failed marriage, her job, and her cancer was necessary and overdue.

Her mouth dropped open as she saw a vase with a dozen yellow roses.

Mark Lawson had struck again. How like him to jerk her heart around! *He must have talked to Kerri and found out I was going to be here.* She closed her fist in disgust. He'd told her he was involved with another woman, but he couldn't stay out of her life . . . or her bed. She supposed that was what kept him coming back. But this was too much. She couldn't allow him to sweet-talk her back into—

She froze as her eyes fell upon a little card. She slipped it from its envelope and read, *With love, Dan.*

She felt a catch in her throat. She lifted the vase under her nose and pulled the drapery away from the window. She had a beautiful view of Lake Michigan. Sailboats dotted the water. A private plane was flying low in an approach to a runway at the water's edge. The sky was nearly cloudless, overall a chamber-of-commerce day.

She wanted to take a walk by the lake, maybe find a quiet place to eat lunch. She checked the minibar. She wanted a bottle of water. Perhaps she could buy one in the gift shop off the lobby.

As she headed for the lobby, she thought about the yellow roses she'd been finding. Was it Dan all along?

As we approached the hotel, Mark wiped the sweat from his forehead. "I didn't expect it to be this hot."

"Why don't you change into shorts?"

He nodded.

"I think I'll buy a Diet Pepsi at the bar. Do you mind taking my book to the room?"

He shook his head and lifted the package from my arms. "I'll see you in a few minutes."

We walked through the lobby, and Mark disappeared toward the elevator. I walked to a small restaurant just off the lobby and sat on a bar stool. After ordering a diet soda, I heard my name.

"Camille!"

I turned to see Tina Kinser.

"Tina? What are you doing here?"

She smiled and shrugged. "I thought you might be able to use a little extra support."

We shared a hug and she sat beside me on a stool.

"You know what's weird?" she said. "I just saw a guy across the lobby that could double for Mark Lawson back at MCV."

"He's here, Tina."

"No, just someone who looks like him."

I shook my head. "No, I mean Mark Lawson is here. He came with me."

Tina's jaw dropped. She looked at me like I'd just escaped a mental ward. "Mark Lawson? The pediatric oncology fellow?"

I smiled. "The one and only." I grabbed Tina's hand and gave it a squeeze. "And you were the one who inspired me to ask him along."

She shook her head. "Wait a minute! You invited Mark here? For me?"

I laughed. "For me!"

We looked at each other for a moment, each searching the other's eyes.

"Tina, what's wrong?"

"Mark. Where is he now?"

I tilted my head toward the elevators. "He went up to our room to change. He'll be down in a minute. Would you like to join us for lunch?"

She stood up and grabbed my arm. "He can't see us here together," Tina said, her eyes steel.

"What are you talking about?"

"We need to talk," she said.

"Sure, but—"

She started dragging me along beside her. "Let's find a private place where we can be alone."

"But Mark will be here in a moment."

"He can wait a minute," she huffed. "Believe me, he can wait." She looked at me and shook her head again, as if in disbelief. "Mark is the boyfriend you've been talking about?"

I beamed, nodding my head rapidly.

She took me by the arm again, and started stomping toward a booth in the back of the restaurant.

Tina muttered. "Son of a—"

Mark looked irritated. "Where've you been?"

I shrugged as I walked back into the lobby from Michigan Avenue. "I walked around the block."

"I looked everywhere."

"I needed to think. Clear my head."

"I'm starving."

I took a deep breath. "Let's go."

We walked two blocks to find a little place with red-checkered tablecloths promising authentic Chicago-style pizza. Mark put a quarter in a jukebox and selected "You've Lost That Lovin' Feeling."

He couldn't have been more on the money. I offered a smile and kept my thoughts to myself.

The pizza was great, what little I ate of it. I had no appetite. I kept fantasizing about pouring the pitcher of beer on Mark's head, stabbing his chest repeatedly with a steak knife, or worse. But Tina and I had made a pact, and I had promised not to kill him at lunch.

I checked my watch. Tina should just about be in place.

I leaned forward so that our foreheads almost touched over the little table, and Mark was sure to get an eyeful of my generous cleavage. I kept my voice low, although I could have practically screamed and been ignored by our neighbors because the music was so loud. "I want you."

His eyes glimmered. He smiled and continued to chew.

"Now, Mark. I want you." I put on my best serious-as-a-heart-attack look. I drew my tongue slowly across my lips. I was going to enjoy this. I could act. And because it was an act, I knew I wouldn't be terrified.

He was intrigued. I could almost see his hormones rising, threatening to take over rational thought.

Mark's eyes widened. "Camille," he whispered. "What's gotten into you?"

"Remember that walk I took to clear my head?"

He nodded with excitement. He reminded me of a bobble-head doll on a dashboard bouncing to the bumps in the road.

"I've been thinking. I've been a fool to let past abuse ruin my present pleasure. If we wait until tonight, after I've had a chance to confront the memories of my father, it's just letting my father win." I shook my head. "I'm not going to let that happen, Mark. I'm through being a victim of my own past. I'm not letting my father win again."

Mark's eyes glanced from the remaining pizza on our table to his plate and back to me. I could tell the testosterone was already scrambling the messages from his higher thought centers. Should I eat the pizza or have sex? Or should I ask the waitress for a take-out box, or will that delay precious seconds of seeing Camille naked?

Mark lifted his hand to signal for a check, and cut the tip off the remaining pizza slice. Oh, the two great loves of the male species: carbohydrates and sex.

"Take me back and teach me," I whispered, running my toe up the inside of his leg.

"Check, please." Mark raised his voice and waved his hand again.

I smiled and acted as if my mouth were watering. I stared at him and touched my napkin to my lips. I looked at my watch. "We've got four hours until the predinner reception."

"Check!"

Mark laid forty dollars on the table. He wasn't going to wait any longer for the waitress.

I smiled. The waitress was a sister. It was probably the best tip she'd gotten all week.

ONCE WE WERE back in our room, I kissed Mark passionately while standing next to the bed. It was funny, I thought. I had no anxiety now because I knew exactly where this was headed.

He quickly moved to pull my blouse out of my jeans, but I backed away, giggling.

"Wait, Mark. Just because I want to be here with you doesn't mean I don't need special treatment."

"I'll give you special treatment," he said, sitting on the bed. He lifted his hand toward me. "Come here."

"Not so fast. Remember, I've got issues," I said, sauntering around the bed and keeping him in my sight. "I still need to be in control." I glared at him, allowing a little of my spite to show before I got back into character. "My psychiatrist said it might be helpful if I played the role of the aggressor, remember?"

He nodded his assent.

"And so I'll need you to lie very still."

I walked over to my carry-on bag and retrieved the sleeping mask the stewardess had given me. I dangled it in the air in front of Mark.

"What? You want me to wear this?" He sounded incredulous.

"Just for a little while," I said in a soft voice. I leaned over and took his hand. "Do it for me." I pushed him backward on the bed. I used a little-girl voice, the one I used to talk to Max, his German shepherd. "Please?"

"Why a mask? I want to see you."

I acted nonchalant. "Men control women with their eyes. They undress them even when they're dressed. Just with a look." I stood up again. Perhaps some distance between us would convince him to cooperate. If I were in his arms, I was afraid I'd lose him to base Y-chromosome instinct.

"It's all part of me being in control, Mark. I don't want to undress in front of you in the first five seconds. You need to let me take this at my own pace. Besides," I said, "I don't want you looking at my every imperfection."

"Believe me, you have no imperfections."

"Mark," I said, backing away and pleading. "You have to let me call the shots. I'll let you take the mask off soon enough."

"OK," he moaned.

I approached again and sat on the bed beside him. I slipped the mask over his eyes. I held two fingers in front of his face. "How many fingers?"

He reached up and grabbed for my hand.

"No fair. I told you to be still."

"Ugh."

At that point, I turned on the radio and rolled up the volume control. I leaned next to his ear and giggled. "I don't want the neighbors to hear if I start screaming in ecstasy."

I started with his shirt, unbuttoning a single button at a time and pausing to whisper in his ear, "Do you like this?"

He was lying on his back, his shirt completely open. I kissed his chest. "Remember, I'm so inexperienced. I need constant feedback."

I pulled him forward so I could remove his shirt, then pushed him back flat again. I moved to kiss his lips and his neck, and then nibbled his earlobe. "How about this? Do you enjoy this?"

"Yes."

I moved to his chest. "This?"

I stopped. "Take off your jeans."

He was eager to cooperate.

I looked up as Tina slipped quietly from the closet. We were both fully clothed, with Mark on the bed clothed only in his boxers, excited and silly all at once.

I kissed his lips and pulled the radio closer to Mark's ear while Tina propped open the door to the hall. He responded by shaking his head to the rock beat, acting goofy. I slid the radio back onto the nightstand before grabbing Mark by the hand. "Stand up," I urged. "I want to look at us in the full-length mirror on the door."

He obeyed, following like a blind man as I led him by the hand. He was a man separated from his brain. I positioned him near the doorway with his back to the open hall.

"Do you like this?" I said, kissing his right cheek, before backing away.

"Or this," I said as Tina kissed him on the left.

"This?" I said, kissing his chest on the right. "Or this?" I said before Tina kissed him on the left.

Mark was giggling, now fully engrossed in my little game.

"Do you like this?" I lifted Mark's right hand to my face. "Or this?" I moved his hand to Tina's.

Mark twitched. A sober expression replaced his smile.

I raised my voice. "Do you like dark meat?"

Tina spoke for the first time. "Or white meat?" she demanded.

Mark instinctually began to back away. I plucked the mask from his eyes just as he entered the hall. "Tina?!"

He lifted his foot to step forward into the room, but Tina and I let out a scream to raise the dead. Long, shrill, and primeval. Mark froze, looking dead in the face of his women.

Together.

I slammed the door, and Tina moved quickly to flip the lock.

Mark, of course, didn't have his pants on.

I high-fived Tina. Our little sting had worked perfectly.

He began to knock and whine as Tina and I dissolved into laughter. She gave me another high five before we leaned against opposite walls in the little entranceway to my room and slid to the floor.

Mark's voice was becoming intense, desperate. "Come on, ladies. Let me in."

My eyes meet Tina's. *It's understood. The door stays shut.*

As if on cue, we stood together and flipped over the privacy lock that allowed the door to open only a few inches before it was arrested by the U-shaped catch.

Mark pounded on the door as I looked at him through the peephole. It distorted his image, making his head and nose look huge. "Open the door, Camille."

We turned the doorknob and allowed the door to fall open against the lock. Tina let fly with another scream. "Fire!"

I'd always heard that if you were attacked you shouldn't yell "rape," but "fire," so people would more readily respond. I joined in, screaming at the absolute top of my lungs. "Ahhh! Fire!"

I could see Mark's face through the crack in the door. Go ahead, I think, put your fingers in the space, and I'll give you something to scream about.

Mark looked desperate. I could hear others in the hallway, perhaps coming to investigate our cries.

Suddenly, a loud voice boomed from down the hall, "You! You're him!"

I saw Mark's eyes widen even more. He stared down the hall at the voice.

Mark suddenly disappeared. I heard footsteps, first louder, then receding. I unlatched the door and peered into the hall with Tina.

"Dan?" she said.

The male duo dashed into the stairwell at the end of the hall, with Mark ahead of Dan Kinser by a hair.

I covered my mouth and laughed. My heart was beating fast. I was almost as exhilarated as I would have been having a lovers' rendezvous.

We shut the door, dazed. What was Dan Kinser doing here?

The phone rang.

Maybe it was Mark, calling in desperation from the front desk. I traded glances with Tina, who held up her hands in an "I don't know" gesture.

I picked up the phone. "Hello."

"Dr. Weller?" The voice was male, one I couldn't immediately place.

"Yes."

"Jacob Richardson here. I wanted to call and welcome you to the Windy City."

"Thanks."

"I have a note here that you informed my secretary that you'd be bringing a guest to the dinner tonight. Could I get a name so we can have a name card made?"

"Oversight on my part, I'm sure," I responded. Without a second's thought I added, "Tina. Tina Kinser will be my guest."

39

E VERY DAY THE Simbas drag in another soldier for Daddy to fix up. He says it's not fair. He hasn't been able to get supplies in over two weeks. I heard him tell Mr. Barnett that if I came down with malaria that he wouldn't even have medicine to treat me.

I haven't always been good about sleeping under my mosquito net, but when I heard that, I made sure the net was down around my bed good.

Some of the Simba soldiers don't look much older than me. The witchdoctor psyches them up with his spells, telling them all the lies about the bullets of their enemies turning into water. It convinces them to run out in the open straight into the gunfire of the national army. Daddy says most of the boys don't even know anything about properly firing a gun. The national army pretty much mows the boys down as they shoot their guns in the air.

Daddy says the pressure of war makes men do stupid things.

It's been two weeks since Momma left. Daddy asked me if I wanted to sleep in his bed, but I told him I wasn't scared as long as Tumi could stay with me.

D AN KINSER STOPPED running when Mark Lawson pushed
through an emergency exit leading to Michigan Avenue.
With the alarm ringing, Dan slipped nonchalantly onto the sidewalk and tried to catch his breath. He wasn't sure what he was
thinking. What would he have done with Mark Lawson even if
he'd have caught him? He chuckled to himself. The sight of Tina's
boyfriend disappearing into a crowd wearing only his boxers was
worth the price of his last-minute plane ticket.

Seeing Mark Lawson had taken Dan by surprise, but perhaps
he should have suspected that Tina would lie to cover up her
little rendezvous. He shook his head. She'd made up some excuse
about coming up here for Dr. Weller.

His hope had been to find Tina alone, out of town, and try to
initiate some communication, something that had seemed impossible back in Richmond. So, on a whim, he'd bought a ticket and
chased Tina to Chicago, booking a room in the hotel where she'd
said she had a dinner to attend.

But after a tiring flight, and losing his luggage, he'd arrived
angry, exhausted, and rethinking his own sanity for following
Tina. When he finally reached his room, only one thought occupied him: What if he'd come all this way and she wouldn't even
talk to him? He'd stuck the key in the door to enter his room.
That was the very moment he'd heard the commotion in the hall
and looked up to see a nearly naked man pounding on a door. He
took a step closer. The man looked strangely familiar. Then recog-
nition dawned and in his frustrated state, he'd flipped.

Dan wiped beads of sweat from his forehead. He needed to
get back to his room and get cleaned up.

Then he would try to find Tina.

WHEN TINA LEFT for her room, I dissolved onto the bed, not caring to stop my tears. This was to be a day to celebrate Mark's love for me, not to discover that he'd been cheating on me and had broken his relationship with Tina only after I'd invited him to Chicago. He didn't deserve my tears, but I cried for the loss of the man I thought he was, not for whom he turned out to be.

After I dressed for the endowment dinner, I plopped Mark's belongings in the hall. I didn't bother to repack for him. I deposited his suitcase, shoes, clothes, and a small leather container of his toiletries in a heap by the door.

I responded to a knock at the door by peering through the peephole. Tina had a smile on her face as she inspected the items on the floor.

I opened the door. "Whoa, check you out, girl."

She held out her hands and pirouetted. "Ready?"

"Now or never."

We walked side by side, comfortable in our new solidarity. I'd operated on her breast cancer. She'd helped me cope with a troubled past. Those were glue enough for us, but getting used by the same man put us in a sisterhood thicker than blood.

It had been a horrible and wonderful afternoon. I was half numb from the abrupt end of my relationship with Mark, but emboldened by the stand we'd made to expose him. Today would be a red-letter day for me. I'd come to confront the memory of my father. Confronting Mark Lawson had given me confidence that I could face my father's ghost with the same cool self-assurance.

I glanced at Tina. "So how do I introduce you?" I held out my hand and smiled. " 'This is Dr. Kinser, my psychiatrist.' "

"Tell them the truth. Say, 'This is my friend.' "

I smiled.

"Dan called my room."

I raised my eyebrows and stayed quiet for a moment. "Well?"

"I agreed to meet him in the hotel restaurant after the reception."

I raised my eyebrows further.

"Just to talk."

"Good," I responded. "You should talk to anyone who chased Mark Lawson out of our lives."

She giggled nervously and gripped my hand.

The reception was in a banquet room that was nearly full when we arrived. Young waiters in black tuxedos came by carrying trays of sparkling champagne. Tina and I had just lifted the glasses from a tray when Jacob Richardson approached with an older man with white hair and a golfer's complexion.

"Dr. Weller, I'm so glad to see you."

I extended my free hand. "Hello, Mr. Richardson. This is my friend Tina Kinser."

He smiled. "I'd like you to meet the man who has made tonight possible." He put his arm on the shoulder of the older man at his side. "This is Dr. Francis Solfelt."

I recognized his name as the donor who had contributed the majority of the money to start the endowment.

Dr. Solfelt took my hand. "It's wonderful to see you again, Camille."

His warmth was catching. I smiled. "Again?"

He nodded. "We were together in the Congo, a long time ago. You've . . . well, you've turned out to be quite a beautiful young woman."

I didn't know what to say.

"So you're a surgeon now." He chuckled. "You're father would be so proud."

I nodded, happy that he was chatting on. I sipped from my glass and the realization dawned that I was sipping sparkling apple juice. I supposed champagne would have been a bit too liberal for the CFW.

"I last saw you when you were about this tall," he said, holding his hand three feet from the floor. "You weren't any taller than that big dog of yours."

"Tumi," I responded softly. "My dog, Tumi."

Dr. Solfelt looked over at Jacob Richardson. "Wouldn't it be something if Camille here became the first surgeon to utilize money from the endowment to donate some time to a hospital back in the Congo?"

Mr. Richardson nodded. "Sounds like a great idea."

They looked at me. I cleared my throat and attempted a smile. "I don't remember applying."

The gentlemen laughed, and Mr. Richardson took Dr. Solfelt away to meet another small group to our right.

The ambiance was about right, I thought. Nice enough to make the patrons feel like they would be getting a little back for their donations, but not so elaborate for them to complain that their money was being wasted. Ornate glass chandeliers hung over tables graced with bouquets of fresh flowers. There were more eating utensils at each place setting than I used in a week at home.

An older couple introduced themselves. "Your father was such a dear friend."

The man chuckled. "He left his signature on me," he said, reaching for his waistband.

His wife swatted his hand. "Don't you dare show her your scar."

The man winked. "Appendicitis. Your dad saved my life."

I smiled, relieved he hadn't pulled up his shirt.

"You're Dr. Weller."

I turned to see an elderly woman at my left elbow. "We're so glad you've come. Your father was a saint."

I smiled again, and then managed to mingle away with Tina through the crowd. I was drawn to a display table at the far end of the room. I gripped Tina's hand as I saw a large black-and-white photo of my father. Next to it was a picture of my father in his white coat, standing beside the bed of a little boy with his leg in traction. Beside that one was a photo of our family: Mom, Dad, me . . . and Tumi.

The tension in my gut was growing. The distance between the man these people praised and the one I remembered was a chasm. My father helped poor African children. My father had kind eyes. How could it be that he hid a dirty little family secret behind a face of compassion?

I looked at Tina and held my glass up. I kept my voice low and spoke into her ear, "I need a real glass of champagne."

Tina squeezed my hand. "You can do this."

We began moving from table to table looking at nameplates. Around us, old friendships were being renewed. People smiled and hugged. Laughter and festivity were the order of the night.

But I felt little of the festive emotion. The more I heard about what a wonderful man my father was, the more I nestled into a conflicted shell.

We found our names and sat at a table near the front, adjacent to a small platform. Jacob Richardson, Francis Solfelt, and their wives joined us.

Mrs. Solfelt leaned over and took my hand. "Francis talks often of your father. They were together in the Congo, you know."

I nodded. The mood for me was surreal. After all these years of not thinking about my father, never meeting any of his colleagues, suddenly I was thrust into a room of people who couldn't praise him enough. Maybe I should blame Aunt Jeanine for that. Or maybe I should thank her for protecting me from hypocrisy for so many years.

Mrs. Richardson smiled. "So you wanted to be just like your father. You followed his footsteps."

I glanced at Tina. "Surgery seemed a natural for me," I responded. "But honestly, I don't remember my father very well."

"What made you want to be a surgeon?" Mrs. Richardson shivered. "I couldn't stand all that gore."

Such a typical opinion from an outsider. What Mrs. Richardson didn't know was that surgeons endure the gore for the excitement of helping someone in crisis. Psychopaths enjoyed gore. The rest of us found it unpleasant.

Fortunately they served the meal quickly, a green salad followed by grilled pork tenderloins, topped with a mango chutney, rice pilaf, vegetable medley, and then cheesecake. Mostly I rearranged the food to make it look like I was eating, that is, until the cheesecake came. I ate that, no problem. Even the anxiety over my father couldn't make me give up that.

Over and over my eyes were drawn back to the pictures on the table, but I failed to have a rush of memories. I wasn't sure what I'd expected, except that perhaps talking with people who knew my father might somehow prod something out of the deep from my subconscious. In all, I guess I hoped to avoid going back to hypnosis to uncover all that horror. I looked at the two men at the table. I realized I'd been too quiet, sitting in the presence of such a potential resource of information. If this was why I'd come, I'd better find my courage and start digging.

I cleared my throat and caught Dr. Solfelt's eye. "What was he like?" I hesitated. "My dad."

He looked at me in a curious way, the look you give to a toddler without a parent in a department store. He was quiet for a moment before asking, "What do you remember? How old were you when he died?"

"Ten."

"The rebellion? Do you remember the Simbas?"

"Not really. I know a little about them from some research I did in college. Personally, I only have the vague memory of bad, scary men."

Dr. Solfelt paused, looking over my head, before a smile came over his face. "I remember two things about your father the most: his sense of humor—I think that's what kept him sane in the Congo—and his love for people. He loved the Congolese people like family."

Jacob Richardson pushed back an empty dessert plate. "To Jack, I believe those people *were* family."

I wondered if they'd turned him into something he wasn't, a posthumous projection of their own ideals, an idol, fulfilling their need for a hero for their little mission to rally around. I blushed at my own thoughts, as I fantasized about blasting down their false image. *Or is it my mental image that is distorted?*

I traded glances with Tina and smiled, but she could see through my facade. Sweet plastic smiles were only window dressing on a house with a cracked foundation. I gave the same look to Dr. Solfelt and Mr. Richardson, but knew they couldn't understand the tension that hid behind my eyes. I enjoyed my little interior monologue. At least it kept me sane to formulate the words I would say if I snapped and let the world really know what I was thinking. I'd used the same technique a hundred times during my residency, when I felt like telling off an attending, but knew if I gave expression to my thoughts, I'd find myself unemployed. So I sat, externally content, internally conflicted, and ready with choice words to spit if the top blew off my emotional volcano.

Jacob Richardson climbed the three steps to the small platform and began a welcome and an explanation of the program in front of me titled "CFW: Outlook for the New Millennium." Good grief. We hadn't even finished 1984 and we had to think about the next thousand years. George Orwell might be surprised to know that Big Brother wasn't watching.

I zoned out while Mr. Richardson droned on. I thought about my life for the past few months. Being an attending was great, but the rose of my arrival had come with a few thorns I wasn't expecting. I'd always dreamed that being at the desk where the buck stopped would be a comfortable spot for me. But when the choices involved people's lives, book knowledge could take you only so far.

The weeks since I'd started leading the trauma service were fun. And horrible. An ironic mix. The residents loved me and the way I'd stood up to the white hairs. If anything would keep me going on this trail, it would be the knowledge that my insights, even if they were borne from struggle, might lighten the load of a sister who followed in my path.

I thought about Nadine Solomon and about a fifteen-year-old boy who had found his way into my heart. I doubted if Kendrick would ever realize how close he'd come to the edge of this life. I shifted in my seat, uncomfortable at the thought that for a little time I was happier about joining the Six-Liter Club than the fact that Nadine got back the boy who "ain't never done nothin' to no one." I thought about the way she prophesized every time she saw me, calling me a Thomas, and confident that someday I'd see the practical evidence that God loved me. It seemed funny somehow, looking around at all the Christians in the room. They all seemed so content and sure about what they believed, both about God and my father. I wanted to believe in God's love. I wanted to believe in an earthly father who loved me. But nagging doubts had built a web that held me captive, unable to believe in the idyllic concept that Nadine had preached.

I thought about how Kendrick ended up dealing with his abusive father and hoped that I could show as much courage in dealing with the memories of mine.

I thought about Kara and how she loved the BoSox and me. I thought it was a crime to have a friend die young. And it was worse that she was one of the few people I'd really been able to share my heart with.

I looked over at Tina. At least something good had come about through all my pain. Tina Kinser and I had bonded for life. When I looked at the woman I was now, I couldn't believe how right Dr. Gilles was: I'd been shut down emotionally for too long, but Tina, Kara, Kendrick, and Nadine had all helped initiate a reversal.

I looked at Mrs. Richardson. She seemed to be admiring her husband, even as he was boring me into a coma. This was to have been the year of the real thing for me, too: Mark Lawson and I would have been perfect together, a combination of looks, personality, and passion that would create a lasting relationship. Fortunately I'd found out about his wandering soul before I'd given him a gift I couldn't retrieve.

My attention was drawn to the platform as Dr. Solfelt replaced Mr. Richardson. I glanced at the program. It said, "Jack Weller, a Tribute."

The lights were lowered as a projector flashed the image of my father onto a screen behind the stage. It was the same picture that sat on the table, the one of my father in his white coat, standing at the bedside of the African boy.

Francis Solfelt cleared his throat to begin. "There's not a Passover that goes by when someone in my family doesn't mention a story about Jack Weller."

The mention of Passover made me think of Kara, and I felt my throat begin to close.

Dr. Solfelt continued, "It was 1964. The communist-backed Simba warriors were in full rebellion against a young Congolese government." Dr. Solfelt's hands trembled as he opened a small bound black book. "I tell the story from Jack Weller's writings in the reports he made for the CFW office back home."

Dr. Solfelt looked around and shifted from foot to foot. "Let me back up," he said. "I should explain that this was a very dark chapter for CFW. The Simbas had gathered most expatriates at a hotel in Stanleyville as a bargaining tool. If the West intervened, the Simbas warned, the expatriates would die. Dr. Jack Weller and his family were left with a handful of CFW missionaries at the Hospital of Light mission station, with the agreement that they could stay if they provided medical care to wounded Simbas." Dr. Solfelt looked up, his voice thickening. "What the Simbas didn't understand is that what Dr. Weller was forced to do at gunpoint, he would have done freely of his own accord." He paused and fumbled with the book in his hand. "Six missionaries and fourteen Congolese nationals lost their lives in one fateful attack on the hospital compound. As UN paratroopers were falling over Stanleyville, the Simbas began a house-to-house slaughter of our missionaries."

Dr. Solfelt coughed. "And now, from Jack's own pen, his account of the attack:

> "For weeks now, the Simbas have come every few days searching our compound for radio equipment. They seem obsessed with the thought that we will signal our governments to intervene, that we will relay the message that will cause the paratroopers to fall in the skies over Stanleyville. They are so suspicious. They seized Mr. Karanja's hearing aid, convinced it was a modern transmitter. A young Simba toting an M-16 rifle crushed it on the floor while the Karanjas watched, saying over and over that they were only here to serve their fellow Congolese people.
>
> "The Simbas have essentially seized the hospital compound. They've taken my Land Rover. The only ones they let in and out are the patients' families as they come and go with food. I managed to have Charity sneak out last month with some letters to CFW detailing our plight and asking for prayers and help."

Dr. Solfelt looked up. "Charity was Jack's wife, a Congolese native. She was later killed by the Simbas." He resumed reading.

> "I would so love to send Camille away, but she is too fair and will stimulate too many questions if she is seen away from the compound. She cannot blend in with the villagers like her mother. Her skin is a curse in these times when anything close to white raises suspicion."

Leaning over to Tina, I whispered, "I never thought he might have left reports."

She lifted her eyebrows in question. "Maybe your aunt Jeanine had secrets of her own."

I nodded as Dr. Solfelt continued reading:

> "We have been preparing for a day like today for weeks now. All the children on the compound have taken to sleeping in their clothes in case a quick escape into the forest at night is needed."

I traded glances with Tina. Was that why I remembered sleeping in my clothes?

> "Today's work at the hospital was slow. I treated one young Simba who shot himself in the foot. I could do little to help him, as the Simbas have cut off our usual suppliers. I had to do an amputation with only morphine for pain relief. Four soldiers had to hold him down. We have only six vials of penicillin left, and I told the nurses to use two for the young Simba.
>
> "Last night, just before eleven p.m., I heard gunfire as I was finishing my daily scripture reading. I lifted my head from the passage in Exodus, the account of the first Passover. I headed out to the front porch to see one of our hospital guards stumble and fall not twenty feet from our door. His name is John Mwangi and he had only recently decided to follow Christ. I ran to his side only to realize that the wound that felled him was a fatal gunshot to the head. I quickly retreated to the doorway of our home. From there, I could see the massacre unfolding. Four doors up, toward the north gate of our compound, I saw a group of Simbas enter the Dicksons'. I heard gunfire, multiple shots, followed by a moving of the group to the Barnetts' next door. To the south, I saw a second band of Simbas moving house to

house. In a matter of minutes, I supposed, the violence would be upon us. It appeared that the Simbas were conducting a house-to-house slaughter. My suspicions were that the UN forces must have landed in Stanleyville, prompting this desperate act of retaliation.

"I looked around, frantic to find a hiding place. I thought of running with Camille through the shambas to the forest, but we would have to pass the back guard gate and I was sure the Simbas would be there.

"Within moments, the Simbas would be at our door. Perhaps it was inspiration from the passage I'd just read. Perhaps I was driven to the brink of madness from weeks of the Simbas' siege of the hospital. Regardless, I gripped a butcher knife from the kitchen and ran to Camille's room where our dog Tumaini slept. I grabbed Tumi's collar and brought him to the kitchen. Tumi sensed danger, but seemed to understand my urgency and cooperated. I moved behind him, talking softly to keep him calm. I lifted his chin, and with all the swiftness and strength I could manage, I slit his throat in one motion down to the bone. I purposefully and methodically spread the blood around the kitchen, first spraying, then allowing the blood to drip from his lifeless body. I carried Tumi to the only closet in our little house, the one in my bedroom. I quickly threw a blanket over his body, and rushed to Camille. Then I took my beloved little one in my arms and hid her in the closet with me.

"When the Simbas entered our house moments later, they saw bloody evidence that the slaughter they desired had already taken place and moved to the next house. I stayed with my little daughter for over two hours in the dark closet. It is my joy to have saved her, but my shame not to have perished trying to save my neighbors."

Dr. Solfelt lifted his eyes from my father's words. "Jake Weller and his wife were killed two days later by a sniper's bullets as the Simbas retreated from the UN forces in Stanleyville."

Tina reached for my hand. The tears that I'd been pushing back all evening found escape. I could not keep them from spilling down my cheeks. I cried not for the pain of a father who had abused me, but for the loss of a man who had loved me with all his heart.

Tina squeezed my hand. I saw that she was crying, too, both of us sharing in silence the significance of a memory long buried. I lifted a Kleenex to my cheeks and tried to regain focus on Dr. Solfelt.

"For us at Christ for the World, our joy and undying aim is bringing the message of the Christ, the Passover lamb, to a world trapped in darkness." Dr. Solfelt's voice cracked. "Thank you, Jack Weller, for sharing your life with me."

A second slide replaced the first. It was a close-up of a tombstone. Dr. Solfelt continued, "Jack Weller was buried in a cemetery beside a small Congolese church, just up the hill from the hospital where he gave his life." He looked over his shoulder at the slide. "In closing, I'd like to read the inscription on his tombstone. It is a quote from C. H. Spurgeon. 'Let me be as the bullock which stands between the plough and the altar, to work or to be sacrificed; and let my motto be, "Ready for either."'"

He turned, his hand trembling slightly as he gripped the small black diary. He walked to the edge of the stage before lifting his index finger and returning to the small podium. "Forgive me," he said, "my age is catching up with me. I've forgotten one important part of this story." He squinted toward the light of the projector. "Could I have my last slide?"

Another image appeared, this one identical to the other on the display table, the Weller family: Mom, Dad, me, and Tumi.

"I wanted you to know about the Weller dog's name, Tumaini. It's a Kiswahili word meaning hope."

40

I DREADED THE PLANE ride back to Dulles, fearing Mark would occupy the seat next to me and try to explain his way back into my heart. The revelation last night may have brought some *tumaini* to my heart, but I wasn't going to give Mr. Lawson any hope for a future with me.

I sat in a grouping of airport chairs across from my gate, pretending to read a magazine. I just wanted to blend in and watch to see if Mark would show. I waited until the loudspeaker proclaimed the last call for my flight, and then, relieved that he must have found another way home, rushed to board. The seat next to mine was empty.

I smiled politely at an elderly man in my row, then pulled on my sleeping mask and planned for a little solitude within the crowded airplane. Only a few days before I had imagined this plane ride home with Mark. I would grip his arm tightly and lay my head on his strong shoulder. There I would rest, happy that we'd enjoyed the consummation of our physical lust. How far that dream seemed from reality now.

Only Tina knew my real designs for this trip. It was ironic, really. I had wanted to confront the demon of my father's memory so I could learn to accept the love of a man. Instead, the only demon I'd confronted was Mark, and the clarification of my troubled memories opened the way for me to accept the love of my father and maybe even the God he served.

On the way home, I pondered the new father I'd found. He did love me. He was a man of passion who lived out his love for God by using his hands to love people. Maybe my old fantasies of him were not so far from the truth. I knew he wasn't perfect, but at least he wasn't the abuser I'd feared him to be.

The event that had brought me so much terror and convinced me that my father didn't love me was actually the evidence I needed to prove he'd loved me all along. I looked out the window at the small checkerboard of fields below me. From up here, even the mountains looked small. Maybe it was what I'd always needed: a higher viewpoint to put things in proper perspective.

I touched the empty seat beside me. Kara was right. I was searching for a love that Mark Lawson couldn't provide. I was so relieved I hadn't slept with him. Even if he had been faithful to me, it wouldn't have worked. I found myself starting to think that Nadine might be on to something. Maybe only God lavished the kind of love I dreamed about.

We touched down at Dulles on Sunday evening. I spent the two-hour drive back to Richmond thinking about the black diary that Dr. Solfelt had given me. It belonged to my father and contained the weekly reports he'd made as a missionary for CFW. Someday I planned to call Aunt Jeanine and ask her why she'd hidden my past from me. I was angry when I thought about it, but I was beginning to understand that the pathology in the family belonged to her and not to my father. She probably had issues. Perhaps she was in therapy, too, just like me. I smiled.

I was glad my relationship with Tina had taken a good turn. My future "in-therapy" days were numbered. Tina was going to be my new best friend.

41

A MONTH LATER, I paused outside the door to the women's locker room and smiled. I was happy to be changing here. I was about to celebrate my third month as an attending—not just surviving, but thriving beyond what the boys' club had predicted. I was confident I had found my surgical home.

After changing, I sat at my desk and pushed aside a copy of patient appointments scheduled for my next clinic. One name stood out among all the rest: Gladys Gilles, the chairman's wife. An evaluation of an abnormal mammogram. *Wow, things really have changed around here.* I imagined either Gladys must be keeping a few secrets from her husband, or he'd come around to my side more than I'd thought possible.

I checked my watch. I still had thirty minutes to get home before Joel Bryan was to arrive. He'd invited me to a special meeting at St. Giles. I shook my head and smiled. Only God could understand why I'd accepted a date from a minister. If anyone would have told me this on the day I joined the Six-Liter Club, I'd have laughed in his face. The surgeon I was didn't need anyone but herself to survive. The woman I was now realized that we all needed each other and God just to make it through a day's worth of trouble.

Life was changing for me. I'd come a long way to opening up emotionally, physically, and now spiritually. Looking back, I couldn't believe I was ever happy as the poser I'd become. Sure, I was safe in my little shell, but safety and love don't always travel on the same train.

Since my fateful trip to Chicago, I'd decided it was time to explore the faith my father had given his life to promote. I spent days reading his mission reports and started reading about the Jesus he loved. Joel directed me to the Gospels and told me to pray as I went, asking for understanding. On Sundays, I even snuck into the back of St. Giles to listen. And slowly, I found my footing again as love chased away fear.

I looked in the compact mirror and freshened my lipstick. I sent a kiss toward my reflection and smiled. Lately, I felt like less of a poser and more of a person comfortable receiving a little of God's grace.

I pushed aside the black diary on my desk and decided that I would do a closer inspection of my makeup at home. Joel was a man worth looking my best for. I felt my heart quicken and smiled. I couldn't believe I was so excited about being with a Presbyterian.

I checked my watch again and decided I had time to do something I'd been meaning to do for a long time.

I called Nadine Solomon. She picked up after a few rings.

"Hi, Nadine, it's Dr. Weller."

"Dr. Weller!" I listened as I heard it repeated over and over in a muffled tone, as if she'd covered the receiver.

I wasn't sure why she was so excited, except that saving her son seemed to have bonded her heart to mine for eternity whether I liked it or not. The thought brought a smile to my face. There were worse things than being bonded to a sister like Nadine.

"What have you heard from Kendrick?"

"He's at my brother's, you know. He's getting along just fine. He told me to tell you he misses you." She paused. "He'll be back for school soon."

"That will be good." I hesitated, picked up the old diary, and rolled it over in my hand. "Nadine, remember how you told me I'd never seen God in action, how I needed to find something practical in order to believe?"

"I sure do, honey."

"I've found it, Nadine," I said, feeling the tears welling in my eyes. "I've found it." The event that precipitated such terrifying memories, once properly understood, provided the practical example I needed to see my Father's love. My earthly one.

And my Heavenly one, too.

I cried with a smile, because I really knew: Everything's gonna be all right.

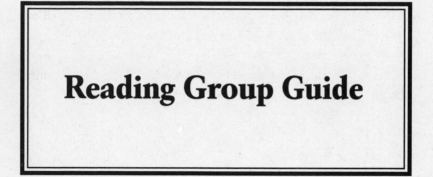

Reading Group Guide

Introduction

In *The Six-Liter Club,* we revisit a time during the 1980s when many personal and professional barriers for women and minorities were yet to be broken. In 1983, Camille Weller, MD, is the first black female in history to attain the status of attending staff at Medical College of Virginia. She is gritty, sexy, and used to excelling over her male colleagues. She was born in Africa, orphaned as a child, and raised by a white aunt in the racially charged South of the 1970s. She is a trauma surgeon and enters the prestigious Six-Liter Club on her first day on the job.

But Camille has difficulties with intimacy. She is troubled by recurrent flashbacks from her youth, growing up in the Congo as a child of an American missionary and Congolese mother during the Simba Rebellion. She becomes convinced by a counselor that she was abused by her father.

In the end, Camille realizes that her father didn't abuse her; he saved her. And the truth opens the way for her to begin to accept the faith of her missionary father, as well as to learn to accept intimacy in relationships.

Discussion Questions

1. What does it mean to be part of the Six-Liter Club? What does it mean to Dr. Weller in particular? How is she con-

flicted after she saves a patient's life and becomes part of the club?

2. After Dr. Gilles questions Dr. Weller's judgment when she didn't ask for help with the six-liter patient (Kendrick Solomon), she makes sure to gather herself and get out of the situation before she starts to cry. Why is it so important to her not to cry in front of her male colleagues? Why is there such a stigma against surgeons who show emotion and how is this stigma magnified by the fact that Dr. Weller is a woman?

3. When Camille is trying to explain to Mark what happened to her parents in the Congo back in 1964, Mark doesn't know what Simbas are. She notes that his ignorance of reality outside his small U.S. life is woefully common among Americans. Is she being too hard on him by expecting him to know about the politics of the country she was born in? Is she overly sensitive about it because her childhood was so tumultuous?

4. Shortly after the "locker room" incident, Dr. Bradford tells Dr. Weller it would be best if she didn't make any more waves and if she played by the rules. Is he right in giving her this advice? Is he looking out for her best interests or the best interests of the status quo? Is he thinking more

about her personal need for expression or the industry's demand that surgeons fall in line?

5. Does it seem easier for Dr. Weller to overcome the fact that she is half African American or that she is a woman in the medical industry? Which of these two defining characteristics do her peers seem to have more of a problem with?

6. At Dr. Weller's welcome reception, her best friend Kara asks her, "Why can't you be who you want to be? Instead of what Gilles expects of his boys?" Why does this statement from Kara bother her so much? Why is she so desperate to be accepted by the doctors in the "boys' club"?

7. Camille starts having debilitating panic attacks, which she discusses with Kara when they go to the Tobacco Company to watch the Boston Red Sox game. At this point, what do you think is causing the attacks? What is Camille afraid of? Failure? The pressure of a new job? Her feelings for Mark? A past she can't remember?

8. When Tina Kinser first comes to visit Dr. Weller, she notes that "Identifying with the emotions of your patients

can make you a more effective healer." How does Tina help Camille change her mind about this notion as time goes on?

9. Does Tina find satisfaction in cheating on her husband, Dan, as he has done to her before? Does she ever truly feel guilty, or is her marriage so over by the time she starts cheating on him that she doesn't feel much regret at all?

10. Why does Camille feel so guilty about Kara's death? Do you agree or disagree that she is to some degree responsible for Kara's death? Should she have been stronger and tried harder to prevent Kara from drinking that night?

11. Mark keeps mentioning to Camille that she is changing. What does he mean by this, and when did this start happening? Is it spawned from her unexpected maternal relationship with Kendrick Solomon? Is it, as Mark suggests, that some mothering instinct has kicked in since she lost Kara?

12. Do you agree with the way Tina and Camille handle the situation with Mark in Chicago after they find out about each other? Do you think it is strange that Camille could

be so in love with Mark and then cut off the relationship with no explanation from him?

13. Do you feel that Kendrick and his father, Clive, being shot by the same gun in similar incidents but Kendrick living and Clive dying is fate? How does this change Camille's opinion on faith and a higher power?

14. Does finding out the truth about her father at the Christ for the World dinner in Chicago give Camille the final closure about her father that she has always wanted?

15. Camille experiences a relatively sudden religious adoption toward the end of the book. What do you think is the major turning point for her? What is the major incident that prompts her religious realization?

Enhance Your Book Club

1. Discuss any major personal obstacles you've had to overcome. Talk about how you overcame the obstacle and how you think that changed you as a person.

2. Camille carries a picture of her mother in her wallet. Bring in a picture of someone who has inspired you. Describe the person and explain how they inspired you.

3. Many professions have their own "Six-Liter Clubs." Is there something similar in your profession? Research other clubs like this in various professions (law enforcement, teaching, firefighting). Discuss what it might have meant for Camille to be part of the Six-Liter Club and what it would mean to be part of those clubs in other professions.